C0-AYC-039

DARKMATTER

More Fiction
by
STEVEN WILLIAM RIMMER

The Order
Wyccad
Coven
Legacy

Eye Of The Dawn

http://www.stevenwilliamrimmer.com

DARKMATTER

Steven William Rimmer

Jam Ink Publishing
Kincardine, Ontario

Darkmatter : by Steven William Rimmer
Copyright © 2007 Steven William Rimmer

All rights reserved. The use of any part of this publication reproduced, transmitted in any form or by any means, electronic, mechanical, photocopying, recording or otherwise, or stored in a retrieval system, without the written consent of the publisher is an infringement on the copyright law. Address inquiries to:

Jam Ink Publishing
1623 Military Road – PMB 203
Niagara Falls NY 14304-1745
USA

Jam Ink Publishing
261 Alice St
Kincardine ON N2Z 2P9
Canada
http://www.jamink.net

Darkmatter
ISBN 978-1-895268-13-3
Steven William Rimmer

Cover design by AMC
Book design by Inside Bestsellers™ 1 800 931-1778
Trade & Bulk Sales Department: 1 888 545-0053 or write to the Publisher.

Darkmatter, an original work by Steven William Rimmer and an original publication of Jam Ink Publishing, is a work of fiction. Any resemblance or similarity to actual persons, alive or deceased, events or occurrences is purely contrived, and in no way represents reality as we know it.

Printing history 11 12 10 09 08 ** 06 05 04 * 02

Printed in China. Published simultaneously in U.S.A. and Canada.

For Megan,
for a lifetime of secrets.

With thanks to
David and Nancy Christie
Scott Hoffman
Joanne Kellock

1

Tuesday, October 10, 1961
Leconfield House, London
Office of the Director, MI5

Someone had no doubt gone to considerable trouble to make these offices a fitting accommodation for a peer of the realm, he reminded himself wearily as he eased himself into his creaking leather chair. He envisioned a minor task force of young men, redolent of shaving soap and hair cream, scurrying about the place with pots of paint and new electrics in the weeks before he'd been installed. He glanced about himself, exhaling forcefully, banishing the claustrophobia he felt in this room. The smell of lemon oil and varnish was still a fragrance in the astringent air, and yet he imagined himself to be in the antechamber of a tomb.

He felt the leather and horse hair embrace him, and he twisted about to enumerate the appointments of his premises — the newly-blackened iron hearth with a discrete electric fire in place of its grate, its chrome carefully polished, an ornate and slightly dated light above his desk, all five of its lamps unaccountably operational, the desk itself, freshly sanded and almost bereft of cigarette burns. He'd been in the city for less than a morning and he longed with every sinew of his being to return to his cottage, to Caroline and her begonias.

One would have thought that after thirty-seven years of marriage he would have been pleased to abandon her for a fortnight now and again. He chided himself wordlessly. He'd not taken her majesty's sword upon his shoulder for being an outstanding actor or the savior of someone's infant daughter from the depths of a well. His labors brought him here from time to time, he considered, and he would do well to accommodate himself to this room.

Pursing his lips, he selected a pipe from one of the drawers of his desk and absently set about the ritual of tamping it with tobacco and setting light to it. He rarely smoked unless he was drawn to London. A pot of smoldering vegetation clamped in his teeth seemed preferable to the reek of furniture polish.

The room had acquired a satisfactory funk of his smoke when he finally demanded of himself some recollection of the reason for his being here. This morning promised to jostle and disorient him amidst its appointments and meetings. It would be well if he were about his tasks. There was a train at 6:47 to return him to his own bed. If his day extended into evening, he would be consigned to a borrowed mattress at his club on a stomach awash with steak and kidneys that had clearly been rejected by the Dunlop company as being unsuitable for use as tires.

His finger paused upon the intercom switch for a moment before he depressed it. The speaker in the unattractive wooden box at the corner of his desk belched impolitely.

"Sir Alistair?" a mechanical woman's voice rattled from within it.

He released the switch. "I believe David Hollings is waiting for me," he said in the direction of the machine.

"Yes sir," the unseen woman replied.

"Kindly send him through."

"Sir," she acknowledged soullessly, and the imperceptible hiss of the speaker fell silent. He gazed overhead. This room required a slow, creaking ceiling fan, he mused, or better still, the all but silent rattle of a punkah waving to and fro. There were no doubt labor laws that would have prohibited his hiring a squatting Indian with a dhoti and a turban to operate it from the next room — perhaps the task could be assigned to whichever of the junior staff had most recently failed to secure his safe.

David Hollings would have been an admirable fisherman in an earlier age, had circumstances not diverted him from the sea into the study of physics. His father and his father's father had taken boats from the Cornish coast, and Sir Alistair recalled hearing that he had several brothers who had followed them past the waves. The man was scarcely into his forties, but he looked as if he'd been staring across the howling of the Atlantic for the better part of a century. He entered without knocking, as he'd been given leave to do some months earlier, but he waited to be offered a chair.

He was carrying a case, Sir Alistair observed, which he chose to regard as an unpleasant portent. Physicists did not carry cases — any matter too complex to be scrawled upon a sheet of paper and thrust into one's pocket was the province of engineers.

Sir Alistair gestured for David Hollings to be seated. After a moment he slid a mahogany cigarette box across his desk. David Hollings glanced at it, and seemed on the point of opening it when he eased himself back into his chair. Sir Alistair smiled, and a moment later David Hollings shared his amusement.

There were few things more disagreeable than the reek of unfiltered Players in a small office with all the windows painted shut, Sir Alistair considered, and while he'd never learned the source of the intelligence, he knew that each of his staff had been briefed concerning his tastes in the matter. The cigarette box was always offered, and had damned well best be politely declined. One day he must really take a moment and see if it contained any cigarettes.

"How was Washington?" David Hollings inquired.

Sir Alistair nodded, steepling his fingers before him. "Quite pleasant at this time of year," he replied. "Not that I had the opportunity to see much of it, I'm afraid."

"Your assistant was saying you took the airship across," David Hollings said.

"I do prefer them," he agreed warmly. "I had the Deutschland III on the return journey. I've stayed in far less well-appointed hotels."

David Hollings nodded his agreement. Sir Alistair felt a tick of irritation at the back of his neck. David Hollings had never traveled further west than the coast of Cornwall.

"I understand we've had another incident," Sir Alistair said, hoping his tone would suggest that what requisite chatter as was called for with his senior staff had now been accommodated.

David Hollings' features stiffened, his eyes narrowing for an instant. "Yes, sir," he said mechanically. "Rather an odd one."

Sir Alistair smiled thinly. "I'm told that your incident disabled the electric power grid of Cornwall and a good bit of Wales for most of yesterday evening."

David Hollings nodded sheepishly. "I don't think this one could have been foreseen, Sir Alistair," he said. "The power requirements were... quite off the scale. I'm surprised we didn't experience more equipment damage."

"I must say, I've read your briefing memorandum and I still don't understand exactly what occurred."

The fisherman with a clerk's hands compressed them together as if he were seeking to crush coal into a diamond. "I'm sorry, Sir Alistair, you weren't intended to. I felt that this incident was too sensitive to entrust to a messenger."

Sir Alistair clamped the stem of his pipe in his teeth and sucked deeply. The tobacco tasted suddenly of ash.

"I understand you've been briefed on the earlier arti-facts," David Hollings said cautiously.

"I believe I comprehend just enough about quantum physics to be a nuisance, but probably not enough to be genuinely dangerous," Sir Alistair prompted him.

David Hollings appeared to permit himself to smile at this. He lifted his case into his lap and pried it open. He reached into its depths and extracted a large black cylinder. After a moment of considering whether it might be incumbent upon him to request permission to do so, he placed it without comment upon Sir Alistair's desk.

Sir Alistair regarded the object for several seconds. It was perhaps a foot long, and several inches in diameter. It was capped at both ends, one of the caps having been affixed with a yellow adhesive that had dripped unevenly across the surface of the material. It was dull black, obtusely unfamiliar. He glared at it for a moment, uncertain what he was intended to be looking at.

"Is it in this?" he inquired.

"This is the artifact," David Hollings said.

Sir Alistair's eyes widened.

David Hollings lifted the cylinder and held it in one hand while he twisted one of the caps which sealed it. The cap relinquished its grasp on the cylinder with a dry squeak. David Hollings upended the object and accepted a large stack of pages that slithered into his hand. He placed the paper on Sir Alistair's desk.

"Was this... inside when you found it?" Sir Alistair demanded.

"It was," David Hollings confirmed.

Sir Alistair considered the manuscript. It was over an inch thick and it had suffered a pronounced curl as a result of its confinement within the cylinder. Each page was dense with type, set in two columns of print.

"Have you read it?" he asked.

"I've had a glance over it," David Hollings confirmed. "There's rather a lot of it."

"I imagine it's something unusual, for you to have driven up here."

"It was decided that the train was insecure."

Sir Alistair pursed his lips anew, uncertain for a moment how he might react to David Hollings' assertion. That one of his scientists might give a moment's consideration to matters of security was beyond his experience.

"Perhaps you could... apprise me of its high points," he requested, in a tone intended to imply that the request was an order.

David Hollings appeared to compose himself, as if he were seeking for a beginning to a rather long tale. The expression was familiar to Sir Alistair, who was called upon to listen to rather more long tales than he might have wished. This one, he sensed, would be either unimaginably dull or starkly disturbing.

"That is a history of the past fifty years or so," David Hollings began. "It's quite detailed, and thoroughly engrossing. The odd thing is that it's not the past fifty years that you or I or anyone else on earth has experienced."

"How's that?" Sir Alistair asked, not having expected the determination of his interest in David Holling's tale to have occurred quite so quickly.

"It begins..." the physicist said, and then he seemed to stop himself. "Are you familiar with Adolf Hitler?"

Sir Alistair considered this. "I don't believe so. He's not one of those American musicians we seem to hear so much of these days, is he?"

David Hollings shook his head. "There's no reason why you should be... I had to look him up myself. He was a minor German politician... turned up after the end of the great war. He became the president of the National Socialist party of Germany in the early nineteen-thirties.

By all accounts he was a gifted speaker... rather fiery. He managed to stir up the Germans at the beginning of the depression, talked about re-arming Germany, violating the treaty of Versailles. Actually, he was a bit too fiery for his own good. On 29 March, 1932, he was in the middle of a speech when he clutched at his heart and fell down dead."

"I could mention a few of our own politicians who might do the same," Sir Alistair said softly.

David Hollings seemed put at his ease by the remark. "The history of Germany for the next few decades was peaceful, of course. Roosevelt insisted on providing her with foreign aid — damned if I know how he persuaded his government to agree to that — and you couldn't ask for a better ally in our current political climate."

Sir Alistair nodded, wondering if he might remind David Hollings that he himself had experienced considerably more of the history of the twentieth century than had his visitor.

David Hollings gestured at the manuscript. "In that history, Adolf Hitler doesn't die," he said coldly. "He becomes the president of the National Socialist party, and in January 1933, he becomes the chancellor of Germany. He completes his rearmament program. In 1939, the German army marches into Poland. A second great war ensues. Germany forms an alliance with Japan. The fighting lasts until 1945. The war is... savage beyond all description."

The blood seemed to have left David Hollings' features. "Steady on," Sir Alistair reassured him, gesturing with the manuscript. "It's not like it actually took place."

David Hollings appeared not to have heard him. "It was savage... eleven million dead. The Germans set about systematically exterminating all the Jews they could find. The author of that... he writes about death camps, mass executions. At the height of the battle there were nightly bombings of London... much of the city was reduced to rubble. The Americans came into the war in 1941."

Sir Alistair was momentarily disquieted by the silent intensity of David Hollings' expression. "I've a difficult time imagining Germany exterminating its Jews," he said in a tone he hoped might be reassuring. "My word, Gustav Braunmann is a Jew, and he's been the president of the German Republic for... it must be twelve years now."

"He would have been put to death by poison gas and burned in that Germany," David Hollings said weakly, gesturing again at the manuscript. The fisherman shook his head as if to purge it of its unwarranted thoughts and he seemed to compose himself.

"The Americans ended the second great war," he continued woodenly. "They spent several years developing a secret weapon. Germany surrendered before they'd a chance to use it, but the Japanese were soldiering on in the Pacific. In 1945, they used their weapon to force Japan to capitulate."

Sir Alistair felt the breath still in his chest for a moment, and he chided himself for becoming engulfed in David Hollings' curious narrative. "Do you mean... the project?"

David Hollings shook his head once more. "No, sir," he replied. "That's one of the remarkable aspects of that history. The scientists of the 1940's... they read Einstein entirely differently than we have. They were interested in a much simpler aspect of his work, you see." He paused, and when he spoke again, his voice was barely audible. "E equals MC squared."

"I don't understand."

"They built an atomic fission weapon," David Hollings explained.

Sir Alistair leant back in his chair and permitted himself to smile. "That's quite preposterous, David, and you know it," he said dismissingly.

"It's not..." David Hollings began.

Sir Alistair gestured expansively. "When I came to head the project, I endured more briefings than I can easily count," he said. "More than a few of them were at your hands. One of them covered the possibility of an atomic fission device. I had the mathematics explained to me in excruciating detail. Were such a device to be detonated, it would set fire to the earth's atmosphere. The first combatant to use one would kill everything on the planet."

David Hollings nodded. "A great many scientists believe that to be true, Sir Alistair," he agreed. "Perhaps those who dissent have kept their silence in appreciation that the world is better off in ignorance of such a weapon. There was a professor at Rome named Enrico Fermi. I spoke with him several years ago, just before he passed away. He has an elegant proof of the possibility of atomic fission... without destroying the world. I've read it, and it works."

Sir Alistair gazed into the eyes of his visitor for a moment and then transferred his attention to the first page of the manuscript before him, reading nothing.

David Hollings appeared to appreciate that their conversation was in grave danger of digression. "The Americans dropped two atomic fission weapons on Japan," he resumed. "Japan promptly surrendered. However, even before the design for the atomic fission weapons was complete, agents of the Soviet Union had created a network of spies to steal it."

Sir Alistair felt a spark climb his spine and illuminate his senses. He struggled for a moment to remain impassive.

"During the second great war, the Germans built rockets to send bombs across the channel in an attempt to force England into submission," David Hollings said. "After the German surrender, the German rockets and the German scientists who developed them were captured –

some by the Americans, and others by the Soviets. By 1947, the Soviet Union succeeded in detonating its first fission weapon, based on the intelligence they'd stolen from the Americans. Within ten years, they had rockets powerful enough to carry atomic fission devices from Russia to targets in the west. The world spent the next thirty years living under the threat of annihilation by those rockets."

Sir Alistair considered reminding David Hollings that the history to which he referred was merely a great many words on a great many pieces of paper. He glanced at the manuscript on the desk before himself and chose not to.

"It's a very different world, from what I've read of it," David Hollings said. "In 1969, the Americans used their rockets to send men to the moon. They had artificial satellites floating around the earth to send back photographs of the Russian interior."

Sir Alistair smiled coldly. "Wouldn't that be the most remarkable thing," he interrupted.

"That history is full of remarkable things," David Hollings agreed. "Some of them defy easy understanding. One of the most remarkable is that as nearly as its author was able to make out, no one appreciated Einstein as we do until the early 1990s."

"That seems difficult to imagine," Sir Alistair suggested.

"It wasn't until the 1990s that the Soviet Union disintegrated, you see," he explained. "Einstein – their Einstein – he'd been instrumental in the development of the atomic fission weapons.

"He was horrified by what his theories had wrought. He died in 1955, while our Einstein is still breathing. Their Einstein never did the work our Einstein did in the mid-nineteen-forties on the cosmological constant and the nature of darkmatter."

"So... these people... never had the project?" Sir Alistair asked, grasping the manuscript.

"Not until 1991, and then it was seven years before they had a working prototype. The author of that history was a scientist who worked on their version of the project."

"Assuming for a moment that I were to believe all this, why would he have written this?" Sir Alistair demanded, hearing a note of irritation in his voice that he might have wished away.

"His name is Ira Rosen. He's an American Jew... a gifted physicist. His grandparents were Germans, and they died in the death camps during the second great war. His father escaped Germany as a child. Rosen writes about being haunted by images... the horror of the genocide of millions of his people. When their version of the project became operational in 1998, he saw himself as having been shown a way to reverse the murder of so many Jews, so many people, at the hands of the Germans."

Sir Alistair realized that he'd come to be leaning forward in his chair, his posture decidedly undignified. He sat upright. The room seemed unaccountably warm, and he daubed at his brow with a handkerchief.

"You have to understand, they had technology we can't begin to dream of... computers vastly more powerful than anything we can build today, a technique for identifying minute samples of genetic material recovered through the time stream. Rosen secretly operated their version of the project..."

Sir Alistair rose suddenly to his feet. He grasped the manuscript, stared at it for an instant, his gaze all but igniting its pages in his fist, before he hammered it into the timber of his desk. "I won't hear this!" he thundered.

David Hollings rose to his feet a moment later, a wild glare of defiance in his eyes. "They had the same grasp of the time stream as we do," he continued, "although

Rosen could target it with unimaginable accuracy. He calculated that it would require the entire electrical output of the eastern United States, and that even so, he could only project a few cubic centimeters of gas that far back through the stream."

Sir Alistair fixed David Hollings in his stare for a moment longer before he willed himself to exhale and return to his chair. David Hollings remained standing. His next words seemed to be spoken from a great distance.

"Ira Rosen located the precise time and place where the heart of Adolf Hitler would be during his speech on 29 March, 1932, and he sent a small quantity of air into it. Hitler fell down dead, the second great war never was and Ira Rosen's grandparents weren't murdered in a German death camp."

Sir Alistair exhaled audibly. He straightened his tie and slid his handkerchief across his brow. He felt himself flush, heard his heart in his ears. After a few moments of silence he leant back in his chair once more. The groan of its leather was comforting.

"I'm... I'm sorry, Hollings," he began earnestly. "I can't say what came over me just now."

"It came over me last evening, Sir Alistair," David Hollings said flatly, with no echo of resentment in his words. Sir Alistair gestured for him to be seated once more.

"You can't... believe this," Sir Alistair said flatly, brushing his hand contemptuously across the manuscript. "It can be nothing other than a fabrication. Why, if it were genuine, it would mean that this Rosen fellow consigned himself to having very possibly never existed."

"He acknowledges as much in the final pages," David Hollings agreed. "It took him months to arrange it all, to learn how to steal enough power to run their project, to gain access to it when it was unguarded. He had a great deal of time to think, to write all that down and consign it to the time stream. As he said, it's all that remains of most of a century of history."

Sir Alistair permitted himself a moment to contemplate the possibility of the manuscript's being authentic. "If this were genuine, David, it would mean that... that... that we are the result of a derivative time stream. While I appreciate that such things have been the subject of innumerable discussions and no small number of jokes, I cannot accept that we are... history's second draft."

"It can't be anything other than genuine," David Hollings said evenly, his certainty unnerving.

"Even allowing that this has actually emerged from the time stream, it could have been written by any one of your people... or any one of the Americans, for that matter. They've sent more objects into the stream than we ever will, and they have the damnedest sense of humor at times."

"I'm sorry, Sir Alistair, it couldn't have been written by anyone from our history," David Hollings said, still speaking with a tone of unshakable certainty. "There are three problems with it."

"Yes?"

"When objects are placed in the time stream, they effectively cease to be for the duration of their stay in the stream. There's a rather complex test involving radioactive cesium to determine how long an object has been in the stream. It's typically accurate to within a few days at worst. The cylinder has been in the time stream for something on the order of six and a half years. The American prototype of the project became operational less than four years ago, and our own several months later."

Sir Alistair's eyes narrowed, and he nodded slowly. "You said there were three problems."

"The other two are material analysis issues, but if anything they're more conclusive still. I had a document specialist examine the title page of the manuscript. That's why it's not included with the rest of the pages. It wasn't printed with ink. His best guess was that the type was formed by baking fine particles of graphite into the surface of the paper. He knows of no printing technology capable of producing these pages."

"And the third?" Sir Alistair demanded.

"The cylinder," David Hollings said, gesturing at the object. "It's made of some sort of plastic. There's a Dupont factory not far from the project site... I've a friend who works there. He's among the best inorganic chemists going. I gave him a sliver of the plastic to work on. I rang him about an hour ago. I can't say I understood everything he told me, but it's safe to say that no such plastic exists on earth apart from this thing."

Sir Alistair lifted the empty cylinder from his desk and considered it. There was a line of faint yellow print along it. "ABS sanitary sew?" he inquired at length?

"Sanitary sewer, I imagine," David Hollings said, a faint smile of amusement creasing his features. "I'd speculate it's made of what would have been commonly-available water pipe in Ira Rosen's version of history."

"It seems as if he should have been able to find something more substantial to protect the last remaining evidence of his civilization," Sir Alistair said absently, as much to the unseen shade of Ira Rosen as to David Hollings.

David Hollings relaxed minutely, easing himself back into his chair. "Will this... will this affect the project?" he inquired.

Sir Alistair regarded him, disturbed from his consideration of the cylinder. "I shouldn't have thought so," he replied. "No one in Whitehall will ever learn of it. I trust your people can be relied upon to maintain security."

"Yes, sir," he said.

"How many of them know of it?"

David Hollings stared blankly into the newly-painted

plaster behind Sir Alistair's head, and he was some while appreciating that his visitor was mentally reviewing the history of the cylinder and enumerating the people who had come into contact with it.

"I'm the only one who knows what was inside it," he said at length. "And now yourself, sir. The technical staff know we had an incident and an anomalous artifact returned from the stream — that's Bernard Oliphant, Arthur Dunross, Charles Owens and James Glass. We've had five previous artifacts. They all know the drill. No one gets to peek, and no one mentions it outside the facility. Everyone at the project knows there's a flap on today, but they'll all assume it's about our excessive electric demands."

Sir Alistair placed his hand atop the manuscript. "It will have to be circulated, of course," he continued. "There will be a very short distribution list. Perhaps we'll have something to learn from the perspective of an author forty years in the future, even if it's not precisely our future."

"I wonder if I might be included on the list, sir?" David Hollings requested. "I've only had the opportunity to glimpse at it."

Sir Arthur nodded. "I shall value your comments," he said firmly, and he rose from his chair. "It's been good to see you again, Hollings, if rather unsettling."

David Hollings clearly hadn't appreciated that he was being dismissed until Sir Alistair reached across his desk to shake him by his hand. He got to his feet and smiled uncertainly. He collected his case and left without comment.

Sir Alistair regarded the manuscript once more. It would have to be transcribed, three carbons, blue MOST SECRET stationary. There was a very short roster of bright young things in the secretarial division cleared to know the contents of such a document, and only one whom he trusted utterly. Alice Woodward, she of limpid eyes and unwatchable fingers, would be called upon to spend the rest of the week alone in a secured, windowless room. Miss Woodward would be displeased, he imagined, but she would not complain. She, too, knew the drill.

2

The air was a haze of cigarette smoke and damp plaster, a prenatal sneeze tickling at his awareness as he stood as absolutely still as he knew how. At the periphery of his attention the spools of a tape recorder rotated, the soft hiss of tape against aluminum machined smooth with use. The recorder's level meters danced lewdly as he struggled to hear what they heard, to see through the wire that linked their airless closet with the Soviet consulate next door.

The headphones clamped over his ears had grown moist with his sweat, their cracked plastic cushions fusing with his hair and flesh as he pressed them more closely to his skull, that he might miss none of what they whispered to him. In the harsh glow of the breathless room's single lamp, Hugh Somerfield struck a match and applied it to his fifth fag of the hour. A luminous coal swelled in the darkness and the slate blue atmosphere grew more unbreathable still.

Alec Grey wrestled with a cough that clamored in his chest, unwilling to surrender an instant of attention to the sound it would make. The consulate was separated from this place by two feet of brick and masonry, he reminded himself, and even if someone therein had had his ear glued to the connecting wall, they'd have been profoundly unlikely to hear him.

He pressed his eyes shut, feeling the cadence of the words in his headphones. He refused to consider what the two unseen men beyond the wall were speaking of. A squadron of overweight émigré women with headphones of their own and electric typewriters would be set the task of transcribing the tapes a day hence.

Hugh Somerfield's chair creaked. Alec Grey opened one eye and regarded the taller man. His colleague had placed his feet on the table before the tape recorder, and was engrossing himself in a ragged copy of News of the World.

Alec Grey shook his head, sundering his concentration, and he tore the headphones from his ears. "It's all bollocks," he snapped abruptly, smiling to himself that he still resorted to whispers in this place.

Hugh Somerfield returned his dusty shoes to the floor and sat upright. "The microphone?" he inquired defensively. "It was working half an hour ago."

Alec Grey shook his head. "The microphone's working," he agreed. "It's just not hearing anything useful."

Hugh Somerfield glanced uncertainly at the level meters on the tape recorder before him, clearly noting that their twitching was consistent with spoken words. He glanced at his watch. The workmen who'd been renovating the building next to the Soviet consulate weren't due to arrive for at least an hour, but they'd all been warned repeatedly to assure themselves of the absence of anyone beyond the false wall that concealed them before they raised their voices, or those of their subjects.

The Americans had enjoyed a period of monumental good fortune when the Soviet embassy in Washington had thoughtfully chosen to relocate itself to larger quarters four years earlier. The trouble with dedicated Marxists, Sir Alistair Fitzhenry had remarked during a later briefing on the operation, was an almost inescapable state of penury. The KGB had employed the craftiest of their engineers to design an embassy compound that would resist the FBI's electronic intrusions, but they'd lacked the resources to have it built exclusively by imported Soviet laborers. The local electricians and bricklayers had included several contractors who'd been drawing their wage packets from J. Edgar Hoover. The Soviets had summoned a brigade of counterintelligence people from Moscow before they'd occupied the embassy, and they'd found all the microphones they'd been intended to find. The more covert listening devices, built into the walls and lamps and plumbing of the new embassy, functioned still.

MI5 had waited for several decades for the Soviet premises in Kensington Palace Gardens to grow similarly inadequate for the requirements of its occupants, thus far forlornly. Sir Alistair was of the opinion that, despite employees of the KGB being compressed into the London consulate with sufficient density to fuse the fillings in their teeth, the Soviet legation lacked the funds to move to more generous quarters. Their current offices enjoyed the prestige of a desirable London address, and perhaps more to the point, they were conveniently located amidst many of the locales upon which the KGB would wish to spy.

It was thus with a considerable flutter of excitement that Alec Grey had been informed that the office building next to the Soviet consulate had been sold, and was scheduled to be extensively remodeled for its intended tenants, The Scottish and Newcastle Insurance Company. He'd scarcely been able to credit his own eyes when he'd driven 'round for a look at the place and had observed that it was physically attached to the Soviet consulate by a common wall.

They'd had only the grace of a weekend and an adjoining bank holiday to locate a suitable closet on the second floor of the building and construct a convincing false wall at its rear — he and Hugh Somerfield and Edward Blair from Technical Services, whose father had actually been a bricklayer, and who, as such, had prevented the work from turning into a vaudeville performance involving three clowns and a mason's trowel. Edward Blair had been all but apoplectic with excitement about leaving the workbench and oscilloscope before which he'd spent the previous seven years of his life and venturing into the field, as he'd chosen to describe the wilds of Kensington Palace Gardens and the Bayswater Road. He'd done a workmanlike job, however, procuring a heap of recovered brick to make the new wall look profoundly Victorian.

As he glanced about the airless chamber now, scarcely large enough for himself and Hugh Somerfield's chair, Alec Grey wondered at the advisability of having had Edward Blair intrude his bricks another two feet further into the dominion of the Scottish and Newcastle Insurance Company. Well they may all have been bespectacled clerks with adding machines for hearts, but they'd certainly not have taken a measuring tape to their stationary closet and noticed the discrepancy.

He sighed abruptly. It hardly mattered. Someone would no doubt be assigned to mind the tape recorder, but it wouldn't be himself or Hugh Somerfield. In another day Sir Alistair would lose all interest in this place, and it would become another dungeon to which he sentenced operatives who'd incurred his displeasure by failing to check the sums in their expense submissions. On some mornings he could still imagine fragments of mortar beneath his fingernails.

"It's all bloody bollocks," he repeated angrily.

Hugh Somerfield regarded him for a moment, and then gestured at the loudspeaker on the table behind the tape recorder. Alec Grey nodded without thinking. The taller man eased one of dials on the tape recorder around its orbit, and the tiny room was gradually submerged in guttural speech.

Alec Grey listened to the two men beyond the wall speaking in clipped, mechanical Russian. He turned to face Hugh Somerfield, who was clearly of the opinion that he might catch snatches of intelligible English in their words if he listened to them with sufficient intensity.

"It all sounds like perfectly grand eavesdropping to me, boss," he remarked, permitting a faint grin to crease his features. "The microphone's working brilliantly."

Alec Grey shook his head, deciding that Hugh Somerfield had genuinely not appreciated the nature of the conversation beyond the wall before them.

"Listen to the words," he suggested.

Hugh Somerfield glanced at him reprovingly. "Some of us don't speak Russian," he observed.

Alec Grey smiled at this. His command of the language was imperfect, and he'd not troubled himself to make sense of the words hissing and coughing from the loudspeaker between them. "It doesn't matter," he instructed Hugh Somerfield. "Listen to the words, not to what that lot's saying."

Hugh Somerfield's brow furled. "Will I need to sit with my legs crossed and my thumbs touching my forefingers?"

"They're not saying anything."

"They're not saying anything in Russian."

"If they're not saying anything, it hardly matters which language they're not saying it in."

"In another ten years you're going to being looking like Sir Alistair Fitzhenry, as well as sounding like him."

Alec Grey resisted the urge to sigh once more. "You've listened to a great many Russians through a great many microphones," he suggested.

Hugh Somerfield nodded.

"Have any of them ever sounded like those two?"

Hugh Somerfield appeared to consider the question. "They're rather more... dignified than most of the Russians I've listened to," he conceded.

Alec Grey felt himself relent to a faint smile. "They're

the most polite Russians on earth. It's been almost ten minutes, and neither of them has remarked upon the sexual activities of anyone's mother. In fact, neither of them has so much as raised his voice. I'm not at all certain we shouldn't be notifying the head of records about it."

"I'm afraid you've lost me," Hugh Somerfield said.

Alec Grey paused and listened intently to the loud-speaker. After almost a minute had elapsed, the cadence of the words oozing from the darkness was broken. The rattle of speech was interrupted by the unmistakable rasp of paper.

"Did you notice that?" he asked.

"The paper?"

Alec Grey nodded.

"We've always assumed the room on the other side of the wall would be someone's office. It follows he'd have papers on his desk."

"A page turns every forty-five seconds or so," Alec Grey said. "If you listen carefully, sometimes you can hear two pages turning at once."

Hugh Somerfield took a long drag of his cigarette. "I don't understand."

"They're reading from a script."

Hugh Somerfield's expression sagged, and his eyes became dark. "A script?" he asked, as if he'd grasped at the faint hope that he'd misunderstood what he'd been told. "You can't be serious."

Alec Grey nodded again. "We've been demoted from the position of spies to that of an audience for a Soviet amateur theatrical," he said, not at all pleased by his obser-vation.

"That's not possible," Hugh Somerfield insisted.

Alec Grey gestured at the unseen loudspeaker, and a stain of defeat seeped into Hugh Somerfield's features. His subordinate exhaled loudly. A few moments later another pair of pages turned audibly in the electronics. Hugh

Somerfield cast his unsmoked cigarette into a cluster of its fellows at his feet and crushed it angrily under his heel.

"They can't possibly have known," he insisted.

"And yet, they do," Alec Grey corrected him, hearing finality in his words. He placed the treasonous headphones on the table before Hugh Somerfield and recovered his coat from a nail in wall behind him.

"Should I switch this lot off?" Hugh Somerfield inquired blackly.

Alec Grey considered this for a moment before he shook his head. "Get it all on tape, and get it transcribed. It might be useful to know what they'd like us to believe. I'll have Edward Blair pop 'round in a few hours to relieve you. If we don't tell him we've been rumbled, he'll probably slip us each a fiver for the privilege."

Hugh Somerfield reduced the volume of the loudspeaker and the two unseen Russians diminished into ethereal Marxist specters. He seemed to notice the mackintosh across Alec Grey's arm for the first time.

"Are you off, then?" he asked.

Alec Grey glanced at his watch without noticing the time. "There's a briefing," he explained. "Office of the Director."

Hugh Somerfield clearly appreciated that he was to be told nothing more. "Black tie and gloves?"

"When Sir Alistair learns of this, I fear it may well be knee pads," Alec Grey suggested, and he crouched to lift the narrow trap door at his feet. The shaft beneath it was stygian, and his toe sought about in the gloom for the iron rung of the ladder Edward Blair had affixed to its far wall.

Access to the secret room had been a matter of some consideration when he and Hugh Somerfield had initially envisioned the project. They'd devised a number of improbable secret doors and ongoing exercises in subterfuge to permit them access to the Scottish and Newcastle Insurance Company's stationary closet on a regular basis. Edward Blair had been a party to none of them, and without being asked to he'd erected a shaft from the floor of the stationary closet through a disused office on the ground floor and into the boiler room beneath them. Alec Grey had been effusive in his praise of the work, and had been some time appreciating that Edward Blair had genuinely thought the solution so obvious as to not have required a mention in the design of the room.

The iron ladder which traversed the narrow shaft was thirty-one feet long. Alec Grey knew it to be so, as he'd noticed it on the bill of materials for the work. He tried not to dwell upon its height when he was climbing into the darkness along it.

He emerged from the basement of the new offices of the Scottish and Newcastle Insurance Company in the Bayswater Road and set himself the task of gesturing disjointedly for a taxi. It began to rain, and he drew his coat about his shoulders, deliberately turning his back on the Soviet consulate that it not be granted the satisfaction of gloating.

3

Another drink had not extinguished the flames in his stomach as he might have hoped. He could still find an occasional grain of pepper in his teeth, still taste the threat of petrol around the rim of his glass. He trudged along the Via Settembre, glaring at the bruised clouds overhead, sheltering himself beneath his preposterous thespian's hat, entombed in a coat which must clearly be in fashion, as it could not be mistaken for being comfortable. He felt himself begin to sweat within its confinement, imagining a more tangible prison. In another week he might well be wearing a coat of masonry and iron.

The street was thick with Fiats and Citroëns, Italian women in clothes that might have been applied with a paintbrush, tourists of a dozen nations who'd lingered too long in the eternal city, unwilling to return to London, New York, Berlin… Leningrad. He was a tourist as well, he reminded himself, if a compulsory one. His colleagues had vied for this posting.

There had been another posting, another British embassy. Fifteen years earlier it had been Istanbul, and he'd worn no hat, no theatrical false beard, no opaque sunglasses. It had been night, and the night had seemed a sufficient disguise.

Konstanin Bolshakov glanced at Villa Bracciano, the British embassy, as he came abreast of the iron arch that suspended an ornate coat of arms above the granite lane leading into the embassy compound. He felt his fingernails claw at the flesh of his palms, clutched about within his coat unthinking, assured himself that the packet of documents remained where he'd lodged it. It had been a single page fifteen years earlier. That page had come within a whisper of costing him his life. The pages he carried with him now boded far, far worse.

Lena had been alive then, and it had seemed vastly more perilous. If Moscow had recalled them, he'd have watched the faceless automatons of the NKVD grasp her by her shoulder for a final time, lead her into the stone chambers of the Lubyanka, as he himself would have been lead away, heard watery screams from the liquid blackness and known in his soul they'd been hers. Lena had found her own way over the curtain, he decided abruptly. Perhaps her ghost awaited him in the west.

It had been raining in Istanbul when he'd at last swallowed enough vodka to extract the list from behind a skirting board in their airless apartment, pour himself into his ill-fitting suit and convince himself that he looked the part of a defector. The night had been as dark as the faces of the Turks he'd brushed past in the street. The embassy, little more than a shadow, had been more substantial than the other patches of lightlessness.

He'd been the Soviet Union's vice-consul in Turkey then, a figure of some urgency, if little authority. He'd sat across from the British vice-consul, C. H. Page, and mentally compared the appointments of the office into which he'd been ushered with the shabby closet that served as his own. The man behind the ornate oak desk had seemed ill-fed, tubercular, an aging school boy with overlarge spectacles affixed to the termination of his nose. He'd perused Konstanin Bolshakov's single page of typescript several times, clearly at no pains to hurry himself despite Bolshakov's periodic request that he be granted a reply and be permitted to leave before his absence from the Soviet consular offices was noticed.

"This seems quite... impressive," the slight man behind his desk had muttered, his words appearing to be directed at his inkwell, rather than to Bolshakov. It had been instantly clear that he'd understood little of what he'd read.

Konstanin Bolshakov had felt himself growing more enraged as the seconds had trickled past him, a rivulet of blood from a newly-opened wound. He'd struggled to still his temper. "It is priceless," he'd growled through a tightened jaw.

Page had smiled thinly. "It's hardly that," he'd remarked. "You said fifty thousand pounds and British passports for yourself and your wife."

Bolshakov had nodded. This had been the third occasion of the vice-consul mentioning the figure. He'd resisted the urge to hurl himself across the immaculate, polished desk and grasp the man by his collars, to shout down his throat that the money would not be deducted from his wages. It had been a handful of kopeks compared to the value of the Soviet documents he'd been prepared to carry with him.

Page had pursed his lips a final time and glanced reprovingly at the list before him. "It's not within my purview to decide such matters," he'd said with sudden finality. He'd smiled, an official smile, timed to the second and then extinguished. "I'll have this sent to London by telegraph this evening."

"In the diplomatic bag, if you please," Bolshakov had insisted. "Moscow Center has been reading your ambassadorial codes for over a year."

The vice-consul's features had stiffened at this, and his eyes had narrowed. He'd nodded sternly. "Very well, then, in the diplomatic pouch. To the attention of the head of counterintelligence at MI6." He'd fixed Bolshakov in his gaze for a moment. "Personally."

Konstanin Bolshakov recalled every pore and a line in Page's face, a decade and a half later, and he could still smell a faint tang of lemon polish on the furniture in his office. He imagined that with some effort, he might still hear a reverberant echo of the thundering of his heart behind his ribs in the instant that the vice-consul had folded the list and smiled unctuously, gesturing toward the door at the rear of his office. The audience had been over, Bolshakov had appreciated, and he'd risen to leave.

"You've not told me your name," Page had said without ascending from his chair.

Bolshakov had turned once more to face the vice-consul. Indeed, he'd realized, he had not. He'd glanced at the list on Page's desk blotter, imagined the lines of type, the inventory of his proposed treason. He'd wanted to include something for the British to taste when they'd read the list, something to entice them into unlocking their bank vaults and showering him with western affluence. There were seven moles in MI6, he'd written, one of them fulfilling the function of the head of a section.

He'd not known the names of any of them, but he'd been certain that the documents he'd proposed to carry with him to the west would have provided British intelligence with sufficient details to have identified the shadows they represented. As he'd gazed at the list, he'd known with a certainty born of vodka and terror that one of them was the head of counterintelligence at MI6.

He'd glanced at the vice-consul, as if lost in thought.

"You've not told me your name," Page had repeated.

"Mikhail Pavlenko," Bolshakov had replied. "I am consular assistant at the Soviet legation."

He'd watched Page write the name on the back of the list, and then he'd hurried from the room.

Mikhail Pavlenko had been an NKVD political officer under diplomatic cover at the embassy, one of the men Bolshakov had been warned from paying excessive attention to. He'd been a venomous ferret, ordering the consular staff about, appropriating what few funds Moscow permitted him, boring into the skulls of Bolshakov's people with his lifeless shark's eyes. None the less, when two men in Russian suits had arrived at the embassy complex and Pavlenko had left, sedated on a stretcher, Bolshakov had spent three days locked in his apartment, his nerves alive with anxious chattering, imagining the screams and pleas of Pavlenko in an unnameable cell in the Lubyanka as he'd protested his ignorance of the charges against him and demanded through cracked lips and a mouthful of blood to speak to his superiors.

No one at the embassy had spoken of Pavlenko from that day until Bolshakov had been posted to Rome, seven years later. No one from Moscow had returned to inquire about Stalin's treacherous servant. Konstanin Bolshakov had personally carried his hoard of stolen documents to the incinerator in the basement of the embassy and burned them to ashes.

None of them would have been worth an English penny today, he thought sourly as he glanced around himself. He drew his arms to his sides and he reminded himself to assume a crouched posture, to look as little like himself as his attire would permit him. Any one of the carefully shaven men in their vacation clothes and expensive shoes might have journeyed here from Moscow Center. The NKVD was the KGB now, but the Lubyanka was where it had always stood.

The dour gray prison was said to be the tallest building in Moscow, in that one could see all the way to Siberia from it. He wondered fleetingly who had first told him the joke in such poor taste.

His stomach boiled within him. If he remained

before the embassy gates for very much longer, he decided, he would either be identified by the KGB despite his costume, or he would expel his lunch and dislodge the glue that affixed his beard to his face.

He permitted himself a final glance along the Via Settembre and then turned to enter the embassy compound. As a point of habit, he shot his cuffs from his sleeves as he walked. Each of the cuff buttons of his shirt had been daubed with curare. He'd applied it himself when his shirts had been returned from the laundry. He'd been doing so for fifteen years, and he'd no doubt purchased enough of the poison since the abduction of Mikhail Pavlenko to have sent every KGB officer at Moscow Center directly to hell.

4

The door closed with a satisfying clap of finality. One of his staff had referred to it as being hermetically sealed. Sir Alistair decided in that instant that he enjoyed the expression, or at the very least that he permitted himself to draw solace from it. He'd arrived to find the last of the technicians who routinely swept the room for hidden microphones packing up his apparatus and preparing to depart for whatever subbasement usually accommodated him. He'd nodded his approval at the integrity of the room, and left without speaking.

Sir Alistair glanced along the table that sprawled before him, at the faces regarding him. He knew the names of most of them without thinking, and he wondered absently if he might not compel the rest to wear badges on their shirts. He placed a leather case on the table and pushed his chair before himself, deciding that this briefing commanded that he remain standing. His subordinates appeared to cease breathing as one.

He took a long draught of his pipe and he glanced at the nearest wall. At the distant end of the room, someone scraped a match to life. The air would be unbreathable in ten minutes, he thought sourly.

"Thank you all for coming," he said, and then he

stopped himself. "It's good of you to be here, even if you all know full well you had no choice the matter."

Several of the faces before him creased with amusement.

"As you're all no doubt aware, if you're at all proficient at your jobs, I've been in America for the past fortnight," he continued. "I was briefed by a department of the American government I hadn't known existed. It's called the National Reconnaissance Office. It's very name is classified top secret. I don't believe the Americans have a classification high enough to classify what it actually does."

Most of the remainder of the faces attending him relented to amusement. The American penchant for secrecy was a matter of some derision amongst his staff.

"I'm going to tell you something of what it does, but before I do, I am required to remind you of the Official Secrets Act, to which each of you has affixed his signature, of the 1948 UKUSA agreement by which we are required to extradite suspected agents of a foreign power to the United States if the Americans believe their secrets have been compromised and of the American love of electric machines... specifically those rather nasty chairs they keep in their prisons."

Sir Alistair leant forward slightly. "If any of you is known to talk in your sleep, this would be the time to excuse yourself from this briefing."

Several of them laughed at this, but as he met each of their gazes in turn, he appreciated that his warning had been understood. He'd been made to sign a formal undertaking to the same effect in Washington.

"I have something I'd like to show you," he said, all mirth excised from his words.

He opened his case and extracted a several large, colorless photographs. He passed them to the man at his left and gestured that they be circulated along the table. He permitted himself to observe the wonder and amazement of each of them as they appreciated what they'd been made privy to.

"Are these from U2 overflights?"

Sir Alistair glanced at the source of the question. Alec Grey had one of the photographs in his hand, and he was gesturing with it to attract his attention.

"No, Mr. Grey, they are not," he replied. "I thought the same thing myself, but as I'm certain you will all appreciate, as I did when I first saw them, no aircraft could have produced these."

"This looks like the Nikolaiev shipyard," Alec Grey said, his attention returned to the photograph. "The entire shipyard, and a substantial portion of the Black Sea."

"That's very perceptive of you," Sir Alistair allowed. "I'm certain you'll appreciate that even the Americans wouldn't dare send a U2 over such a target, and that an aircraft-mounted camera couldn't have covered an area that large in a single image."

Alec Grey handed the photograph to the man beside him and directed his attention to Sir Alistair. "If not an aircraft..." he began.

Sir Alistair smiled, permitting himself a moment of enjoyment. He imagined himself having dressed up to play Father Christmas to a room full of expectant children.

"These pictures were made by an American project code-named CORONA," he said, appreciating as he did that the word would mean nothing to the other men in the room.

"It's been a joint effort with a group of German engineers. It uses a very large rocket to send a mechanical camera outside the atmosphere of the earth. The camera floats over the Soviet Union and takes holiday snaps until its film's all used up. Then it spits out a capsule that returns to earth and is snagged on the way down by a C-119 aircraft over the Pacific ocean."

The room descended into silence, and each of the men fortunate enough to have possession of one of the photographs regarded his prize with renewed interest. Sir Alistair regarded Alec Grey, who was clearly doing sums in his head as he considered an image before him.

"One hundred miles above the surface, sir?" he inquired.

"Apparently the exact altitude of the camera is one of its many features about which the Americans have chosen to remain silent. I believe it's something like that."

"Are there more images?" Alec Grey asked.

Sir Alistair nodded. "The Americans have successfully orbited three CORONA cameras… or satellites, as they choose to refer to them. Each camera records about fifteen hundred images. We have access to the lot, although out of consideration of not causing the airship I returned on to list dangerously, the entire archive did not accompany me. Arrangements are being made to deliver copies of all four and a half thousand. I might also note that another camera is scheduled to be sent up in less than a month."

Another photograph waved from the back of the room to attract Sir Alistair's attention. "I wonder if I might interrupt," its owner asked, his voice crackling in the aftermath of a lifetime of too much drink and too many cigarettes smoked to the fag end.

"Mr. Philby?" Sir Alistair acknowledged.

Several of the younger men turned slightly to regard the bemused features of Kim Philby. He was dressed in what Sir Alistair took to be a suit from Saville Row, and the parting in his hair might have been installed with a straight edge. The head of anti-Soviet counterintelligence was a common sight at high level briefings, but it was unusual to hear him speak.

"I wonder what the Soviets know of this… CORONA?" he inquired. Philby had spent three years in Washington as the MI6 liaison with the CIA and FBI. Sir

Alistair decided that his Cambridge accent had acquired a faint drawl.

"The Americans are of the belief that they know nothing and suspect less," Sir Alistair replied. "It's a poorly-kept secret that the Americans have been experimenting with rockets at one of their air bases in California, but as it happens, they managed to explode the first twelve attempts at launching the CORONA cameras. Even the German engineers who designed the rocket motors weren't told what they were to be used for. If anyone took any notice of the rockets, they would have concluded that they were suitable largely as fireworks."

"I only ask because this would seem to be a potential provocation for Mr. Khrushchev," Philby observed. His voice seemed to deflate itself to a loud whisper. "As were the U2 overflights," he added.

Sir Alistair sighed. Kim Philby had issued at least a quire of agitated, ill-composed memoranda concerning the instability of the Soviet premier and the potential effects upon his demeanor of the Americans' surveillance aircraft invading the airspace of the Soviet Union. The U2s danced upon the upper reaches of the atmosphere sixty-thousand feet above the ground, and their American handlers were convinced that none of the current generation of Soviet jet fighters could fly sufficiently high to intercept one.

"I'm certain you'll take no small measure of comfort, Mr. Philby, to learn that President Nixon ordered an immediate cessation of U2 overflights upon the recovery of the first CORONA capsule."

"If Khrushchev learns of this..." Philby persisted.

"...he'll be hard pressed to shoot one of them down with a MiG-21," Douglas Harvey interrupted him. A cloudburst of restrained laughter rattled though the confined briefing room. Douglas Harvey was the liaison with GCHQ.

Sir Alistair turned to address Douglas Harvey.

"What about it?" he inquired. "Anything in the Soviet signals intelligence to make us think they've sussed CORONA?"

Douglas Harvey regarded Sir Alistair myopically, his features clamped to his skull by a pair of large, impenetrable spectacles. "I believe we'd have noticed," he replied earnestly. "I can instruct my staff to search the recent decrypts."

Sir Alistair shook his head. "Were you to, I would with the greatest of reluctance be required to extradite you to the United States for summary execution, Mr. Harvey. Please don't compel me to do so."

Douglas Harvey fell silent, his expression suggesting he was uncertain whether he was having his leg pulled or measured for a set of leather restraints. "I could search the decrypts myself," he suggested.

"There's a good lad," Sir Alistair agreed. "If you find anything significant, you may brief me and I shall brief Mr. Philby. As Mr. Philby has rather more experience in Washington than I, perhaps we'll let him break the news to the Americans."

This engendered more laughter than most of Sir Alistair's earlier remarks. He surveyed the men before him, feeling for an instant like a gratified music hall entertainer. Kim Philby was laughing as well, but he clearly wasn't entirely pleased by the suggestion.

He felt himself touched with muted anger, a poorly-mended tear in the fabric of his suit coat caught in the corner of his eye. Reminders of his nation growing increasingly beholden to its former colony seemed bent on intruding upon his morning. Unbidden, his moment of pique swelled and bubbled as he recalled sitting in this room six months earlier when one of the secretarial staff had closed her notebook and inquired absently whether he thought parliament would permit the Church of England to sell Winchester Cathedral to an American businessman.

He'd learned later that day that the FCO had in fact assisted in brokering the transaction. The building was scheduled to be dismantled in the spring of 1962 and shipped to someplace named Orlando, in the state of Florida.

He'd been wed to Caroline thirty-seven years earlier in St. John's Chapel – she'd been quite beside herself when she'd learned that the site of their vows was poised to cross an ocean.

The briefing continued for another fifteen minutes, by which time Sir Alistair decided that most of the intelligent questions had been put to him and answered or politely deflected, as he'd been requested to do in Washington. He signaled its conclusion by unlocking the door and pulling it open. A visible cloud of blue smoke was driven before him into the corridor beyond. Each of the recipients of the briefing filed past him, and he set about refilling his pipe. At length he appreciated that Alec Grey had contrived to be the last to rise from his seat. Alec Grey no longer appeared in the slightest bit amused, or even greatly impressed by the revelations of the CORONA project. His expression had become markedly dour, Sir Alistair decided, and he harkened back to his Scots ancestors.

"May I have a word, Sir Alistair?" he inquired.

"I'm never entirely at my ease with you when you undertake to be deferential, Mr. Grey," Sir Alistair said as he lit his pipe. He nodded his agreement.

Alec Grey closed the door to the briefing room. "I'm afraid PAPER HAT has been blown," he said mechanically.

Sir Alistair was several seconds recalling that this was the code name for a project to place a microphone in an office of the Soviet consulate. He remembered being briefed about it in the flutter of audiences and files before he'd departed for Washington.

A chill touched him. "Are you certain?" he asked, his teeth clamped to the stem of his pipe.

"Reasonably certain," Alec Grey replied. "I'll be able to confirm it when we have the tapes transcribed. They'll turn out to have been staged for our benefit."

Sir Alistair withdrew his pipe. "Blast," he muttered. "Do we know how it was rumbled?"

"We know it wasn't the team and it wasn't the microphone," Alec Grey said defensively. "I was there when Hugh Somerfield installed it. He bored through the brick and the plaster on the other side of the wall an eighth of an inch at a time with a hand brace. I examined the bit myself when he finally reached the consulate. There was no paint on the side of it. He successfully positioned the microphone behind the paint on the cornice board in the room across from our listening post. Even if the Soviets swept the room, the microphone would have registered as another nail in the woodwork."

"And yet it was rumbled," Sir Alistair said didactically.

"Yes it was," Alec Grey agreed, a note of accusation in his tone.

Sir Alistair felt his hair prickle. "I do not wish to hear the word 'mole' spoken in my presence," he said sternly.

Alec Grey almost smiled at this. "I'm not sure I wish to speak it," he agreed. "I doubt there's another word that covers the likely cause of our being discovered. We could call him a Soviet infiltrator if you prefer."

"There is no 'him' at this point, Mr. Grey," Sir Alistair cautioned him sternly. "There's just a blown operation, and no evidence that it was compromised internally."

Alec Grey nodded. "I agree," he said. "The POST-CARD and GOLD WATCH operations showed no evidence of having been compromised internally either."

Sir Alistair regarded Alec Grey coldly for a moment, but he sensed a creeping disquiet descend upon him. He permitted himself a long draught of his pipe before he spoke. "I want proof," he said quietly. "I want something tangible, and I don't want a blasted mole hunt."

"Yes sir," Alec Grey said, and he smiled thinly. He turned to leave, and then seemed to recall something else he'd meant to ask.

"At the moment, the only people who know about PAPER HAT are myself, Hugh Somerfield and yourself. Until the transcripts are circulated and it all becomes patently obvious, I wonder if we might keep it that way."

"Yes," Sir Alistair agreed. "Yes, of course."

Alec Grey smiled once more and opened the door of the briefing room, slipping into the gloom beyond it.

5

T he book shop was suffocating. The rain had arrived unbidden an hour earlier, and damp permeated the Dickensian building. The inner surfaces of the sooty windows at the front of the shop had grown slick with condensation. He wondered absently how it was that the shelves of old volumes didn't rot in these conditions.

Perhaps it was their contents, he mused. Perhaps even the corruption of damp and mildew had its standards. Perhaps the ugliness of this place kept lesser decay in the street beyond the shop.

The damp was preferable to the dust, he considered as he pretended to peruse the books before him. The shop had been tomb-like on the occasion of his previous visit. It had occurred to him that he'd been inhaling particles of the books around him. He'd been seized at the time with the uncontrollable desire to run from this place, to fill his lungs with the automobile exhaust and smoke and sewer fumes of the city.

The shop reminded him of what had euphemistically been called a 'gentleman's club' he'd visited in Limehouse ten years earlier, one of the many opium dens Her Majesty's government licensed and gratefully collected taxes from. The tang of putrefaction had been heavy between its walls as well, but at least its proprietors had known the courtesy to set fire to its source.

He reminded himself that no one he knew would come anywhere near this shop. He would not be observed here, and later questioned about his odd predilections. His colleagues were hours away, behind a high fence, in a con- crete building, more carefully guarded than convicts.

There was a card in his trouser pocket with his name on it, and an expressionless photograph. The man who was Arthur Dunross was anonymous save for that card. He was required to carry it about with him, to present it when he approached the locked gates and begged leave to enter or to return to the world beyond the fence. The picture barely resembled him. He looked like an adolescent's crude ren- dering of something vaguely sexual in that photograph.

He squinted at the faded gold leaf that filled the embossed title of one of the books on the shelf before him. The light was deplorable. After some time he realized that the title was in French. All the books on the shelf were in French. He glanced anxiously about himself, to ascertain whether he'd been observed. The shop was deserted.

His arm had grown numb clasping the book he'd brought with him. He'd carried it thus for hours, on the train up to London, through the tube, along the Strand to this cavern. He'd dared not relax its confinement, lest the obscenities within its cracked leather covers ooze from their imprisonment and infect the drably-clothed women and bored clerks with whom he'd shared his seats. He'd come to imagine it as having the smell of decay about it, the metallic wetness of blood, the sweat and saltiness from between a woman's thighs.

The book was revolting beyond words, he thought bitterly, and who better to know it in all its depravity than he, who'd read carefully its every word.

He stepped quietly from between two of the book cases that stood like ill-kempt dominoes across the floor of the shop. The man at the till observed him for a moment before he smiled. He looked like someone's Latin master, Arthur Dunross decided. He was of no specific height, with light hair of no particular color, a chin notable by its absence, a rather shabby woolen sweater that looked as if it hadn't been washed since the book under his arm had been printed. The book under his arm had been printed in 1892, he recalled, and no doubt rowed across from France under the cover of night.

Arthur Dunross approached the till and struggled to return the man's smile. His features defied him. He imagined the ancient paper slowly decomposing around him to be emitting something toxic, gradually poisoning his nerves until all the muscles of his body banded together in mutiny. He sighed as he raised his burden to the counter between them and prised his fingers from its covers.

The man behind the till was Peter Kroger. Arthur Dunross allowed that he was uncertain whether it was his real name, and considering the nature of what took place in his shop, it seemed unlikely. He spoke oddly, clearly not a native of London. At times it had seemed he was an American pretending to be English for the sake of his fellow party-goers, an intentional parody.

"It's good to see you again," Peter Kroger said, his eyes clearly on the book, rather than meeting those of Arthur Dunross. "Was the work to your liking?" The man behind the till tapped the cover of the book gently with the tips of his fingers, the gesture both reverent and salacious.

Arthur Dunross scowled despite himself. "It was sickening," he muttered.

Peter Kroger seemed genuinely distressed for an instant, appearing to have allowed his benign mask to topple from his features. His hand caressed the book. "It's quite rare, you know. It was written by a man known to us Jules d'Anjou. He most certainly suffered for his art. When the French authorities of the time became aware of his writings, he spent twelve years in an asylum. It wasn't the sort of place you'd send your worst enemy back then."

Arthur Dunross felt himself grow unaccountably angry with the peculiar man before him. When he spoke, his voice had dropped to a harsh whisper, a rasp of escaping steam. "You didn't tell me there'd be descriptions of a fourteen-year-old girl being... outraged. If I'd been caught in possession of this, I'd be spending twelve years locked up."

Peter Kroger smiled beneficently. "Now now," he said, "the police can't be troubled by what they don't know." He slid the book toward himself and opened it. There was a small brown envelope attached to the flyleaf with sticky tape. He scowled and glanced up at Arthur Dunross reprovingly. "This book is over half a century old... I do wish you'd treat these works with the respect they deserve."

Arthur Dunross leant minutely closer to Peter Kroger. "They deserve to be burnt," he growled.

The man behind the till appeared to ignore him, his attention occupied with the removal of the offending sticky tape from his book. At length he opened the envelope it had been securing and regarded its contents. They consisted of ten photographic negatives, each comprised of several pages of text and diagrams. He smiled fleetingly and returned them to their slumber.

"The Center will be entirely satisfied, I'm certain," he said as he began glancing about his shop. "I'll give you another book to carry the next consignment in. Is there anything in particular that strikes your fancy?" He turned to catch Arthur Dunross' eye. "No fourteen-year-old girls being outraged this time... I promise."

Arthur Dunross drove his fist into the polished wood between himself and Peter Kroger. "I don't want another book," he said coldly. "You owe me for this lot and the two this past summer. I'll take it all now, in cash."

Peter Kroger's expression sagged and he withdrew his attention reluctantly from his books. "I'm afraid I can't do that," he said.

"My agreement with your... employers... was that I get paid when I deliver."

The shop fell silent for some time. Arthur Dunross regarded Peter Kroger, watching a parade of expressions each take possession of his features and then relinquish them in favor of its successor, a surreal queue of jugglers and acrobats seen through a peep hole. Somewhere at the periphery of his attention, a hitherto unnoticed clock ticked, the swinging of its pendulum almost audible as well as it ploughed furrows in the liquid air.

"I'd certainly like to oblige you," Peter Kroger said at length. "The Center hasn't forwarded me the funds, you see, and there's nothing I can..."

Arthur Dunross hammered the counter once more. "I'm taking a bloody great risk doing this and I expect to be paid," he barked.

"There's a good deal more to this work than mere money," Peter Kroger said, with waning conviction.

"Perhaps for you bolshies," Arthur Dunross said.

Peter Kroger forced himself to smile. He'd clearly known little experience with dissatisfied customers. The men who came into this place were hardly likely to complain about the quality of their purchases to the editor of the Times.

"What would you have me do?" Peter Kroger asked, a decided note of pleading in his voice. "I can't pay you if the Center doesn't pay me. It's just that simple, and..."

Arthur Dunross held up hand, and the man behind the till fell silent. "Your name is Peter Kroger," he began. "You've a wife named Helen. You live in a bungalow at 45 Cranley Drive in Ruislip. You run a pornographic book-shop and you're a spy for the Russians. What do think would be the longest it would take Scotland Yard to have a

squad of men around here were they to receive an anonymous letter in tomorrow morning's post to that effect?"

Peter Kroger stared at him, unwilling to speak for a
moment. "I don't believe you're serious," he said at length.
"You'd be cutting your own throat as well."

Arthur Dunross smiled coldly and shook his head.
"You don't even know my name," he said. "Lonsdale, the
fellow who put me onto you... he won't have told you. I
know how you lot operate."

Peter Kroger sighed. "Yes, I can see that you do," he
said. He considered the man before him for a moment and
then nodded his head. "You're quite right... you've not
been dealt with fairly. You understand, it will take me a few
days to get a message to the Center and have them forward
your money."

"I shall be back in London Tuesday week," Arthur
Dunross said, his jaw taut. "I shall come with a letter to
Scotland Yard prepared and ready to post."

Peter Kroger nodded, saying nothing. Arthur
Dunross stared into his eyes for a moment longer before
he turned to leave. They seemed inappropriate for the
remainder of his face. His face was jovial, guileless, the
image of a banker gradually relenting to jowls and a distended belly. His eyes alone burned beneath his flesh.
Arthur Dunross realized that Peter Kroger's eyes had witnessed things he himself could wish had remained forever
hidden.

6

"I'd bend over a table and do naughty things with Alec Grey 'til I couldn't stand up straight," Julie Gardner said, her voice touched with ribald amusement at the thought. She spoke without permitting her attention to be diverted from the street before her, the hive of other cars, the dark blue Ford Anglia several cars ahead of her own. A hulking black taxi was crowding her, threatening to overtake her. She eased minutely closer to the center of the street, confining it. Its driver thrust two fingers into the air behind his largely opaque windscreen and cursed.

"I didn't know you fancied him," the woman in the seat beside her remarked. "From what I've heard of him, I wouldn't have said he was your type."

Julie Gardner forced herself to recall that the woman in the seat beside her was Margaret something. This was the third new girl in as many weeks. She'd called the second one by the first one's name on several occasions, and the air between them had become quite testy.

She decided she was amused by her inability to remember the common, pronounceable English names of her colleagues without some effort when that of Valentin Maksimovich Chervenkov, the driver of the Anglia, rolled from her tongue like a poem she'd memorized in junior school and subsequently never forgotten. With far less effort than would have been required to summon Margaret's surname, she could have repeated everything British intelligence knew about Valentin Chervenkov, or at the very least, everything his file at A4 had confided to her.

"You'd fancy him and all, if you realized you owe him this job," she said.

"Really?" Margaret said. "I don't think I ever met him. I thought A4 was run by Mr. Dixon."

"Andy Dixon owes his job to Alec Grey as well," Julie Gardner said. "He's one of Mr. Grey's chaps."

In the corner of her eye, Margaret appeared to consider this. Julie Gardner forced herself to recall her initial months with A4, her almost perpetual confusion over the hierarchy of an organization patched together over several decades by a succession of administrators who'd each thought it unlikely to survive another year.

Valentin Chervenkov moped through an intersection before her, catching a traffic signal as it turned amber. Without thinking, she downshifted and felt the car around her surge forward. The Volvo P1800 was unquestionably her favorite of A4's livery. She traversed the intersection as the traffic signal became red, hearing the protest of several horns rattling as she passed them. They were immediately swallowed by the undulating stomach growls of the city.

The Anglia was half a block ahead, too distant for its driver to have observed her, she decided. She permitted the Volvo to return to its languid progress, imagining a note of reluctance in the rapidly diminishing throat of its engine.

Margaret's features had grown bloodless in the previous few seconds.

"So have you actually... been out with this Alec Grey bloke?" Margaret inquired uncertainly.

Julie Gardner shook her head. "I've a husband and a daughter," she replied, and she removed her left hand from the Volvo's steering wheel long enough to display the ring she wore on it. "He wouldn't understand. Not even for the best job in England."

This seemed to amuse Margaret. "Is it?" she asked. "The best job in England, I mean."

Julie Gardner felt herself frown. "Of course it is," she replied. "You get to drive around London all day without paying for petrol, in cars you couldn't possibly afford, keeping the realm safe from Russian spies, nice wage packet at the end of the week, thanks of a grateful nation even if it doesn't know you exist... and one of those." She gestured to a small leather folder on the console between the seats.

Margaret held it before herself and regarded it, clearly not appreciating it.

"One of what?"

"A police pass," Julie Gardner explained. "When you go out by yourself you'll have one too. Show it to any copper who thinks you must have had a few to be driving like this and he'll get on his bike and leave you alone."

Margaret smiled, clearly impressed.

"Will I get one of these cars?" she asked.

"A4 only has one of these cars," Julie Gardner replied, in what she hoped was tone to suggest that the Volvo had been spoken for. "A girl could find herself assigned to Camden if she tried to pinch it."

The expression of the woman beside her grew dark. "No fear of that," she hissed. "Do you know what they've done to the streets there?"

There were few of A4's watchers who were unfamiliar with the peculiar transmutation of the London street map. The previous summer the National Trust had succeeded in persuading the office of the mayor of London to restore several of the city's historically-significant locations to their original medieval names. What had once been Grape Street was referred to as 'G Street', as its residents considered Gropecunt Lane to be somewhat impolite. It had been the preferred address for brothels in the middle ages.

Margaret gestured through the windscreen, dispelling her amusement. "I think he's turned into Halsey Street," she said. Julie Gardner was pleased to observe that Valentin Chervenkov had indicated before he'd turned, something he'd have been unlikely to do if he'd suspected he was being pursued.

"I still don't understand who Alec Grey is," Margaret said at length. Julie Gardner turned into Halsey Street and found the Anglia where she'd anticipated it, half a block distant.

She permitted herself to relax in the embrace of the Volvo's seat. Margaret was the first of her charges thus far to inquire about matters beyond their current speed and direction, and the nature of the Russians they were keeping under surveillance. Julie Gardner decided that while attaching a dedicated historian to A4 would no doubt have violated the Official Secrets Act in a sufficient number of places to have sent the historian in question to Wormwood Scrubs prison for the remainder of his natural life, she might nominate herself to the post for a brief while, within the secret chamber that was the passenger compartment of her borrowed car.

"I started with A4 in the wireless room," she began. "That was when Tony Roberts was still head of A4. Tony was a lovely fellow... he'd have walked on broken glass for anyone who worked for him, but the first week I was there I knew the whole thing was a joke."

Margaret looked decidedly shocked.

"Someone said Tony only knew how to say three things," she continued. "Fancy a cuppa, God bless the queen and S.O.P."

"S.O.P?" Margaret asked, her expression suggesting she appreciated she was intended to.

"Standard operating procedure," Julie Gardner explained. "Everything we did back then came out of a book. The problem was, the Russians had the book too."

"Do you mean we had a Russian spy?"

Julie Gardner shook her head. "We had Tony Roberts," she said. "He was all the Russians needed."

"Now you've lost me."

Julie Gardner reasserted her attention upon the street, assuring herself that Valentin Chervenkov hadn't eluded them. The Anglia was where she expected it to be.

"We've a flat in Kensington Palace Gardens, across from the Russian embassy," she said. "There are always at least two of our people up there, watching everyone who enters or leaves the building."

"I've heard of it," Margaret agreed. "I've not actually been assigned there yet."

Julie Gardner smiled coldly. "You'd do well not to volunteer for it," she warned the woman beside her. "It's about a foot deep in fag ends and coffee cups, and eight hours of looking at Russians through binoculars is a lot like being dead, only less exciting."

Margaret seemed puzzled by her unglamorous description of the watchers' observation post, and Julie Gardner appreciated that her superior, Andrew Dixon, had probably begun his subtle recruitment of his new staff member for what was at best an unloved assignment.

"When I started, the men in the flat watched the Russians, and whenever anyone left the embassy, they'd identify him and radio in a five-digit number, along with the direction he was last seen traveling and whether he was on foot or in a car. Someone like me would write down the information and watchers would be dispatched to follow him."

"Isn't that what we do now?" Margaret asked.

Julie Gardner considered this. "Our operating procedures are a lot less standard," she replied. "The Russians have a wireless room of their own, and they could listen to the watchers' radios just as well as we could. Since they knew who was leaving the embassy, they eventually sussed the code numbers we'd assigned to everyone on their staff. They knew who we'd assigned watchers to follow."

"Wasn't that... rather pointless?"

Julie Gardner glanced at Margaret, trying to decide whether the woman beside her was endeavoring to be sarcastic.

"Yes it was," she agreed at length. "Everyone who worked for Tony Roberts arrived at work neatly shaven, in a clean suit, wearing a proper hat. A4 sent them out to follow the Russians in a fleet of dark gray and navy blue Vauxhall Victors. Every car had three men it in... one to drive, one to work the radio and one to read the maps. I imagine the Russians could have identified them with a blindfold on."

"Did we know they knew about us?" Margaret inquired, her expression suggesting that she was finding the bureaucracy of counterespionage to be more perplexing than she'd anticipated.

"It depends on which 'we' you mean," Julie Gardner replied. "Tony Roberts was of the opinion that Russians are thick as two short planks, and they could never have thought of listening to our radios."

"And... and Alec Grey?"

Julie Gardner smiled, amused by her memories of her first encounter with Alec Grey.

"One day about two years ago, this chap Alec Grey arrived from Leconfield House with a letter from Sir Alistair Fitzhenry and one of his very tall fellows, Hugh Somerfield. He walked into Tony Roberts' office without asking leave, and Tony... Tony wasn't in the best of moods. I couldn't see it all from the wireless room, but I was told later Alec Grey put a stack of photos of Russians coming out of the embassy on Tony's desk, every one with a five-digit identification code on it. Tony wanted to know how he'd found the codes, as they were supposed to be for A4 people only. Alec Grey said he'd sat in a car outside the embassy with a camera and a radio, listening to the watchers."

"And had he?" Margaret asked.

Julie Gardner considered the Ford Anglia in the distance. It seemed for a moment that Valentin Chervenkov was considering parking his car, but after some consideration he signaled to turn into Milner Street. Julie Gardner followed discretely.

"As the story goes, he had fifty photos, and every one of the codes matched our own," she said.

"This Tony Roberts chap... was he angry?"

"Alec Grey didn't give him much time to be angry. He came into the wireless room and he said he needed someone to be an impartial witness. I was the closest to hand. I remember Tony saying that I couldn't be spared, and Alec Grey telling him that if I missed any calls while I was away from my station, the Soviet embassy would catch them for me."

Margaret put her hand to her face to conceal her amusement.

"Hugh Somerfield had a wooden case with him. He opened it and took out a peculiar electric lamp and a very long lamp flex. We all went into the garage where the Vauxhall Victors were kept. Alec Grey said he'd spent the last week wandering around the city, looking for watchers' cars. Every time he thought he'd found one, he marked it with a special chinagraph pencil. He had it with him. You couldn't see the mark it made in normal light, but it glowed blue under the special lamp. Alec Grey led Tony Roberts through the garage, shining the lamp on the boot of each of the cars."

"How many had he marked, then?"

"All of them."

Margaret pursed her lips. "I'll bet he wasn't half furious," she said.

Julie Gardner considered this, recalling the two men standing at the distant end of the garage. The air had been foul with the exhaust of the cars that had returned from their assignments, and dank with the musk of the underground. Several of the overhead lamps had been dark, with their few remaining comrades casting shadows like shards of glass across the features of the two men. Hugh Somerfield had switched off his lamp and begun walking back toward the front of the garage, coiling its flex around his elbow. She'd been uncertain whether she was intended to follow him or remain where she'd been discarded.

They'd both been livid, she remembered, standing like male caryatids bearing the whole of England upon their heads. Predictably, Tony Roberts had demanded of Alec Grey how he and the other mandarins from Leconfield House had dared trespass upon his patch, hindering the vital efforts of his people. Alec Grey had said nothing in response to this. Alec Grey had said nothing for a very long time, and when he'd spoken his voice had hardly been louder than the distant rumble of traffic in the street beyond the garage.

"Every report that's come out of this place in the last year has been written for you by Moscow Center," he'd said, not turning to face Tony Roberts. "It took me three days to rumble your entire staff. The Soviet embassy has had a good deal longer than that."

"Where the hell do you think..." Tony Roberts had begun, the pitch of his voice having risen noticeably.

Alec Grey had interrupted him with an envelope he'd extracted from his coat pocket, and Tony Roberts had accepted it without comment. He'd torn it open as he'd unwrapped the newspaper from the egg and chips he'd favored for his tea.

She turned to consider Margaret for an instant before she forced her attention to the street once again. "Alec Grey gave him a list," she continued. "I asked him what it was when I had my interview with him the next week. He told me it was a list of changes to be made to A4. Tony Roberts read the first line, chucked it on the ground and told Alec Grey to get stuffed. Tony'd been given the sack when I came in the next day. I think he's been posted to Iran."

"Did Mr. Grey tell you what the first line on the list said, then?" Margaret inquired.

Julie Gardner smiled. "Yes he did, and he said I could tell anyone else in the shop I pleased. It said that henceforth, A4 was to employ women as watchers."

She watched Margaret's features darken in the corner of her eye. "I thought there've always been women watchers," she said uncertainly.

Julie Gardner shook her head. "Tony wouldn't stand for it... said the wives of his lads would go spare when they learned their husbands were spending eight hours a day alone in a car with another woman. That was Tony... anything for his people, even if it did make us all look like clowns to the Russians."

Margaret leant back in her seat, regarding the pedestrians swimming past her window. "What I don't understand is, we still have chaps in that flat in Kensington Palace Garden, and they still have numbers for all the Russians who leave the embassy. I worked in the wireless room when I was first hired."

"No, you didn't," Julie Gardner corrected her. "You worked in Alec Grey's theater."

"In what?"

"That's how his mind works, Alec Grey," she said. "He kept the old system in place, and he's kept the Russians thinking it's still active. There's several dozen of them who pretend to come and go at the embassy, thinking they're keeping us occupied. When the wireless operators at the Soviet embassy hear the code number for someone who's just left the building, they assume he's being followed. If someone leaves the building without a code number being announced on the radio, they think he's slipped his minders... like Valentin Maksimovich up ahead."

"But this car has a radio..." Margaret began, now clearly perplexed.

"Yes it does," Julie Gardner agreed. "It has a taxi radio, and all genuine communications between us and Regent's Park are to sound like calls for taxi drivers. You're to be briefed on the system next week."

Margaret appeared to be on the point of drawing a diagram to keep track of what she'd been told. "So there are dozens of Russians walking around London thinking they're occupying the time of... almost a hundred watchers... when in fact all the watchers are following Russians who don't think they're being followed at all."

"...and that's down to Alec Grey," Julie Gardner observed.

"And who's this Valentin chap we're meant to be watching?" Margaret inquired, perhaps grateful to have a lone Russian upon which to focus her attentions.

Julie Gardner watched the new subject of Margaret's inquiries turn into Draycott Avenue.

Margaret would not have been briefed on the Soviet personnel who were currently known to be at large in London, Julie Gardner reminded herself. That facet of her training would occupy months, and there was a considerable likelihood she'd prove inadequate to the task. Remembering the nuances of the uncountable photographs in A4's books of known Soviets was interminable, soul-destroying. Many of the new staff who'd come to A4 in the wake of Tony Roberts' departure had subsequently accepted other postings and left the Georgian manor house in Regent's Park that now served A4 as a headquarters with obvious relief.

"He's relatively new," she replied, "and we don't know a lot about him. He's very low-level so far... he just drives about fetching things, as close as we've been able to discover. Either that, or he's terribly clever and he's managed to keep us from spotting what he's really up to."

"Which do you think he is?" Margaret asked.

Julie Gardner parted her lips to reply when she noticed the blue Anglia ahead. It was as it had been for the past hour, unhurried, its driver clearly unaware of her presence. She regarded the number plate, squinted to discern the shape of Valentin Chervenkov's head in the awkward rear window. Without speaking, she stopped the Volvo and reversed into a laneway.

Margaret turned to stare at her. "What are you doing?" she demanded. "He's getting away."

Julie Gardner put her finger to her lips, and then gestured into the street. She hardly dared breath. Three full minutes elapsed before the blue Anglia appeared and drove past the mouth of the laneway. She permitted it twenty seconds, and then she let the clutch of the Volvo out and resumed her place behind it.

"Hang about," Margaret said. "It drove off. I saw it drive off."

Julie Gardner gestured at the car half a block before them. "And yet, there it is."

Margaret stared at the Anglia, and then at Julie Gardner. Another minute elapsed before she spoke. "I don't understand this," she said quietly.

"That would be two of us," Julie Gardner agreed. "We've just watched a Russian do something they've not done before."

"How's that?"

"That was a lovely piece of driving you just saw," she explained. "There were two blue Anglias. They had identical number plates. One of them was parked. When Valentin Chervenkov turned, he had enough time to exchange places with the parked car before we reached the corner. By the time we came into Draycott Avenue, Valentin was stopped and the other car was driving off."

"That seems like a lot of bother for someone who just runs around and fetches things, and doesn't think he's being followed. Have we been rumbled?"

In the distance, Valentin Chervenkov indicated to turn. Julie Gardner shook her head. "It was a precaution," she said. "It was clever, but they must know that the first one of us who sees it will spoil it. Whoever Valentin Chervenkov is, he must want rather badly not to be watched."

Margaret appeared to consider this. "If you don't mind me asking," she said at length, "how did you rumble the duplicate car?"

Julie Gardner's attention was entirely on the blue Anglia. "The real one's been driving about for half the day. Its gotten quite dusty. I imagine the replacement's been parked for almost as long. It was clean."

Margaret stared through the windscreen at Valentin Chervenkov's car for some time, saying nothing.

7

One of the pleasures of being the director, Alec Grey mused as he pushed the door of Sir Alistair Fitzhenry's office closed behind him, was that his rooms had been painted more recently than the late Mesozoic period. He found this remarkable, in that his own office looked like a coal cellar and gave every indication that it would continue to do so long after he was drawing his pension. All of Sir Alistair's lights worked, as did the electric fire, he imagined. Perhaps it was as Hugh Somerfield had suggested — in time he would look like Sir Alistair. He might well be able to occupy these rooms if such a transformation occurred.

Their rightful occupant smiled benignly from behind his desk and gestured to an unoccupied chair. There was a secretary in the other, Alec Grey observed, and he wondered fleetingly what made his second summons to Leconfield house this day so formal as to require a stenographer.

He'd all but descended into his chair when the secretary sniffled, and she hid her features behind her hand. Alec Grey glanced at her without thinking, noticing that she lacked a writing pad and pencil. He looked uncertainly at Sir Alistair. The director's attention had been drawn to the woman before him, his expression avuncular.

"I'm sorry to drag you up here again, Mr. Grey," Sir Alistair said.

He waved dismissingly, a gesture which Alec Grey had long since come to appreciate indicated that Sir Alistair felt no such thing, but that he was aware of rites and formalities attached to his position which could not be dispensed with for the sake of expediency.

Alec Grey nodded, feeling himself smile despite his uncertainty. He glanced at the secretary.

"This is Alice Woodward," Sir Alistair explained. At the mention of her name, the woman removed her hand from her face and regarded Alec Grey. "She's one of our confidential typists."

Alec Grey smiled as disarmingly as he could manage. "I don't believe we've met," he said, wondering if it would be appropriate to offer her his hand to shake. The geometry of the two chairs seemed to preclude it.

"Miss Woodward has had a rather nasty time today," Sir Alistair continued. "She's had an encounter with someone from behind the curtain."

Alec Grey felt his eyes narrow at the mention of Sir Alistair's current euphemism for the Soviets. There was a hint of accusation in his tone, suggesting that Alec Grey and his staff bore responsibility for maintaining a respectable distance between agents of a hostile foreign power and the decent women employed by MI5.

"She's shown considerable courage in bringing this... matter... to my attention so promptly," he continued. Alice Woodward smiled fleetingly. "I think it would be best if I let her tell you what's happened."

Alice Woodward glanced at him, her features tinged with startled unease. "Me, sir?" she asked.

Sir Alistair smiled. "I think it would be best," he repeated. "You may tell Mr. Grey everything you told me." He directed his attention to Alec Grey. "Miss Woodward types up much of what you read from this department. She has the highest clearance, and probably knows more secrets than the two of us combined."

Alec Grey nodded. This had been a feature of all the meetings he'd taken with the director. He'd been informed discretely what he might and might not disclose in Alice Woodward's presence.

Alice Woodward seemed to compose herself by degrees, daubing at her eyes and squaring her shoulders against the back of her chair. She would have been an attractive woman in another context, Alec Grey thought idly, had she not found herself ensnared in something ugly left dangling by the Russians.

"I usually take my lunch in a park several blocks along Curzon Street," she began. "There are trees and some benches to sit on. It hadn't begun raining yet, this morning, so I took my sandwiches there."

She raised her eyes until they met Alec Grey's, as if she'd just recalled being instructed to do so.

"Shortly after I began eating today, a man sat on the bench beside me. He knew my name. He said he wanted to show me something. He… gave me an envelope with some photographs inside."

Alice Woodward glanced imploringly at Sir Alistair, who appeared to consider her wordless request. When at last he spoke, his voice was a harsh whisper despite the remote likelihood of anyone beyond the walls of his office having access to their conversation. "Miss Woodward's visitor gave her pictures of her brother, Charles Woodward. He's a chemist… he works for the… Ministry of Agriculture, I believe." Alice Woodward nodded. "He's also secretly homosexual."

Alice Woodward appeared stung by Sir Alistair's explanation, and she was some time forcing her eyes to again meet Alec Grey's. "Charlie's very careful," she said quietly. "I don't think he even… goes with anyone… at the moment. Last summer… he went on holiday to Spain.

I think that's where the pictures were taken... him and another man. They were... horrible..."

Alec Grey felt himself exhale, unaware that he'd been anticipating the woman's reaction. He'd expected her to succumb to a fresh draught of tears, and he permitted himself to be impressed by her composure.

"The man said he intended to post them to the police unless I did as he said. Charlie would go to prison... I don't think he'd survive in there."

"What did he want you to do for him?" Alec Grey inquired.

"He wanted me to take photographs of some of the papers I'm given to type," she replied. "He gave me a packet with a camera."

Wordlessly, Sir Alistair opened one of his desk drawers and pushed a large brown envelope across his blotter. Alec Grey emptied it into his lap. Its contents consisted of several typed pages, a package which he imagined would be film cassettes and a small silver block that expanded into a camera when he pulled it apart. He glanced over the pages, and then returned his attention to the camera.

"Minox B," he observed, regarding the object in his hand. He'd encountered several of them. They used 9.5 millimeter film, and they could be set up to copy documents by anyone with at least two working fingers and reasonable eyesight. The Soviets were greatly enamored of them.

"He said... that is, there's instructions for using it," Alice Woodward continued, "and a list of subjects he wanted me to look for."

Alec Grey nodded. "Did he tell you how to get the film to him once you'd done as he instructed?"

She nodded. "I use the Bond Street tube station," she said. "He knew where I live, and how I come to work. He told me how to find a loose tile near the top of the stairway. I'm to put the film behind it, and make a chalk mark on a lamp post a block further along. When he's collected the film, he'll make a different chalk mark on the lamp post, and I'm to collect fresh film for the camera from behind the tile."

"A dead drop," Alec Grey observed. "Your visitor knows what he's about. He's chosen a location that will be difficult to observe, with several ways to leg it if he thinks he's been rumbled."

"I did get the sense he'd done this before," she agreed quietly, her voice portending further tears.

Alec Grey leant back in his chair, listening to the leather and horsehair protest beneath him. He turned to meet Alice Woodward's gaze. "You'll no doubt have heard what we do here referred to as 'the great game,'" he said evenly. "It may seem preposterous, but even our game has rules. Your visitor has violated several of them. I feel certain Sir Alistair is less than pleased."

She turned to regard the director for an instant, clearly unsure what she was to make of his displeasure.

"It's a great deal easier to obtain forgiveness than permission," Alec Grey continued, his voice having acquired a conspiratorial rasp. He leant minutely closer to Alice Woodward. "I shall hazard to say that we can promise you nothing will befall your brother, even if the pictures you saw should find their way to the police."

He turned to regard Sir Alistair, who seemed to be a moment appreciating what was expected of him. He nodded cautiously, as if he feared being manipulated into conceding some aspect of the conversation as yet unspoken. "Shall I alert the local nick, Mr. Grey?" he inquired warily, using the expression as he might have consumed an unfamiliar wine of questionable vintage.

Alec Grey smiled fleetingly and returned his attention to Alice Woodward. He was pleased to see her return his smile, to permit her shoulders to relax into the back of her chair.

"I'd like you to know that if you wish, you can leave this room in about five minutes and never hear another word about the camera, the man who interrupted your lunch or the compromising pictures of your brother. One of my lads will fill your dead drop, we'll find a way to put it under surveillance and we'll catch your visitor when he arrives to service it. He'll be in prison or on an Aeroflot back to Moscow in a fortnight."

Her eyes flashed, and she seemed to appreciate that he was poised to ask something more of her.

"What would happen if I don't leave the room in five minutes?" she inquired.

Alec Grey grinned, uncertain if he was pleased with her or with himself. "If you don't leave the room, you can do exactly what your visitor meant to blackmail you into doing. I'll give you back the camera, and you can spy for the Soviet Union."

She stared at him, genuinely shocked.

"There's actually something preferable to preventing the Soviets from spying on us," he explained. "We're particularly fond of providing them with disinformation."

She regarded him curiously. "I don't understand," she said at length.

Sir Alistair coughed. "We'd very much like them to think you're spying for them, when in fact you'll be photographing documents we prepare." He turned to address Alec Grey. "I presume that is what you had in mind."

"Something like that," he agreed, and he returned his attention to Alice Woodward. "You'll be provided with papers to copy, and situations to take pictures of them without anyone else being likely to observe you."

Alice Woodward's eyes widened. They were sea-green eyes, he observed, without the darkened rings about them that scarred the veterans of Sir Alistair's legions. She'd come here in response to a suggestion over sherry and cigars one evening, he imagined, a hushed conversation between Sir Alistair and Lord Woodward or Sir Woodward or Doctor Woodward or whatever her father answered to. Some other lord or sir or doctor of her family's liking would squire her away in a year or two, and she'd be well removed from this place.

She'd not imagined she'd have to touch the sinister little camera, or skulk about as her new controller had instructed her. He watched her expression resolve, permitting himself to observe a flash of anticipation fused with her distrust.

"I don't think I could," she said nervously. "I wouldn't know what to do. I... I mean, if that man were to sit beside me again in the park..."

"He won't," Alec Grey assured her. "He's taken a substantial risk making contact with you. He's set up the dead drop to be sure he won't have to take another. In the event he makes a liar of me, he'll have one of my people to deal with."

She appeared to consider this. "Your people?"

"I'll assign someone to keep an eye on you every minute of every day until we pick up your visitor," he continued. "I wouldn't have said there was much of a chance you'll see him again, but he's proven he's not bothered by breaking a few rules. It's possible he'll get a bit stroppy if he discovers he's been messed about."

Sir Alistair's expression creased in the corner of his eye, clearly disturbed by the direction their conversation was taking.

Alice Woodward regarded him for almost a minute, her features ineffable. At length she nodded, her eyes never leaving his. "Very well," she said evenly, no echo of her previous sobbing now audible in her words. She turned to Sir Alistair, as if to solicit his permission. The director said nothing.

Alec Grey permitted himself to smile. "It won't be anything like as exciting as you imagine," he said.

This clearly amused her, and she glanced at the far wall, a moment of ill-concealed embarrassment touching her features.

"Do you mind if I ask where you're living?" he inquired.

"I've a house in Adams Row," she replied. He decided that he must have betrayed a moment of surprise, as she smiled apologetically. "It's my family's house," she added quickly. "I get teased about it... about living in Mayfair."

"Who else is living there with you?" he asked.

"I'm there by myself. The rest of my family is up at the country house at Windermere."

Alec Grey was uncertain how he might imagine her living arrangements, deciding that he would be substantially impressed by the 'country house' if her family maintained such a home as a *pied à terre*.

"Do you have any friends who come by regularly?" he continued. She shook her head. "Domestics, tradesman... a boyfriend?"

His last suggestion appeared to embarrass her once more. "No one," she said quietly.

"Would it be possible for us to install someone at your house until this is over?" he asked.

"Oh yes," she said. "There are plenty of extra rooms. I've often thought I should be taking in a lodger, but my father wouldn't hear of it."

"Perhaps you will do for a time," he agreed.

Alec Grey glanced at the director, who seemed on the point of berating him for some as yet undisclosed violation of protocol or procedure. Sir Alistair would not wish to be troubled with the details of Alice Woodward's domestic considerations, nor would he want to contribute to the operation she was rapidly becoming mired in. In another day or two he would receive a memorandum with a code name and a considerable number of aliases, and Alec Grey knew he'd do well to keep it to a single page.

He returned his attention to Alice Woodward. "The director and I will have to plot and scheme behind your back for a time," he explained. "Can I ask you to wait outside until we've finished playing at being spies? I'd like to have you look at some photographs to see if you can recognize the man who gave you the camera."

She rose from her chair, brushing the creases from her skirt as she got to her feet. She appeared to have known considerable practice at being dismissed.

"Miss Woodward," he said as she was turning to leave.

She paused and glanced at him.

"I wonder, have you told anyone else what you do here?" He watched her expression darken in the corner of his eye.

"No, sir," she replied quickly. "I'm not permitted."

"What about your family? You must have told them something."

"I told them I work for the ministry, but I've not said what it is that I do."

He heard a note of disquiet in her words, and he wondered if he'd offended her.

"Thank you," he said, and after a moment's hesitation she left Sir Alistair's office.

Sir Alistair scowled at Alec Grey for a moment. "I'm not at all pleased with any of this, you know," he said, his voice a dire rumble in the otherwise silent office. "She's a fine young woman... she shouldn't be involved." He stabbed at Alec Grey with his finger. "And you... took a considerable risk, offering to let her walk out of here without agreeing to play the Soviets for us."

Alec Grey smiled, wondering for an instant whether the director was having him on.

"There was no risk to speak of," he said at length.

"She's not a coward... if she had been, she wouldn't have come to you at all."

Sir Alistair appeared to consider his assertion. "You rely too heavily on patriotism," he said dismissingly. "You'd do well to remember that some of the people who work here do so largely for a wage packet."

It seemed pointedly unlikely that Alice Woodward might ever be called upon to do anything largely for a wage packet, Alec Grey considered, wondering if he would do well to say as much aloud. He shook his head, dispelling the thought of a baronial castle in Windermere and a family with more money than the queen.

"She didn't agree to assist us out of patriotism," he observed. "The Russian who interrupted her lunch gave her a damned good fright. She agreed to assist us because she'd enjoy getting her own back."

Sir Alistair's features creased with amusement, and he glanced at the closed door behind Alec Grey, as if he sought to peer through it, to reassess whatever secrets might be hidden behind Alice Woodward's sea-green eyes.

"I don't imagine I need remind you that her safety is on your head," he said. "How do you propose to keep her away from the Soviets?"

"I'm not sure," Alec Grey replied. "I imagine it will depend on who she identifies as her controller. We've photographs of all of them... I'm quite certain he'll turn up." He paused and willed himself to relax into his chair once more, to grant himself a moment's intoxication under the influence of fumes from the leather and the furniture polish. "There are two rather more pressing issues."

The director's brow creased, his expression suggesting that the likelihood of Alice Woodward coming to harm and he subsequently being called upon to explain her situation to her family could have little that was more urgent.

"Mr. Grey?" Sir Alistair prompted him.

Alec Grey exhaled. "The Russians undertook a considerable risk contacting one of your staff," he began
thoughtfully. "They'd have known there was a substantial
likelihood that whoever they tried to co-opt would do precisely what Miss Woodward did... or that she'd get to her
feet and shout for a policeman. They risked having one of
their embassy people blown and deported... or more likely,
an illegal who'd be given the choice of talking to us or
doing a long stretch in Wormwood Scrubs. They chose to
take that risk because they knew Miss Woodward has
access to sufficiently valuable material to justify it."

"I'm aware of that," Sir Alistair said, his voice tinged
with irritation.

"Shall we trust her when she says she's not told
anyone on the outside what she does here?"

The director nodded, and Alec Grey was puzzled for
an instant that Sir Alistair had clearly not appreciated what
was so obvious to him. The director had a godlike touch
upon the tiller of his organization, but he'd neither
wrapped himself in the cloak nor grasped the dagger. He
was unquestionably the most well-chosen political
appointment to head MI5 in living memory, but his subordinates did well to remind themselves that he was a political appointment none the less.

"The Soviets chose the ideal target for recruitment,"
Alec Grey explained. "The only way they could have
known that she was the ideal target would have been if
someone told them. Someone on the inside."

Sir Alistair glanced away from him, his eyes incandescent in the shadow of his brow. "Your preoccupation
with moles could become tiresome, Mr. Grey," he said.
Once again, Alec Grey was uncertain whether the director
was having him on. "You will recall from our earlier conversation that I require proof of the existence of an agent
in our midst."

"I believe it just left the room," Alec Grey said.

"A name would be of no small assistance."

Alec Grey nodded. "I'll see what I can do."

The director smiled at length. "You said there were two issues," he said.

Alec Grey placed the camera, its packet of film and the papers that had accompanied it on the director's desk. After a moment's consideration he slid them across his blotter. "The last page is a list of the subjects the Soviets are interested in," he said. "Miss Woodward is presumably to look out for files that pertain to them and photograph their contents. You should pay particular attention to the third entry from the top."

Sir Alistair flipped through the papers before him and he began reading the page in question. His expression grew perplexed. "Items referring to element ninety-seven, also known as Berkelium, to the ionic bombardment of Americium 241, to the refinement of Uranium 235 from Uranium 238 by the process of gaseous diffusion," he read aloud. He glanced up at Alec Grey. "What the hell is that about?"

"Sir?" Alec Grey replied. "I'd have thought it would have made more sense to you than to me."

"I'll be the first to admit it's been a very long time since I was at school, but I don't believe there is an element ninety-seven."

The room grew increasingly still. The director withdrew his pipe from one of his desk drawers and began filling it, apparently without it occupying his awareness. Alec Grey regarded the object malevolently, having observed on past occasions that whatever the substance Sir Alistair chose to bring to combustion within the bowl of his pipe, its vapors were not intended to be a balm upon the lungs of the unwary.

"When I was briefed about the time stream project, you sent me to Cornwall to attend several days of lectures by David Hollings. Perhaps you remember him."

Sir Alistair gestured with the stem of his pipe. "Of course I do," he said absently. "As it happens, he was sitting in the same chair you are just this morning."

"I was comforted at the time in thinking that you'd been subjected to much the same lectures," Alec Grey continued.

The director nodded and he permitted a wicked grin to crease his features. "I'd be lying if I said I was conscious during their entirety," he said.

"As would I," Alec Grey admitted. "Perhaps if we'd planned the thing better, we might have fallen asleep during alternating portions of his talk, such that we'd now have a more or less complete understanding of the matter between us." This moment of shared conspiracy appeared to please Sir Alistair.

Alec Grey watched the director apply a match to his pipe and he felt the first tendrils of smoke rasp in his throat. "The thing of it is," he continued, "there's one part of it I do remember. I imagine it stuck in my mind because it could be understood without a doctorate in quantum physics. It has to do with the materials that make the time stream accessible."

"Oh yes?" Sir Alistair asked, perhaps having appreciated that he was about to be availed of an aspect of the project he too might understand. He'd remarked on numerous occasions to anyone who would listen and had sufficient security clearance to be permitted within earshot that he knew no small measure of discomfort at being in charge of a facility that was responsible for the disposal of billions of pounds, and for which he could not have provided a convincing description of its function.

"In the late 1930s, two German scientists discovered it was possible to cause the atomic bonds of the element Uranium to break, releasing a substantial amount of energy," he said. "Having achieved passing grades in

A-level high school physics, I actually understood that bit of the explanation without having to ask any questions."

The director gestured for him to continue.

"Uranium occurs naturally predominately as Uranium 238, but it's possible to refine natural Uranium to extract Uranium 235. The simplest way to refine it is by using a series of electrical magnets. The more complex way, but by far the most effective..."

"...will no doubt turn out to be by the process of gaseous diffusion," Sir Alistair interrupted.

"I believe so," Alec Grey agreed. "Once one has Uranium 235, it can be bombarded with alpha particles to produce a number of new, synthetic elements. One of them is called Americium. Americium, in turn, can be bombarded to produce Berkelium, which has an atomic number of ninety-seven."

The director regarded him balefully. "Mr. Grey, I did a great deal more than achieve passing grades in A-level high school physics, and I believe I'm growing bored none the less."

"Berkelium is the material that drives the time stream project," Alec Grey said, and in an instant the director was clearly no longer bored.

Sir Alistair glanced uncertainly at the page before him. "Do you mean to imply that the Soviets have begun research on the time stream?" he asked, his tone suggesting that Alec Grey would do well to think carefully about his reply.

"No, sir," he said. "It's possible to produce Uranium 235 in small quantities with a modest laboratory. According to Mr. Hollings, the apparatus to bombard it with alpha particles to create a trace amount of Americium is elaborate but reasonably accessible. The early research into the properties of the time stream was carried out with minute amounts of Berkelium... on the order of a millionth of a gram. The first darkmatter time stream displaced a few hydrogen atoms in time by several tenths of a second."

The director took a long draught of his pipe and permitted the smoke to ooze from between his lips, a coiled serpent about his shoulders. "If they're not doing time stream research..." he began, and then seemed to think better of the question.

"If I recall Mr. Hollings' talk, Berkelium only exists for about four and a half hours after it's created. In order to displace something of a useful size in time, you need a great deal of it. The procedure is to bombard a lot of Americium with a lot of alpha particles to produce a sufficient volume of Berkelium to get the job done, bung it in whatever they call that thing they've built in Cornwall, light the blue touch paper and switch on. The only practical way to get enough refined Uranium to end up with sufficient Berkelium is to refine it through gaseous diffusion."

The director gestured once more with his pipe. "What are you telling me, Mr. Grey?" he demanded.

Alec Grey struggled for a moment to arrange his thoughts, to trace a map for the man before him through the thickets and undergrowth of conspiracy. "If Miss Woodward had in fact become a Soviet agent, she would have been exceedingly valuable. She would also have had a short working life. Every time she photographed a file or filled her dead drop, she would have risked being blown. The Soviets know that, and they wouldn't have employed her to obtain information unless it was of practical and immediate importance to them. The fact that they asked about the technology to create substantial quantities of Berkelium suggests that they have an immediate use for substantial quantities of Berkelium."

Sir Alistair's features grew hard, and he glared at Alec Grey.

"David Hollings assured me that there is no other known use for Berkelium," he continued. "If the Soviets want it, it's because they have a working time stream pro- totype and it's ready to become operational."

Sir Alistair shook his head angrily. "That's quite pre- posterous," he snapped. "I've been told on good authority that the Soviet Union lacks the scientific talent to develop the project independently. The best estimates have them taking another twenty years to bring a working prototype on stream. The Americans are convinced they'll never suc- ceed."

"I agree," Alec Grey said. "Which brings me back to the first issue."

"Which issue would that be?"

"If they couldn't have developed it themselves, the only way they could have it is if one of our lot gave it to them," he said. He reached across the director's desk to touch the Minox camera that rested between them to emphasize his point, but he appreciated as he did that it had been unnecessary.

8

D avid Hollings peered through the window of the unfamiliar car that bore him through a London he'd thus far only read of. The rain was gray acid, bubbling and hissing from the unseen night sky, scalding the anthracite bricks and greasy windows of a quarter of the city he imagined only emerged in the silent hours after midnight. The darkness beyond his window was stygian, punctuated by imitation gemstones of neon and incandescence, deluding no one as to their true worth.

The journey had been interminable, and he resisted the urge to consult his wristwatch yet again. He ran his hand across his chin without thinking, finding his day's growth of beard unsettling. He'd last shaved in his cottage on the Cornish coast, and he would very much have enjoyed being back there now. He would certainly be in no fit state to drive in the morning, if the night that subsumed this place ever knew morning.

The car braked suddenly and he reached forward to steady himself. It had done so half a hundred times earlier, and he was several seconds appreciating that its driver meant to stop for a time at its current location. The granite hulks of several other dark, ineffable vehicles had gathered in the gloom beyond the windscreen before him.

Shapes which seemed laughing parodies of men darted amongst them, sheltering from the rain.

He stared once more through the window and forced his eyes to resolve the sign on the nearest building. The Strathmore Hotel appeared in keeping with the structures that confined it at its current address. Its lighted signboard had lost several of its bulbs, its single tiny window was streaked with the bile of a perpetual netherworld. He shuddered within his coat, unwilling to imagine the men who returned to such a place each evening.

Someone unlatched his door as the constable beside him switched off his engine. As he eased himself into the street, he noted that another constable had appeared, an official manservant, craning his arm to poise an umbrella above the car's open door. He nodded his appreciation to the gray, sightless eyes of the young man and quickly crossed the ragged cobbles to the door of the Strathmore Hotel.

The man who awaited him looked nothing like what he'd anticipated of a London policeman. His features were leaden, framed by thinning hair that appeared to have been combed to camouflage more of his scalp than it might have presumed to. He seemed skeletal and unwell, his age an unmentioned lie. When he spoke, it was with the accent of Docklands through a mouthful of teeth the color of rotted wood.

"Doctor Hollings?" he asked, withdrawing his hand from the pocket of his coat. David Hollings accepted it with a moment's concern that a vigorous shaking might dislocate it.

"Bloody sorry you had to come out here this late, sir," he continued. It was unclear whether his air of deference was genuinely affected, or merely a garment he drew about himself for occasions such as this one like a second ratty coat. "I'm DC Hayes. We spoke on the telephone."

David Hollings smiled thinly, feeling himself awash

with fatigue. His day at Leconfield House had been exhausting, and he felt as if he'd hardly crawled into his unfamiliar bed when he'd been awakened and summoned to the telephone. His tongue tasted as if sheep had been grazing on it during the interval.

"Are you sure it's..." he began.

The detective nodded, his lips bloodless. He gestured at the tiny lobby of the hotel and the staircase beyond it. Behind the desk, a bearded man with a cigarette struggling from between his teeth malevolently eyed them both. The hotel was awash in a funk of cigarettes, rising damp and stale lager.

"There was a card in his pocket, sir," DC Hayes explained as they came abreast of the staircase. The detective gestured for David Hollings to precede him into the gloom. The light on the landing above them had clearly been a cousin to the extinguished lamps in the hotel's sign. "It had his name and a photograph, and a number to ring if he was in trouble. I don't suppose anyone could be in much more trouble than he is. Only, I've seen cards like that before, and I recognized the number." The detective's voice was reduced to a harsh, conspiratorial whisper. "It rings MI5."

He had such a card himself, and he knew full well where the telephone number printed on it rang. He was still uncertain why MI5 had chosen to ring him. He'd long since accepted that the work of his days was to be the province of the intelligence agency, but he'd thus far insisted with reasonable success that his nights were to remain his own.

"What was the name on the card you found?" he inquired, mounting the stairs. He felt the ancient boards sag and creak beneath him.

He heard the pages of a notebook flipping behind him as the detective followed him up the stairs. "Dunross," DC Hayes read mechanically. "Arthur Francis Dunross."

David Hollings paused and turned to regard the shadowy features of the detective. "Damn," he spat, uncertain whether it was for the benefit of the detective or himself. "Is he injured?"

The detective shook his head. "I'm sorry, sir," he said. "I thought I explained on the telephone. He was found dead earlier this evening."

David Hollings felt his eyes widen, and he parted his lips to speak. The vapors and fumes of the hotel cloyed in his throat and he turned to resume his journey up the narrow stairs.

There was a constable outside room eleven, his uniform a sculpture of obsidian in the glare of one of the few functioning lamps in the corridor. DC Hayes nodded to him as they passed him and entered the room. The man said nothing, his expression vacant.

The room in which Arthur Dunross had died was an above-ground catacomb. Its walls were of cracked plaster, stained with innumerable shades of age and filth. A bare light bulb dangled from a ragged flex in the center of the room. A dented iron bed clung to one wall, its bedclothes tumbling into a puddle on the floor. The stink of malfunctioning plumbing vied with the coppery wetness of blood, now grown faint with the passing of hours.

Arthur Dunross lay on his back staring at the cobwebs and scarred plaster above him, his lips drawn back over his teeth in a final snarl. He was wearing trousers and a white shirt, unbuttoned at his neck. There were two craters in his forehead, one perfectly positioned between his eyes and the second an inch to its right. The wall behind him was dark with what David Hollings realized were his colleague's brains.

He glanced around the suffocating room, imagining its walls on the point of dissolution to admit the fanged avatars of Hades into their midst to gloat, drooling upon their handiwork.

"Is this Arthur Francis Dunross?" DC Hayes asked, gesturing at the body scattered before them.

David Hollings nodded. "Yes," he said weakly. "Do you know... what's happened to him?"

The detective seemed as if he were on the point of saying something impolite, that the state of Arthur Dunross must have been obvious even to someone with letters after his name. At length he smiled coldly and nodded.

"We have a very good idea what happened to him, sir," he replied. "Some time between half eleven and midnight, a man came to his room. Mr. Dunross answered the door. The man drove Mr. Dunross back into the room with his foot and shot him through the head with a Walther PP handgun fitted with a silencer. The man then left the hotel."

David Hollings considered this, allowing that it was a somewhat more specific answer than he'd anticipated. "I'll have a written report sent along in the morning," DC Hayes added.

"Can I ask how you can be so certain of... of the details... of how he died?" David Hollings asked, refusing to permit his eyes to meet those of the detective.

"Police work," DC Hayes replied. "This one didn't call for much of it, mind. There's the impression of the sole of a boot in the front of his shirt, with the toe cleanly visible. That's how we know he was pushed back into the room. The door has a bolt, which was drawn. That's how we know he came to the door... rather than having his killer kick it in. The fellow on the desk skaved off down the pub at half eleven for a quick pint. One of the other... tenants here... he found Mr. Dunross a few minutes after midnight."

"And the gun?"

DC Hayes appeared almost pleased with himself. He turned to the bed and lifted a dark, menacing object from it, dangling from the end of a pencil. "He chucked it on the bed when he was done with it."

"I see," David Hollings acknowledged. He regarded the thing for a time. "It seems... old."

The detective nodded. "It is... I believe this one dates back to the middle of the nineteen-thirties. Our firearm experts will be able to say for certain in the morning." He paused and returned the gun to its place on the bed behind him. "They're quite common. The German police bought them by the lorryload over the years. There won't be any fingerprints on it, and I imagine it will turn out to've been nicked from somewhere, and quite untraceable. Whoever killed Mr. Dunross knew what he was about."

David Hollings put his hand to his face, wishing for an instant that he might cover his eyes with it, to see no more of the squalid room in which Arthur Dunross had died. "I can't imagine why anyone would wish him dead," he said, as much to himself as to the detective. "I can't imagine what he'd have been doing here."

DC Hayes eyed him curiously, as he might have done a wayward American tourist disconcerted to learn that automobiles drove on the other side of the street in these longitudes. "Mr. Dunross signed in under the name of James Smith," he said. "It's not very original, but you'll find a surprising number of Smiths and Jones in the guest book of the Strathmore. The management isn't much bothered, as long as everyone has a picture of the queen to vouch for them."

"He told me he was coming to London to visit his sister," David Hollings muttered.

The detective gestured dismissingly. "I can't say what he came here for, sir," he said quickly, "and I've been instructed not to ask." He reached into an inside pocket of his coat. "About an hour ago, a fellow arrived and gave me this... says I'm to give it to you when you arrive." He proffered an envelope to David Hollings. "I'd one as well," he added. "It had very specific instructions."

David Hollings accepted the envelope uncertainly. "Instructions?" he inquired.

"One of my men has collected your things from your hotel. You'll be driven somewhere to get a few hours sleep. You've a meeting first thing in the morning. I'm to have all of Mr. Dunross' things sent on as well. I'm to tell you not to say a word about any of this to anyone, including me."

The room grew silent, and David Hollings stared at the detective. The man had become motionless, a carving of flint and fabric occluding the wounds in Arthur Dunross' forehead.

"I... I don't understand," he said at length.

"I don't either, sir," DC Hayes said, and he gestured toward the door. "It was made clear to me earlier I'm not meant to."

9

Wednesday, October 18

Tea was intended to be drunk from a glass, not a cup — not an effeminate, insubstantial cup with a handle too small to insert one's finger through, and a volume inadequate for a reasonable swallow. Tea was not intended to be adulterated with cow's milk and sugar until it tasted of a sweet shop. There hardly seemed a great deal of purpose in boiling the stuff at all.

Yuri Modin glanced absently about the tea room, peering over the edge of his cup. The interior of the place looked like it ought to have been the coffin for someone unusually large and offensively bourgeoisie. The windows were veiled by lace that reminded him of something a spider might have wrought. The tables were small and uncomfortable, a farthing on legs.

The room was deserted save for two aged women near the front of the shop, engaged in a lackadaisical conversation about nothing. He shifted his wrist imperceptibly, glancing at his watch. STANLEY was rarely punctual, but he was yet to miss an agreed-upon meeting. In another three minutes he would be compelled to assume that STANLEY had been compromised, or had chosen to abort.

He was still gazing across his cup of tea when the door at the front of the shop clattered, its wisps of lace fluttering in the draught it admitted. The man who stepped through it could not have looked less like he'd belonged in the tea shop if he'd been wearing a British grenadier's uniform and carrying a musket.

STANLEY glanced into the darkness at the rear of the tea shop, clearly willing his eyes to become adapted to the tepid light. He shrugged his overcoat from his shoulders and draped it across his arm. After a moment's consideration, he smiled thinly and began to navigate the erratic reef of tables that bobbed and lurked between them.

STANLEY looked like shit, Yuri Modin considered as the man approached him. He willed the thought from his mind. STANLEY had been Moscow's best-loved subject of the British empire for several decades, and he'd certainly looked worse. STANLEY had clearly not observed the peculiar British custom that strong drink was reserved for the afternoon or evening. Yuri Modin had long since appreciated that meetings with STANLEY were best not conducted in pubs, however much more comfort the crush of people might have afforded them both.

He observed the figure stumbling toward him, wondering desperately whether he was about to be confronted by the morning after or a continuation of the night before.

It's time you left for Moscow, he'd once told the man who now navigated the tea shop. It had been 1956. STANLEY had looked like he'd spent a month in the Lubyanka being questioned by experts. The dark, haunted eyes had peered at him, as if through someone else's spectacles, and STANLEY's head had shaken woodenly. He'd resembled a mechanical toy left to wind down, no longer an amusement to the child who owned it. STANLEY had insisted his value to Moscow was far from exhausted, and in the fluttering of a heartbeat Yuri Modin had nodded, questioning what madness had overtaken him in his moment of compassion for his agent. Moscow would have welcomed STANLEY with vodka and ceremony, and dispatched the instigator of his arrival to a shallow grave outside the city.

STANLEY was 49, an age only ten years removed from his own. For an instant he wished for a mirror to inspect his own features, to reassure himself that his face was not so scarred and veined as the one that lowered itself into his awareness.

STANLEY took the chair opposite him and glanced toward the kitchen of the tea shop, the gesture habitual, instinctive.

"Sorry I'm late," he said, his tone suggesting that he cared little for his tardiness. STANLEY knew his worth, Yuri Modin reminded himself. When STANLEY finally did accept an invitation from the Kremlin, he would have an apartment, a dacha outside the city and a Zil limousine to see him on his travels. One day he would find his likeness on a postage stamp. Yuri Modin had long since appreciated that his years upon the soil of his enemy had been far more comfortable than anything he would know upon his eventual return to the *rodina*.

He'd come to Britain in 1947, and not returned to the Soviet Union until 1954. He'd spent two years in Moscow, and by the time he'd arranged his return to the west, he would have cheerfully accepted a posting to the Outer Hebrides.

"It is good to see you again," Yuri Modin said. He willed himself to smile.

STANLEY nodded. "It's been too long," he agreed.

Dead drops and telephone conversations regulated by a stop watch were hardly a substitute for friendship. It had been different when they'd all been friends, he and his five spies.

"I was not certain you would come," Yuri Modin continued uncertainly. "I did not believe you would contact me through such an unusual channel. I have not heard from JOHNSON for… for quite some time."

STANLEY's features creased in irritation. He detested the use of code names, as much as he accepted the prudence inherent in their application. His own code name was PETER. HICKS, another of the five, had observed that in his time in America, he'd been told that both 'johnson' and 'peter' were used to mean *khuy,* a man's penis. HICKS had found the observation pleasingly vulgar, in keeping with his character.

"I telephoned... JOHNSON... because there wasn't time for the usual dog and pony show to establish contact," STANLEY said with barely disguised irritation. "Chalk marks on lamp stands are all well and good when the navy starts talking about a new submarine... I think you'll agree this was rather more p-p-pressing." He glanced slowly about the tea shop, as if to reassure himself that they were unlikely to be overheard.

Yuri Modin smiled, wondering if he would do well to reassure STANLEY that all the other occupants of the place would require fresh batteries in their hearing aids to present them with a tangible threat of discovery. His stammer had returned, a harbinger of his disquiet.

"Did you study the photograph I gave JOHNSON?" STANLEY demanded harshly.

Yuri Modin nodded. "It is in Moscow now. I am surprised you did not hear them scream when they first saw it."

STANLEY appeared genuinely amused by the suggestion, a rare enough thing in recent years.

"I have had a long briefing from Moscow Center... what I was to ask you when next we met. They assured me that I need not rush you... any time in the next half hour would be fine." He smiled at his own joke, but STANLEY appeared to have ignored it.

"So they agree it's a serious threat?" STANLEY insisted.

Yuri Modin nodded. "Oh yes, my friend," he said quietly. "They agree it is serious. They just cannot agree on what it is."

"It's the N-N-Nikolaiev shipyard," STANLEY explained, a note of irritation in his voice.

"Yes, of course it is," Yuri Modin agreed. "They were at a loss to explain how the photograph could have been created."

The briefing he'd been sent from Moscow Center had in fact expressed very little confusion, and a great deal of outrage. Unable to imagine that the photograph they'd been sent could have been genuine, they'd persuaded themselves it was a clever forgery woven together from American U2 photographs, and imposed upon them as an attempt at disinformation.

STANLEY leant closer to the table. "The Americans have invented a camera that flies outside the atmosphere of the earth," he said.

Yuri Modin blinked and stared at the man opposite him for a moment, imagining himself to be a wire recorder replaying what it had overheard. He exhaled, feeling his fingers grow taut about his tea cup. "Are you certain?" he inquired. He too glanced about the tea shop. He'd all but convinced himself that the urgent meeting with STANLEY had been a ruse to press him for money, or merely a desire on the part of the ruin of a man opposite him for a moment longer of shared conspiracy, a reminiscence of the thrill of his youth.

STANLEY nodded. "I've been briefed by Alistair Fitzhenry, MOST SECRET, matter of the utmost security," he replied. "I had a word with one of his bright young men afterward. There's no possible way that photograph could have been taken from an aircraft."

"Still, it was very hard to make out," Yuri Modin said, as he'd been instructed to. "It was hardly possible to decide what it was at first."

"The photograph you saw was taken with a Minox in less than ideal conditions," STANLEY said. "The ones I was given to inspect during the briefing looked like they'd been

etched in g-g-glass. I understand that the original negatives are two feet across and sharp as tacks."

Yuri Modin felt his eyes widen despite his resolve
merely to converse with STANLEY. "There are more photographs, then?" he inquired uneasily.

STANLEY's features creased with the specter of
amusement. "I'm told there are almost five thousand of
them," he said. "Copies of the entire collection arrived in
crates at Leconfield House yesterday. The Americans plan
to shoot another camera up some time soon."

Yuri Modin stared at him for a moment longer before
he permitted his attention to return to his cup. "Moscow
will not be pleased," he muttered.

"I should damn well hope Moscow won't be
pleased," STANLEY agreed.

"Moscow was not pleased with the U2s," Yuri Modin
said, "but they knew it was only a matter of time before
one was shot down, and the Americans could be made to
stop sending them over Soviet territory. This... this is
much worse."

STANLEY nodded, apparently satisfied with himself.
STANLEY clearly looked forward to seeing his face upon a
Soviet postage stamp.

"The Center has instructed me to ask you when you
can provide additional photographs," Yuri Modin said.
"Perhaps you could be supplied with a better camera."

"Can't be done, old son," STANLEY said, and he
eased himself back in his chair slightly. "It was only by
a fantastic bit of luck that I arranged to be left alone
with the one I did get to copy. Alistair Fitzhenry has instituted a level of security around those pictures that would
make the c-c-crown jewels look positively unguarded by
comparison. From what I'm told, one would have to
submit a request to the director himself to see them, and
then there would be two men to keep an eye on them at
all times. As the story goes, the minders have to request

permission to visit the lavatory, so a replacement minder can be sent for."

Yuri Modin scowled into his tea. This was not the response he'd anticipated. STANLEY rarely disappointed his controller, and after a moment's consideration he appreciated that his agent was almost certainly telling him the truth.

"Is there anything I can tell Moscow about this... flying camera?" he asked, suddenly appreciating that he would leave this meeting with little to show for the risk of contacting STANLEY.

STANLEY appeared to observe him, the man's eyes diminishing into reptilian slits in the dark folds of his skin. "Alistair Fitzhenry has been less than forthcoming. You understand, my current position doesn't require I know how the thing works. I don't have a convincing reason to ask for details." He paused and adopted a posture of res-ignation. "Fact is, my current position doesn't require I have access to the collection of pictures, even with two minders in the room."

Yuri Modin wished with all his being that he might curse STANLEY aloud in the coarse Russian his father had employed when the old man had been furious. *Sukin syn...* son of a bitch. He'd be up half the night devising a way to make STANLEY's intelligence palatable to Moscow. He willed himself to be calm, to imagine the features of the man before him glued to the corner of an envelope with '5 Kopeks' printed below it, the lines of age and drink erased by its engraver.

He poured the dregs of his tea over his tongue, smelling the rot of soaking vegetation in the vapors from his cup. At another time, decades earlier, he would have enjoyed idling the morning with STANLEY, before his agent's mind had become sodden with whiskey. He glanced at his wristwatch, suddenly uncomfortable with his surroundings.

"What of ENORMOZ?" he asked, hearing a flicker of hesitation in his words.

STANLEY's expression remained dulled and impassive. "W-W-What of it?" he asked tonelessly.

Yuri Modin leant across the table. "Moscow requires intelligence on the current developments in the... time stream research," he hissed, pleased that he'd overcome his training to speak only in code names on this occasion. STANLEY's eyes flashed, as if he'd been told something forbidden.

STANLEY leant forward as well. "Did you know that MI5 doesn't have its own code word for the project?" he inquired absently.

Yuri Modin stared blankly at him, wondering for an instant whether STANLEY had understood his request.

"I imagine the damned thing is so profoundly secret that there's no need to refer to it. If one is called into a briefing concerning it, one always knows, as there's only a handful of people allowed to speak about it."

Yuri Modin smiled, struggling to veil his growing irritation. "I believe it is what is discussed at those briefings that Moscow would like to know."

STANLEY nodded. "As would I, old friend," he agreed, a note of resignation in his words. "I'm barely permitted to know the bloody thing exists."

"Surely there is something more..." Yuri Modin began.

STANLEY shook his head. "I haven't seen so much as a single-page memo pertaining to it in over six months," he said.

"Moscow..." Yuri Modin began, but STANLEY's head was shaking once more, solemn, pedagogical, final.

"I believe your best hope in that area would be in the talent I spotted for you," he interrupted. "Have you done anything about her?"

Yuri Modin glanced away from him. "Yes," he

replied. "She did not prove to be a great deal of trouble. We anticipate her first consignment today." He stiffened his jaw, realizing that STANLEY was awaiting the conclusion of his response. "Moscow is most assuredly in your debt for her."

A smile flickered across STANLEY's features, an expression which might have been mistaken for a moment of gastric distress by someone less observant. "One day we'll meet in R-R-Red Square and laugh about this place," he said, gesturing around the room.

STANLEY too glanced at his watch, and both men rose from their chairs as one. A woman with a tea cup and a battered metal pot had appeared from the distant shadows, clearly intent upon STANLEY. Yuri Modin deposited several coins on the table between them and gestured for her to return to the darkness which had dispatched her.

"One day we will certainly meet in Red Square," he agreed, and STANLEY turned for the door.

10

"**I** hardly know what to think, Mr. Grey," Sir Alistair said, a note of mirth in his words despite what he must have surmised would be a disquieting half hour. "I believe this is the first time in living memory you've actually scheduled a formal meeting. I've almost become accustomed to having you storm my office unannounced."

Alec Grey rose from his chair at the briefing room table, wondering if the director's remark warranted a show of amusement. The old man's sense of humor was convoluted at best, and knowing with certainty whether Sir Alistair was pulling one's leg oftentimes required half a dozen agents, a week of laboratory analysis and substantial computer time.

He smiled despite his uncertainty. "I felt we might benefit from a room without telephones," he said.

The director pushed the briefing room door to and took his customary seat at the head of the table. "I can see a new level of security classification arising out of this," he mused as he withdrew his pipe and pouch of tobacco from his pocket. "CONFIDENTIAL, SECRET, MOST SECRET… and now, not for discussion in a room with a telephone." He looked up suddenly and caught Alec Grey's eye. "Do you think all that would fit on a rubber stamp?"

"It would have to be a very large one," Alec Grey allowed, wondering if there was an officially-sanctioned duration for japes and liberties before the serious portion of an audience was undertaken. It was as Sir Alistair had suggested — he could claim little experience in organizing events such as this one. The director lit his pipe, and he chose to accept the summoning of fire as the ceremonial commencement of these proceedings.

He pushed a ragged paper folder from beneath his elbow into the center of the table. "You asked to be kept informed about the status of my investigation," he said.

"This would be the mole hunt, then?" the director asked with affected displeasure. Alec Grey nodded. His memorandum to Sir Alistair requesting the meeting had said as much.

"We have a list of seven names," he said.

The director's eyes narrowed, all fragments of mirth suddenly driven from his expression. "How solid is this list?"

"One of the names on it belongs to an employee of Moscow Center," he said firmly.

The director took a draught of his pipe, its contents glowing angrily for a moment. After several seconds he withdrew the stem from his teeth and gestured at the paper folder. "I trust you'll appreciate that I would wish to understand how the seven names in question came to be on your list. I've been involved in mole hunts in the past... they're remorselessly corrosive, and I'll be damned well certain we have a mole to hunt before I authorize another one."

Alec Grey met the director's gaze. "I can walk you through everything we did to assemble the list," he began. "I'm afraid it's all rather boring, though."

Sir Alistair leant back in his chair. "You have my permission to bore me, Mr. Grey," he said.

Alec Grey smiled, and he permitted himself a

moment to review the briefing he'd assembled for the director in the event that Sir Alistair proved ill-disposed to accept his findings. Hugh Somerfield had wagered him a guinea that he'd leave the briefing room five minutes after the director entered it.

"We began by assembling a list of everyone who knew enough about PAPER HAT, POSTCARD and GOLD WATCH to have blown them to the Soviets. We fed them all a barium meal."

The director's brow creased. "You did what?"

"I'm sorry, sir," he said. "It's a rather tasteless expression, I imagine. We fabricated several classified documents we felt would interest the Soviets, distributed them in groups to the individuals on our initial list and we waited to see which ones reached the Soviet embassy."

Sir Alistair nodded uncertainly. "I see," he said, his tone suggesting that he did not. "How exactly did you know when one of them reached the Soviet embassy?"

Alec Grey glanced about the otherwise deserted briefing room. When he'd had occasion to occupy one of its chairs previously, he'd located himself with a strategic measure of displacement between his lungs and the fuming cauldron that was the director's pipe. At present there was little more than an arm's length separating them, and he felt the first murmurings of a cough in his words.

"In point of fact, we don't know when things reach the Soviet embassy," he admitted. "However, having done so, they're immediately sent on to Moscow, and we can usually tell when that takes place."

The director looked mildly unsettled, as if he'd been subtly reminded once again that he occupied his present chair wholly by the sufferance of the faceless men in Whitehall who'd assigned him his current title.

"Mr. Grey, I've taken the trouble to review the cryptographic facilities at GCHQ," he said. "Were it possible to read the coded transmissions between the Soviet embassy and Moscow Center, I believe I would have been informed. We could have dismissed three quarters of the staff."

"It's not quite that simple, sir," Alec Grey said. "In fact, it's the most profoundly boring aspect of this investigation."

Sir Alistair leant forward. "I repeat my leave for you to bore me," he said coldly.

Alec Grey nodded. "When Soviet embassies communicate with Moscow Center by radio, they encrypt their transmissions using Hagelin machines." He paused and glanced at the director, who clearly did not recognize the word.

"They're quite primitive by current standards. The basic machine was developed in 1923 by a Swede named Boris Hagelin. It amuses the chaps at GCHQ to remind anyone who'll listen that Boris's parents were actually Russian."

The director smiled fleetingly.

"The Hagelin machine was intended for use by banks and private businesses to transmit secret information between their offices. Its trade name is Enigma." He opened the paper folder on the table between them and removed a large black and white photograph of what appeared to be a peculiar typewriter. After a moment's consideration he slid it across to the director.

"The Enigma uses a keyboard, a set of lights behind glass slides with letters printed on them and three mechanical rotors behind the lights. The rotors have a ring of contacts on each side, with one contact for each letter on the keyboard. The contacts are wired internally so none of the contacts on one side of the rotor is connected to the corresponding contact on the other side. When you press a key, an electric signal passes through the three rotors and illuminates one of the lights. The rotors then turn, so the signal from the next key takes a different path and illuminates a different light."

Sir Alistair studied the photograph for a time, and his expression grew suddenly brighter. "I understand," he said at length, clearly pleased with himself. Alec Grey exhaled, cheered by the prospect of not having to discuss the inner workings of Enigma in detail, a subject he found mind-numbing at best. The abstruse machinations of intelligence frequently eluded the director, but in reflection, the machine in the photograph would have been something very much in keeping with his background.

"Having encrypted a message with Enigma, it can be decoded by sending the encrypted letters back through the rotors to return it to plain text," he continued. "There's actually nothing very mysterious about how the machine is wired internally."

"I imagine you're going to tell me that the only real problem is knowing how the rotors are initially set before the machine is used," Sir Alistair said, a note of triumph in his voice.

"That's exactly right, sir," Alec Grey agreed.

The director glanced at the ceiling, clearly occupied with his own thoughts for a moment. "I reckon there to be... seventeen-thousand or so possible permutations for three rotors having twenty-six positions."

Alec Grey smiled, impressed with the director's calculation. He glanced at his notes. "17,576... or so the chaps at GCHQ tell me."

"That would make the prospect of discovering how the Soviets have set up their Enigma machines somewhat daunting," the director said, and he sucked noisily on his pipe. "Do they change the rotor settings often?"

"Every morning," Alec Grey replied. "As we understand it, there's a master list of rotor settings for each day of the month, which is sent from Moscow in diplomatic bags or by messenger to each of its embassies. We've never actually seen one."

The director met his gaze. "All of which means that

you haven't a prayer of reading the Soviets' message traffic," he said admonishingly.

Alec Grey smiled and shook his head. "Enigma has a flaw," he said.

The director regarded the photograph before him, as if he were looking for evidence of a weakness visible in the device. "From what you've described, I hardly think that likely."

"The flaw in Enigma is that it encrypts every letter entered into it."

The director appeared puzzled. "I would expect nothing less of an encrypting machine," he said.

"The flaw in Enigma is that it will never display the same character as one types on its keyboard. I can't say how long it took the fellows at GCHQ to appreciate how to exploit it."

"I'm afraid you've lost me, Mr. Grey," the director sighed.

Alec Grey considered how best he might explain this peculiarity of Enigma. Upon reflection, he allowed that he would have done well to have included in his folder an example Enigma message, and the tools by which the Soviets' secret transmissions could be broken into.

"Imagine an Enigma message printed in a single line on a very long strip of paper," he began. The director nodded. "Now imagine that we suspect there's a known phrase somewhere in the encrypted text. We call these phrases 'cribs.' We'll write the crib phrase in a single line on another strip of paper." The director nodded once more.

"If the crib is placed below the message, with the first letter of the crib and the first letter of the message aligned, the corresponding letters in the message and the crib can be compared. We know Enigma scrambles every letter, so if any of the letters in the crib and the part of the message being compared are the same, we haven't found the part of the message where the encrypted version of the crib is. We'll move the crib along by one letter and try again. Eventually, we should find a place in the message where none of the letters in the message are the same as the corresponding letters in the crib. We'll assume that's what the text of the crib looks like when it's been encrypted."

The director stared at Alec Grey for a moment longer, and then returned his attention to the photograph. He seemed at odds to decide whether his understanding of Enigma was as vital as he'd originally anticipated.

"Having found the location of a crib," Alec Grey continued, "it's possible to work backward through the message and determine how the Enigma's rotors would have had to have been set up in order to encrypt the text of the crib into the letters of the corresponding portion of the message. Once the rotor settings are known, the whole message can be decrypted... as can all the other messages sent between Moscow and all its embassies on the same day."

The director scowled at him for a moment longer, and his face suddenly erupted into a broad grin. Alec Grey appreciated that the older man's expression was familiar. He'd seen it appear across the features of numerous cryptographers at GCHQ when they'd broken into a hitherto occluded transmission intended exclusively for Moscow Center.

"That's quite brilliant," Sir Alistair said, as much to himself as to Alec Grey. He appeared to be dividing his kudos between the nameless men who'd first appreciated the weakness of Enigma, and himself for understanding their discovery.

"It's actually not as useful as it might seem," Alec Grey cautioned him. "The Soviet transmissions are typically rather terse, without many salutations or other predictable phrases. We rarely have worthwhile cribs to work with. Of course, that's hardly a problem when we're searching through Soviet transmissions for the text of our own documents. We can have cribs several pages long if we need them."

"Still, it must take days to break into a single message," Sir Alistair said.

"I imagine it did at one time," Alec Grey agreed. "The initial successes against Soviet Enigma traffic in the nineteen-thirties were performed entirely by hand. Several years ago GCHQ developed a computer program to search for cribs and break into Enigma messages. We can send them messages by teletype and the decrypts and rotor settings come back in several hours if the program's successful."

Sir Alistair held the photograph of an Enigma machine before himself for a time, as if he were regarding a fascinating but highly venomous snake from behind a pane of glass. "Do the Soviets know of this flaw?" he inquired at length.

Alec Grey considered this. "We're not entirely sure," he replied. "I met Boris Hagelin last year... he's a curious old bird. He sussed the flaw thirty years ago, but he was of the opinion it was a theoretical weakness at worst. Boris thinks in terms of switches and lamps. We suspect the Russians have much the same problem."

"I'm certain they have a number of bright young men behind the curtain, even if we aren't entirely fond of their politics," the director said.

"I'm certain they do as well," Alec Grey agreed. "What they lack are computers."

The director's eyes narrowed. "Is that so?" he asked, and exhaled a fresh billow of smoke.

Alec Grey leant back in his chair, realizing as he did that he'd have done well to have carried a portable oxygen supply to this meeting. He nodded, wondering if Sir Alistair would notice him through the translucent atmosphere that had enshrouded the few feet separating them.

"Most of the significant technology the Soviet Union possesses owes more to its spies than to its bright young men. You'll recall the Tupolev TU-4."

The TU-4 had been a poignant intelligence embarrassment to the American military. The first Soviet long range bomber had been observed in 1947, an aircraft which had appeared identical to the American B-29 Superfortress. It had proven to have similar flight characteristics as well, on those occasions when it had been seen by western pilots. The Americans had belatedly realized that it had begun its life when a B-29 had crashed during a surveillance flight from Japan over the Kamchatka peninsula. Josef Stalin had personally assured Franklin Roosevelt that the aircraft had been destroyed. In fact, it had been quietly dismantled, transported to Andrie Tupolev's design bureau in Moscow and meticulously duplicated. A dedicated factory had been built on the Volga river to produce twenty TU-4 aircraft. One of them had crashed in 1955 near Kautokeino, Norway, and had been recovered by the Americans. The B-29 had been slavishly reproduced with Soviet components, with the exception of its tires. Unable to duplicate them, Soviet agents had succeeded in buying surplus tires from a scrap dealer in New Jersey.

"It was rather before my time," Sir Alistair said, "but I've read the file. Have they not managed to do the same with computers? I don't suppose one would have to actually crash land in Siberia for them to be able to take it to pieces and see how it works."

"The boffins at GCHQ assure me that a computer is vastly more complex than an aircraft," Alec Grey said. "You can't just disassemble one and make more of them. You'd have to actually understand how the thing operates, and how to create programs for it. We're quite comfortable in the belief that doing so is well beyond the Russians."

The director seemed troubled by this. "I've read several reports which indicated they've successfully bought computer equipment in the west and smuggled it back to Moscow," he said.

"I'm certain they have," Alec Grey agreed. "We believe there to be between six and ten working computers in the Soviet Union at the moment, or about as many as would be owned by a small British bank. They'll very likely manage to smuggle a few more of them over the border in time. If they're attempting to duplicate the time stream project, they'll have dedicated every one of them to their research facilities."

"I believe we may have strayed from my original question, Mr. Grey," the director said. "I asked whether the Soviets know of the weakness in their Enigma machines."

Alec Grey nodded slowly. "It's possible that they, like Boris Hagelin, appreciate the theoretical possibility of breaking into Enigma messages with cribs. It's also possible, in that almost nobody else uses Enigma machines any longer, the problem never seemed relevant to them. However, it's a safe assumption that those few computers the Russians do possess aren't being occupied with verifying their own cryptography. It's probably never occurred to them that a computer could exploit this particular theoretical weakness. It's not how their people think."

Sir Alistair smiled warily. "I wouldn't like to discover five years hence that they've been leading us about by the nose with concocted secret messages the way we've been leading them about by the nose with our concocted watcher radio transmissions."

Alec Grey felt himself touched by amusement. "I think it unlikely."

"I have a difficult time imagining the KGB, easily the

most suspicious organization on earth, entrusting their secrets to a coding system they know can be broken into."

"I had a very long chat with Boris Hagelin," Alec Grey said. "He told me any number of stories he probably shouldn't have. He told me about two men with rather obvious Russian accents approaching him in the summer of 1959, interested in buying a substantial quantity of his current encryption machines. They initially wanted ten of them to get on with."

"Did Mr. Hagelin sell the KGB his machines?" the director prompted him.

"No, sir," Alec Grey replied. "He's dealt with Soviet intelligence for years. He required payment in full before he shipped the encryption machines. Their order arrived at Hagelin's firm, Crypto AG, their check was promptly dishonored by their bank and he never heard from them again."

11

The American deported himself with the air of a god, was spoken of with the reverence accorded to a god and possessed the middle name of a god. Lawrence Downs had disliked him on sight. James Jesus Angleton was the director of counterintelligence for the CIA. He resembled a twig in an expensive suit — men who shook him by the hand for the first time were said to be fearful of snapping his off at its wrist. He was wont to smile benignly for the benefit of those with lesser security clearance than he carried. The effect was largely undermined by his dark, hooded eyes peering through his horn-rimmed spectacles. He drew suspicion about himself like a theatrical cloak.

His suspicion buzzed and hummed above his slicked-back hair now. Lawrence Downs wondered fleetingly why the Americans' most revered spymaster had apparently as yet failed to appreciate the reason for his presence in this room.

James Angleton was clearly not impressed by his surroundings. He had the apprehension of a man who wished to excuse himself and remove his suit coat, that he might assure himself nothing had crawled into his clothing and begun fabricating a nest for itself. He glanced about the small, airless room for what seemed like the dozenth time in the past quarter of an hour before he appeared to will his attention back to the scowling man sitting across the table from him.

A single bare lamp hung from its flex above the table, casting the features of the director of counterintelligence and the overweight Russian before him into stark relief. The Russian glared at him for a moment, his lips pursed into a fleshy creature clawing its way through the pallor of his cheeks. The lamp had been located to render the features of the men confronting the Russian as little more than discordant shadows.

James Angleton twisted in his chair, causing its legs to squeal threateningly. The room only included a single comfortable chair, and it was occupied by Lawrence Downs. The American's presence had not been anticipated, and the only available chair had been crafted for use by someone else like the Russian.

Mikhail Sergeyevich Zakharov had been a major in the KGB. It had been the KGB's misfortune that he'd awoken one morning eighteen months earlier and found himself unable to recall being anything other than a major in the KGB. Mikhail Zakharvov had ascribed his lapse of memory to the length of his tenure at a very small desk pushing very small files around a very small office in the Lubyanka. Lawrence Downs had ascribed it to his consumption of a quantity of vodka which would have been excessive even for a member of Soviet state security.

The thought of being presented with his pension book and a pocket watch twenty-five years hence, still wearing the insignia of a major in the KGB, had apparently filled Mikhail Zakharov with a degree of loathing and dread which had, by his account, left him little choice but to defect to the west. He'd slipped through the curtain with his mistress, a substantial number of cigarette lighters and a small tin box which had originally contained cough lozenges, but which he'd stuffed with microfilmed copies of every document that had crossed his small desk.

Mikhail Zakharov glanced at his wrist now, and reminded that he was no longer permitted to wear a watch, scowled still more resolutely.

"I have seen enough," he said abruptly. His present silence had suffocated the tiny room for several minutes. James Angleton had clearly anticipated him remaining wordless until he was addressed. The American started visibly in his uncomfortable chair.

Lawrence Downs leaned into the puddle of light cast upon the splintered surface of the table that separated himself and James Angleton from Mikhail Zakharov. He slid a large photograph of a document toward the Russian.

"I'm afraid you haven't, Mikhail," he said quietly. "You know we have a great deal more material to get through. We've discussed barely a tenth of the papers you brought with you on film."

Mikhail Zakharov appeared for a moment as if he might dissolve the damp hush of the room with a string of Russian obscenities, as he'd done most days when he'd been confronted by more of his purloined secrets than he'd cared to burden himself with. He clearly imagined the language to be his alone, that his pique might only be guessed at by his British interrogators. Lawrence Downs had thus far chosen not to reveal his own command of Russian, nor the existence of the microphone in the lamp socket dangling above Mikhail Zakharov's balding head.

The Russian's fist pounded the table. "I did not leave the KGB to find myself being questioned by its English equivalent," he growled.

Lawrence Downs smiled benignly, and he reminded himself of the volume and timber of the voice he'd fashioned to speak to Mikhail Zakharov. "You knew when you joined us that you'd be debriefed, Mikhail," he said. Mikhail Zakharov had 'joined us' rather than 'defected,' and he was being 'debriefed' rather than 'questioned.' His active file included several pages of expressions which were and were not to be uttered in his presence.

James Angleton's countenance grew minutely darker, but he said nothing.

"I cannot be expected to review every page that I photographed," the Russian insisted. "There are thousands of them. I have not seen daylight in three months. I have not seen Lana in at least that long. I demand..."

Lawrence Downs shook his head, and Mikhail Zakharov ceased his protest as if an unseen attendant had reached under the translucent fabric of his shirt and removed the batteries that operated his face.

"You know I'm not authorized to agree to any change in your status until the debriefing is complete," he said, pleased with the polish he'd applied to his words. "I can assure you that Miss Kyuzis is well and looks forward to being reunited with you."

Lawrence Downs forced himself not to smile beyond what he permitted himself in addressing Mikhail Zakharov. Svetlana Kyuzis, the Russian's lady friend at the time of his hasty departure from the Soviet Union, was something of a puzzle to him. She was quite a stunner, and there was little doubt why the former KGB officer had enjoyed her presence in his bed. She was, however, also empty-headed to a degree which Lawrence Downs would have insisted with undeniable certainty a year earlier was impossible for any creature more highly evolved than a tapeworm.

Unlike Mikhail Zakharov himself, Svetlana Kyuzis had clearly offered western intelligence no prospect of secret information, insights into the machinations of the Kremlin or the identities of Soviet agents ensconced within this green and pleasant land. It was a particularly good day when she could recall her own name without deep concentration. In that there had been little call to subject her to the mental stresses being inflicted upon her lover, she'd been installed in a secure apartment with a television set and a supply of fashion magazines, which appeared to be all she'd ever asked of her life.

A week earlier, submitting to a dare by one of his colleagues, Lawrence Downs had contrived to visit her. As the myth which had grown up around her had suggested, she had indeed answered her door entirely in the nude, and she'd invited him inside and offered him tea before she'd excused herself to wrap herself in a towel. The officer who'd been assigned to teach her English was said to be experiencing a measure of difficulty in that Svetlana Kyuzis had only barely mastered her native Russian.

"Perhaps if I could go for a walk for just one hour," Mikhail Zakharov said tonelessly, staring into the surface of the table between them. "You could send guards to accompany me."

"I can submit your request," Lawrence Downs sighed, brushing his words with a note of impatience. "I believe we both know what the outcome is likely to be." He touched the photograph, and after a moment's consideration he pushed it several inches closer to the Russian. "The sooner we crack on with these documents, the sooner you'll be able to leave this facility and enjoy your new life in the west."

Mikhail Zakharov glanced up at him, his expression that of something which had been so long at the zoo as to have scant memory of the jungle from which it had been abducted.

Lawrence Downs touched the photograph thoughtfully and gazed into the rising damp which had discolored the wall behind the Russian. After several seconds of further consideration he retracted it.

"There was something more pressing I wanted to ask you about, Mikhail," he said abruptly. The man before him seemed to withdraw minutely from the funk into which he'd submerged himself by mid-morning most days.

Lawrence Downs made a point of addressing him by his given name only on those occasions when he genuinely wished the Russian to apply his mind to a question, rather than to repeat what he'd said a fortnight earlier.

"What can you tell me about Konstanin Bolshakov?" he asked.

Mikhail Zakharov put his hand to his chin, his eyes suddenly alight. "He is... he is nobody... an *apparatchik*. He is a minor diplomatic official in Istanbul."

"Rome," Lawrence Downs corrected him. "He was stationed in Istanbul some years ago, but his most recent posting has been Rome."

Mikhail Zakharov smiled apologetically. "Yes, of course, Rome," he said. His eyes narrowed, and he clearly appreciated that he'd been caught out in an inconsequential deception. "What are you interested in Bolshakov for?"

"He's come over to us," Lawrence Downs replied, and he leant back in his chair. "It was something of a rush job. I understand he's brought some genuinely interesting material. We were hoping you would lend us the benefit of your considerable experience as we attempt to verify some of it."

The Russian shook his head with affected amusement. "I will be happy to help you, but I can tell you now that if whatever Konstanin Bolshakov gave you appears to be important, he is lying to you. He would not have been permitted access to anything more than low-level diplomatic papers."

Lawrence Downs smiled to himself. Somewhere in another safe house in another quiet London street, Konstanin Bolshakov was probably sitting before another cigarette-burned, ruined table in another merciless chair beginning his tale. Whoever had been assigned to question him would ask him about Mikhail Zakharov in time. Unless Konstanin Bolshakov turned out to be very different from the others who'd slipped the curtain of late, he would say much the same thing, denouncing all the defectors who'd come before him as worthless. Lawrence Downs considered it to be a fundamental aspect of the character of those men who were driven to betray their countries in windowless chambers such as this one.

He glanced once more at his watch. Mikhail Zakharov had been occupying his chair for a little over three hours this morning, which he'd long since concluded was about the limit of his attention. In another hour the Russian's voice would acquire a distinct whine to it, and he would become alternately belligerent and obsequious. More to the point, he would begin fabricating details of his career with the KGB, and Lawrence Downs would be obliged to point out the inconsistencies between his present version of events and that which he'd recounted a week earlier. He'd learned that pressing the Russian beyond the limits of his patience was rarely fruitful.

The afternoon's session would be considerably more productive, he reminded himself. He replaced the photographed document which he'd presented to the Russian in the folder from which it had emerged, hoping as he did that Mikhail Zakharov would appreciate he'd not seen the last of it. After a moment's consideration he closed the folder and rose from his chair.

"Hold on a minute," James Angleton said, his voice betraying a note of irritation.

Lawrence Downs considered the director of counterintelligence, deciding as he did that in more refined circles he might well have been regarded as genuinely impolite.

"I do beg your pardon," he said, and he returned to his seat.

"I have a document I'd like to show Mr. Zakharov," James Angleton said. He withdrew a large brown envelope from a briefcase which had rested, unnoticed, beside his chair.

Mikhail Zakharov turned to consider the unfamiliar voice, and his eyes narrowed. "I... I do not know who you are," he said defensively.

James Angleton smiled coldly, and he leant forward into the incandescent puddle which spilled over the coffee rings and cigarette burns and pencil drawings that pocked the surface of the table. His features became alabaster, his eyes blackened pearls set behind crystal. "Don't you?" he asked absently.

Mikhail Zakharov's expression grew alarmed, and he appeared to curse under his breath. He leant back into his chair, as if he sought the succor of the gloom that bubbled and oozed beyond the grasp of the lamp. He glanced accusingly at Lawrence Downs.

The American removed a photograph and a sheet of typescript from his envelope and pushed them across the table until they glowered at the Russian. "This is one of the documents you brought out," he said icily.

Mikhail Zakharov regarded the photograph for a moment. It was of a printed page with several complex drawings interspersed with Cyrillic type. The typescript would be an English translation of the Soviet document.

"Perhaps," he agreed. "I photographed a great many documents..."

"When did you photograph this one?" James Angleton demanded.

The Russian shook his head. "I do not remember," he replied. "There were a great many documents..."

"What can you tell me about it?"

Mikhail Zakharov glared at the American. "I... I do not know," he said, his jaw taut above his collar. "It is very technical... I do not understand it."

"This is a diagram of small cyclotron designed to bombard the element Americium with alpha particles, for the purpose of producing the element Berkelium," James Angleton explained. His tone suggested he was conversant with the rarefied language of the document before the Russian, and that he would brook no dissembling to the effect that the man before him was less so.

Mikhail Zakharov gestured awkwardly at the photograph. "I will take your word for that," he said, and he again glanced at Lawrence Downs, his expression imploring on this occasion.

"Why does the Soviet Union want to build a cyclotron, Mr. Zakharov?" James Angleton inquired harshly. "What interest does a country that has a hard time making decent steel have in the production of Berkelium?"

"I do not know," the Russian repeated. "I do not understand what that document is about."

James Angleton seemed to ignore Mikhail Zakharov's reply. "How is the Soviet Union refining the Uranium required to initiate the process of large scale Berkelium production?"

The Russian stared at him blankly. "I do not know what any of this means," he pleaded, wresting his attention from James Angleton and addressing Lawrence Downs. "Why is he asking me this?"

"Because this is a very serious matter, Mikhail," Lawrence Downs replied. "Mr. Angleton has arrived at it before we did, but you will require an extensive debriefing on the subject. Perhaps you should answer his question."

"I do not know..."

"That's not an answer, Mikhail."

A rivulet of perspiration plodded across the Russian's forehead and hurled itself, unnoticed, into the darkness. His gaze staggered between the faces of the two men before him. His hands had affixed themselves to the table, iron clamps upon the wood. His fingers seemed as if they might snap themselves into kindling.

"It is just a document I photographed," he pleaded.

"It's not the only one on this subject, Mr. Zakharov," James Angleton snapped.

"I do not understand…"

James Angleton stared at the Russian for a moment longer before he retrieved his photograph and returned it to his briefcase. Wordlessly, he rose from his chair and turned to leave the room. Lawrence Downs considered Mikhail Zakharov for a moment longer before he followed the American into the narrow corridor beyond the tiny room. The door locked behind him. A soldier stood at attention beside it, deliberately ignoring the two men.

James Angleton walked several paces along the corridor, clearly wishing to be out of earshot of the man guarding Mikhail Zakharov. At length he turned to address Lawrence Downs.

"He's full of crap," the American said, his expression tinged with dark amusement.

Lawrence Downs permitted himself to smile. "I believe he's more than half full of crap at present," he said. "The questioning process shovels it all out in time."

James Angleton nodded uncertainly, and he leant against one of the walls of the passage. "Is this how you normally interrogate defectors?" he asked. "It all seems damned unusual to me." He gestured at the narrow corridor, his hand growing indistinct in the shadows between the overhead lamps. "This place looks like a cheap hotel."

"As it's intended to," Lawrence Downs agreed. "We hired a chap who designs sets for the Pinewood film studios to make it look like this."

The American's eyes narrowed, and he clearly did not appreciate the purpose of such a deception.

"It was the idea of one of our fellows, Alec Grey," Lawrence Downs continued. "He reckoned that most of the defectors come across motivated largely by their egos. They arrive thinking they're going to save western intelligence all by themselves. Mikhail Zakharov demanded that he be permitted to take tea with Her Majesty the queen when he arrived. This place... it knocks them down a peg, illustrates their place in the world."

James Angleton glowered at him for a moment, his expression suggesting that two large men with leather truncheons would have knocked Mikhail Zakharov down a peg with considerably greater efficacy.

"I find it strange I was... invited here this morning," the American continued, his words muted in the stillness of the passage. "We've asked for direct access to your assets for years."

Lawrence Downs felt himself smile uncomfortably, and he chose to grant the director of counterintelligence a moment of pique. "I'm afraid your presence here is as much for our benefit as for yours," he allowed. "When it was learned you'd be arriving in London yesterday for discussions with Sir Alistair Fitzhenry, we appreciated that your presence would be of assistance in... motivating Mikhail Zakharov. We felt you'd make some use of the audience as well... as, in fact, you have."

"What are you talking about, Mr. Downs?" the American snapped.

The air in the passage was close and damp. Lawrence Downs sighed. "When Major Zakharov first came across to us, we asked him a lot of predictable questions, and he provided us with a lot of predictable answers for the most part. One of the things we asked him had to do with why he'd chosen to defect to us, rather than to your lot. His answer was... unexpected. It appears the KGB has put a rumor amongst its officers that the CIA is particularly unpleasant to Soviets who come through the curtain. He feared being imprisoned and interrogated for years, questioned under the influence of drugs, physical torture... and finally being sent into internal exile in a small town in Montana or Wyoming, with full-time guards to see that he stayed there."

James Angleton laughed, the sound dark and reptilian. "Congress would have us before a firing squad," he remarked, his expression suggesting he sincerely wished it were otherwise.

"The intent in circulating such a rumor is somewhat transparent," Lawrence Downs said. "None the less, it was a useful insight into the character and motivations of Mikhail Zakharov. Several weeks later, when the major was behaving especially poorly and throwing one of his tantrums, I suggested that perhaps he would be better suited to working with the CIA. He stopped his playing up immediately, and he was a good little spy for the rest of the day."

"Then what am I doing here, if all you had to do was mention the agency to make him settle down?"

Lawrence Downs smiled fleetingly. "The effect became less pronounced with repeated use," he replied. "We appear to be reaching a critical stage with Major Zakharov. I felt, and my superiors agreed, that some additional reinforcement of our threat would make him more... cooperative."

He braced himself to be berated by the director of counterintelligence, but James Angleton merely smiled. "Glad I could be of help," he said coldly. He glanced back along the passage toward the door that confined Mikhail Zakharov. "You know he's a Soviet plant, don't you?"

"Is he?" Lawrence Downs inquired, affecting a note of mild surprise.

James Angleton had become legendary in intelligence circles for his revelations about Soviet double agents and disinformation. It was his belief that, unable to intimidate or capture its defectors, the Kremlin had sought to render them impotent by sending false defectors to the west in their wake. These double agents, or 'plants,' were said to have called into question the revelations of genuine defectors.

It was a perfectly reasonable assumption, Lawrence Downs considered, save that it was impossible to know whether it was true, and if it was, which defectors were authentic and which were Soviet plants.

"Of course he is," James Angleton said. "Listen to the man. He gets sent highly sensitive material about what has to be part of the Soviets' time stream project that he says he isn't qualified to understand. Why would he be sent papers he couldn't understand? Either he's lying about not understanding them, or he's lying about how he got access to them."

"I see," Lawrence Downs said, nodding, appreciating as he did that he'd used the same tone as he applied to his interviews with Mikhail Zakharov.

"We know he was a paper-pusher for the KGB," James Angleton continued, "an *apparatchik*, as the Russians like to say. The Kremlin wouldn't have been sending him time stream documents."

"Are we to assume Major Zakharov breached the Kremlin's internal security and gained access to those papers?"

James Angleton sighed with obvious annoyance. "We are to assume he was given the documents to photograph before he pretended to defect," he snapped.

Lawrence Downs nodded again. "I fail to see why the Soviets would wish us to know they're further along in their research than we hitherto suspected." He forced himself to smile faintly. In point of fact, he fully appreciated the reasoning behind the Kremlin planting such documents, if in fact it had done so. He and Alec Grey and several other senior people from Leconfield House had debated much the same theory. Alec Grey had denounced it as the product of a dark and twisted mind, while acknowledging that the mind responsible for it had been his own.

"Because they damned well want us off our guard,"

James Angleton said harshly. For a moment Lawrence Downs imagined that he might hammer his fist into the passage wall to emphasize his statement, and he considered mentioning that the concrete had been the work of genuine masons, not the decorator from Pinewood film studios.

"They want us to think they have everything they need to move ahead with their research, so we'll stop worrying about keeping our progress top secret. They don't have anything like it. My people tell me a high school student could have drawn the plans for the cyclotron. Knowing how the thing works in theory is a hell of a long way from being able to build one."

He permitted himself a flicker of amusement, pleased that the director of counterintelligence for the CIA had come to much the same conclusion as his superiors had done when Mikhail Zakharov had first imposed himself upon them. Regrettably, James Angleton had not chosen to disregard the theory with the benefit of subsequent consideration.

"Golitsyn reviewed his material," James Angleton continued. "He agrees it looks like it was cooked up by Moscow."

Lawrence Downs felt himself wince. Major Anatoli Golitsyn had been a KGB officer stationed in Helsinki when he'd defected to the CIA the previous year. He'd informed James Angleton that there was a mole within the CIA. The director of counterintelligence had warmed to him immediately. Regrettably, Lawrence Downs considered now, he'd been unable to name the traitor, or to provide sufficient details about his activities to suggest where he might be sought. He'd succeeded only in stoking the already belching furnace of James Angleton's suspicion and paranoia.

It was known that James Angleton frequently granted his most favored Soviet defector access to highly classified material from a variety of western intelligence sources. It was troubling to think that transcripts of Mikhail Zakharov's debriefings, currently among the most secret intelligence Leconfield house shared with the CIA, had traveled directly from the desk of the director to that of a former employee of the Kremlin.

"You do understand that much of what Major Zakharov has provided us with thus far has proven accurate," Lawrence Downs said quietly.

"Of course it has," James Angleton said. "Moscow knows it'll have to wrap the lies it wants us to believe in enough truth to disguise them."

Lawrence Downs nodded his agreement. The American was clearly on the point of excusing himself for his meeting with Sir Alistair Fitzhenry, and he appeared greatly comforted to be preparing to leave this place. He wondered absently if Leconfield House had chosen not to reveal the full extent of the damage Major Zakharov had done to the Soviet espionage apparatus in Great Britain, or if the director of counterintelligence had simply failed to read the major's file in its entirety.

Mikhail Zakharov had thus far compromised a network of five illegal agents loosely connected with the Soviet legation in Kensington Palace Gardens and a senior engineer at the Guided Weapons Research and Development Division of the Air Ministry. Lawrence Downs had little doubt that Moscow was infernally devious and quite heartless when it came to expending its resources to further its ends, even when the resources in question were human beings. None the less, he considered it beyond even the machinations of the Kremlin to burn assets in quite the numbers that Mikhail Zakharov had thus far proven himself capable of doing.

12

The woman in her constable's uniform appeared to have been carved from the living rock upon which this stygian cavern of a police station had been built, and placed in her corner of this room by the blind, hunched trolls responsible for its construction. She might have been the image of their overweight, ashen-blond goddess of fertility, or inexpensive lager. She stared blankly at a stain on the far wall, just to the left of the locked steel door.

Gina Caroll lit a fresh cigarette from the glowing corpse of its predecessor and infused her throat with its smoke. She felt herself become lightheaded for an instant, pleased by the sensation. Her legs were growing numb in the uncomfortable chair they'd given her to sit in. The table between herself and the door was scarred by countless cigarette ends, and she vowed to add to its misery. She directed her attention to the motionless constable.

"Do you know how much longer I'm to be kept here?" she demanded.

The woman shook her head mechanically. "I'm afraid not, ma'am," she said lifelessly.

"Any chance of a cup of tea?"

The woman shook her head once more, the gesture little more than a continuation of her previous regret.

"I'm not permitted to leave the room," she replied.

"Has my solicitor been sent for? He should have been here by now."

"I couldn't say."

The constable returned her attention to the far wall. They'd engaged in roughly the same conversation on two previous occasions throughout the morning.

She'd consumed her cigarette and was most of the way through another when she heard the door at the far side of the table rattle. She glowered at it, willing it to open, willing the overweight, overpaid attorney she retained for outrages such as this one to waddle through it in one of his best Italian suits and spirit her away from this medieval battlement. The man who stepped from the glare of the corridor beyond it looked nothing like him.

He glanced at her for a moment before he seated himself across the table from her and placed a small leather case between them. As if by a trick of telepathy or electrical control, the woman constable strode to the door and left the room.

"And who might you be?" she snapped. "Are you the one responsible for me being banged up in here for the past three hours?"

The man nodded. He seemed to be in his late thirties, but he was subtly unlike the men of her acquaintance. He regarded her as he might have done an unexpected curiosity in a familiar shop. After a moment's consideration he opened his case and removed several papers.

"My name is Alec Grey," he said, his attention on the pages before him. "I've had you invited here..."

"I wasn't invited here, Mr. Grey," she said icily. "I was arrested in my home, handcuffed and pushed into the back of a police car."

"To answer multiple charges of solicitation," he said, still reading from his papers.

"I asked to have my solicitor sent for," she said, her

teeth clasped upon the end of her cigarette. "When can I expect him?"

Alec Grey smiled. "He won't be attending this inter-view, Miss Caroll," he replied. "I thought it best that this matter be private for a time. I believe you'll agree with me."

She felt her eyes narrow, her jaw stiffen. "You're not a policeman," she said uncertainly.

"No, I'm not," he agreed. "I'm with MI5."

She leant back in her chair. "If you're not the police, you can show me the way to the street," she said.

"We enjoy the assistance of the police. The charges of solicitation are quite genuine."

"I've been charged before," she said.

"I'm fairly certain you would be found guilty on all the counts in this arrest, Miss Caroll," Alec Grey said. "My understanding is that you'd be looking at four years."

"I want my solicitor," she growled.

He smiled faintly, and his eyes bored into her own. "Your solicitor wouldn't be of very much help to you, Miss Caroll," he said. "This is a matter of the defense of the realm."

She coughed, feeling her chest tighten. "I've no idea what you're on about."

"I've arranged to have you arrested because Her Majesty's government requires your assistance," he said formally. "In the event that you choose to provide it, you'll be free to leave here. Failing this, there's a real policeman on the other side of the door behind me prepared to take you into custody and have you formally charged."

"What sort of bastard are you?" she demanded, aware that her voice had risen in pitch.

His smile broadened. "The usual sort," he said, and he returned his attention to his papers.

"Tuesday last, you were collected outside your flat by a Russian named Valentin Chervenkov, driving a dark blue Ford Anglia. Mr. Chervenkov drove around Chelsea for over half an hour, and eventually arrived at a house in Abbots Close, where he drove into a private courtyard. An hour later, Mr. Chervenkov emerged from the courtyard in his Anglia, with you in the rear seat, drove around Chelsea for half an hour and finally dropped you outside your flat. Yesterday you and he engaged in the same performance. The house in Abbots Close is owned by another Russian, Ivan Vasilievich Nikonov, a colonel in the KGB, currently stationed at the Soviet embassy in London."

"I don't know the name of the driver," she said, hearing her voice flutter with uncertainty. "The man who lives in the house told me his name is Gerald."

Alec Grey removed another clutch of papers from his case. They proved to be six large black and white photographs. He spread them before her. Each of them was of a different man, similar in appearance, taken from what she considered were peculiar angles. "Is one of these a picture of Gerald?" he asked.

She touched the second picture from the right, and Alec Grey nodded. "That would be Colonel Nikonov," he said. He returned the photographs to his case.

"I trust you visit Colonel Nikonov in a professional capacity, Miss Caroll," he continued.

She nodded stiffly.

"May I ask how you came to meet the colonel?" Alec Grey inquired. "Our understanding of him suggests that he wouldn't have engaged the services of a common streetwalker."

"I'm not a common streetwalker," she snapped at him. "I service a select group of important clients. You probably work for some of them."

He smiled thinly. "No doubt," he agreed, perhaps remotely amused by the thought. He elevated his gaze as if it were a gun turret and bored it into her. She was a moment appreciating that he was awaiting a reply to his question.

"One of my... one of my other clients gave him my telephone number," she said.

"And he would be?"

She felt her eyes narrow. "And he would be none of your concern," she hissed.

"I would be concerned which of your clients is sufficiently familiar with a Soviet agent operating on British soil to share your services with him, Miss Caroll." His voice had rumbled with an undercurrent of threat.

"Mr. Portland," she said, watching his expression flicker. "Mr. Douglas Portland."

He wrote the name on one of his pages. "An assistant undersecretary of... something I don't recall," Alec Grey said, as much to himself as to her. He paused. "You understand that we'll need you to identify him from a set of photographs later."

She nodded.

He pushed the photograph of the Russian she'd identified earlier across the table to her. "I'd like to return our conversation to this fellow," he said.

She scowled at him, wondering if she would do well to remind him that what was occurring between them was entirely removed from a conversation, and bordered on an inquisition. At length she nodded again, and he smiled once more.

"How long have you been acquainted with Colonel Nikonov?"

"Six months," she replied. "Perhaps longer."

"How often do you visit him?"

"When he sends for me. It's been several times a week, and then I won't hear from him for a fortnight."

"Has Valentin Chervenkov always collected you?"

"I think it's been the same driver. I've never had a proper look at him."

He glanced at her. "Why is that?"

"It's part of the instructions. As soon as I get in the

car, I'm to put on a large hat and dark glasses that've been left on the rear seat. The glasses are completely black, and I can't see anything. The hat makes it impossible to see around the sides of the glasses."

This clearly amused him. "So you've no idea where the house you're taken to is located."

"I now know it's in Chelsea," she said.

He considered one of the pages before him. "Please describe in detail what happened the first time you were brought to Colonel Nikonov's house."

She felt herself smile despite her growing anger at Alec Grey. "I'd have thought a clever fellow like you could have imagined that," she said.

"If you would," he prompted her.

She sighed. "I was brought through a rear door into the kitchen. There was no one else about except for the driver. He walked ahead of me, and I never saw his face. We climbed a flight of stairs until we reached a door on the second story of the house. I went through the door. Gerald... or whatever his name is... was in the room beyond it, wearing a smoking jacket. He had a cigar. The room was posh. He gave me a glass of wine, and then he told me to go into the next room and undress. There was a bed. He came in a few minutes later. The rest of it's predictable."

"When you were finished?"

"When we were finished, I got dressed. He told me there was an envelope with my money in it on a table in the next room. I took the envelope and left. The driver was waiting. He took me back to the car, drove around for a time and left me at my flat."

"How long was it until Colonel Nikonov sent for you again?"

She considered this. It seemed a remote epoch of her past. She willed herself to recall the silent, dusty interior of the house, the oddly mismatched furniture, the slender, balding man with an unplaceable foreign precision in his voice. "Two days," she replied at length. "Perhaps three." "And was it much the same as the first time?" She nodded. "He didn't offer me a glass of wine." "And the third time?"

She felt her breath catch in her chest. Without thinking, she lit a fresh cigarette from the glowing end of her last one and gasped through it. She glared at Alec Grey through a billow of smoke.

"The third time he told me that he'd increased my payment by a quarter," she said coldly. "He told me that he'd be having me anally, and that I could use his lavatory to prepare myself." She observed a flicker of disquiet in the features of the man across the table from her. "You needn't look shocked, Mr. Grey," she said, pleased by his moment of surprise. "It's a service I perform for several of my clients, and most of them don't pay me half so well. It's painful... men enjoy that." She met his gaze for a moment before she permitted herself another draught of her cigarette. "Some men," she added.

"He'd clearly done it before," she continued. "There were pots of cream and petroleum jelly on the back of the wash basin, objects of various sizes to be... inserted, to make it easier for him to..." She paused, feeling herself grow unaccountably angry at her inability to describe the distasteful hour she'd spent with her client. "I wrapped a towel around myself and went out into the bedroom. He had me lie over the edge of the bed. He took an unusual amount of time... when he was done with me, he told me I could use his lavatory once more... to staunch the bleeding."

"Is that all?"

She regarded him, and after some consideration she decided he was genuinely uncomfortable with his task, requiring that she recount her humiliation for the benefit of his superiors. He'd written nothing during her

description. There was a tape recorder running somewhere, she imagined.

"He told me in future I should make more noise,"
she replied coldly.

"I trust he sent for you again, then."

"It was the next week... but he had me... in the usual
way, and the time after that."

"And the time after that?"

She stared into the surface of the table between
them, and when she could no longer prevent herself from
imagining sprites and monsters writhing in its details, she
permitted herself a glance into the shadows that sulked in
the corners of the airless room. "He told me my payment
would be increased by half," she whispered. The features
of Alec Grey swam in her tears.

"What did Colonel Nikonov expect for his money?"
he asked.

"He... tied my hands and legs... he put a cloth over
my eyes, and another in my mouth... and he beat me with
a cane," she replied, conscious that her words had been
barely audible.

"And the next time?"

She felt herself relent to sobbing. "Don't you understand?" she cried. "Every time he sent for me, I couldn't
know if he meant to... I entered the room waiting for him
to tell me that he'd increased my money... I wanted to run
out the house, tell him to stuff his money and run out the
house..."

"Why didn't you?"

She felt her jaw grow taut. Wordlessly, she unfastened her blouse. There was a thatch of angry welts and
sores across her breasts. She'd refused to confront them in
her mirror that morning, but they'd clawed at her and rent
her flesh as she'd been led from her flat by the police.
"Yesterday he doubled my money." she said, hearing her
voice shatter.

"May I ask what he expected of you?"

She took a final draught of her cigarette. "I'm not certain I recall everything he did to me," she said quietly. "I was tied up... he beat me... he touched me with a live lamp flex... I think I passed out... he had me several times. When it was over, and he'd untied his ropes and given me back my clothes, I said I couldn't return, that he wasn't to ring me again. He pushed me down over the bed and... and he took a pistol from a drawer in a table beside his bed. He tore off my knickers and pushed it inside me. After a few seconds he pulled the trigger."

She willed herself to meet his gaze, to return his stare. "It wasn't loaded. He pulled it out of me and stood me up. He told me where I lived, the name of the market I got my shopping from, the pubs I visited. He told me that if I didn't come when he sent for me, the pistol would be loaded the next time, and the sound of its trigger would be last thing I'd hear. Then he told me to leave and collect my money."

Alec Grey considered her, his face devoid of the pity or disgust or contempt she felt certain he must hold for her. She was aware that she'd begun sobbing during the previous few minutes. She daubed at her eyes.

She stared at the smoldering fag end between her fingers and glanced accusingly at the empty cigarette packet on the table before her. Without thinking, she crushed the cigarette into lifelessness in a cracked glass ashtray and she returned her attention to the figure across the table.

"Have you arrested him... Colonel... whatever you called him?" she asked uncertainly.

"No," he replied.

"Will you?"

"It's unlikely. Ivan Vasilievich Nikonov carries diplomatic credentials. The most we could do is pack him off to the Soviet Union."

"Why have you brought me here?" she demanded, feeling the chill of the room clutch at her hair, as he'd done while he'd been sodomizing her for the second time the previous afternoon.

Alec Grey pushed his papers into a single pile before himself. "You've been of considerable assistance," he said, his tone suggesting that he'd deliberately deflected her question.

"He'll know," she said angrily. "He'll bloody well know I've grassed him out to you lot."

Alec Grey regarded her, his eyes featureless pools in the tepid illumination of the room.

She leant forward. "He'll kill me," she pleaded, hearing once more the muted snap of the trigger of his pistol where it had protruded from between her legs. "When he finds out..."

"One of my staff is waiting outside," Alec Grey said evenly. "She'll want to go over your account of your contact with Colonel Nikonov in somewhat more detail. When she's done... and assuming you're as helpful with her as you've been for me... several of my lads will return with you to your flat. There's to be a removal van waiting for you. You'll be taken to another city, provided with new accommodations, a different name... we can arrange to find you work, if you don't mind abandoning your current profession."

"The hell they bloody will," she cried.

"You may wish to consider the alternatives."

She was about to speak, to tell him what he could do with his lads and his removal van. She willed herself to be silent, to still the incandescent rage that howled within her.

Alec Grey got to his feet, collected his papers and pushed his chair under the table. "I'm genuinely sorry for what Colonel Nikonov subjected you to, Miss Caroll," he said into the shadows. "As you'll appreciate, I'm not permitted to disclose what we have in mind for him. If it offers you any comfort, I can tell you that by the time he returns to Moscow, you'll have exacted more than ample revenge."

13

"In another few minutes my teeth chattering will be audible outside, and we'll be blown," William Montrose said, as much to himself as to the ill-defined figure before him. The confined interior of the works van stank of petrol fumes and stale breath, cigarettes smoked to the fag end, take-away coffee and inexpensive whiskey. This was the fourth occasion of his occupying it. The first had been at the height of summer, and he'd been compelled to violate security on that occasion to stagger outside and be ill.

"Please bloody do." Victor Speaks turned momentarily from the viewing lens that protruded through the side of the van. He withdrew a battered silver flask from his boiler suit, unscrewed its cap and raised it to his lips. His words were beginning to slur. In another hour he'd crumple against the back of one of the seats and fall asleep. "I'd suffer a ragging out by that poncy little shit if it'd get us out of this bloody soup tin."

William Montrose sighed, wishing as he did that he'd kept his discomfort to himself. Victor Speaks had taken to punctuating his expressions of displeasure with swallows of drink all morning. In the event that the objects of their interest finally did rouse themselves from their bed and begin their journey, as they were scheduled to do, Victor Francis Speaks would require rolling across Mayrick Road and dragging into the house in question.

Victor Speaks had been seconded from F Branch. In an earlier epoch, F Branch had been all but autonomous, and Victor Speaks had probably had leave to do as he pleased. The new head of F Branch was a rather short-tempered former policeman named Harold Newcomb. Harry the Nick was said to have dominion over his fief, but few of his charges were under any illusion as to his true disposition in the great chain of being. He reported to Alec Grey, and it was rumored that Alec Grey reported to God.

William Montrose reported directly to Alec Grey, which he considered to be a situation identical to that of Victor Speaks for all practical purposes, save that it was somewhat less time-consuming.

"You'd do well to remember that poncy little shit kept you on when half of F Branch got the chop," William Montrose said, watching his breath form into diaphanous clouds before his face, colorless wraiths in the gloom of the van.

"He couldn't bloody well have given us all the sack," Victor Speaks muttered, returning his eye to the viewing lens. William Montrose knew precisely what his colleague was looking at. Mayrick Road had been a swirling bazaar of middle-aged businessmen in conservative suits several hours earlier, as they'd each left their redecorated Georgian homes and debouched into the outflow pipe of Dollis Hill tube station. It had subsequently taken on aspects of the valley of the kings, motionless and sepulchral. Perhaps the wives of those businessmen didn't rise until late afternoon, he mused.

"Of course he could have." Alec Grey had performed what had been referred to in polite circles as 'weeding,' and in various pubs in an Official Secrets Act whisper as 'butchery.' "Cambridge rolls hundreds of you lot off the

assembly line every year, all neatly packaged in wood shav-
ings and brown paper."

Victor Speaks turned from his lens once more, those
few shards of his expression as were visible in the errant
light from the windscreen of the van ineffable. William
Montrose wondered fleetingly if he'd had his colleague on
about his expensive upbringing once too often.

"You can't replace experience," he said coldly. "I've
been doing this work…"

"…since you were personally hired by Sir Francis
Walsingham," William Montrose interrupted him, gestur-
ing impatiently. "I know… I've read your file." Victor
Speaks' features erupted into a twisted grin. Francis
Walsingham had been educated at Cambridge as well, and
he'd risen to head the British espionage services of his day.
His day had been during the reign of Elizabeth I, however
— he'd died in 1590.

William Montrose indicated the abandoned viewing
lens, and Victor Speaks returned his attention to it once
more.

"He's as bad as that pratt of an MP in the 1940s,"
Victor Speaks muttered. He paused, clearly struggling to
recall a name. "Carlyle… Malcolm Carlyle… the nutter
who persuaded the government to put that green border
around the union jack. I saw one of them flying over a
junior school this morning. Carlyle's been dead a good ten
years, but he's left us all with his night soil to scrape up.
It'll be the same with Alec bloody Grey. They'll be trying to
hire back the F Branch people he's sacked for the next ten
years."

"Perhaps they could get work sewing new flags,"
William Montrose suggested. Victor Speaks turned
momentarily to glare at him.

The next half hour passed in silence, save for William
Montrose's teeth, which he grew increasingly certain
would be a cause for concern over possible earthquake

damage to several nearby homes. He'd largely convinced himself that the feeling would not return to his lower extremities for at least a fortnight when Victor Speaks again permitted himself a sip from his flask.

"Bloody hell," he muttered.

"What is it?"

"His lordship and madam appear to have stirred their stumps and roused themselves from their bedclothes," he continued, affected awe in his voice. "He's actually wearing a bowler hat, the great girl's blouse. They've just locked the front door and they're coming down the steps." He paused, and William Montrose willed himself to his feet. His legs began to tingle, a harbinger of the pain that would shriek at him a moment hence as his blood began to thaw.

"His lordship appears to have correctly identified which of the objects in his garage is his car," Victor Speaks continued, having assumed the mannerisms of a football announcer. "He's entered the car... his good lady wife has entered the car... the car has started... the car has emitted a cloud of smoke sufficient to blanket London for at least a week... and they're off."

The rattle of a badly-tuned engine was audible through the steel walls of the van as it approached them, turned abruptly and vanished along Mayrick Road in an uneven cacophony of misfires and clashing gears.

"That car wants seeing to," Victor Speaks concluded.

"A good communist does not repair his car," William Montrose chided him. "A good communist allows his car to go to rot, and then buys a new car to provide employment and glorious prosperity for the working masses."

Victor Speaks smiled, his eyes narrowing. "You'd do well to take care who you say that to, sunshine. Rumor has it that some of them back at Leconfield House voted labor."

The couple Victor Speaks had referred to as his lordship and madam were Reginald and Evelyn Childers.
They'd been described by Alec Grey as either a political
inconsistency or the worst sort of hypocrites — affluent
Marxists. They'd been active in the Communist Party of
Great Britain since they'd been at school. They raised
funds, organized meetings and took periodic sojourns into
the Soviet Union for what they'd described as 'cultural
exchange.' It was unlikely they engaged in any genuine
espionage, Alec Grey had insisted, as it was doubtful either
of them could spell the word. None the less, they unquestionably rubbed elbows with any number of genuine spies.

Eighteen months earlier, the Childers' status in the
party had shifted. The party's headquarters in King Street
had been burgled — remarkably, not by MI5 — and the
party had clearly decided that its many secrets were no
longer secure in the yellowed stone building it had occupied since the nineteen-twenties. Chief amongst these had
been its membership lists, which were reputed to include
over fifty thousand names. Reginald Childers had been
deemed worthy to safeguard this most holy of relics. Alec
Grey had speculated on whether Reginald Childers had
been thus honored because he'd proven himself trustwor-
thy, because he'd seemed an unlikely subject for the attentions of MI5, or merely because he'd owned the nicest safe.

In point of fact, Alec Grey had continued at the
briefing for this operation, it had taken over a year of mail
intercepts and telephone taps to ascertain who'd been
granted custody of the list, and there was some concern
that the party had in fact adopted what would have been a
breathtakingly clever strategy of shifting it from one
guardian to another at intervals more frequent than once
every forty years. The operation to obtain it had been laid
on with no small measure of haste for this reason.

They remained in the van for fifteen minutes after
the cacophonous departure of Reginald and Evelyn

Childers, should the lady discover that she'd forgotten her handbag, or his lordship his copy of Das Capital. The couple did not reappear. Intelligence from sources not explained in detail to William Montrose had indicated that they were destined for Birmingham, to attend Evelyn Childers' mother's funeral.

Victor Speaks sighed, and he took a final draught from his flask. He smelled of a distillery, William Montrose considered uneasily. Without consulting the other man, he unlatched the rear doors of the works van and stepped uncertainly to the cobbles beyond it. Mayrick Road was lifeless, a disconcerting watercolor from a more somber age. Brittle leaves crackled under his boots like distant gunfire, and he accepted his tool chest from Victor Speaks.

The two men crossed Mayrick Road with the unhurried gate of tradesmen who were being paid by the hour. Victor Speaks was expending no small measure of effort to prevent himself from staggering. William Montrose glanced at him as they came abreast of the Childers' home. He'd joined F Branch before William Montrose had entered his freshman year at Oxford. If word of his state of inebriation reached the ears of Alec Grey or Sir Alistair Fitzhenry, his career would vanish like a wisp of breath on a chilly morning such as this.

They slipped through the lane from which Reginald Childers had driven a quarter of an hour earlier. Nothing stirred. The day drew in upon itself, a narrow corridor of scrubbed brick, fresh tarmac, a small window with recent double glazing. They reached the rear of the house. The door was exactly as the photographs they'd been presented with at the operation briefing had promised it would be.

William Montrose reached inside his boiler suit and then stopped himself. After a moment's consideration he peeled the door mat from the slate upon which it rested. The impression of a key was visible in its rubber underside, but the key itself was absent. He smiled to himself and returned his hand to his shirt pocket. He withdrew a leather folder and selected a suitable lock pick and a tension wrench.

Picking a lock, he'd been taught, was to be considered a last resort. He knelt before the door and inserted the tension wrench in the lock before him. It was a new Yale, fitted within the last year judging by the shine on its brass. Reginald Childers had undertaken his duties as keeper of the list with some measure of concern.

Picking a lock was to be considered a last resort because it was all but impossible to pick one without causing it some minute degree of damage. None the less, he'd been trained by some of MI5's most skilled technicians in the finer points of burglary. He applied a gentle pressure to the wrench and carefully slipped his pick into the barrel of the lock, locating the rearmost pin. It slid minutely, paused, and then broke. He smiled to himself. It had four fellows still to be defeated.

Someone dismantling the Childers' lock would most certainly have been able to detect the scratches made by his pick. His skill was such that he would leave no visible spoor for a less thorough inspection.

The lock required just over a minute to vanquish. When he finally rose to his feet and pushed the door before him, he noticed that Victor Speaks had grown decidedly uneasy. The man from F Branch had very possibly spent his entire working life crouched in works vans and other places of concealment. This was probably his first direct encounter with the lodgings of one of his subjects.

Victor Speaks followed him into the kitchen of the Childers' home. The air was thick with fumes of a coffee pot, vapors of toast and marmalade. Victor Speaks was glancing about the kitchen, clearly seeking their source.

"Don't touch anything," William Montrose said sternly. "This is all for nothing if they suss we've been here."

Victor Speaks scowled at him, saying nothing.

"The safe's in a closet in the master bedroom, on the second floor," William Montrose continued.

"How can you possibly know that?" Victor Speaks hissed.

William Montrose smiled, wondering if he might remind his colleague that they'd watched the occupants of the house depart, and there was arguably no call to whisper.

"One of our lot found the chap who fitted it." he replied.

The operation briefing had called for Victor Speaks to wait outside the door of the master bedroom while William Montrose defeated the safe, and then assist in photographing whatever documents were discovered within it. The safe might have called for a quarter of an hour's effort, and as William Montrose considered the man before him, he decided that leaving Victor Speaks adrift with nothing to occupy him for that time would be patently unwise.

"I'd like you to have a quick butchers of the place," he said. "Start with the top floor. Let's be certain there isn't a maiden aunt sleeping in one of the other bedrooms, or a two-hundred-pound dog no one's thought to feed for the past week."

Neither prospect concerned him remotely. The house had been under surveillance for the previous fortnight, and it was unlikely that it contained anything larger than a virus without a file at the registry.

"I'll call you when I've finished with the safe."

Victor Speaks nodded and left the kitchen.

The safe, too, was where the briefing documents had predicted it would be. It lurked behind a hedgerow of all but identical suits. It was a particularly venerable Mosler to which someone had welded steel brackets, that it might be fitted into the rear wall of the closet. William Montrose suppressed the urge to laugh at it. He opened his tool chest and extracted a pair of cotton gloves and a modified doctor's stethoscope. Unthinking, he noted the position of the dial before he touched it, that he might return it to its original position when he was done with it.

He was listening for the arid click of the third tumbler when he heard Victor Speaks scream.

"Christ," he muttered, and he returned his stethoscope to his tool chest. He quickly returned the dial of the safe to its original position and ran for the staircase to the third floor of the house.

Victor Speaks was standing in the doorway to a bedroom. His features had been pressed from linen, bloodless and immobile. He stared into the room beyond. Only his breathing was audible. When he finally spoke, all trace of his whiskey had been driven from his voice.

"What the hell is that?" he gasped, gesturing into the room.

William Montrose stepped uncertainly past him. The room seemed impossibly bright after the gloom of the rest of the house. Its walls were white, its floor encrusted with ivory lino. A pair of florescent tubes had been affixed to the ceiling, driving the cowering shadows of the room into its furthest corners.

The only substantial item of furniture in the room was a bed, and it was occupied. William Montrose knew without consideration that the man who lay upon it must be dead. As he approached the immobile figure, he permitted himself to wonder that such a thing might ever have drawn breath.

He circled the bed warily, chiding himself silently as he did. There was no immediate threat in this room. Whatever hazard the man before him might once have posed had fled this place some time earlier in the day. That which had wrought the ruined creature, however, unnerved him.

The occupant of the bed would have died quite hor-ribly. His flesh appeared to have been burned, swelling in angry violet blisters across his neck and chest. His bed-clothes had been removed, perhaps as he couldn't tolerate the touch of fabric against his inflamed skin. He was hair-less, shriveled, a deflated airship. His eyes had been left open to gaze sightlessly at the florescent tubes overhead. His lips seemed about to fling themselves apart, to admit a final shriek into the room before his soul was reclaimed by his heartless god.

"What the hell happened to you?" William Montrose whispered to the motionless corpse.

An intravenous bottle dangled from a polished steel support beside the bed, its contents depleted. There was a small steel table before it, its surface cluttered with glass bottles, dressings, syringes. He gathered one of the bottles into his palm, studying it. It had contained morphine sul-fate. There were at least dozen like it on the table. They all appeared to have been emptied. The man in the bed had known considerable pain.

"Is he dead?" Victor Speaks inquired. William Montrose withdrew his attention from the bed. His col-league was still poised in the doorway, clearing unwilling to enter the room without being summoned.

"Of course he's dead. The question is how he got that way."

Victor Speaks' eyes widened for an instant. "He's not part of our brief," he said.

"No, he's not," William Montrose sighed. "Still, you'll agree that he's not the sort of thing we've been led to expect in the home of an upper-middle-class bolshie."

Victor Speaks ran his hand through his thinning hair, his mood becoming more agitated. "I don't bloody want to know how he died," he said quickly. "Let's do the safe, copy the contents and leave him for the Childers when they return."

"He won't be here when the Childers return," William Montrose said, curious that Victor Speaks hadn't appreciated it. Despite his affinity for drink, he was an observant enough fellow when his mind wasn't elsewhere.

"He's unlikely to get out of bed and take the tube into the city."

William Montrose permitted himself to smile grimly. "The Childers would hardly have left a dead body in their home for several days, knowing it would have begun to rot by the time they returned. There are limits to what even the most dedicated party members are likely to subject themselves to for the cause. They gave the spare key under the mat to someone so he could come by and collect this poor beggar."

Victor Speaks stared at the body across the room. "When?" he demanded.

"That would be convenient to know, wouldn't it?" William Montrose mused. He wrested his attention from the bed. "I'd like you to fetch the camera from my tool chest," he said suddenly.

Victor Speaks glared at him. "Why? It's for the party list in the safe."

"We've plenty of film," William Montrose said. "At the very least, this chap could well be of some use one day, if it becomes necessary to have a serious talk with the Childers... they might be more comfortable betraying a few secrets than explaining how a dead man was lodging in their spare room." He paused. There was a metal tablet hanging from the foot of the bed with a ragged clutter of papers attached to it under a spring clip. He strode to the end of the bed and lifted it from its hook. While it clearly wouldn't have been up to the standards of Charing Cross, it was a medical record of sorts. He flipped quickly through its pages, glancing at records of morphine administrations, fever, symptoms reported by the dying man. It would prove to be of far more interest than the party membership list, he decided, and he sought for a comfortable location to photograph it.

Victor Speaks departed for his camera. They'd be done in under an hour, and he willed the nameless, trace-less phantoms who'd been tasked with disposing of the body before him to have another pint and perhaps a spot of lunch before they came to discharge their responsibilities.

14

The effervescent trickle of flowered dresses and bluish-gray suits and cardigans and tennis shoes and handbags babbled over the stairs descending to the tube station, eddying past him, a clouded stream swirling around a stone. He glanced at the nearest of them, and then the one beyond her, and beyond, seeking for a flicker of recognition. They were all twigs and leaves in a mill race, flung into the reverberant cavern behind him. He took a step toward the daylight, and then another.

Andrei Mikhailovich Bogdanov permitted his hand to pass once more across the imperceptible bulge in the pocket of his overcoat and he felt himself smile fleetingly, willing himself to suppress the flush of satisfaction that threatened to wash over him. He took another step up through the tangle of supplicants to the underground and filled his lungs with the chill and petrol fumes of the street beyond. He turned his face to the wall beside him, thinking as he did that he might have done well to have worn a hat.

When this assignment was over, he promised himself, and if the object of his current affection had not succeeded in securing for herself a twenty-five year prison sentence, he would visit Alice Woodward and offer her

heartfelt thanks for her services to the Soviet Union. He
would get her drunk on the best vodka to be found in
London, buy her a meal if she would permit him, and fuck
her until she could no longer stand. He smiled despite
himself, recalling her as he'd sat next to her the previous
week, trembling within her heavy coat. She'd been so
unlike the shiny black and white photograph, so unlike his
imagination of English women.

She would oblige him in bed, he decided, every bit as
enthusiastically as she'd done in a private corner of
Leconfield House. He felt the package in his pocket, trying
to imagine how many Minox film cassettes it must contain.

He ascended into the gray, squalid daylight of Bond
Street. Shop windows were arranged like gold teeth, as
lurid as whores waiting outside one of Moscow's more dis-
reputable hotels. He drew his coat about himself, feeling
his eyes sting in the sudden brightness. A volley of rain-
drops assailed him as he strode from the entrance to the
tube station.

No one was observing him. He glanced along the
street, into the reflections in the nearest windows, into the
glass scales that decorated the flanks of a passing red bus.
No one was observing him. He sought for his bearings,
struggling for an instant to orient himself before the identical shops, the featureless pedestrians. They were clearly
piss-awful shops, he considered, smiling to himself, in that
no one was queued up at their doors. No self-respecting
shop in Russia would open its doors without an untidy
straggle of impatient, weary customers beyond it.

No one was observing him. There was an overweight, untidy man in a red telephone box with his back to
the tube station, a grandmother with a pram from which
was heard the screaming of a discontented child, several
conjoined young women in clothes that would have seen
them arrested in the Soviet Union, an old man with a
newspaper and an overly-large pipe clearly waiting for

someone to arrive in a car and collect him. There were uncountable hundreds of them, but none of them had noticed him, he assured himself, and none of them was employed by MI5.

He turned into Oxford Street and began to walk.

He was in sight of Debenham's department store when he heard his name being shouted over the ululation of the street. He glanced at the glass facade of the building, wondering for an instant if he might ignore the summons, vanish through its portals as he'd intended, buy a fresh coat, a shifted appearance, and continue on his journey to Kensington Palace Gardens. His heart clutched at his throat and he paused between strides, glancing uneasily around himself.

"Andrei Mikhailovich," a voice amidst ten thousand other voices muttered. It was a familiar salutation, a Russian form of address. He was a moment longer acquiring the owner of the voice. The figure approaching him was quietly familiar, his features more of a cerebral itch than a memory. He was portly, unshaven, shabbily dressed amidst the scrubbed, fashionable dwellers of Oxford Street. His shirt-tails billowed from his trousers, his feet scuffing the concrete beneath them as he walked uneasily against the tide of pedestrians.

"Andrei Mikhailovich," he repeated, a note of urgency in his voice. Perhaps it was amusement. He smiled broadly, gesturing above the cluster of dour, middle-aged women he appeared to have become mired in.

Andrei Bogdanov felt his shoulders sag, his features relent to a forced smile as he gestured his acknowledgement. The man's face grew increasingly familiar. He'd watched it become concerned, bemused, triumphant and ultimately flushed with drink over the span of a sweaty afternoon the previous summer, separated from his own by a cracked wooden chess board littered with unassuming plastic rooks and pawns. They'd encountered each other in

a filthy émigré Russian cafe called the Potemkin, somewhere in the darker fringes of Soho. The man had surprised him — he'd been brutish and unkempt on the occasion of their earlier acquaintance as well, but he'd won
more games than he'd lost.

He considered losing himself in a particularly dense
thicket of businessmen approaching him, and then sprint-
ing for the department store. The man shouted his name
once more and he decided that it would be preferable to
renew their acquaintance for a few minutes rather than
having the fat lout draw attention to him.

Malenkov, he remembered absently. Dmitri, or
perhaps it was Georgi. Men who'd deported themselves
as this one did hadn't possessed names in the Soviet
Union. The fellow deserved little better, having fled his
homeland.

He raised his arm as if in surrender and turned to
approach the man.

"Andrei Mikhailovich," the fellow said again as they
met on the sidewalk, and for a moment he was concerned
that the man in his filthy clothes might embrace him.

Andrei Bogdanov forced himself to smile thinly,
wondering how to address the man. Georgi Malenkov, he
decided. *"Dobriy dyen,"* he said, and he shrugged.

Georgi Malenkov shook his head, his expression
admonishing. "This is England. You should speak in
English. Your English was so much better than mine."

Andrei Bogdanov nodded his submission. The man
had taken him to task over his deplorable lack of fealty to
his adopted homeland when they'd played chess. "Good
day," he repeated woodenly. Georgi Malenkov smiled his
approval.

"It has been several months. We have all missed you
at the Potemkin," Georgi Malenkov said.

"It is my work... it leaves me little time for anything
else."

The man before him permitted his expression to sag for an instant before he relented to a broad grin. "You should not look so unhappy, Andrei Mikhailovich," he said suddenly. "You should be grateful that in this country you have work to do, you take home a decent wage at the end of the week... in pounds, not in worthless fucking rubles, yes?"

Andrei Bogdanov smiled and nodded once more. He suppressed the urge to tell this ungrateful *mandavoshka* that rubles had paid for his upbringing, paid for the state which had supported him until he'd treacherously fled from it. He imagined himself adjusting his personality about himself as he might have done a new suit before a shop mirror.

"What brings you up here?" he inquired of Georgi Malenkov, deciding as he did that a few moments of pointless conversation would serve to dismiss the fellow and permit him to continue with his journey.

The man gestured along the street. "I had a delivery... there is a shop near Sedley Place, it sells *antieekvarniy...*" He appeared to struggle for the correct word in English. "...antiques. The owner... he wanted his own men to unload the crates. He said I should return in an hour to collect the truck."

"You drive a truck?"

Georgi Malenkov smiled again and he slapped Andrei Bogdanov across his shoulders. "I own the fucking truck," he said, clearly pleased to be able to do so. "When I lived in Leningrad I drove a truck that would not be fit for scrap metal in this country... now I own my truck."

He met the man's gaze for an instant and attempted to mirror his appreciation. Georgi Malenkov clearly deserved to have been shot at the Soviet border while attempting to escape, but perhaps the country was better without him. If the zenith of his aspirations was the ownership of a truck, England was welcome to him.

"And you," Georgi Malenkov said. He stepped back a pace and affected an air of contemplation. "What brings you to Oxford Street?" He cocked his head thoughtfully. "I do not think you are here on business. You are too well dressed. I think you have a woman here."

Andrei Bogdanov felt his features grow taut. He glanced at the man before him through narrowed eyes, suddenly unconcerned by the squall of pedestrians with whom he shared the sidewalk. Georgi Malenkov stood before him, leering like a drunken idiot staggering along the Old Arbat. For an instant he regarded the man with opaline clarity. No one could be so profound a fool without months of practice.

His thoughts rattled behind his eyes, clamoring for his attention. How was it that a man with hardly the education to sign the application for a British passport had come to live in this country, he considered. He recalled Georgi Malenkov recounting his flight across the Finnish border during a blizzard. The Finns would certainly have had enough truck drivers amongst their own citizens, and he felt certain that the situation would have been much the same for the English.

How unlikely was it that the man he'd idled a few afternoons with in Soho half a year earlier might appear before him on this of all days, he mused, with the first package of documents from Alice Woodward secreted in his pocket.

He smiled thinly at Georgi Malenkov. "No," he said, "not a woman. I... I am supposed to meet a man here today about some work he wants me to do for him."

The fellow nodded, clearly pleased to have his impressions of his adopted homeland affirmed. There was work here for everyone, even if some of it was at the behest of MI5.

Georgi Malenkov could be nothing other than an agent of British intelligence, he decided abruptly. He glanced around himself, forcing his mind to consider his situation.

MI5 could not know of his meeting with Alice Woodward. He'd be locked in a very small concrete room now if they did. That meant he hadn't been observed during his contact with her, and she hadn't summoned the nerve to burn him to her employers. He considered Georgi Malenkov once more. At worst he was with the A4 division — what the English liked to refer to as 'watchers.' Andrei Bogdanov had been briefed on the activities of A4. Despite his cover of a Russian émigré, he'd been warned to expect a measure of surveillance by MI5's watchers.

The man had not come from the tube station, so he'd not been observed servicing Alice Woodward's dead drop. This meeting could be little more than routine interest in him by the English.

He scratched his head, stretched his back and permitted himself another careful observation of Oxford Street. He was certain no one else was paying him any attention.

"You say you drive a truck?" he asked Georgi Malenkov suddenly, infusing his voice with a note of surprise.

The man nodded.

"Would you... that is, could you do some work for me?"

Georgi Malenkov's smile seeped into his features. "Yes... yes, of course. What do you need moved?"

Andrei Bogdanov smiled suddenly and passed his hand across his chin. "It is a complicated business," he said, and he gestured along Oxford street. "Come... I want you to meet the man I will be working for. He is a proper gentleman. You will like him. It is fortunate I have run into you today. You could save me a lot of trouble."

He led Georgi Malenkov to Harewood Place, and they turned south. When he'd first devised the dead drop he'd created for Alice Woodward, he'd spent several days becoming familiar with Oxford Street and its attendant neighborhoods. He knew every exit and dark hole within running distance of the Bond Street tube station.

The lane he sought was an untidy accretion of shadows and filth, stretching back into the buildings surrounding it like the throat of a sleeping beast. It was hardly wide enough for one man to walk through without his shoulders scraping the flaking bricks that confined it. He preceded Georgi Malenkov into it, his hand seeking about in the pocket of his coat for the knife. Its surface felt cold, oily in the darkness of his clothing. When he could no longer hear the scuffle of passing traffic and the rattle of passers-by in the street, he paused, turned abruptly and drove the blade into Georgi Malenkov's chest.

The fat, unwashed pig stared at him for an instant with bovine eyes, wet with shock and agony as his arms thrashed at the cloying air. His legs seemed to ooze from beneath him like columns of pitch left too long in the sun. He collapsed, first to his knees and then onto his back, a cry of distress still-born in his throat. He raised a bloody hand for a moment and kicked feebly at the gloom that awaited his silence.

Andrei Bogdanov glanced once more along the lane, assuring himself that he'd not been observed. He felt for Alice Woodward's package beneath his coat and he began walking briskly toward the distant exit.

15

Sir Alistair Fitzhenry slid a folder across his desk toward the crouching form of Alec Grey with the solemn gravity of the issuing of a death warrant. The silence that enshrouded his office might have been mistaken for the sudden onset of deafness. He'd said nothing as Alec Grey had entered the room and pushed the door to behind himself, watching him as he'd taken one of the leather chairs. His pipe was clamped between his flint lips, seething, toxic.

Alec Grey considered the folder for a moment before he accepted it. The director was clearly in a mood, he appreciated, but he was at some disadvantage to ascertain which of his selection of moods he'd chosen to costume himself with this afternoon. He'd lacked the opportunity to observe the previous visitor to this office leaving, something which had provided him with insight into Sir Alistair's likely disposition in the past.

He regarded the folder for a moment longer before he opened it. It was a fresh folder, unmarked, without any trace of sticky labels obscuring its previous identities. The director's secretaries didn't squander virginal folders lightly.

There were four large, rather grainy photographs before him, and it was not until he regarded himself peering blankly from the fourth at the camera which had taken them that he appreciated what they must be. He permitted his fingers to idle through them a second time. His attention was drawn to a slightly out-of-focus depiction of Hugh Somerfield's amplifiers, and of a boiler suit and a mason's trowel that Edward Blair had forgotten in the secret room at the Scottish and Newcastle Insurance Company's new offices.

"Bloody hell," he muttered under his breath. "Bloody hell."

The director was observing him, he realized, and he glanced away from the folder in his lap. The older man's features were partially occluded by smoke. "Mr. Grey?"

"The Soviets knew the whole damned time," he said, struggling to suppress his swelling anger. "I can't believe they had a camera in there with us."

"Can't you?" Sir Alistair inquired, his tone curiously without rancor.

"They must have sussed it when we were building the room... to have hidden a camera in the masonry," Alec Grey continued.

"Must they?" the director asked.

Alec Grey glanced at Sir Alistair for a moment, appreciating as he did that something was amiss. The director was decidedly amused. Having discovered a Soviet camera in one of his intelligence operations would not have amused him. It required a moment longer for Alec Grey to finally and conclusively determine the chosen mood of the afternoon. He'd clearly failed to ask the most salient question.

"How did we come by these pictures, sir?"

The director removed his pipe from his teeth and smiled broadly, as if he'd spent the day awaiting those words. "Ah," he said, and he turned his attention to the intercom console on his desk. He depressed one of its switches with the stem of his pipe, the gesture clearly affected. "Would you be so good as to ask Mr. Hollings to join us?" he spoke into it, and then released the key.

Alec Grey unthinkingly closed the folder in his lap, a Pavlovian response to the impending presence of someone of indeterminate security clearance. The director shook his head dismissingly.

David Hollings entered the room and eased himself into the unoccupied leather chair before the director's desk. He smiled as he caught Alec Grey's attention, his gaze descending to the folder.

"What did you think of them?" he asked, a note of anticipation in his words.

Alec Grey regarded him curiously, a growing whine of corroding orthodoxy rattling the varnished floor of the director's office. He could imagine no good reason why the director should have made the contents of his folder known to the head of the time stream project, a scientist with no meaningful involvement in intelligence gathering.

He stared blankly at David Hollings, whose smile sagged momentarily.

David Hollings turned to address Sir Alistair. "You've not told him," he said accusingly.

"I thought you might wish that honor for yourself," the director replied.

David Hollings cast Sir Alistair a reproving glanced. He reached across the chasm between the two chairs and took the folder from Alec Grey's lap. "He probably had you believing the Russians were spying on you lot, I shouldn't wonder."

Alec Grey permitted himself a twisted smile, feeling himself suddenly to have been the butt of a joke he'd yet to fathom. He watched as David Hollings placed the folder on the director's desk and spread the four photographs before them.

"They're by no means the best we've had out of this camera," he said. "Still, the light in your little room was quite dreadful... we've had to push the film... you'll have noticed the grain." He gestured at one of them. "Despite the significant distance variations, you can clearly make out this equipment in the background, part of your face in the foreground and what I take to be Mr. Somerfield's overflowing ashtray in the far corner."

Alec Grey ignored the photograph and returned his attention to David Hollings. "You took these?" he asked accusingly.

The man nodded. "Yes," he replied. "Yes, of course we did. That's rather the point."

"Can I ask how you came to know about the secret room?" Alec Grey asked coldly.

"Well, we didn't," David Hollings said, as if it might have been obvious. "At least, not until today, when Sir Alistair explained what you were doing there."

Alec Grey leant back in his chair. "That's nonsense," he said. "These pictures were taken two... perhaps three weeks ago. The room hasn't looked like this for some time."

"Oh no, these pictures were taken yesterday," David Hollings said.

Alec Grey was about to speak when he noticed that the director was gesturing for his attention with the stem of his pipe. "Mr. Grey, perhaps you would do well to remind yourself what Mr. Hollings and his colleagues down in Cornwall spend their days toiling at," he suggested.

Alec Grey paused, regarding the four photographs. At length he lifted the one which included his face and regarded it in greater detail. "You can't be serious," he whispered.

"With the volume of Her Majesty's treasury which has disappeared into Mr. Hollings' work, I should very much hope that he is."

He handed the photograph to David Hollings with

what he hoped would be an air of finality. "I'm still not certain I understand," he said. "Perhaps you would explain
how you came to photograph a room you didn't know was
there three weeks after you took the pictures."

David Hollings grinned broadly, his expression suggesting that he'd journeyed from Cornwall solely to do so.

"I should begin by pointing out that this is our first
series of tests involving sending a mechanism through the
time stream," he began. "One of our chaps, Stuart Alwin,
worked up a mechanical camera with a clockwork motor.
It can be sent through the time stream, pop out somewhere... and somewhen... take four holiday snaps on a
two-inch square of film and then drop back into the time
stream before anyone notices it. It's all a bit complicated,
working out exactly when it will emerge from the stream,
of course... keeps our lads busy for days calculating it."

Alec Grey regarded him, suddenly beyond speaking.

"We didn't know about your secret room," David
Hollings continued. "We were aiming for the Soviet consulate in Kensington Palace Gardens. One of our lads
appears to have allowed a small error to creep into his calculations. Still, we're pleased with it as a first result. We
did have to know where the camera appeared, however,
and as you were recognizable in one of the photographs, I
arrived hoping the director could tell us where you would
have been when the camera emerged from the time
stream... which he's done, of course."

Alec Grey exhaled. "I fear I'm about to be made
redundant," he said. "You've actually got a machine you
can send back in time to spy on the Soviets for us."

David Hollings nodded uncertainly. "Well, yes... at
least, in theory," he said.

"Those pictures seem rather more than theoretical,"
Alec Grey observed.

"They do... but they required almost a fortnight's
production of Berkelium to achieve them, and we still can't

target the camera with any accuracy. We might just as well have taken four photographs of the women's lavatory at Harrods."

"Weren't you at all concerned that the Soviet consular staff might take exception to a camera appearing in one of their offices?"

David Hollings shook his head. "We can only project it out of the time stream for a little over a second," he replied. "By the time anyone noticed it, it would have retreated back into the stream and essentially vanished."

"A great many of my staff are about to be made redundant as well, I see," Alec Grey remarked. "How long will it be before you can send me back to October of 1917 so I can put a bullet between Josef Stalin's eyes and put an end to this business before it begins?"

David Hollings smiled once more. "I'm afraid it doesn't work quite that way," he said, clearly having said much the same thing frequently of late. "There is neither enough energy on Earth nor enough Uranium in our galaxy to project something with the mass of a human being through the time stream to a distance of several decades... and we're reasonably certain a living organism wouldn't survive in the stream if there were. The Americans are supposed to have sent insects into the time stream... it's my understanding that what emerged wasn't even recognizable, not to say alive."

"Are you likely to be able to put one of your cameras inside the Soviet consulate in the next while, then?" he asked.

"I believe so."

"The Kremlin?"

"Possibly."

"The American time stream facility in Utah?"

This amused David Hollings. "I'd not thought of that," he said. "I'm sure there's some manner of treaty that forbids us from doing so."

"How certain are we the Americans believe that?"

David Hollings appeared to be a moment appreciating what Alec Grey had suggested. He'd clearly not considered the possibility that the Americans might have used their own time stream research, believed to be several years more advanced than the work at the facility in Cornwall, to spy on its allies.

The director coughed, obviously requiring the attention of the other two men in his office. "There's something I've been rather curious about since you brought me these photographs, Mr. Hollings," he said. "This little camera of yours emerged from the time stream in Mr. Grey's secret room... what might have happened if it had emerged inside one of the walls surrounding that room?"

David Hollings said nothing for a moment, and when he finally spoke, his voice had lost its earlier mirth. "That's a matter of some debate, sir," he replied softly.

"I see," Sir Alistair said, and he permitted himself a lengthy draught of his pipe. "Shall I take this to mean that you don't know."

"There are two theories. I'm of the opinion that it's impossible for an object to exit the time stream if the exit aperture is located within solid matter. The physics of the time stream suggest that the aperture would attempt to slide around until it encountered an area not occupied by solid matter."

"That's most obliging of it," the director said. "What's the other theory?"

David Hollings pursed his lips. "The Americans favor an explanation in which the exiting object's sub-atomic particles would become intertwined with the sub-atomic particles of the solid matter in which it emerged, creating an artificially dense atomic structure. The resulting matter would be extremely unstable, and it couldn't exist for more than the briefest fraction of a second."

"What would become of it, Mr. Hollings?" the director asked him, his expression making it clear that he knew precisely what the scientist would say.

"An explosion, sir," David Hollings whispered. "An unimaginable explosion."

16

H ugh Somerfield had never been entirely comfortable with the thought of visiting Fulham Hospital as a patient, in that it backed onto Hammersmith Cemetery. One could admire the potential efficiency of its location without necessarily approving of it. As he strode now through its tiled corridor, breathing a heady admixture of carbolic and ether, he decided that he was no more comfortable about attending it in his present capacity.

The ceaseless clatter of illness echoed and swelled in the concrete intestines of the place, bubbling around him like a serving of ploughman's lunch that hadn't entirely agreed with its owner.

Heads would roll for this day's misadventures, he appreciated, and having just had his hair trimmed at considerable personal expense, he was determined that they not include his own.

He loomed forward, descending upon a woman in a white smock who glared at him with the authority born of years of expensive medical training and an intimate familiarity with bodily components best not mentioned in civilized company. He was all but atop her when she finally stepped from his path. He could imagine her eyes boring into his departing skull as he proceeded around the next bend in the corridor, a gleaming surgical implement wrought entirely of outrage.

Without thinking, he reached into his coat and sought about for his packet of cigarettes. He'd extracted them before he recalled being admonished for the one he'd been smoking when he'd entered the hospital, moments earlier, and had been compelled to discard well before its time. It was at moments such as this when he wished for Sir Alistair Fitzhenry's pipe and the countenance that typically smoked it, that he might cast a single eye upon his oppressors and watch them beetling off for a suddenly-recalled tea break.

He paused and permitted his attention to stroll the corridor before him, struggling to recall the clipped, impatient directions the sister two floors below him had uttered, unwilling to prise her attention from her file drawer as she'd replied to his questions. She'd clearly been on the point of inquiring as to his authority for investing the private keep of the hospital when he'd thanked her in mid-sentence and vanished into a lift.

He was several minutes longer locating the room he'd been summoned to, and as he regarded its featureless door in the heartbeat between his discovery of it and his shoulder brushing it aside, he wondered where next he might be summoned, when he was brought to kneel before his gods and explain the wretched business to Alec Grey. This was a cockup of sufficient magnitude as to be posited in the rarified presence of Sir Alistair Fitzhenry himself, with Alec Grey assuming the office of courtier or lord high executioner, as circumstances dictated.

The rattling of the corridor slipped from him as might a barrister's wig snagged upon a nail as he entered the hush of the room, and he pushed the door to behind him. He'd expected a scrum of physicians arranged in an attractive topiary about the lone bed before him, and perhaps the regular inhalation of machinery. The room was silent, luminous with a superabundance of lighting.

A man in an untidy gray suit rose from his visitor's chair, depositing his newspaper on its seat as he did. He might have been cherubic in an earlier life, his features subsequently having relented to a career of egg and chips and take-away coffee. He appeared to have been too long without sleep and recourse to a decent razor. Nigel Rigby rarely looked markedly better, Hugh Somerfield reminded himself.

He turned for an additional moment's contemplation of the waxwork figure in the bed between them, and then he glanced at the ceiling above Nigel Rigby's head, running his hand over his chin. "What the bloody hell were you lot thinking?" he asked softly.

Nigel Rigby glared at him, his eyes narrowing. "What was that?" he snapped.

Hugh Somerfield took a step forward, passing the foot of the bed. "I asked what the hell you were thinking," he repeated, gesturing absently at the bed.

"You don't look a thing like Alec Grey," Nigel Rigby growled.

Hugh Somerfield felt his fingernails clawing at the flesh of his palms. He paused, reminding himself that cracking the man's jaw would entail his devising a creative explanation when the whole sordid business reached the desk of Sir Alistair Fitzhenry. There would be quite enough creativity surrounding this afternoon without his own contribution.

"You should be bloody grateful I don't look like Alec Grey, son," he said quietly. "If I did look like Alec Grey, you'd be strapped to a table as we speak, rolling along to surgery to have your balls cut off."

Nigel Rigby's features reddened. Hugh Somerfield took a step closer to him. The other man was almost a head shorter than he, and he'd come to appreciate that his stature was of little value if he couldn't employ it to intimidate his wayward colleagues from time to time.

Nigel Rigby stabbed at him with a porcine finger. "Don't think for a minute you'll be putting this down to me or any of my lads," he said. "We couldn't have expected this."

Hugh Somerfield smiled thinly. "No, I don't imagine you could have," he agreed. "It's not something anyone would expect to have happen in the heart of London." He paused, and stared into the other man's eyes, and when he resumed speaking he was all but shouting. "That's why no one with a working brain would take a Soviet defector out for a damned walk!"

Nigel Rigby glared at him for a moment longer before he turned to regard the shadows at the distant end of the room. "You lot have no idea," he muttered.

He grasped the man by his shoulder. "Explain to me why you took Konstanin Bolshakov for a walk so a Soviet assassin could kill him, Mr. Rigby," he said evenly. "You'll be wanting a proper explanation for the director by morning. Consider this an opportunity to practice your performance."

"He's not dead," Nigel Rigby snarled.

"Yet," Hugh Somerfield corrected him. "He's not dead yet."

The distinction seemed of singular importance to Nigel Rigby.

Hugh Somerfield addressed his attention to the occupant of the bed. His were the sort of features one properly anticipated coming upon in a hospital ward. He was portly, his cheeks a skein of purple veins from a lifetime of drink. His thinning gray hair seemed as if it had been carelessly applied an hour earlier, a whim of a balding man. His eyes were seeled with wrinkled lids crushed shut. The sheet that covered him rose with the ragged shuddering of his chest, mechanical and lifeless.

"Konstanin Bolshakov was on the Soviet consular staff at Rome," Hugh Somerfield said, as much to himself as to Nigel Rigby. "A few weeks ago he walked into the British embassy with a handful of papers. We pulled him out twenty-four hours later.

"You'll have been briefed on the difficulty and extreme risk surrounding his extraction. You'll not have been briefed as to the nature of the papers he was carrying. You'll also not have been permitted access to his subsequent interrogation. Did that in any way make you suspect that Mr. Bolshakov had brought us some unusually valuable material?"

Nigel Rigby glared sullenly at the man on the bed. "That's not something I'm paid to know about," he muttered.

"Why did you take Mr. Bolshakov out for a walk?" Hugh Somerfield asked, his tone affected to be suitable for communication with a petulant child. "Why did you let a vital Soviet defector wander blissfully along Ganton Street, gazing into shop windows and other capitalist delights so a Soviet assassin could fill the poor bastard full of poison, Mr. Rigby?"

"It wasn't bloody well like that," Nigel Rigby barked, his features suddenly woven from taut steel cables. "We had him covered."

"I don't care if you had him surrounded by an entire squad of her majesty's beefeaters armed with automatic weapons. He was placed in a safe house for a damned good reason. The Soviets have a good deal more trouble killing our defectors with several feet of mortar and bricks to shoot through."

Nigel Rigby shook his head wearily, clearly appreciating that in another day he would be called upon to engage in much the same conversation with Alec Grey or Sir Alistair Fitzhenry. Hugh Somerfield was empowered to do little more than berate him. The manifestations of retribution at the disposal of the director were spoken of only in whispers.

"He wasn't shot," Nigel Rigby said quietly. "He was poisoned."

"More's the pity," Hugh Somerfield observed. "Gunshot wounds are very often survivable."

"He just wanted to get some air," Nigel Rigby said defensively. "He'd been at it since he arrived. He'd been entirely cooperative. The chap you brought in to debrief him was finished for the day. Bolshakov asked if he could spend an hour looking at the city he was going to live in when we'd done with him. We put four minders on him, front and back, ten feet away. It was broad daylight."

Hugh Somerfield stared at the man for a moment longer and then turned to regard the motionless form of Konstanin Bolshakov. He decided that he would do well to listen to the man's explanation. There was every likelihood he'd be present when Sir Alistair Fitzhenry administered a complete verbal disemboweling for Nigel Rigby and his people. The director was considerably more skilled at such matters than he himself could aspire to.

"How did they get to him?"

He watched Nigel Rigby smile coldly in the corner of his eye. "A chap in a business suit stuck him in the leg with the tip of his umbrella," he replied. "We didn't appreciate it was an attack for several minutes... the bastard with umbrella was long gone by then. Bolshakov complained of feeling ill. By the time we got him back to the house, he'd chucked up his tea and he was doubled over in pain. They've had to sedate him."

Konstanin Bolshakov looked well beyond mere sedation, Hugh Somerfield considered. The Soviet defector appeared to have expelled the force of his continued life along with the contents of his stomach.

Nigel Rigby was silent for a time, and when next he spoke his voice was almost childlike. "Am I likely to be sacked for this, do you think?" he inquired.

Hugh Somerfield regarded him for a moment. Nigel Rigby's immediate career options seemed of trifling conse- quence. "I shouldn't count on it," he replied, much of the venom bled from his voice. "I believe Alec Grey will want to have you assigned to a listening post in one of the less fashionable quarters of Yemen... he can't very well do that if you're on the dole."

Nigel Rigby's face creased with his appreciation of the jest made at his expense, and he said nothing.

Hugh Somerfield permitted the room to be overrun once more with the reverberant silence of the hospital, hearing the distant clatter of wheelchairs and rolling beds in the corridor beyond Konstanin Bolshakov's room. At length Nigel Rigby returned to his newspaper.

The doctor who arrived twenty minutes later to con- sider the earthly form of Konstanin Bolshakov looked as if he too had been awake longer than the present state of his mental processes would permit him to recall. His cheeks were a forest of coarse stubble, his white coat glowering with smudges of blood. He smiled briefly at the two men and then directed his attention to the figure in the bed.

Nigel Rigby pushed himself from his chair. "This is Doctor Meyer," he said tonelessly. "He's signed."

Hugh Somerfield considered whether he should offer the doctor a hand to shake. It seemed unwise, con- sidering where a physician's hand typically found itself before one had the opportunity to grasp it. The man had used one of them to sign the Official Secrets Act, however, and as such he presumably knew enough about Konstanin Bolshakov to be of more use than Nigel Rigby. He intro- duced himself, and the doctor smiled professionally.

"What's to become of him?" Hugh Somerfield inquired, gesturing at the motionless figure of Konstanin Bolshakov.

The doctor shook his head with a gesture of finality.

"I shouldn't think he'll live to morning," he replied. His manner suggested that he was accustomed to such pronouncements. "A man of his age... perhaps if he'd been younger, in better health..."

"He's not," Hugh Somerfield interrupted him, casting about for an expression to put the doctor at his ease. "The young healthy ones always defect to the Americans."

The doctor appeared to permit himself a moment of dark amusement. He consulted a chart hanging from a clip at the foot of the bed, and then returned to gaze at Konstanin Bolshakov's features. Wordlessly, he prised back one of the defector's eyelids and peered into the unseeing lens behind it.

"Do you know what's been used to poison him?" Hugh Somerfield asked.

The doctor held up his finger, suggesting that he required a moment longer to conclude his examination of his patient. Without returning his attention to Hugh Somerfield, he withdrew two objects from the pocket of his white coat and placed them on the bed. Hugh Somerfield retrieved them.

"That's what was used to administer the poison," the doctor explained. "I took it from a wound in his right leg."

Hugh Somerfield considered the objects in his hand. A small glass vial, apparently empty, was dwarfed by a metal cylinder that resembled a particularly obese fountain pen. He shot a questioning glance at the doctor.

"Look through the microscope at the contents of the vial," the doctor instructed him.

He was several seconds ascertaining the correct operation of the small microscope, and a minute more appreciating that the vial did indeed contain something. He squinted through the eyepiece until he'd located it, a minute metallic sphere pocked with round openings. It resembled a diver's helmet wrought for single-celled organisms.

"What am I looking at?" he inquired at length.

"I surmise it was filled with poison earlier today," the doctor said. "It's small enough to have fit through a large hypodermic needle. From what your colleague has told me of my patient, I imagine there was a mechanism in the tip of the umbrella used in the attack to push the metal pellet through the victim's skin."

Hugh Somerfield glanced angrily at Nigel Rigby. Signed or not, the doctor had been told somewhat in excess of what he'd needed to know that he might minister to Konstanin Bolshakov.

"Have you been able to tell which poison was used?"

The doctor appeared satisfied with his examination of Konstanin Bolshakov. "Ricin," he replied, "perhaps a derivative of it, considering how quickly it appears to have acted."

Hugh Somerfield shook his head, appreciating that unless the doctor had replied with something from an Agatha Christie, he'd have been unlikely to understand his answer. He placed the vial and the microscope on the bed beside Konstanin Bolshakov.

"Ricin is actually a relatively old poison," the doctor explained. "We don't see it much... too hard to make, too easy to avoid... no common commercial applications. It's derived from the seeds of the castor bean plant. The seeds are harmless if they're swallowed... the stuff has to get into the blood stream to be toxic."

"And there's no antidote, I trust," Hugh Somerfield said.

The doctor shook his head. "In a younger patient, we would have tried to stabilize him... keep him alive until his body broke down the poison. This fellow... he won't live long enough. This variant of Ricin works rather more quickly than the references suggest it should... makes me think that it's something special, made especially for killing people."

Hugh Somerfield glanced at his watch. Konstanin Bolshakov had arrived at the hospital slightly more than three hours earlier. Even with Sir Alistair Fitzhenry tele-phoning every twenty minutes to reaffirm the urgency of the matter, he was reasonably certain the doctor would not have been able to complete an analysis of the poison used to kill the defector in that time.

"Could it have been a different poison?" he asked absently.

"I think it unlikely," the doctor replied. He retrieved the glass vial and his microscope, handing the vial to Hugh Somerfield. "That's the third one of those I've taken from someone of eastern European origin this year. The first two had traces of Ricin in them... I'm quite certain this one will as well."

17

A gramophone record of a lone saxophone played aimlessly from the shadows, a disembodied street-corner musician. Alice Woodward appeared to consider the label on the bottle of wine she'd chosen for them before she tipped it gently over his glass. The wine was the color of ancient wood in the leafy shadows of her sitting room, catching the reflection of a candle on the table before them. It sounded like laughter as she poured it.

When she'd filled his glass, she poured one for herself.

He wondered for an instant if there was a social observance for this moment. He'd not enjoyed her upbringing, not been raised to know instinctively which fork to use for the salad course, which years represented the desirable vintages for French wines. He touched the glass to his lips, feeling liquid smoke upon his tongue.

"How does it taste, Mr. Grey?" she asked quietly. He glanced at her, discerning amusement in her features despite the paucity of light in the room. She'd taken to addressing him in a formal manner to remind him that he'd grown silent or serious.

"Expensive," he replied, and he leant across the settee to kiss her. The gesture was awkward, and he struggled for a time to maintain the crush of his lips upon hers without upending his glass across her lap. He antici- pated her disentangling herself from him after a respectable few seconds, but she seemed only to lose her- self more deeply in him. He imagined himself to have become quite breathless when at last they parted.

She smiled broadly, and she touched his glass with her own. "I suspect it is," she said. "My father has a man come and restock the larder and the cellar at the start of the month if anyone's staying at the house. I've never been privy to which of them selects the bottles." She appeared to permit herself a sip of her wine as if it were an indul- gence she'd not yet received official dispensation to enjoy.

"Do you know much about wine, then?" he asked her.

She nodded. "Never use the bottles from the rack at the back of the cellar. My father's put them by for special occasions."

He eased himself into the embrace of the settee, holding his glass that it not be upset by the tidal motion of the furniture. She slipped, catlike, into the crook of his arm, clearly more expert than he with the disposition of her drink.

"Is this an occasion for expensive wine?" he inquired, the fragrance of his glass vying with her scent.

"It's our anniversary," she replied at some length, her tone infected with a note of mock reproach. "This will be a whole week since we've met."

He considered this. "It would be eight days as I reckon it."

She sighed. "I refuse to consider a quarter of an hour in Sir Alistair's office with me sobbing and speaking nonsense as the day we met," she said, a flutter of amuse- ment in her voice.

He found himself unable to recall the girl she'd been as she'd clung to the arms of the director's leather chair, gazing uncertainly at the malevolent silver camera that had been forced upon her and the two men who'd come to possess it. He'd noticed her eyes at the time. They would be liquid spheres machined from the stuff of night now, were he to gaze into them.

"Do you think Sir Alistair would be terribly upset if he knew what we were getting up to?" she inquired softly.

He permitted himself a dark smile. "I believe Sir Alistair would be terribly upset if he knew we were thinking about getting up to this," he replied. "Were he to discover what we were in fact getting up to, his head would explode and Whitehall would be compelled to appoint a new director of MI5. It would not go well for us... I'm certain there's a regulation somewhere prohibiting senior staff from bringing about the explosion of the heads of their superiors."

"Isn't he likely to find out?" She had clearly elected to participate in his moment of depraved absurdity. "He is the director of a spy agency, after all."

"That doesn't actually make him a spy," Alec Grey explained. "The position of director of MI5 is most often a political appointment. Sir Alistair's unquestionably one of the better ones in recent years, but I shouldn't think he's a tangible threat to us."

"Then he isn't likely to discover that all the officers who've been assigned to guard me for the past week have been you?"

"Not unless one of my lads tells him, and they're unlikely to do that as long as I'm available to approve their postings to the Sudan."

"Have any of your people requested postings to the Sudan?" she asked, her words suddenly touched with curiosity.

"Not that they're aware of," he replied, and he enjoyed another swallow of his wine.

She twisted unhurriedly against him, clearly seeking

a more comfortable position. She let her head droop against his shoulder. He decided he was probably too ill-fed to afford a woman the optimum degree of padding in a situation such as this.

"I've wanted to ask you about something," she said at length, disturbing the silence of the room. "The other morning, as I was leaving to catch the tube, there were some of your men in here with... odd-looking wireless equipment, I think. Were they checking to see if the Soviets had hidden microphones in the house?"

He nodded. "The entire building is swept every day," he said quietly. "I've asked them to see to it while you're at work."

"Then we're in no danger of being overheard," she continued.

"Not by the Soviets," he assured her, "or are you still concerned about Sir Alistair?"

She clearly had not come to the purpose of her query. "I've been wondering... are we permitted to speak of things... from work?"

He turned to regard her, to the extent that the furniture would permit him to do so. She seemed amused by her question, and he was a moment appreciating its complexities.

"Sir Alistair would no doubt quote the act," he said with mock gravity. Sir Alistair was overly fond of citing the Official Secrets Act when issues of security were put before him. He seemed to regard it as a writ etched in stone by his malevolent, officious god and handed down to him from whatever the mountains in Cornwall were named.

"The thing of it is," she continued, "you're permitted to know almost everything there is to know, so you can go about spying on the Soviets, and I'm permitted to know absolutely everything there is to know because I'm made to type it all up with two carbons."

"I was under the impression that confidential typists were trained not to read the things they typed."

She touched her glass to her lips. "I've never understood how they could do that," she admitted.

"If I recall the act, it gives itself a great deal of unrest and aggravation over the disclosure of the nation's secrets. Even the faceless mandarins of Whitehall would have some difficulty with the notion of disclosing secrets to someone who's known them since they became secret."

"That's a comfort," she said.

"Unless I'm wrong, in which case we both risk being shot as enemy agents," he added. "What did you fancy talking about?"

She ventured another sip of her wine and appeared to consider this. "Actually, I've been burning with curiosity about the dead drop today," she replied. "You did know I filled the dead drop at the Bond Street tube station?"

He smiled at this, noticing that during the previous week she'd acquired the argot of espionage to accompany her miniature camera. "Seven of my lads watched you at it," he said. "One of them was in a telephone box, describing it to me. You tripped on the stairs as you were pushing the tile back to hide your packet of film cassettes... nearly went arse over tip down the tube. I'd have been there to watch over you myself, but it's almost certain the Russians will have acquainted their people with the likes of me."

"I barely stumbled," she corrected him. "I think I did quite well, considering I could hardly keep my hands from shaking."

"As I'm to hear it, you handled it masterfully," he said. "You could do a year at the embassy in Moscow."

"No fear of that," she whispered. "Did the man I identified last week turn up to collect the film?"

"Andrei Mikhailovich Bogdanov," he said. "He looks just like the photograph you chose. He barely paused climbing the stairs... he's clearly done this sort of work before." Andrei Bogdanov's afternoon had become markedly more eventful after he'd exited the underground, but Alec Grey decided that Alice Woodward would be comforted by not knowing what the Soviet agent had occupied himself with.

"So he's a proper spy, then?"

"I'm not sure a spy can be proper," he mused. "He's unquestionably working for Moscow, if that's what you're asking. He arrived about a year ago with a German passport the KGB had knocked up for him. The Germans have a crafty system of changing the color of the type on the first pages of their passports, depending where they're issued and in which month of the year. Moscow clearly hasn't noticed this… A4 had Andrei in a box before he left Heathrow."

The box that A4 prided itself on erecting around Soviet agents consisted of four watchers, two walking in front of the subject of their attentions, and two behind. Skilled watchers could alter their appearance with reversible jackets, a variety of hats and such to follow their subjects for days if needs be.

"To his credit, Andrei led our lot a merry chase for several hours before he legged it to Kensington Palace Gardens," he added.

"Are the Soviets likely to believe all the papers I photographed about the time stream?"

He felt himself start at the mention of the project, and he was a moment willing himself to remember that Alice Woodward was routinely trusted with confidential material out of Cornwall that even he would have had difficulty obtaining access to.

"We had David Hollings working on them… he reckons we gave them enough genuine intelligence to make them believable, but nothing they can actually use. If they follow the research you provided them, they'll spend at least half a year learning that it's all utter nonsense."

"They won't be pleased," she said, a whisper of genuine concern in her words.

"No they won't," he agreed. "However, the Russians
are usually fairly good sports about such things. A substantial number of KGB officers will be summoned to the
Kremlin, and one of them will almost certainly be assigned
the task of shooting Andrei Bogdanov."

He glanced at her through the corner of his eye,
wondering for a moment whether he'd summoned the
drooling, unwashed brute of her recent terror into the hush
of their evening together.

"Good on him," she whispered. "Will you be wanting me to fill the dead drop again?"

"I should think so, if you're not too uncomfortable
with it."

"I don't mind… it was actually rather exciting."

He'd no doubt permitted himself to become jaded
by the defense of the realm, he allowed. The work had
excited him as well, some years earlier. Hers had been
a sterile, contrived species of excitement, a fun-fair ride
with a great deal of screaming and little genuine threat
of even minor bruises. He felt his arm grow taut about
her for a moment as he considered that Andrei
Mikhailovich Bogdanov was afoot in the city this night.
The Soviet agent had proven himself capable of far darker
forms of excitement.

"Did you have a meeting with Sir Alistair?" she
inquired.

He dispelled his unsettled reverie. She was smiling at
him, peering through the distorted lens of her glass.

"I'd several, as it happens." he replied.

"Only, I've had his notes from one to type, and they
said that you'd actually summoned him. I didn't think you
were permitted to summon the director."

"I believe I'm granted special dispensation if he's in
a good mood. I wasn't aware he kept notes of his meetings.

Shall I ask what they said, or would you have to begin quoting the act as well?"

"I don't know," she answered him quietly. "I'd only just started on them when it was time to leave for the day. He'd underscored a great many of the things he wrote, so I imagine it was terribly important."

He was some while recounting his discussion that morning with the director. He was amused to learn that even Sir Alistair's typist was familiar with his aversion to mole hunts. The old man hadn't been at all pleased with his conclusions, and had spent almost half an hour seeking fruitlessly for alternate interpretations of his findings.

"Perhaps I haven't understood correctly what you told Sir Alistair," Alice Woodward said. "You've found seven men, one of which must have communicated your fabricated intelligence to the Soviets."

He nodded.

"Would it not have been more effective to have given each of the men you suspected a different set of documents?"

"It would have taken ages to create forty-nine believable sets of papers," he explained, "and high-level intelligence officers aren't permitted to discuss classified papers amongst themselves, but we know full well they do so none the less. That many secret, eyes-only files appearing suddenly would have caused grave suspicions amongst a fair few of them. We assume the mole is traitorous, but not stupid."

"I can't imagine Sir Alistair not taking your investigation seriously."

He sighed and finished his wine. Wordlessly, she extricated herself from his embrace, refilled his glass for him and returned to her place on the settee. "In point of fact, he does appear to take it seriously. I might have hoped he'd have done so for more compelling reasons."

The director was a political appointment, he reminded himself, as he'd observed to Alice Woodward earlier.

She smiled and glanced up at him.

"Did you type up his notes for his high-level staff meeting last week?" he asked her.

"Are you asking if I'm permitted to know about the CORONA camera?"

He returned her smile. "Yes, I imagine that was what I was asking." He paused, wondering if another swallow of his wine would begin to get to his head. "The matter which commanded the director's attention was the observation that all seven of the men on the list of possible moles were in attendance at his briefing about CORONA. Whichever of them is actually working for the Soviets, Moscow now knows about the CORONA project."

"Oh dear," she whispered. "The Americans will not be pleased."

"Sir Alistair has expended a great deal of political capital on the UKUSA agreement by which we share intelligence with the Americans. If they were to learn we'd handed their most holy relic to the barbarian hordes, they wouldn't trust us with their great aunties' recipes for fried chicken."

"Oh dear," she repeated. She clearly appreciated the gravity of the matter.

He relented at length to the blandishments of his wine glass. "I'm dreadfully sorry," he said. "I don't imagine this conversation is entirely in keeping with the evening."

She seemed amused by his apology. "No, I don't mind," she said quietly. "It's all rather fascinating... and I've never actually been able to speak to anyone about what goes on at work. It's quite frustrating, you know, to be asked what one does for a living and to have to smile like an idiot and try to change the subject as quickly as possible."

"You'll develop a talent for it in time," he assured her.

She twisted herself from beneath his arm for a moment to kiss him. The brush of her lips upon his was unexpected, the taste of her pungent with the fragrance of her drink. He heard a flutter of her laughter and she vanished from before him, settling herself back into the hillocks of the settee.

"I shall have to," she agreed. "One of the other women at work will no doubt ask me if I've anyone I'm seeing. The danger of it is that so many of them will have taught themselves to smile like an idiot and try to change the subject as quickly as possible, and they're quite likely to recognize me doing it."

"Is there no professional courtesy amongst the ladies of counterintelligence?" he asked, hearing a note of amusement in his words.

"I suspect there's considerably more amongst sharks," she replied, "or Soviet agents."

He was several moments appreciating that he was enjoying their mutual conspiracy of shop talk as well. He'd not been granted the opportunity to natter on about the labyrinthine machinations of his work. The sudden liberty to speak of the most occult secrets of his days without the need to periodically inquire about the security clearance of the girl beside him was considerably more intoxicating than his wine.

"I... I've heard a secret about you," Alice Woodward said after some time, her voice barely audible above the gramophone.

"If it's at all salacious, it's unquestionably a lie," he said.

"One of the other women at Leconfield House... said that you were married."

"That's true," he said. He felt her shoulders grow taut beneath his arm, and he appreciated that he might have phrased his response more gracefully. "I was married."

"Was?" she asked.

"As in 'was, but no longer.'"

Her shoulders drooped, and she seemed to flow into the cushions at her back. "Did you leave her, or have I just spoiled our evening because she's died?"

"We left each other," he said evenly. "It's something of an occupational hazard. Spending all hours chasing Russians about and plotting the downfall of the Soviet Union is rather hard on a marriage. Hugh Somerfield's gotten through three of them. He's of the opinion that most of the cars he's owned have lasted longer."

"It's my understanding that Hugh Somerfield has had more girlfriends than he's had hot suppers," she whispered, glancing away from him.

"That probably hasn't helped," he agreed.

She turned to face him, her eyes opaline and liquid. "It wasn't particularly thoughtful of me to ask you..."

He shook his head. "MI5 prizes curiosity," he interrupted her. The phrase had appeared as the title of a document he'd been given when he'd been recruited to the intelligence service. He could no longer recall what the text beneath it had said. Her features erupted into a grin, and he appreciated that the service was clearly still providing the same document to its new employees.

She sipped her wine, gazing at him over the lip of her glass. "I feel as if I've asked you something uncomfortable just the same," she said at length. "If you fancy asking me something uncomfortable one day, you can remind me of tonight and we shall be even."

He smiled into the shadows of the room, and for an instant he felt his heart in his chest, wondering that it might not be audible to her as well. "I've thought of asking you if you'd like to come away with me for the weekend," he said into the darkness, unwilling for an instant to watch her expression. "Hugh Somerfield's mentioned an hotel by the seaside in Kent... it's open year 'round, and he says it's quite beautiful in the autumn."

In the corner of his eye her breast swelled for a moment beneath her sweater, and she glanced at him. "I should like that very much," she said. Her words had been dark with surprise, and he spent some time wondering that they should be so.

The final notes of the saxophone moaned from across the room, to be replaced by the slow waltz of the gramophone's needle ticking. She rose to her feet and turned the record over. The saxophone returned, this time accompanied by a cornet.

"Have you had a rather large file typed on blue paper in the past few days?" she inquired absently as she folded her legs beneath herself and cloaked herself once more in his arm.

He considered her question, realizing at length that he'd received the papers she was referring to that morning. He'd pushed them into the unseemly clutter of his safe, where he had every expectation that they'd eventually turn to coal under the seismic pressure of later secret memoranda from the office of the director.

"I have," he replied. "I trust this is more of your handiwork."

"Have you read it?" She smiled reprovingly, and clearly she knew before he spoke that he'd not.

"I've had rather a busy day," he said defensively. "It's not something I'd confess to just anyone, but if I'm the last name on the distribution list for files, I've been known to ignore them for weeks... especially the thick ones."

"You shouldn't ignore this one," she said.

He felt his eyes narrow. "And why is that?"

She parted her lips to reply to his question, and then seemed to think better of it. "I shouldn't say," she said, an

odd note of bemusement in her voice, "but it will unquestionably be the most remarkable file you've ever been
sent."

18

Friday, October 20

I t was apparent as Hugh Somerfield opened the door of Edwina Pearson's office that she should have been Dame Edwina. The room appeared to have been sealed and locked in 1880, and just recently redis-covered. Its furnishings whispered of the sort of refine-ment which only accompanied advanced years or a great many hired decorators. The walls were ramparts of book-shelves splashed with incandescent daylight from an immense circular window at the distant end of the office. An ornate oak desk stood like a Norman fortress, a gran-ite enclave steeled against the spears of barbarians.

Edwina Pearson seemed to be just over one hundred years old. She grasped an elongated cigarette holder between two fingers that might well have served as the claws of a small flightless bird in another life and glanced up at him as he entered. She removed a pair of gold pince-nez spectacles from the bridge of her nose and replaced them with a rather larger pair of conventional eyeglasses set with lenses that appeared capable of permitting anyone with normal vision to count the craters on the surface of the moon. She smiled agreeably and closed the book she'd been studying.

"Are you the fellow from MI5?" she inquired, her voice considerably more robust than her person.

Hugh Somerfield pushed the door to behind himself

and nodded. "Yes I am," he replied. "Thank you for agreeing to see me."

She glanced at a clock beside her desk. "Are you certain? I've not known one of you to arrive on time in the past."

He permitted himself to be amused. "It's not difficult to be punctual for one's first appointment of the day," he observed.

"You studied at Cambridge," she said, her words bearing a distinct whisper of accusation.

"Yes, that's right." He was uncertain why she might concern herself about the locale of his education, and upon further reflection, how she'd come to ascertain it.

"Alec Grey studied at Oxford," she added.

"So I understand."

"I lectured at Oxford, you know."

He regarded her features, considering the possibility that either she was having him on or that Alec Grey had dispatched him on this errand as some manner of punishment for an offense as yet unclear to him.

"Is that how you came to know Alec Grey?" he asked.

She nodded. "He was a clever student. The government should be grateful to have him."

"I'm certain it is," he said uncertainly. "At least, it appears to be so when the wages are paid."

She regarded him for a moment through her heavy lenses, and then she smiled thinly. "May I offer you some advice?"

"Yes?"

"You should make it your practice to observe the appointments of a room such as this when you enter one," she said quietly. "The most difficult aspect of conversing with old people is that it's so very tricky... ascertaining which of them are merely eccentric and which of them actually have porridge where their minds used to be.

You're no doubt too polite to say as much, but you've been having concerns to this effect since you arrived."

"What would I wish to observe?" he inquired slowly, deciding as he did that he would have been foolish to have denied her implicit accusation, or at the very least ill-mannered.

"The books," she said, gesturing at the walls of her office. "Senile old people invariably have them upside down, some with their spines facing in, a few others replaced with cheese and onion sandwiches they put there a few months earlier and forgot about. Eccentrics are orderly as a rule."

He glanced about the room, permitting his attention to light upon her innumerable volumes. They were, as she'd suggested, all orderly, and showed no sign of having been interspersed with discarded crusts of bread.

"Would you like to have a chair, Mr. Somerfield?" she asked, gesturing to a wooden visitor's chair before her desk. He accepted it wordlessly. The timbre of her voice had shifted minutely.

She opened one of the drawers of her desk and extracted a small white envelope and a large set of silver tweezers. She opened the envelope and withdrew its contents with her tweezers. A triangle of paper fluttered before her, a geometric butterfly emboldening itself for its appointment with a pin and a long Latin name, and she eased it to the surface of her blotter.

"I believe this is what you've been sent for," she observed.

He considered the object for a moment. It bore the number 217, and three truncated lines of type. The first was the words 'resembling Venus,' the second the single word 'ivory' and the third a mere two letters, 'nt.' He'd seen a photograph of it several days earlier. The obverse bore the number 218, he recalled, and some additional text.

"I've been informed you've learned something of it," he said curiously.

"I believe I've learned virtually everything of it," she corrected him. She returned her tweezers to their place in her desk. "Am I permitted to ask how you came by this?"

"It was found on the body of a murder victim a week ago. I'm afraid I'm not allowed..."

She raised one of her skeletal hands and he fell silent. "You need not explain, Mr. Somerfield. As I alluded to earlier, you are not the first supplicant from MI5 to grace my threshold."

"Alec Grey seemed to think it was... unusual," he prompted her.

"It would depend a great deal upon who owned it," she explained. "I trust I would not be telling you anything you don't currently know if I informed you that it's a corner from the page of a book."

"That's about all we do know," he agreed.

She leant back in her chair. "Let us begin with the paper, then. You will have observed that it's rather heavy paper, and that it has an irregular edge on two sides. The third edge is quite straight, but we may assume that it has recently been torn."

He nodded, and she continued.

"The paper has a substantial rag content, which indicates that it was relatively expensive and of high quality. Its surface is distinctly gray, which tells us that it was not subjected to bleaching, as modern paper is. The wood fiber used in its production is almost certainly German spruce."

"Shall we assume, then, that it was manufactured in Germany?"

"France," she said, as if it might have been apparent. "At the time this paper was made, the German timber industry was enjoying a great deal of prosperity supplying spruce wood to firms across Europe which built a variety of musical instruments. This entailed felling a great number of trees, only a very few of which were suitable for the instrument builders. The remaining trees were, on the whole, exported to France, where they were boiled into pulp and used to make paper."

"Does that tell you when the paper was made?" Hugh Somerfield inquired. He decided as he did that the question was almost certainly irrelevant, as what Leconfield House was most concerned with was the name of the murdering bastard who'd put a hole in Arthur Dunross and left him in a Docklands hotel with this scrap of paper in one of his pockets.

"It was made in 1892, as it happens," she said. She leant forward and smiled conspiratorially. "Shall I tell you how I've come to know that?"

He regarded her for a moment. "I think perhaps you should."

"You'll have noticed the text on this scrap of paper," she continued, returned to the embrace of her chair. "It's an unusual typeface."

"Is it?" He considered the paper once more, but its few characters appeared unremarkable.

"You'll notice the slight bulging in the vertical stalks of the letters, and the oval serifs on the lower-case characters. The descender of the letter G seems unusually deep."

"I shall take your word for it."

"This is a typeface called Vestal Gothic. It was designed in the middle of the nineteenth century by a Swiss typographer, Edvard Schoeffer. With the advent of the first Linotype mechanical typesetting machines, he reintroduced it in 1889. It's rather notable in typographic circles."

"Is it?" Hugh Somerfield repeated, as he appreciated he was intended to do.

Edwina Pearson nodded. "It's singularly ugly, you see, and it was one of most unsuccessful commercial typefaces in history. For reasons which he chose not to record for his descendants, Schoeffer spent a sizeable fortune promoting Vestal Gothic to various printers and publishers across Europe... I believe he virtually bankrupted himself. He sold eleven sets of it in all, of which only three appear to have been used to print anything."

"This being the work of one of them, I trust," he suggested, indicating the scrap of paper.

"Of the three sets of Vestal Gothic, one was sold to the British gardening book publisher Trentham and Sons, one went to a Swedish weekly newspaper which still uses the typeface for its masthead... most unaccountably... and a third was bought by a French publisher call *La Presse du Chat Noir*... the Black Cat Press. Would you care to speculate upon the nature of their works, Mr. Somerfield?"

"Veterinary guides, perhaps?" he suggested.

A smile flickered across her features and was dispelled. "Most unlikely," she said sternly. "*La Presse du Chat Noir* printed rather distasteful pornography. It was begun in Paris by a man named Phillipe Maistre, who produced his first works using hand-set type on a manual press. He wrote under the name Jules d'Anjou. He was rather clever about promoting his books... he put it about that Jules d'Anjou existed in a continual state of arrest, incarceration... I believe he was said to have been imprisoned for a time on what the French referred to as the Devil's Island penal colony in Guiana."

"None of which was true, I trust."

"Of course it wasn't. Phillipe Maistre was arguably mentally ill, judging by what he wrote, but he was a shrewd businessman. His books were written in English, for export to this country. He paid his taxes... and a suitable number of bribes... and he enjoyed a comfortable relationship with the French authorities. In time he became so successful as to be able to afford an automatic printing press and a typesetting machine... very much the height of innovation in those days. He immediately set about printing his latest work, entitled The Reluctant Maiden. It was thoroughly abhorrent. Jules d'Anjou was said to be living in chains in a medieval dungeon at the time, or some such. The book sold extremely well, through several dozen printings."

Would this have been in 1892?" Hugh Somerfield inquired.

"Yes it would," she said, clearly pleased that he'd been paying attention.

He regarded the scrap of paper with renewed interest. "What you said about the unusual typeface earlier... it would make this one of the naughty books this fellow printed. How can you say that it was the particular book he printed in 1892?"

She regarded him for a moment before she returned her attention to the paper. "A hand printing press produces type with a perfectly clean edge all the way around each character, as pressure is applied evenly from above. An automatic mechanical printing press rolls a metal drum over a flat galley of type, and in so doing produces type with a slightly irregular edge in the direction of the moving drum. I can provide you with a lens if you wish to examine the type on your fragment of paper."

"I'll take your word for it," he conceded, deciding as he did that he'd come to enjoy the arcane detective story she'd sprawled across her desk on his behalf. "That would place this printing in 1892 or some time thereafter."

"The Reluctant Maiden was Phillipe Maistre's only work printed on his automatic press. As I'm to understand it, the book made him quite wealthy. His later works were all printed by hand, a process which he appears to have enjoyed. Mercifully, they were distributed in very limited numbers."

Hugh Somerfield leant back in his chair and waited until Edwina Pearson had done the same. "This doesn't fit with what I've read about... the murdered man who was discovered with that bit of paper in his pocket. He was a respectable scientist... he had a wife and children. Our people searched his home and his office... if something like the book you've described had turned up, it would have been noticed."

"If I'd had a copy of The Reluctant Maiden, I'd have found a very safe place to hide it. You must understand, Mr. Somerfield, we are not discussing Lady Chatterley's Lover. From what I know of it, it was a wholly revolting work, replete with the most unimaginable depravity. I'm not certain if owning such a book is in itself illegal at present, but it would unquestionably attract the attention of the authorities."

"Would it be valuable, this book?" Hugh Somerfield asked.

Edwina Pearson put her hand to her chin. "It would depend upon who was selling it," she replied thoughtfully. "As I say, Phillipe Maistre printed innumerable copies of it, and I dare say most of them still survive today. I would imagine antiquarian booksellers who trade in such works periodically convince unwary customers that it's somehow rare, and as such worthy of a high price. Why do you ask?"

"As a rule, I would have said that collectors of rare books would be unlikely to rip away parts of their pages."

She glanced thoughtfully at the scrap of paper, clearly not having considered this.

"As I was examining this fragment of paper... and having provided such assistance as I've been able to Mr. Grey in the past... it occurred to me that your people might wish to ascertain where this unpleasant book could have come from," she said.

"You're not going to tell me you can deduce the shop that sold it, are you?" Hugh Somerfield said, permitting himself to smile.

"Perhaps," she replied, and she opened one of the drawers of her desk. After a moment's consideration, she extracted a single sheet of paper and pushed it toward him. "I'm afraid I shall have to require that you work for your answer, however. There are a great many dealers of rare books in London, of course, but I don't imagine very many of them would wish to be found in possession of anything bearing the imprint of *La Presse du Chat Noir*. I've written out a list of those few exceptions... booksellers who deal in pornographic works. If your murder victim acquired The Reluctant Maiden from a private source, this will be of no help to you. If you're correct in saying that he did not collect such books, however, then it would be unlikely that he'd have moved in such circles. He would have had to buy it from a shop." She touched the page before herself. "One of these shops."

Hugh Somerfield folded the list and slipped it into the pocket of his suit coat. "This has all been rather fascinating, Mrs. Pearson," he said. "You're like one of those archeologists who discovers a hundred-thousand year old finger bone and goes on to reconstruct the entire man who originally owned it, right down to what the fellow favored for breakfast."

She shook her head, her features creased with amusement. "I shouldn't think so, Mr. Somerfield. Archeologists are all such dreadful frauds."

19

He permitted his umbrella to slip behind him for an instant, feeling the assault of rain across his face. It tasted of cinders and treachery, he mused, raising his free hand to shield his eyes. The gaunt man walking toward him carried no umbrella. His head was encysted in a black ushanka, the fur hat the Soviet army issued to its officers. This one had had its Soviet insignia removed, but its origins might well have been displayed in flashing red neon. Its owner seemed unconcerned by his translucent anonymity.

He stepped quickly into man's path, the other pedestrians oozing around him like treacle. The ushanka twisted in the gray morning as if it were manipulating the legs far below itself. The man glanced around, seeking for a fissure in the crush of passers-by.

"Colonel Nikonov," he said evenly.

The man glanced at him, a flash of recognition in his expression for a moment before he looked away. He said nothing.

"Ivan Vasilievich Nikonov," he said again.

The scowling figure paused, glaring for a moment, his eyes suddenly alight with unease. He froze in mid-stride, a tide-wall against the rush of people clattering about him.

"What do you want?" he growled, his voice barely audible above the shuffle of feet and the roaring of traffic in the street.

"There's a cafe a few minutes further along," he said. "I'd like to buy you a glass of tea and have a quick chat."

Colonel Ivan Nikonov's jaw stiffened, and he clearly seemed to be struggling with the diffuse light in the lee of the umbrella before him. "Who are you?" he demanded.

Alec Grey lowered his umbrella and removed the dark glasses he'd been wearing. A flash of recognition tainted the colonel's expression. Alec Grey replaced his glasses out of consideration for the man before him. It would serve neither of them if another officer of the first directorate of the KGB identified the party who'd struck up a conversation with Ivan Nikonov.

The cafe was ill-lit and crowded, thick with fumes of hot fat and stale cigarette smoke. As they entered, Edward Blair rose from his seat at a table in a far corner and made his way to the lavatory, leaving the table unoccupied. Alec Grey watched the colonel's eyes, smiling fleetingly to himself as the Soviet officer appreciated he'd been seconded to a troupe of wandering thespians. Edward Blair had clearly been struggling to dominate his ribald excitement at his second field assignment in little more than a fortnight.

Alec Grey gestured for Colonel Nikonov to take the chair in the corner, that he might enjoy some small measure of comfort in not having to sit with his back to the room. Alec Grey had installed three men in the cafe to watch his own back. He furled his umbrella and at last removed his preposterous dark glasses.

"I find this highly unusual, Mr. Grey," the colonel said quietly.

Alec Grey permitted himself to smile. He'd not previously had occasion to meet Ivan Nikonov, but he was certain he knew more about the man before him than all but the most trusted officers of the KGB. He was also certain the colonel enjoyed an equally detailed file on him.

"You've taken meetings with British subjects before, Colonel," he said. "We have photographs and tape recordings of some of them."

Colonel Nikonov gazed at him malevolently. He was a slender man, especially for an officer of the KGB. Hugh Somerfield had postulated that in a nation which demanded its common citizens queue for three hours to buy bread, gluttony and its attendant conspicuously large trousers were all but unavoidable for those party members sufficiently highly placed as to be able to delegate their shopping to subordinates. The colonel's features seemed deflated, his flesh undulating with plummeting valleys and creases of worry. His dossier observed that he was not yet fifty, but he looked at least a decade older.

The man who glared at him now seemed to consider denying the casual accusation cast onto the greasy surface of the table between them, and then to think better of it. "What is it that you want, Mr. Grey?" he asked, his eyes narrowing. He'd clearly appreciated that he would not enjoy the reply to his question.

"You're assuming I don't wish to defect," Alec Grey said, permitting himself to be amused by the thought.

The man before him blinked, touched by a flicker of confusion. "I think I will assume that, yes," he said at length.

Alec Grey reached into the pocket of his overcoat. There were two packets secreted therein, and he was a moment ascertaining which was the one he wished to reveal first. He extracted a small brown envelope and placed it on the table before Colonel Nikonov. The Soviet officer paused for a moment before he opened it and emptied several black and white photographs onto the table.

"What are you showing me, Mr. Grey?" he asked, his voice touched with affected irritation.

Alec Grey decided that his own irritation would become authentic momentarily. Colonel Nikonov was a professional, he considered, and he felt he was due a minimum of theatrics.

He arranged the photographs before Colonel Nikonov and touched each of them in turn. "This first one is of a rather expensive prostitute of your acquaintance, by the name of Gina Caroll. This second one is of a house in Abbots Close which you arranged to purchase eighteen months ago whilst pretending to be a German businessman named Willie Fuchs. The third is of Valentin Maksimovich Chervenkov, whom you've had collect Gina Caroll from time to time and deliver her to your house." He allowed the colonel to regard the photographs for a few moments before he gathered them from the table, replaced them in their envelope and returned them to his pocket.

"We've photographs of several other young women you've employed as well," he added.

Colonel Nikonov regarded him warily. "Is the British intelligence service at such a loss for things to occupy it that it has sent you to charge me with the hiring of prostitutes?"

Alec Grey caught the eyes of the man before him with his own, staring through them into Ivan Nikonov's skull. "I've not come out in the rain this morning to trade pleasantries, Colonel," he said coldly.

"Perhaps you should tell me what it is you have come for, Mr. Grey," the colonel said.

"Blackmail," Alec Grey replied.

Colonel Nikonov stared at him, smiling thinly. He shook his head slowly. "You have wasted your time, Mr. Grey," he said, "and mine as well. I have blackmailed no one."

Alec Grey matched the smile that had twisted the features of Colonel Nikonov. "I'm sorry, Colonel," he said.

"I didn't mean to suggest you had. I've come to blackmail you."

The colonel leant back in his chair as if he anticipated Alec Grey reaching across the table and grasping him by his collars. "What are you talking about, Mr. Grey?" he demanded. He'd sought to affect a note of irritation once more, Alec Grey appreciated, but he'd been singularly unsuccessful.

Alec Grey sighed. He'd summoned the illusory hope an hour earlier that the colonel would be sufficiently astute to comprehend the box into which he'd locked himself without a laborious description of its every rivet and weld. Were he present, Hugh Somerfield would no doubt remark upon the lamentable standards by which officers rose to positions of influence in the KGB

"Your government habitually beggars itself to supply the first directorate of the KGB with sufficient western currency to fund its intelligence operations abroad," Alec Grey explained evenly, his manner intentionally didactic. The wisp of condescension was not lost on Colonel Nikonov. "It's my belief that were your superiors to become aware of your rather bourgeoisie accommodations and your use of them... no doubt purchased with their meager allotment of pounds... they would recall you to Moscow just long enough to have you kitted out in cold weather gear."

The color had slipped from Colonel Nikonov's lined features and he stared blankly at Alec Grey for a time. Some aspect of the threat placed before him seemed to have proven elusive, and Alec Grey wondered if he might be called upon to repeat it.

"You cannot be serious," the colonel said at length.

Hugh Somerfield would have been dancing on the table, Alec Grey thought fleetingly, and he experienced a moment of genuine disappointment that he'd not undertaken to record his conversation with Ivan Nikonov.

"Yes, I can be serious, Ivan Vasilievich," he said quietly, "and I'm being serious now. Whilst it is not considered to be the proper behavior of gentlemen, agents of my government have from time to time arranged to entrap agents of your government in compromising situations to exploit them as sources of intelligence. You represent the first occasion of an agent of your government thoughtfully entrapping himself for us. You must agree we'd be utter fools to waste this opportunity. I don't believe you regard us as fools."

The colonel shook his head wearily, his eyes haunted and vacant. "What... what is it that you want of me?" he asked quietly, his words barely audible over the murmur of the cafe.

Alec Grey reached into his pocket once more and removed the other package he'd brought with him. He reached under the table and placed it upon the knees of Colonel Nikonov. The man's expression grew startled as he felt its touch, appreciated what it must contain.

"I'm certain you won't require instruction in the use of a Minox camera," Alec Grey said, relenting to amusement despite the growing horror of the man before him. "The package also contains a supply of film cassettes, details of the operation of your dead drop and a list of topics about which we're keen to know more."

"You cannot be serious."

"I believe I've addressed that matter."

Colonel Nikonov leant forward, his voice little more than a whisper. "If I am caught, I will be executed," he hissed.

Alec Grey put his hand to his chin. "Surely the likelihood of your being caught spying for us is preferable to the certainty of your being found to have embezzled funds from your embassy should you fail to do so, Colonel," he said.

He sought for rage or deceit in the face of the man

before him, but he witnessed only the lifeless stare of the vanquished. He was not looking into even the most distorted reflection of Alice Woodward's sea-green eyes. The colonel would do as he'd been instructed, for the alternatives were unthinkable.

An aging waitress approached the table, a sullen wraith with graying hair in the corner of Alec Grey's eye. He ordered coffee for himself and tea for the colonel, who seemed beyond sensible communication with the woman. She said nothing and evaporated into the gloom of the cafe.

"What is it you think I have access to, Mr. Grey?" Ivan Nikonov inquired softly. "My function is to gather intelligence. I am not required to be briefed on the secrets of my government. Anything I am privy to will have been obtained from yours."

Alec Grey smiled. "We're particularly interested in ENORMOZ," he replied.

The colonel appeared to have forgotten to breath for a time. "I... I do not know what you are referring to," he said at length. His body seemed on the point of trembling.

"You know quite well what I'm referring to," Alec Grey corrected him. "We have our moles in your organization as well, Colonel." In fact, GCHQ had thoughtfully passed along a decrypted briefing document it had intercepted, intended for Colonel Ivan Nikonov at the Soviet embassy in London. It had chanced to arrive several hours after one of the concocted files Alec Grey had circulated in an attempt to identify the Soviet mole within MI5, and the Enigma rotor settings that had been revealed by the MI5 file had served to decrypt the rest of the day's transmissions.

"I have been made aware of little more than the existence of the... ENORMOZ project," Colonel Nikonov protested. "I have no requirement for the details of the research. I can give you very little."

Alec Grey pretended to consider this. He leant forward, adopting an air of conspiracy. "We have a source within your research complex, Colonel," he said softly. "He provides us with a great deal of intelligence about ENORMOZ. We'd like to be certain we can trust him. Your material will help us verify his."

The colonel drew his palm across his brow, his expression having grown bloodless. He seemed to be gathering fragments of appreciation of his increasingly bleak situation. He'd just been informed that he would have scant opportunity to provide MI5 with concocted intelligence, that anything he brought out would be compared against secrets from another agent. He would begin hammering his fists against the wall of the cafe in another five minutes, Alec Grey mused, pleading for his release.

He'd spent some while crafting the intricate fantasy with which he would confront Colonel Nikonov, and as he watched the life slip from the older man's eyes now, he allowed that he was darkly pleased with his labors. In the unlikely event that the colonel did risk the caustic ire of his superiors and burn MI5's attempt to suborn him, the KGB would presumably sear its own time stream facility to ashes as it sought for MI5's imaginary agent.

The waitress returned and placed stained white mugs before each of them. Coffee slopped from the one nearest Alec Grey. Colonel Nikonov clutched his in both hands and emptied half its contents in a single swallow. He clearly would have preferred that it had dispensed vodka.

"If... if I am found out," he said at length, his words barely audible above the noises of the cafe, "If I am found out by my government... would you permit me to defect?"

Alec Grey smiled. "That's not something I'm permitted to decide, Colonel," he answered. "I feel certain that if the material you provide us with is worth the film it's photographed on, my superiors would consider bringing you over."

The Soviet officer's shoulders sagged, and Alec Grey appreciated that he'd genuinely believed the promise of asylum in Britain. He imagined proposing the defection of Ivan Nikonov to Sir Alistair — the director would no doubt laugh uneasily, suspecting himself to be the butt of a joke in poor taste and highly questionable judgment.

The coffee was truly foul here, Alec Grey mused as he considered Colonel Nikonov for a moment longer. He forbade himself speculation as to how the gnomes who scuttled about the kitchens of this place rendered it so. The Russian suggested a small animal staring into oncoming headlamps.

"There are two other things, Ivan Vasilievich," he said at length. The colonel was clearly beyond taking umbrage at the untoward familiarity in the use of his Christian name. "As you will appreciate, we can't have you disposing of your house in Abbots Close and attempting to bury the evidence of your naughty behavior. You understand that one of my lads will keep an eye on it. If anyone resembling an estate agent crosses your threshold, your lot in Moscow will be given an opportunity to bid on the property."

The colonel nodded slowly.

"In addition, you'll need to look elsewhere for ladies to entertain you. I'm aware the women you hired were whores, but they were English whores. The realm I'm charged with the defense of includes them as well."

20

The steward gestured wordlessly across the room at a solitary figure in a leather chair large enough to have provided housing for a family of four. His face was shrouded by a copy of the Times, and crowned with a halo of cigar smoke that seemed on the point of growing solid and raining down about his shoulders. The man in his chair appeared oblivious to his surroundings, which Sir Alistair considered to be very much out of keeping with his former calling.

Sir Simon Turnbull had occupied the office of the director of MI5 for seven years before he'd been deposed by the mandarins of Whitehall in favor of Sir Alistair Fitzhenry. Sir Simon's own predecessor, Sir Percy Sillitoe, had retired from the director's chair to pursue diamond smugglers on behalf of the De Beers company in South Africa. Sir Simon had chosen to pursue the Times crossword, an undertaking for which he was said to be poorly qualified.

It was a periodic source of irritation to Sir Alistair that he shared a club with the former occupant of his office. He'd contrived to encounter Sir Simon on only the rarest of occasions by observing that he appeared to have been granted a one hundred year lease on his favorite chair, which he rarely vacated and was never unfaithful to.

He was loath to violate their unspoken anonymity on this occasion, touched as he was with the nagging fear that the rabid hostility Sir Simon had expressed for him on the occasion of his being elevated to his current posture might have cooled, and the former director might one day deliberately seek his company. Sir Simon Turnbull was an offensive, salivating toad of a man who appeared to have been made flesh from a caricature of an over-privileged Englishman in a Victorian newspaper cartoon.

It was rumored that Sir Simon had been installed upon the board of the recently reborn East India Company. Alec Grey was wont to refer to it as having been 'exhumed.' The original Elizabethan trading company had closed its offices and sold off the last of its clipper ships during the reign of Victoria. Upon the third and presumably final denunciation of Indian independence from the British Empire by its citizens in 1951, and the subsequent defeat of Nehru's government, the great tyrant from across the sea had been roused from its slumbers by a group of Scottish investors. The freighters which now sailed from Pondicherry and Bombay did so with their holds packed with transistor radios and television receivers rather than spices and silk.

Sir Alistair nodded to the steward, who turned wordlessly and vanished to seek other duties. After a moment's hesitation, Sir Alistair entered the room and approached the man before him. The funk of his cigar was almost palpable, something burned by a tribe of headhunters to overcome the stench of their leftover dinner.

He eased himself into the chair facing Sir Simon Turnbull. The newspaper between them hardly rattled. He considered for an instant the possibility that he was to be spared an awkward conversation by the man's recent demise.

"I wonder if I might trouble you for a moment, Sir Simon," he said at length.

The paper crumpled between two porcine hands, lowering itself until its owner could peer over its summit at the author of this intrusion upon his privacy. Sir Simon Turnbull's eyes glowed like coals in the caverns below his brow, flickering with unease or outrage.

"You," he muttered, his voice a scattering of gravel on concrete.

"I require a few minutes of your time," Sir Alistair insisted.

The newspaper resumed its former location, rattling with sense of finality.

"If they've sent you over to inquire about my bill, you may inform the steward I'll settle it at month's end," Sir Simon growled.

Sir Alistair felt his jaw grow taut. He'd been assured by a solicitor whom MI5 retained for such concerns that he had sufficient authority to have Sir Simon Turnbull uprooted from his chair by force of arms and carried bodily to Leconfield House for a summary conversation and as much cold tea as the former director could stomach, should the matter become sufficiently disagreeable.

The likelihood that the former director would burst every significant blood vessel in his brain were he to be subjected to an outrage of this magnitude was not lost on Sir Alistair, and he was reluctant even to threaten Sir Simon with it.

"I'm afraid I need to speak to you in an official capacity, Simon," he said patiently. He resisted the temptation to glance at his wristwatch and assign the civil portion of this conversation a time limit.

The newspaper between them descended once more. The entirety of Sir Simon Turnbull's features grew visible, veiled only by the smoke of his cigar. "I can't see how that would be possible," he said, his words liquid and ragged as they struggled around the cigar. "I haven't an official capacity any longer."

Sir Alistair sighed and leant back in his chair. "This is a matter of some urgency," he said.

During his tenure as the director of MI5, Sir Simon Turnbull had armored himself in legend with his volcanic temper and his frequent use of language which would have been regarded as barbaric in Docklands. He appeared to be on the point of giving flesh to the tales that ennobled him.

The overweight man leant forward, compressing his newspaper into his lap. "Nothing is urgent to me any longer," he hissed.

"This is a matter of some urgency to the ministry," Sir Alistair insisted.

"Then I suggest you sort it out," Sir Simon coughed. "The ministry has left you in charge." He seemed to be on the point of cloaking himself with his copy of the Times once more, a signal that their brief discussion had been concluded.

Sir Alistair peered into the man's eyes. Those eyes had been said to spit fire at MI5's officers during Sir Simon Turnbull's reign as director. Their fires had clearly been banked, but they smoldered yet and they showed no sign of being extinguished.

"I'm afraid I must insist, Simon," he said coldly.

The features before him smiled, a crease of fleshy lips affixed to two pendulous jowls. Sir Simon leant further forward. "Go to hell," he whispered.

The gesture seemed decidedly overacted, Sir Alistair considered, as they two were the only occupants of the room. He appreciated that it would serve the former director if he were to lose control of his temper and begin shouting.

"Are you certain that's what you wish, Simon?" he inquired earnestly. "I'll be of very little assistance to you in the fires of Hades, and you're shortly to require my assistance."

"I don't need anything from the likes of you," he said, but his words fluttered with uncertainty.

"Need I remind you that it wasn't I who caused you to lose your position as director?" Sir Alistair asked, his tone suggesting that his inquiry did not require a reply. "Your dismissal came from Whitehall."

Sir Simon Turnbull's eyes narrowed. "Perhaps you should ask Whitehall whatever you've come here for."

"Are you certain you'd wish Whitehall to be reminded of your name?"

Sir Simon pushed his newspaper to the floor. "What are you on about?" he demanded.

"It wasn't I who caused you to lose your position as director," Sir Alistair repeated. "You have Mister Burgess and Mister Maclean to thank for that, Simon, and they in turn have you."

Sir Alistair regarded the man before him, allowing as he did that his feint had been something of a gamble. Sir Simon Turnbull had no doubt known innumerable silent hours in which to contemplate the agents of his downfall. It seemed unlikely that he was at peace with the events which had driven him from Leconfield House.

Guy Burgess and Donald Maclean had been friends from their days at Cambridge during the 1930s. They'd almost certainly been recruited by agents of the Soviet Union during that time. They'd known careers in British intelligence which their Soviet controllers must have regarded as stellar.

Guy Burgess had been the son of an officer in the Royal Navy. He'd read history, graduated with distinction and by 1939 he'd been employed by MI6. He'd also been flamboyantly homosexual, an aspect of his character which had attracted the displeasure of his superiors. It had very likely disturbed his Soviet controllers as well.

Despite his oftentimes outrageous behavior and a

monumental capacity for drink, Guy Burgess had ascended the hierarchy of MI6. Major General Sir Stewart Menzies, the director of MI6 until the early 1950s, had had a bellyful of Burgess, but he'd found him sufficiently well-connected to be difficult to dismiss. He'd undertaken what he'd later described as a bargain with the devil and diverted him to MI5.

Donald Maclean had been as unlike Guy Burgess as he'd been able. He'd graduated Cambridge and applied to the foreign office. He was posted to Washington as first secretary at the British embassy. By 1951 he was the head of the American department of the Foreign Office.

The volume of intelligence passed to Moscow by Burgess and Maclean remained a matter of speculation, save that it was vast. They'd been highly-situated agents-in-place for well over a decade. They were ultimately to be revealed by a fortunate American cryptographic break-through, which had successfully compared Donald Maclean's activities through much of the 1940s with a series of intercepted Soviet radio messages.

Someone had warned Burgess of Maclean's immi-nent doom. On the Friday before he'd been scheduled to appear for questioning, Guy Burgess and Donald Maclean had hired a car, driven to Southampton and taken a ferry to France. They'd traveled by train to Paris, then to Berne, and finally to the Ukraine, where they were met by Soviet agents and smuggled across the border into Russia. Maclean's wife Melinda had joined him in Moscow several years later.

"I had nothing to do with Burgess or Maclean," Sir Simon Turnbull snapped. "They were well before my time."

"That's hardly true," Sir Alistair said. "MI5 is responsible for vetting officers of all of the intelligence services and employees of the foreign office with access to sensitive information. You know that as well as I do. You'd have caught the pair of them if your people had looked beyond that rag at your throat."

Sir Simon's features grew incandescent, his hands clawing the arms of his chair. Much had been made of his having worn the same Cambridge school tie which had granted Burgess and Maclean entry into the secret chambers of government. Sir Alistair feared for a moment that the huge figure before him might hurl itself across the few feet that separated them and crush him to death.

"Damn you..." he snarled.

"I lie awake some nights imagining how many Burgess and Maclean damned with the secrets they provided to Moscow," Sir Alistair said.

Sir Simon seemed on the point of rising from his chair. "I've heard as much of this as I care to..." he began.

Sir Alistair gestured for him to remain where he was. "Guy Burgess knew we suspected Maclean," he said. "It has never been determined how he came to know."

"Damn you..."

Sir Alistair paused, putting his hand to his chin as he regarded the man before him. He leant forward, and he waited until Sir Simon did the same. When he again spoke, very little of his former civility remained in his words.

"Listen to me, you arrogant little bastard," he said coldly. Sir Simon's lips had parted to speak, but he appeared to have been shocked into a moment of silence. Sir Alistair approved of the effect of his sudden change of demeanor, and he continued. "You allowed two Soviet agents of whom we know to get past you, and Christ knows how many others of whom we don't. I remain under considerable pressure to devise suitable cause to bang you up somewhere very deep and very dark until it can be determined whether you were working for Moscow or just criminally stupid. I have thus far resisted that pressure, but I am increasingly amenable to changing my mind. I've come here this morning to request your assistance, and you are damned well going to provide it."

Sir Simon Turnbull took a long draught of his cigar, the coals at its extremity pulsating very much as his eyes appeared to do. At length he extracted it from between his teeth and deposited it in an ashtray beside his chair.

"What is it you want?" he asked.

Sir Alistair sighed and he permitted himself to relax against the back of his chair. He removed a folded sheet of paper from the inside pocket of his suit coat and handed it to the former director.

"One of my people has convinced me that we have an active mole," he began. "His investigations have produced a list of seven names. Three of the men we suspect date from your tenure as director. I've read their files. All three of them went to Cambridge. All three of them come from impeccable families. All three of them had your unquestioning approval. I need to know whatever you chose to omit from their files, Simon."

He watched the former director unfold the list and consider its contents. "I need to know the truth," he added.

"This is bloody nonsense," Sir Simon said at length.

"This is the defense of the realm," Sir Alistair said harshly, and Sir Simon Turnbull glared at him with narrowed eyes. The former director had clearly perceived the threat cast onto the oaken floor between them. In the defense of the realm, the shadowy figures who answered to Sir Alistair had license to trample civilized behavior under foot without so much as an apology to its next of kin.

Sir Simon slapped the page derisively with the back of his hand. "Look who you've chosen as suspects," he said. "These men have served the nation for decades."

"As had Burgess and Maclean," Sir Alistair reminded him.

Sir Simon scowled at him. "I knew these men personally." He stabbed the list with an immense index finger. "Peter Willes was my assistant director of counterintelligence. He was a captain in the Royal Air Force. His brother is a personal friend of Prince Philip. He attended Christ's College at Cambridge, as did I."

"He keeps a mistress twenty years his junior," Sir Alistair interrupted him. "There are those on my staff who would no doubt applaud his initiative, but they're perceptive enough not to do so within my hearing."

The former director regarded him uncertainly, clearly reluctant to denounce the accusation. Sir Alistair gestured at the page, prompting him to resume.

"This next one is positively laughable," Sir Simon continued. "Nigel Thurloe's family dates back to Oliver Cromwell. He's served in a dozen postings around the world, taken tea with God knows how many prime ministers and presidents. He owns stock in half the major firms in Britain. He's hardly cut from left-wing cloth."

"Were you aware that Donald Maclean's father was a member of parliament?" Sir Alistair inquired. "He was knighted in 1916."

Sir Simon Turnbull's expression grew darker. He returned his attention to the page in his hand. "Finally, we have Kim Philby. I've known Kim for twenty years. His father was an assistant commissioner in India... he worked for MI6 in Saudi Arabia during the great war. Kim Philby would walk through fire for this country. He's gifted, intelligent... a Trinity College man. He's very highly regarded in Washington."

Sir Alistair sighed. "I wonder if I might ask the magnitude of your outstanding bill here," he inquired absently.

Sir Simon Turnbull glanced at him uncertainly, his expression suggesting that he feared he'd misheard the question.

"What's that?" he demanded.

"I can have a word with the steward if you'd prefer," Sir Alistair continued. "I'm certain he'd confide the figure to me in a discrete whisper."

The man before him glowered across the space between them, his expression growing minutely more perplexed.

"In a day or a year, my people will reduce the list from seven names to four, to two and finally to one. In the event that the last man standing turns out to be Willes, Thurloe or Philby and you've not seen fit to unburden yourself of your secrets, you will either be occupying a cell at Wormwood Scrubs or you will be receiving your mail in Moscow for the rest of your days. In either eventuality, I shall feel compelled to make good on your bill. I would be comforted in knowing the magnitude of my potential obligation."

Sir Simon Turnbull said nothing, and at length Sir Alistair got to his feet. "I believe you know how to contact me by telephone," he said. "The fellow who's busy with that list most assuredly does. You'd do well to make yours the first voice I hear."

He turned to leave the smoking room without indulging in a final glance at Sir Simon Turnbull. The oily silence was rent by the hiss of a match across the edge of its matchbox, and the all but inaudible gasp of breath through a fresh cigar.

21

What did the division manager of an engineering firm look like, Peter Kroger wondered uneasily. He could no longer suppress the growing suspicion that the face which had regarded him from his mirror this morning wasn't it. He'd had far too little time to prepare for this interview, and it was hardly his forte in any case. His palm had grown sweaty about the handle of his briefcase.

In the far corner of the broad office he'd arrived at, a secretary in a dress as gray as her hair assailed her typewriter with glassy-eyed malevolence, the staccato of its keys like machine-gun fire. Peter Kroger was not comforted by the sound, imagining a flight of bullets hurling toward him. He reminded himself that Great Britain was not disposed to executing agents of a foreign power.

His wife Helen had struggled to calm him as he'd left their bungalow that morning, reassuring him that he was to undertake a conversation with a businessman, not an interrogation by MI5. She'd seemed bemused by his formless dread, and he'd snapped at her to keep her smile to herself. It wasn't she who would be play-acting.

Moscow Center required too damned much from him. He glanced across the office at the secretary, who'd clearly forgotten his existence somewhere over the previous five minutes. The wait was unnerving him, and he considered instructing her to inquire of her superior how much longer he'd be expected to remain quiescent in the uncomfortable visitor's chair he'd been directed to. One of the telephones on her desk growled at her, the sound jarring and unfamiliar. She lifted its receiver, listened to it for a moment and then replaced it in its cradle. She smiled, a flicker of illumination maintained for a precise interval and then extinguished.

"Mr. Singleton will see you now," she said, and she gestured at a windowless door to his right. He got to his feet and the door opened.

Carl Singleton was an unremarkable fellow, Peter Kroger decided as he entered the man's office. He wore an inexpensive suit which hung on his flesh like a sausage skin. His hair consisted of a few strands of aging ginger across a scalp that appeared to have been groomed with a blowtorch. A pencil protruded from behind one ear. The most regrettable aspect of the man, he decided as he shook Carl Singleton's hand and permitted himself to be directed to a still more uncomfortable chair, was that the pencil clearly belonged where it was.

He glanced about himself. Much of the office was occupied by a sprawling green drafting table which luxuriated beneath the rays of an overhead lamp. It was littered with drawings, pens, a slide rule. The far wall was encrusted in books, and without being able to read their titles he knew with dreadful certainty that not a single page of them described anything remotely having to do with young women, leather restraints or instruments of pain.

Carl Singleton seated himself behind an untidy desk. "Mr. Kelly," he said, his voice coarse with the accent of Newcastle.

Peter Kroger illuminated the distressed smile he'd practiced earlier that morning. He shook his head. "Epstein," he corrected the man. "Abraham Epstein. I'm terribly sorry... John Kelly is one my engineers. He was injured yesterday evening... we had a beam fall..."

Carl Singleton's face grew darker. "I'm sorry to hear that," he said, clearly affecting concern for the fictitious man he'd never spoken with. "Is he... that is, was he seriously..."

Peter Kroger shook his head. "I'm told he'll be back at work in a fortnight," he said evenly. He'd practiced this phrase as well, with Helen performing the role of Carl Singleton.

The man behind his desk eased himself back in his chair. "You might have rung me... I'm sure I could see your Mr. Kelly when he's mended."

"John asked me to take this meeting in his place," Peter Kroger said. "He assured me that your time is quite valuable... and I'm afraid we have a deadline bearing down upon us."

Carl Singleton smiled. It was the perfect smile, Peter Kroger decided, the requisite countenance for a man who'd been granted a moment of status and then brushed with the camaraderie of the perennially over-worked.

It had been Helen who'd fabricated his character for him, and he permitted himself an instant's pleasure now at her perspicacity. He'd resigned himself to daubing himself with the wig and greasepaint of the performance of a genuine mechanical engineer, hoping to keep his audience with Carl Singleton sufficiently brief as to skirt any matters which might have revealed him for the fraud he'd have been. Helen had pointed out that far from not knowing how to operate a slide rule, he was uncertain what one was used for. She'd suggested that he portray instead an engineer's boss, that he might be granted leave for his ignorance.

He regarded himself now as an engineer's bookkeeper, which he decided granted him a suitable deportment.

"What is it that I can help you with, Mr. Epstein?" Carl Singleton asked.

Peter Kroger nodded. "I'm not certain what John will have told you," he began. "Our firm is installing the new hydrocracker facility at the BP refinery at Grangemouth, as I'm certain you know."

Carl Singleton knew no such thing. Peter Kroger hadn't known what a hydrocracker was a day earlier, or that BP had had a refinery at Grangemouth. He'd spent a quarter of an hour with a folding map before he'd ascertained that Grangemouth was in fact located in Scotland. The man before him nodded sagaciously none the less.

"We'll be sourcing a number of components which I believe your firm manufactures, but the matter we're most pressed for just now is high-temperature pressure access covers."

He watched Carl Singleton's eyebrows dance for an instant. "I know," he continued, "it's rather trivial, but as I understand it, we're in a tight spot and John Kelly was certain you could accommodate us... before his little mishap."

He regarded the man before him, cataloging the expressions that paraded across his face. "Well, yes," Carl Singleton said at some length, "it's nothing we can't handle, of course."

"And John will be back on his feet in a few weeks to deal with the heavy valves and plumbing," Peter Kroger added. The man's features softened perceptibly.

"What exactly is it that you need, then?"

Peter Kroger poised his briefcase upon his knees, opened it and extracted a page of handwritten notes. They were largely meaningless to him, having been prepared at his behest by someone at the Soviet consulate. He passed it across Carl Singleton's desk.

"This is what John asked me to refer to you," he said,

hoping his tone would suggest that he served in the capacity of messenger to those more enlightened.

Carl Singleton spent several minutes in silence before the page, tracing its scrawl with his finger as he read. Peter Kroger felt himself begin to perspire, imagining his sweat dissolving the tissue-paper mask of his assumed identity and exposing him. Carl Singleton clearly failed to notice him. He opened one of the drawers of his desk and withdrew a thin white booklet, which he proffered to Peter Kroger.

"I believe this will serve your needs," he said. "It's high carbon stainless steel, capable of withstanding three times the pressure you've specified. It uses a six-pin locking wheel mechanism with detent... we've sold a number of these to one of the Shell facilities in Holland."

Peter Kroger accepted the booklet and fanned its pages before himself for a moment, and then placed it in his briefcase. The specifications of the device were of scant interest to him, but they included drawings that described in detail the locking mechanism.

"We constructed a facility for the government down in Cornwall," Peter Kroger said as he closed his case. "I believe you supplied these for that project as well."

Carl Singleton smiled, the expression smug and reptilian. "You know as well as I do we're not allowed to discuss that project, Mr. Epstein."

"I do indeed," Peter Kroger said apologetically as he rose to leave.

22

Alec Grey drove his fingers through his hair, conscious of the rain that still nested within it. He pushed the door to behind him, averting his gaze from the glare of the lighting which ennobled the briefing room. The director regarded him indulgently from his customary throne at the head of the long table, not troubling himself to rise to his feet. Edward Blair stepped uncertainly before him, clearly discomfited by what the technician regarded as a shrine for which his cindered feet were hardly worthy.

"Sir Alistair," he said. He placed a large brown file on the table. "This is Edward Blair from Technical Services. I believe he's been mentioned in dispatches." He turned toward the younger man. "Mr. Blair, this is the lord your god Sir Alistair Fitzhenry. It's inadvisable to permit yourself to gaze directly upon his countenance for extended periods, lest you be struck blind. Crossing yourself in his presence is permitted."

Edward Blair seemed at a loss as to whether decorum required that he offer to shake the director by the hand. After several seconds of indecision, he accepted the chair Alec Grey indicated for him.

"You seem inordinately taken with yourself this morning, Mr. Grey," the director said, perhaps bemused by his introduction.

Alec Grey smiled and took the seat to the right of Sir Alistair. "The forces of light and order have known some small victories this day," he said.

"Have I been called here to learn of one of them?"

Alec Grey nodded, deciding as he did that he was seeing entirely too much of this room of late. Were he to permit this to continue, he feared, he would presently discover that he chose socks to match the rest of his attire, rather than merely selecting the ones that appeared reasonably clean.

"And Mr. Blair?"

Edward Blair clearly had the capacity to cause the director a degree of unrest. The pale-skinned, hulking trolls of Technical Services were scarcely granted sufficient security clearance to use the lavatories in this section of Leconfield House.

"Mr. Blair has come along to explain a spot of research he undertook at my behest," Alec Grey explained.

The director appeared to consider this, and as if his hands were being manipulated by an unseen party below the floor, he filled his pipe and lit it. He gestured toward Edward Blair with its stem at length. "Young man," he prompted the technician.

"Sir," Edward Blair said.

Alec Grey extracted a long slip of paper from his folder and slid it across the table to coil like a serpent that had chanced to nap upon the M1 motorway. Sir Alistair flattened it, regarded it, and then turned it over to see if its obverse was any more revealing. His expression grew questioning.

"It's not entirely blank, sir," Alec Grey explained in response to his unspoken query. "If you look closely, you'll notice a line of black spots along one edge."

The director examined the paper once more, and he appeared satisfied that it was as it had been described. He returned his attention to Edward Blair.

"It's a radio spectrograph," the technician explained hastily. "At least, I'm reasonably certain that's what it is."

"Is it?" the director asked, his tone making it clear that he wished a more detailed explanation.

"Mr. Grey provided me with that paper, sir," Edward Blair continued, his expression growing increasingly distraught at his proximity to the most dreadful power in the universe with which he was familiar. "He suggested that it might be a radio spectrum, and he instructed me to…" He paused, his features crumpling for an instant. "Perhaps I might begin again."

"Perhaps you might," Sir Alistair agreed.

"If you wished to know if a radio signal was present, you would switch on a wireless and tune it to the frequency of the signal," Edward Blair explained.

The director nodded.

"If you wished to know if a radio signal was present somewhere in the range of the wireless, you'd switch it on and tune it across its entire band until you found the signal."

The director nodded once more.

"I believe that paper was made by a machine to do much the same thing. It scans across the radio spectrum of interest, with a small lamp connected where its speaker would be. As its scans, the lamp moves over a strip of photographic film. When it finds a radio signal, the lamp is illuminated and it leaves a spot on the film."

The director regarded the paper for a moment longer. "I believe I understand, Mr. Blair," he said tonelessly.

"Due to its being classified, Mr. Grey was unable to inform me where this spectrograph was created," the technician continued, "but he provided me with a list of known radio transmitters in the area, and their relative strengths. You'll observe, sir, that some of the black spots are larger than others, indicating stronger radio sources."

"I do observe this, Mr. Blair," the director agreed, and Alec Grey appreciated that Sir Alistair had permitted himself a level of interest in the proceedings.

"Based on the information Mr. Grey provided me with, I've concluded that the spectrograph represents a range of one thousand to three thousand megacycles. If one assumes this, all but two of the black spots on the spectrograph represent radio sources that were included on the list Mr. Grey provided me with. One of the unknown ones is at 1420 megacycles, and the second is at 2840 megacycles, which I assume is the first harmonic of the 1420 megacycle source. The 1420 megacycle source is the largest spot... this indicates that it's the most powerful radio source."

The director glanced at the strip of paper for a moment longer and then released it, permitted it to coil itself once more.

"Is that all, Mr. Blair?" he inquired.

"Yes, sir, unless you have any questions."

"I do not," the director said.

As he'd been instructed to do, Edward Blair got to his feet and left the room, pulling the door to behind him.

The director sucked on his pipe, and he glanced after the departed technician as if he were considering the future employment prospects of a particularly backward grandchild. "I have no doubt, Mr. Grey, that you will expand upon what I've just been told until it enthralls me, but I must say, this is one of those occasions when I'm exceedingly grateful the taxpayers of Great Britain remain unaware of how we are disposing of their surplus pounds."

"I believe I know where the Russians have built their time stream research facility," Alec Grey said, and he heard a note of childlike anticipation in his own voice despite the gravity of his discovery.

"Do you indeed?" Sir Alistair said, his expression suddenly alert.

The director's attention alighted upon the brown file on the briefing room table, the only object between them save for the hulking specter of a tin of tobacco so toxic as to be reputed to corrode the metal which confined it if it were not smoked within a month of its purchase. Alec Grey chose to ignore the latter, and he disgorged the contents of the file across the table.

"Those appear to be CORONA photographs," the director said accusingly.

"Some of them," Alec Grey agreed. "Some of them are U2 overflights."

"We have a procedure in place for the examination of the CORONA material, Mr. Grey," he continued, his words growing more stern. "How did you manage to get those past my security people?"

Alec Grey felt himself become minutely irritated at the distraction. "The contents of each file containing CORONA photographs are counted before an officer is granted access to a section of the library, and then again after he leaves. I don't believe anyone actually looks at them, however. At the moment, some of them have been replaced with holiday snaps Hugh Somerfield took when he went to Tenerife with one of the girls in the registry this past June. I promise I shall return them as soon as we've finished."

Sir Alistair's expression darkened, and Alec Grey fleetingly imagined the men charged with the defense of the CORONA room being publicly flogged, or posted to the south pole. He decided that he would do well to reaffirm his purpose in abducting the photographs before the director began to consider including him in his scheme of divine retribution. He extracted one of the photographs and slid it across the table until it rested before the director.

"All the CORONA images made by the second and third cameras the Americans shot into space have a line of black spots along one edge of the image," Alec Grey said.

The director squinted at the picture before him, and at length he nodded. "I've seen them as well," he agreed. "I assumed they were some aspect of the process of creating the photographs while the CORONA cameras were in space."

"I initially thought so as well," Alec Grey agreed. "However, what little information the Americans have provided us about the CORONA KH-1 cameras indicates that they're all identical. In that the lines of spots don't appear in any of the photographs from the first CORONA camera, we must assume that the second and third cameras were modified to produce them."

"I trust I am to assume that these lines of spots are the radio frequency plots which you had Mr. Blair come by to explain."

"Yes, sir, they are," Alec Grey replied. "Edward Blair lacks sufficient clearance to see the CORONA images, of course, but I felt he could be trusted with a copy of one of the lines of spots. The one I gave him is from the picture you have now."

The director held the image before himself. Each of the CORONA photographs was indexed, and a master list referenced the index numbers to geographic locations. Without recourse to the index, Sir Alistair was clearly unable to ascertain which portion of the Soviet Union he was observing.

"It's the Murmansk naval base at Polyarnye," Alec Grey explained. "We know the radio frequencies used by the Soviet radar installation there, and of a number of radio sources nearby in Finland."

"I remain at something of a loss as to how this locates the Soviet time stream research facility for us," Sir Alistair said, "allowing that one does indeed exist."

Alec Grey willed himself to restrain his growing exasperation. "It has to do with the process of accessing the time stream," he explained. "David Hollings went on about it at his briefing. The apparatus emits considerable radio frequency energy at the natural resonant frequency of hydrogen, which is 1420 megacycles."

"And this accounts for the large spot on this photograph for which you have no other explanation," the director suggested, his words alight with skepticism.

"It does."

"It does if we assume that these spots mean what you and Mr. Blair believe them to mean."

"It does," Alec Grey insisted, "and the Americans clearly concur."

"What makes you say that?"

Alec Grey leant back in his chair, grateful for a moment's reprieve from the director's pipe. "Because the Americans didn't build CORONA to surveil the Soviet Union. They built it to find the Soviet time stream project. It's the only explanation for the cameras being equipped to generate radio spectrum plots in this portion of the spectrum. I couldn't help noticing that while the second CORONA camera was tasked to observe a variety of targets across the Soviet Union, the third one took the bulk of its pictures in the north west."

"You're implying that the Americans also suspect a Soviet time stream project exists," the director said.

"I was hoping you might inquire with Washington, sir," Alec Grey suggested. The director's eyes narrowed. He clearly found the prospect of approaching the CIA with a begging bowl in hand distasteful.

Sir Alistair shook his head as if to dispel an errant thought. "This photograph represents thousands of square miles, Mr. Grey," he said. "Even if there is a Soviet facility down there, this hardly provides us with its precise location."

Alec Grey smiled coldly, and he spread the remaining photographs from his file across the table. "I agree, sir," he said. "I had a look through some of the additional

photographs to see if we might narrow the scope somewhat."

He slid the first of his pictures toward the director.
"This one is from a U2 overflight in May of 1958,"
he began. "We're looking at a relatively uninhabited region
of Murmansk, not far from the Finnish border. You'll
observe the steep valley in the lower left corner, with a substantial river running along it."

"I do," Sir Alistair agreed uncertainly. Alec Grey
permitted himself a moment's sympathy for the director.
The images in the overflight photographs required considerable effort to interpret.

"What's of interest in this photograph is that nothing had been constructed in this valley as of the middle of
1958."

Alec Grey offered a second photograph to the director, this one of a considerably larger area. "This is a photograph from the first CORONA camera. Unfortunately, it
doesn't show the valley from the first image... the valley is
several miles beyond the lower edge of the picture.
However, you can see substantial electric power lines running into the image from the lower edge. The power lines
run to a large installation near the center of the photograph."

"That tells us that the Soviets need a great deal of
electricity for something," the director agreed. "They
could be manufacturing tractors."

Alec Grey felt himself touched with amusement. "It's
unlikely, sir," he said. "It's brutally cold up there. The
Soviets maintain a naval station in Murmansk because it
gives them access to the Barents Sea. They perform little
heavy manufacturing there, owing to the cost of maintaining their people in the extreme arctic. That's not the issue,
however."

"Perhaps you would explain what the issue is, Mr.
Grey," the director prompted him.

"Based on the size of the electric transmission lines in that photograph, the power station they're connected to is capable of producing power on the scale of Battersea... perhaps five hundred million watts. The most recent Soviet hydroelectric project of which we are aware required eight years to complete, and it was capable of generating less than fifty million watts. The Soviets built this one in just over two years, in one of the most inhospitable places on Earth, and in a region which appears to have electric demands that would scarcely call for a hundredth of this power. I am informed that there is no single civilian industry in Britain which could account for this much electric power."

"Our Mr. Hollings could no doubt mention a use for it," the director muttered.

"Yes, sir, I believe he could," Alec Grey agreed.

Sir Alistair put his hand to his chin and regarded the CORONA photograph. "It seems an odd place to put their time stream facility, Mr. Grey," he mused.

Alec Grey leant back in his chair. "Yes, sir, it does," he said coldly. "That's what makes this so troubling."

The director glanced up at him.

"There aren't all that many locations within the Soviet Union that would have been suitable for this installation," he continued. "They would have had the same requirements we did when we constructed the project in Cornwall... a substantial electric grid, water for cooling, somewhere that could be made secure with a military presence close by..."

"And they have all those things here," the director conceded, "but they're within shouting distance of the Finnish border. Moscow was quite aware of the U2 missions when they began this. They must have known it was only a matter of time before we learned of their activities. I find it difficult to believe they couldn't have located it in a more inaccessible area."

Alec Grey nodded, pleased that Sir Alistair had arrived at an appreciation of the problem before them without the necessity of his expanding upon it.

The director glanced at Alec Grey. "Perhaps this one might be a... a red herring," he said. "The Americans built their time stream project in the middle of the Utah desert, with access to neither abundant water nor a great deal of electric. There might be a second, more secret one somewhere else in the Soviet Union."

Alec Grey pretended to consider the suggestion. He'd raised it with his own people several days earlier, and he'd subsequently agreed with a variety of dissenting arguments. "It seems certain that the Americans chose to build their project in the desert because it's effectively impregnable... even if none of our people can imagine how they've made it work out there. I think it unlikely the Soviets will have penetrated it." He paused, and reached across the table to touch the photograph before the director.

"The one in Murmansk," he continued, "is emitting energy at 1420 megacycles. It's not a deception... it's clearly operational."

"You've not explained why the Soviets don't appear to care whether we learn of its existence."

Alec Grey was silent for a time, and when he spoke he heard a distinct ripple of uncertainty in his own voice. "You're quite right, sir," he said. "I've no explanation. The only occasions of the Soviets not being concerned with their own security have involved undertakings which they intended to construct, utilize and then discard before their lack of security became an issue."

"I hardly think that's likely of their time stream facility," Sir Alistair said. "These things take years to build, a fortune to operate and no one knows how long to reach a state where they're anything more than a wind-up toy for scientists. They're not something you'd build to use once and then abandon."

"We certainly wouldn't," he agreed.

23

The taste of blood was lurid upon his tongue, a metallic syrup like something he'd sampled once as a child and loathed thereafter. He felt a leaden trickle of it drool from the corner of his mouth. His belly threatened to defy him, and he resisted the urge to vomit, to disgorge the cauldron of blood and bile that was his stomach.

Andrei Bogdanov permitted himself a flickering glance at the ill-defined features of the man before him. He was a creature of iron and shadow, his eyes like waning coals. He tightened a glove across the knuckles of his right hand, his arm as taut as a bowstring. His teeth flashed in the ragged light, ivory and stainless steel.

Somewhere in the far distance, a gout of steam exploded from a relief valve, the exhalation of something blind and godlike. He felt the crush of machinery in the gloom, desperate to know to where he'd been brought. He willed himself to affix his attention to the man before him.

The man behind him was a ghost, ineffable, known only by the hands which pinned his arms like manacles, alternately winching him from the steel chair they'd provided for him and hurling him back to its embrace at a nod from his tormentor.

He met the man's gaze for a moment as his arm tensed once more, determined to transfix him as his gloved fist again burrowed into the bruised flesh of his belly. He grunted, a cloud of blood spat from between clenched teeth. His flicker of defiance appeared to have gone unnoticed.

His knees threatened to betray him, but the hands that protruded from the darkness at his back were immobile, unyielding. He coughed, feeling himself begin to choke.

"Comrade?" the man said, as if he were inquiring about the health of an acquaintance. Andrei Bogdanov glanced at the dark form, his vision awash in his tears.

The interrogation was being conducted in English. He'd observed as much before his beating had begun, when he'd addressed his captors in Russian and been rebuked for his use of what he knew to be their common language. Someone else was listening, he decided, or there was a tape recorder's spools revolving amidst the other machinery of this place.

Someone English was listening. He felt a new flicker of humiliation amidst the embers of his pain. His beating was a Russian affair, not to be shared by foreigners even if it was taking place on their soil.

The man before him grasped him by his hair and drew his head back, staring into his eyes for a moment as if he were seeking an encrypted message written on the inner surface of his skull. "Comrade?" he repeated.

"Yes… comrade," he replied, his words thick, oozing past the mire in which his tongue wallowed.

The man smiled coldly. He raised his fist to be sure Andrei Bogdanov could view it clearly and he made a point of adjusting his glove.

Andrei Bogdanov summoned what little resolve as remained to him, willing himself to gaze into the man's eyes, to ignore the fist.

The KGB scripted its beatings, anticipated the per-
formances of its prisoners with every bit as much precision
as a choreographer at the Bolshoi. Generations of men like
this one had worn the gloves, assumed the expression of
contempt, spoken the words in a harsh stage whisper,
nodded to their unseen subordinates. His role in this
drama called for him to begin to whine and plead and
babble and confess, to hurl himself to the bloody concrete
and contort himself into the aspect of a dog being pun-
ished for its lack of fealty. He'd worn the gloves himself
once, and as he recalled the sensation of the leather across
his own knuckles, he thought it a lapse in the preparation
of the man before him that he'd not been suitably briefed.

The ones who pleaded for their lives invariably lost
them, or wished as much.

A gloved hand touched his cheek, minutely adjusting
the posture of his face.

"What have you to tell me, comrade?" the man
inquired.

He considered the immobile features swelling in his
awareness. "I have nothing to tell you that was not in my
report, comrade," he replied mechanically. "Nothing that I
failed to tell you an hour ago."

The words oozed like darkening blood across his
lips. He could no longer recall how many times he'd
repeated them.

His tormentor drew back his own lips, revealing a
still greater wealth of steel teeth. He raised his fist until it
was a centimeter from Andrei Bogdanov's nose, until it
deflected his ragged breath and grew damp with the vapors
of his stomach.

Had this cavern of pipes and pumps and valves been
less stygian, he might well have been able to ascertain
whether the expression before him was one of anger or
swelling desperation. He would assume the latter, he
decided abruptly. His guts would survive few additional

blows without serious injury, and he resented the prospect of submitting himself to the ministrations of an English doctor.

The KGB interrogator had superiors as well, and he would be called upon to submit a report to one of them. Was that sweat forming upon the man's brow, he wondered, refusing himself permission to smile.

"Comrade," he said at length. The man lowered his fist minutely. "*Pazhalsta,* permit me to request a favor, comrade. If it is not your intention to kill me, I ask that you not strike my face. My usefulness will be greatly diminished if I appear injured... people will be more likely to notice me if my face is bruised. You understand."

The man's eyes widened for an instant, and he withdrew his fist. His expression grew minutely darker. This was clearly not an aspect of the performance for which he had rehearsed. Andrei Bogdanov drew a flicker of solace from his mounting confusion.

His tormentor stepped back into the darkness, turned and gazed for a moment into the tangle of machinery. His form became an aspect of the rust and oil, ill-defined, wrought of ancient steel.

"Why did you kill the English scientist, Arthur Dunross?" he barked into the gloom.

"Comrade, it is as I have said, my instructions..."

The man strode angrily from the shadows, his gloved fist suddenly alight, a centimeter from his nose. "Why did you kill the English scientist, Andrei Mikhailovich?" he repeated, his snarl both homicidal and ludicrously overacted. "What exactly were your instructions?"

Andrei Bogdanov paused, and he sought for the man's eyes. This was a variant of his questioning which had not occurred previously. The performance had progressed to a new act. His interrogator had abandoned his effort to entrap the subject in a deception, and now sought information. He permitted his shoulders to relax minutely.

"I received a telephone call at my apartment," he began. "The caller said one word, *nozhneetsi*... scissors... and then he rang off. This told me to visit a dead drop in Notting Hill. The dead drop contained a folded sheet of paper, coded with a one-time pad. When I decoded the message, I found instructions to visit Arthur Dunross in his hotel room and liquidate him."

"The voice on the telephone... did you recognize it?"

Andrei Bogdanov sighed. "No, comrade, but this is not uncommon when I am contacted in this manner."

"Was it a Russian speaking?"

He paused to consider this, surprised for an instant that it had not occurred to him to do so earlier. "I... I cannot say for certain. It was a single word."

"It could have been anyone, then, Andrei Mikhailovich," the man said, his tone growing decidedly accusatory. "It could have been the British themselves."

He shook his head minutely. "You forget the message, encoded with a one-time pad. Only I and my controller have copies of the pad. The British could not have correctly encoded the message... and I hardly think they would have wished their own scientist killed, even if he was betraying them."

The man nodded, and he said nothing for a time. When he again spoke, he sounded very much unlike the KGB thug he'd thus far portrayed. "You understand, comrade," he said softly, "you have killed perhaps the most valuable asset the Soviet Union had in the British time stream research project. Someone must be accountable for this inexcusable error."

"I followed my instructions... comrade," he said sternly, as he had done several times earlier. "I followed my instructions as a good Soviet citizen would. If you find the owner of the one-time pad that corresponds to mine, you will know who sent me to kill the English scientist."

"Have you retained the message you collected from

your dead drop?" the man asked, a wisp of anticipation in his question.

He forced himself to gaze into the lifeless shark's eyes before him. "Please, comrade," he said, a deliberate note of reproach in his words. "I burnt it the minute after I read it."

The face before him exhaled audibly, its breath foul with *gallupsi,* bitter cigarette smoke and coffee. "You cannot imagine the shit you have kicked up." The interrogator regarded him thoughtfully for a time. "If I was permitted, I would see to it that you left this place in pieces."

"If you did, comrade, Moscow would lose a loyal servant," Andrei Bogdanov said evenly, touched with renewed concern over the man's intentions.

He waved dismissingly. "Moscow is buried up to its arse in loyal servants." He nodded to the owner of the unseen hands which pinned Andrei Bogdanov's arms. Fingers bit more deeply into his flesh, and he felt himself being thrust into the chair once more. The metal frame protested menacingly, twisting beneath its burden.

The interrogator loomed above him, his features distorted by the odd perspective. Andrei Bogdanov permitted a smile to flicker across his features before the man returned his attention to his labors. The performance had resumed. He was intended to contort himself in his uncomfortable chair, to assume an aspect of supplication before his tormentor. He gazed blankly at the buckle which restrained the man's trousers.

"There is another matter, Andrei Mikhailovich," the voice rasped from the blackness above him. He resisted the urge to face its source.

"Yes, comrade," he acknowledged.

"You have a new asset. She is known by the code name FINCH."

Andrei Bogdanov felt his eyes narrow and the hairs at the back of his neck rise with curiosity. FINCH was Alice

Woodward, and the fact that his interrogator referred to
FINCH as female suggested he knew as much. It disturbed
him that this animal had been granted access to so sensitive a fragment of intelligence. Upon further consideration,
it disturbed him still more that whoever was listening to
this conversation, or whoever would be permitted to hear
a recording of it, was to be admitted into the secret of Alice
Woodward's betrayal of MI5.

"Yes, comrade."

"She has brought us some useful information, but I
am instructed to tell you that it is all too vague. Moscow
requires a great deal of additional information about the
British time stream research, and especially about the
process of Uranium refinement."

"Yes, comrade," Andrei Bogdanov agreed. "She has
only made one drop to date. Perhaps her next package of
documents..."

"Perhaps will not be satisfactory," the interrogator
interrupted him. "Moscow requires specific intelligence,
and it requires it immediately. You are instructed to make
contact with FINCH and motivate her to surpass her earlier
efforts."

"I will do as I am instructed, comrade," Andrei
Bogdanov said, sensing the approaching termination of his
interrogation. He felt his heart flutter in his chest as he
permitted himself the realization that he would remain
breathing at its conclusion. "I am uncertain how I will persuade her to increase her activities."

The man before him must have nodded once more,
as Andrei Bogdanov felt the hands that pinioned him to the
chair relax and then vanish from his arms. Something
dropped into his lap. He clutched at it, regarding it in the
shards of light which haunted this place. His interrogator
had removed one of his leather gloves.

"I suggest you use that," the man before him said,
and he turned to leave.

24

W hen Alec Grey had first been shown his present office, its desk had been uncluttered save for a neat stack of memoranda. Upon inspection, the pages had been from his predecessor to Sir Simon Turnbull, the previous director of MI5, complaining about the Lilliputian dimensions of the room and its appointments. Alec Grey had been unsuccessful in ascertaining who had provided him with these documents, but he'd understood their intent well enough. The previous occupant of this room had protested its inadequacies for much of his tenure, and had accomplished nothing more than a stack of papers.

He considered the office to be the antithesis of the one Sir Alistair Fitzhenry was wont to summon him to from time to time. Little more than a windowless telephone box with pretensions, most of its interior space was occupied by a cramped steel desk upon which various previous tenants appeared to have vented their displeasure with unnameable blunt objects; a substantial iron safe inconveniently located at the far side of the desk, but which was too heavy to shift; an oak chair on wheels that clearly dated back to a period in the history of the empire when people were considerably shorter, and had no feeling in their backsides; and a steel visitor's chair from which most of the stuffing had emerged, and which Alec Grey used in the absence of a file drawer.

Hugh Somerfield was considerably more affronted by the office on Alec Grey's behalf than he himself was. He spent little time behind its door. A more substantial office would have implied an obligation to keep it tidy.

The office resembled a rubbish tip at present, he chided himself absently. He'd compelled one of his more substantial towers of low-priority files to vacate the visitor's chair in favor of David Hollings. Bereft of suitable accommodations on his desk, it now languished in several smaller heaps across the floor.

Alec Grey leant back in his medieval chair for a moment and gazed at the rotted plaster of the ceiling and a dusty lamp in which a single remaining bulb wheezed toward its imminent demise. David Hollings withdrew a packet of cigarettes from his suit coat and began to glance uncertainly about the clutter of Alec Grey's desk for an ashtray.

"I shouldn't light that," Alec Grey said without turning his attention to the scientist. "Technical Services informs me that with the door closed, there's only enough breathable air in here for two people to survive for about fifteen minutes. Their calculations clearly don't allow for a source of combustion."

David Hollings smiled and returned his cigarettes to his pocket.

"How's the weather in Cornwall?" Alec Grey inquired.

"I'll let you know if I'm ever permitted back there."

Alec Grey detected a note of rebuke in the tone of the man before him. "I'd have thought a few spies would have been a welcomed diversion from all those pipes and computers. A fellow could grow bored with just one thing on his desk, year after year."

David Hollings regarded the chaos of Alec Grey's

desk with an air of distrust. "It has a wealth of possibilities, our time stream," he mused.

Alec Grey raised his eyebrows, diverted by the thought.

"Bernard Oliphant... one of our senior research people... he maintains that one day women across Britain will be pulling the Sunday roast out of darkmatter cookers," David Hollings suggested. Alec Grey considered whether he was intended to take the notion seriously.

"There was an American engineer a few years ago," David Hollings continued. "He noticed that his sweets had melted in his trouser pocket after he stood beside a working radar set. Bright spark that he was, he put the magnetron valve from a radar into a box and made it into a cooker. The radio waves vibrate the water molecules in food, heats them up and supper's ready in no time. The Americans call them microwave ovens."

"Impatient lot, the Americans," Alec Grey observed.

David Hollings appeared to have ignored him. "The fundamental substance that makes the time stream accessible is darkmatter. We don't know what it is, or where it is... Mr. Einstein tells us that it must exist, and that it's tremendously massive. In that we know it's necessary to make the time stream go, and the time stream does in fact work, we're reasonably certain it's out there somewhere."

"It sounds rather like what we do here with the Soviets," Alec Grey observed.

"Bernard Oliphant has a drawing for a darkmatter cooker... he's convinced it would work, if some darkmatter could be found to power it. It places food between several pieces of the stuff and switches the gravitational fields from the darkmatter on and off very quickly... vibrates the water molecules just like a microwave oven, but it uses almost no electric."

Alec Grey nodded, deciding abruptly that he was unlikely ever to ascertain whether David Hollings was serious. "It sounds like a brilliant invention," he said dryly. "Imagine the advantages to a thing like that."

David Hollings appeared surprised by his enthusiasm. "Do you think so?"

"If something went wrong and you were to burn the Sunday joint, you'd have almost everything you needed to send it back in time and try again."

David Hollings scowled briefly, and he began to torment his packet of cigarettes. He glanced around the office that confined him as if to remind himself of his purpose here. At length he returned his attention to Alec Grey.

"Sir Alistair mentioned you had some photographs to show me," he said, "but he didn't seem to know what they were."

"I think it best to keep it thus for the time being, out of consideration for the director," Alec Grey mused. "They point to a conspiracy of the sort that's wont to try Sir Alistair's patience."

"I would've thought he'd have been keen to know of any conspiracies on his patch."

Alec Grey smiled. "I'm quite certain he is. It's the ones he merely suspects that get his knickers in a twist." He permitted his chair to return to its upright posture. After a moment's consideration he opened one of the drawers of his desk and withdrew a file.

"You'll recall the briefing I received when I was indoctrinated into the project," Alec Grey continued. "You conducted it down in Cornwall on my behalf... lasted for slightly less than a century, by my recollection." He smiled accusingly.

"I don't remember the duration, but I've been told we have peculiar ideas about time," David Hollings replied. He was clearly pleased with himself over his observation.

"I'm concerned with a specific portion of it at the moment," Alec Grey said. "I'd like you to cast your mind back to your talk about the materials involved in accessing the time stream... specifically, to Uranium."

David Hollings nodded uncertainly. "It's the precursor element in the production of Berkelium."

"Yes, I recall. It's the only naturally-occurring one of the lot... all the others are derived from it."

"I'm not certain I'd describe the Uranium we use as 'naturally-occurring,'" David Hollings said. "There's a frightfully complex refining process to separate the Uranium 235 we use from the bulk of natural Uranium, which is predominately Uranium 238. Less than three quarters of one percent of natural Uranium is actually of any use to us."

"Yes," Alec Grey agreed. "That's what the conspiracy is about, to some extent." He touched the file on his desk. "One of the other things I recall from your briefing was that Uranium 235 is quite poisonous."

David Hollings shook his head. "I believe you recall me mentioning it was toxic," he said. "It's not quite the same."

"Toxic, then," Alec Grey allowed. "You said at the time that living tissue that got close to the stuff would be damaged... that the effect would be similar to severe burning."

"Yes, that's correct. We have elaborate procedures for handling it. After refining, it's stored in lead containers to prevent the staff from being exposed to it."

"Do you know if anyone's been exposed?" Alec Grey inquired.

"There are no cases of which I'm aware," David Hollings replied. "We hear all manner of rumors out of Utah, of course. It's my understanding that the Americans have done some experiments with animals."

"What became of them?" Alec Grey asked. "The animals, not the Americans."

David Hollings leant back in his chair. "Oh, they all

died, of course. Exposure to substantial levels of radioactivity is invariably fatal."

"Is that what you call it?"

"Radioactivity," David Hollings confirmed, and he
smiled indulgently. "It was covered in the briefing."

Alec Grey chose to ignore the mild rebuke. He
opened his file and pushed several photographs across his
desk toward David Hollings. The scientist accepted them
without comment and he began to consider them. His eyes
widened.

"Is that what someone who died of exposure to
Uranium would look like?" Alec Grey asked.

David Hollings paused for a time before he replied.
"I... I can't say for certain, you understand, but it does
seem probable. Who was this poor bastard?"

Alec Grey shook his head. "We don't know as yet.
I'd harbored some hope that he might be familiar to you."

"I'm not certain he'd be familiar to his own mother
in this state. Was he admitted to hospital?"

"No.. and that's one of the troubling aspects of this
business," Alec Grey replied. "Two of my lads were doing
a spot of burglary for queen and country when they came
upon this chap. One of them had the presence of mind to
photograph him."

David Hollings regarded the photographs in silence
for a time. His attention appeared drawn to one of them in
particular, and he spent some while staring at it, clearly
growing more disquieted by the inhuman figure it portrayed.

"I believe we have something of a problem," he said
at length. His words were cast into the gloom of Alec
Grey's office like a pronouncement of the impending end
of the world.

"I'm certain we do... at the very least, the fellow in
photographs does."

"No, you don't understand," David Hollings continued, and he returned the photograph to Alec Grey's desk. The dead man it depicted stared blankly at the ceiling through eyes crushed to slits. "This chap didn't just die of exposure to Uranium. He died of exposure to our Uranium."

Alec Grey permitted his attention to be drawn to the picture, despite his having scrutinized it for some time prior to David Hollings' arrival. He'd succeeded in convincing himself that the dead man in Mayrick Road could have come by his demise from no other source, but it startled him none the less when the scientist gave voice to his suspicions.

"How can you be certain?"

David Hollings leant forward and indicated the left hip of the figure in the photograph. Alec Grey had noticed it earlier. While much of the visible flesh of the dead man appeared scorched, there was a roughly circular area just below his waist that was as black as night. "This is one of ours," he said.

"What is?"

David Hollings appeared to wish to drive the image of the dead man from his awareness. He leant back in his chair once more, removing it from his immediate perception. "When the initial work began on the project, we constructed an apparatus to refine Uranium, and then to handle it so it could ultimately be converted into Berkelium. We required a standard-size mold to form the blanks of Uranium. The size and shape weren't greatly important, so long as the blanks were of a consistent size. Philip Wymark, our machinist... he used a saucepan to make the original mold. All the later apparatus that's involved with Berkelium production was designed around disks of material nineteen centimeters in diameter... that was the size of the bottom of the saucepan."

Alec Grey considered the photograph. Nineteen centimeters was about seven and a half inches. It seemed to match the area of the dead man indicated by the circular burnt area.

"What I can't understand is how he'd come to have placed the Uranium blank next to his hip like that," David Hollings said, his tone suggesting that no one in his right mind would imagine doing so.

"He carried it for some time in the pocket of his overcoat," Alec Grey explained, without glancing up at his visitor.

"He'd have had to've been mad to do such a thing."

"It was just a lump of metal to him, I imagine. We may surmise that if he'd been briefed as to its true nature and the lingering death he could expect as a result of his contact with it, he'd have refused to have anything to do with it." Alec Grey wrested his attention from the photograph. "Is it possible the Uranium that caused this could have come from another source... the Americans, perhaps."

"The Americans would be the only other source of refined Uranium," David Hollings said, "but, no, it couldn't be theirs. They form refined Uranium into rods. Their Uranium rods would be too large for a man to carry about secretly, even if he were mad enough to wish to do so."

"They might be onto something. You say our Uranium blanks are stored in lead containers... how large would one of them be?"

David Hollings held his hands before him and indicated a box slightly more than two feet on a side.

"What would one weigh?"

"Forty or fifty kilograms, I believe."

Alec Grey smiled. "In English, for those of us who didn't read physics at university."

"Eighty to one hundred pounds."

"So a man could conceivably lift one without assistance if he were reasonably fit and somewhat motivated," Alec Grey suggested.

"He could... although none of our lot fancies getting near the stuff. When it's moved about, we use trolleys."

"How difficult would it be for someone to pinch one of the Uranium blanks?"

David Hollings regarded him wordlessly for a moment. When he spoke, his voice seemed to have been put out of tune. "I don't imagine it would be unthinkable to get one out the building. Getting it past the gate guards would be well nigh impossible, though. They've orders to search everything leaving the facility... overcoat pockets not excepted."

"I wouldn't imagine the chap in the photos is the one who removed it, and I'm quite certain it wasn't transported through the gate. If I had to guess, I'd say it was taken from your facility, carried to the perimeter fence and chucked over so our friend here could retrieve it later."

David Hollings put his hand to his chin. "None of our people would dream of doing such a thing," he said coldly.

"Arthur Dunross is our current favorite," Alec Grey said, meeting the scientist's gaze. "I'd be the first to agree that his connection to the fellow in these pictures is somewhat tenuous, but he's beginning to appear to be a proper fit for the frame."

He watched a parade of expressions creep across David Hollings' features. The man clearly did not wish to believe his deceased colleague had been capable of espionage and treason. There was a Mrs. Arthur Dunross somewhere in the countryside of Cornwall, Alec Grey recalled, and it might well fall to David Hollings to explain some aspect of her husband's secret life to her.

"What does a Uranium blank look like?" Alec Grey inquired, deciding that David Hollings would be of considerably greater assistance were he not granted leave to swim in the mire of his own thoughts.

The man before him appeared to seize upon the offer

of a query he could answer definitively. "Uranium is a silvery metal, almost white in daylight. You wouldn't see it, however... the blank would be housed in a casing of borosilicate glass, which is brown."

"Is that to shield your people from the... radioactivity?" Alec Grey asked.

"No... as I said, that requires a hundredweight of lead. The borosilicate absorbs neutrons from the Uranium. If it were left to its own devices, the Uranium would emit neutrons, which would cause a cascade reaction. It would grow increasingly hot as more and more neutrons were released. Some of our chaps are of the opinion that an uncontrolled Uranium reaction could burn right the way through the crust of the Earth."

"I find myself growing less comfortable by the minute with the thought of the Russians having this stuff," Alec Grey observed. He leant back in his chair once more, and he resumed his consideration of the deplorable state of his ceiling. "Would one blank be sufficient to run your time machine?" he asked.

David Hollings disliked having the time stream apparatus referred to as a 'time machine,' Alec Grey knew, and he heard the scientist sigh. "It would depend upon the nature of the time stream access one required," he replied. "A sufficiently small object could be projected into the stream for short distance with the Berkelium derived from one blank of Uranium, yes. Accessing the time stream for a distance of any reasonable interest would require two or more. However, even if the Russians have a chunk of Uranium, they don't have the apparatus to utilize it."

Alec Grey glanced at David Hollings. "Yes," he said. "Yes, in point of fact, I'm convinced they do."

"You can't be serious," David Hollings said, his eyes narrowing.

"I seem to get told that a great deal of late, and I'm invariably quite serious at the time. I'm not permitted to disclose the intelligence upon which my belief is based, but I'm reasonably certain it's sound."

"Christ," David Hollings whispered.

Alec Grey was silent for several minutes as he considered his ceiling. In the corner of his eye, David Hollings withdrew his packet of cigarettes, extracted one of its contents and then appeared to recall his earlier admonition to refrain from lighting it. He returned the cigarette to its confinement and then set about tormenting the cellophane that enshrouded it.

The office had grown quite still by the time Alec Grey again leant forward in his chair and addressed his visitor.

"You concocted a set of documents for us to feed to the Soviets," he began slowly, "to sidetrack their time stream research."

David Hollings nodded, appearing to permit himself a measured smile. He'd clearly enjoyed the diversion from his usual responsibilities, the shared conspiracy of a taste of spycraft. Alec Grey recalled fleetingly that Alice Woodward had described her part in the journey of David Hollings' fabrications behind the curtain as 'exciting.'

"How difficult would it be to create a second set for us?" he continued. "This one would do somewhat more than just sidetrack them."

"I'm not certain I'm following you."

"I'm convinced the Soviets have a working time stream facility, or nearly so. I believe that all they're missing is a sufficient supply of refined Uranium to bring it on stream and complete its final adjustments. I'm quite certain they've managed to steal every bit of it from us."

David Hollings appeared genuinely shocked at the suggestion.

"I'm not permitted to explain the nature of our intelligence, but based on the technology and science we know they've been after for the past few years, I'm certain they barely understand what they've built. They've no one of the

caliber of you or your people... just a few competent engineers, and a smattering of physicists."

He watched as David Hollings reluctantly nodded
his head. "I imagine it would be possible... given suitable
plans, one could make a stab at reproducing the Cornwall
facility. The amount of information required..."

"It would be unwise to underestimate Moscow's
capacity for acquiring information," Alec Grey interrupted
him. "I'm occasionally called before the director for half an
hour of ritual embarrassment as a result of my doing so."

"What is it you want these documents to contain?"

"I should like to know if it would be possible for you
to create a set of believable papers dealing with the final
stages of the assembly and fine-tuning of a time-stream
apparatus which, if followed blindly, would result in its
destroying itself."

David Hollings stared at him as if he'd been slapped.
He leant forward, resting his elbows upon the edge of Alec
Grey's desk.

"You don't know what you're asking," he said, his
jaw rigid.

"I know precisely what I'm asking, and I'm afraid I
know a great deal more about why I'm asking it than I'm
able to say."

David Hollings shook his head. "This goes way
beyond the last lot. It's one thing to confuse the bolshies...
what you're suggesting will almost certainly kill people."

"Yes it will," Alec Grey agreed.

"I don't have a problem with pulling their legs and
messing them about, but I'm not sure I can murder the
poor bastards just because they've copied a few of our
papers."

Alec Grey sighed. "I'd have agreed with you until
quite recently," he said, surprised that he heard very little
rancor in his own voice. "You, Sir Alistair, the
Americans... everyone was certain that we'd all be long in

our graves by the time the Soviets developed a working time stream facility. Sir Alistair jokingly suggested that we let them have the basic design of the thing so they'd have a proper understanding of the magnitude of what they were up against. Unfortunately, it's turned out that every bloody one of you was wrong."

"How can you be so certain?"

"Because in the past week or so the Soviets have begun burning assets like matchwood to acquire refined Uranium, or the technology to create it. Not plans for the cooling system, not schematics for the control computers, not specifications for the metallurgy of the reactance chamber... they're not after the design of the car, they want the petrol to make it run. The only reasonable con- clusion to be drawn from this is that they have the machine."

David Hollings stared blankly at him, and upon regarding the scientist's expression he suspected he might well have worn it himself when he'd first appreciated the magnitude of the Soviet penetration into the time stream project. "How close are they?"

"We can't know for certain."

David Hollings eased himself back into his chair and covered his face with one of his huge palms, glancing about the office through its fingers.

"I was most impressed with your photographs of our secret room in Kensington Palace Gardens," Alec Grey continued. "I have no difficulty imagining Moscow pop- ping little mechanical cameras out of the time stream in this building, and upon consideration, I suspect that will become the least of our worries if they bring their project on stream." He drove his fist into the top of his desk to be certain he had David Hollings' complete attention. "I must ask you again, David... can you create a set of documents the Soviets can steal, follow to the letter and destroy their project with?"

David Hollings stared at him for a moment longer before he nodded. "Yes," he said, his voice all but lifeless. "Yes... yes, it's all we can do to keep the whole works from going up in smoke most days, and we know what we're about." He glanced around the office, clearly considering the problem. "We can instruct them to reduce the magnetic restraining density by a factor of ten... the time stream flow would tear them apart before they knew what hit them."

"What sort of damage would... whatever you've just said cause?"

"I can't say for certain... for reasons I'm sure you'll appreciate, it's not something we've attempted ourselves. If such a thing were to take place at the Cornwall facility, the main reactance chamber would be destroyed by the shock and most of the rest of the facility would be severely damaged. Everyone not killed outright would die of exposure to radioactivity... as your friend in the photographs did."

"Can you be reasonably certain it will work?" Alec Grey asked.

"If it's as you've described, and they'll follow any instructions they pinch from us, yes, I'm quite certain it will work," David Hollings replied, "but... it's bloody barbaric."

"Yes," Alec Grey agreed coldly, "yes it is... bloody barbaric. The only thing that could make a civilized man imagine such an act is the level of barbarism the Soviet Union will inflict upon the rest of the world if they find themselves with access to the time stream."

David Hollings nodded his agreement. "Does Sir Alistair know what you have in mind?"

"I intend to have a word with him when we're finished here," Alec Grey said, feeling a moment of dread at the idea. "He's arguably the sharpest director MI5 has enjoyed in living memory. He's not known to shrink from taking difficult decisions... this will be his opportunity to justify his reputation."

"I shall know some small comfort in your being the one to bring this to him, rather than I," David Hollings said.

Alec Grey smiled ruefully. "What's the soonest you could complete the documents?"

The scientist looked thoughtfully at the wall behind Alec Grey. "If I drive back to Cornwall this evening and I work through the weekend, they could be ready by Sunday night, or Monday morning at the latest."

"Splendid."

"Shall I ring you when they're complete, then?"

Alec Grey permitted himself to smile once more. "I'll have Hugh Somerfield accompany you. When you're done with them, he'll drive them back to London. I intend to be unavailable for the weekend."

25

Saturday, October 21

It had been raining for several minutes before he encountered a lay-by to pull into. The car's seats were all but at the level of the tarmac it rode on, and he'd been occupying his for what seemed like most of the day. He reached over the door for the release handle, pried himself from the machine's leather embrace, shook the water from his hair like a spaniel and set about raising the top.

Alice Woodward looked decidedly less sodden than he felt as he returned to his seat. He'd been quite taken with the car when he'd collected her at daybreak, but it seemed now like an antique ride at a fun-fair no one visited willingly. The canvas of its top hovered a hand's breadth above his head, growing damp even as he released the handbreak.

"This is a wonderful car," she said, smiling. He glanced at her, deciding as he did that she wasn't having him on. Her hair was strewn across her face like hay, her lips a slice of a species of exotic fruit that was only glimpsed in holiday photographs. She leant over the hand-break lever and kissed him.

"It's decidedly more wonderful if the sun's shining," Alec Grey suggested.

She eased herself down in her seat. "I think it's quite

exciting, driving with the wind in your face. I've not been in a car without a roof before."

"I should have thought sports cars were all the rage up at Windermere," he suggested. He released the brake and eased the car back onto the road from whence it had fled the deluge.

"I'm certain they are, in some circles," she agreed. "My father prefers... a more dignified car."

"A Rolls?"

"A Bentley," she sighed. "It's very much like a Rolls, actually, only larger and grayer."

He smiled at her obvious reservation. It was momentarily beyond him to imagine her being disappointed by an automobile that was worth about as much as his salary from Leconfield House was likely to provide him with over the next two or three decades.

"Has he always driven a Bentley?"

"He's always driven a gray Bentley Continental... at least, for as long as I can recall. He might have been born driving one. He gets a new one every few years." She leaned toward him, her features twisted with affected conspiracy. "There's an unconfirmed rumor below stairs that next time he might go completely mad and buy a light gray one... perhaps even with a hint of blue."

Alec Grey felt himself touched with amusement. He glanced into the wing mirror as a rivulet of rainwater broke from the cover of his hair and scattered itself across his forehead. "Perhaps the interior leathers go well with gray," he suggested.

She shot him a reproving glance. "They could hardly do otherwise. They're gray as well."

She pushed her hair from her face and peered over the dashboard at the serpentine maze of the road. The car slipped between two hedgerows as old as time, punctuated by rusty farmers' gates and unnameable laneways.

"I'd not have imagined you owning this car, Alec

Grey," she said at length. Her voice was alight with amusement or curiosity.

"In point of fact, I don't," he said. "It belongs to
Kenneth Bryan. He was one of my lads until he took a
posting to Panama this past spring. He's asked me to keep
his car ticking over for him in his absence, take it out for a
spin every now and again. I hope he'd approve of our use
of it today."

"I believe I've met him at Leconfield House," she
said uncertainly. "What made him want to live in
Panama?"

The car crested a rise and he hurled it around a blind
corner, allowing himself a moment of gratitude that no one
else had manifested an interest in this stretch of road.
"He'd a particularly ugly divorce," Alec Grey replied. "He
fancied a different view for a few years. I arranged to have
him seconded to MI6. Most of my lads begin to imagine
Russians in the shadows after a while. I fear Ken Bryan
was beginning to imagine his former wife, which was a
good deal worse."

"That's rather sad," she said, as much to herself as
to him.

"He thought so as well," Alec Grey agreed. "He'd
just finished restoring his car when his wife's solicitor set
about trying to claim it."

She glanced about the interior with renewed interest.
"What sort of a car is this?" she inquired.

"1954 MG TF," he replied. "He spent a year of weekends under it. I used to dread Mondays if Ken Bryan was
to be about. I feel as if I know every bolt and wire in this
car as if they were my immediate family."

"He's done a lovely job," she observed.

"When he finishes his time in Panama, I shall have
him tell you about the carburetor. Ken can do a fortnight
on carburetors, given a willing audience."

"Did his wife divorce him because he spent all his

time spying on Russians, or because he kept going on about his car?" she inquired, repressing a smile.

"That's still a matter of some speculation."

Alec Grey peered through the windscreen, deciding that he'd probably enjoyed more time behind the wheel of the MG than had the man who owned it. Ken Bryan had spent his weekends concealed under his car, his face camouflaged with bearing grease and his body disguised in the gillie suit of a mechanic's overalls. Neither the Russians nor his wife had sought him there.

A village appeared from the mist and rain beyond the windscreen, and Alec Grey geared the car down as it swelled before them. It appeared scarcely more populated than the deserted road had been, its high street a ruined watercolor of stained brick and obsidian cobbles running with silver threads of rainwater. A colorless figure beneath a black umbrella emerged from one of the shops, crossed the street and flowed into an alley. Alice Woodward pressed her face to the glass beside her, peering into the gray morning.

They'd slipped though a dozen such places on their journey to the coast, sepulchral houses, a blackened market square, the signboard of a shuttered pub, a glowering church behind a phalanx of gravestones and then back out into the countryside, winding unceasingly toward the sea. She seemed entranced by each of them, and he permitted himself to wonder how the villages in the vicinity of Windermere deported themselves.

"It would be ever so easy to stop here," Alice Woodward said quietly at length. Her voice was barely audible above the thunder of the tires over the road. "Park the car, find a farmhouse for sale... not return to London." She turned to face him, her expression touched with imagination. "I feel certain the realm would be defended quite admirably without us."

"I believe I should have left off telling you about

filling your dead drop until Monday morning," he suggested.

She smiled and glanced away from him. "Am I that
obvious?" she asked. "I'm clearly not qualified to be a spy
if you can tell what I'm thinking."

"I've had some practice of late," he suggested. He
permitted his attention to be drawn by a particularly
intriguing laneway that slipped past the car. "Do you think
there'd be a reasonable selection of farmhouses for sale out
here?"

This appeared to please her, and she resumed her
consideration of the blur of hedgerows beyond the windscreen.

When Alice Woodward again spoke, her voice had
resumed its earlier note of amusement. "Is it considered
polite to speak of things from the office during a romantic
weekend?" she inquired.

He affected an air of consideration. "Perhaps if
they're not genuinely treasonous," he suggested.

"Only, I've been curious whether you've read the
large blue file we spoke of the other evening."

He permitted himself a glance at her before he
returned his attention to the road. They'd nattered on
about far more disturbing aspects of their increasingly
shared conspiracies during the course of this day's peregri-
nations, and he wondered fleetingly why she'd wished his
dispensation over this particular fragment of conversation.
"I did," he replied, smiling to himself. "Once I got stuck
into it, it occupied most of a morning."

"Isn't it quite the most remarkable thing?" she continued. "Did you read Doctor Hollings' attachment, about
how it couldn't be anything other than genuine?"

"And some additional notes from Sir Alistair about
how he'd welcome suggestions from anyone on the distribution list concerning arguments that it be otherwise," he
added. "If we are, as Sir Alistair remarked, history's

second draft, I can't help thinking history made a much better go of things the second time around."

She appeared to consider this. "Do you think it's possible... the world as it's described in that file?" she asked quietly.

"I've difficulty imagining it. If I recall correctly, their Soviet Union included most of eastern Europe... Poland, Czechoslovakia, Hungary, Rumania... I can't recall all of them... and a good bit of Asia as well. Can you imagine Gustav Braunmann presiding over half of Germany, with the Soviets running the other half?"

She smiled coldly at his suggestion. The German president was a stalwart exponent of German sovereignty in the face of a growing call for an economic union of European nations. His steely gaze from beneath granite brows had become familiar to every Briton with a television receiver, and his habit of drumming his fists on whatever flat surface he found himself before when he spoke no doubt the nemesis of television sound engineers on two continents.

"I believe the file described the city of Berlin as having been divided between the west and the Soviets," she said, "with a concrete wall keeping them apart."

"Herr Braunmann would have the thing down with his fingernails if needs be," Alec Grey offered. He'd attended several meetings with Gustav Braunmann over the previous few years. He allowed that he enjoyed the image of the German president assailing the Soviets with his bare hands. It was considerably more comforting than his conclusion upon first reading the file, that Gustav Braunmann would almost certainly have perished in a death camp during the second great war.

He'd found the description of the atomic bombs and the missiles constructed to deliver them to be the most unsettling. To have survived with the daily understanding that death might rain from the clouds at any moment, leaving nothing but ash — he'd imagined nations of people driven mad with apprehension and lifetimes of uncertainty. The author of the file had asserted that citizens of both sides of the cold war had disposed themselves to live with the threat of immediate annihilation — he doubted that he could have done as much.

The prospect of the Soviets obtaining access to the time stream was potentially far more terrifying, he considered fleetingly, and he drove the thought angrily from his awareness.

"I'm not certain I understand why the director insisted the file be classified MOST SECRET," Alice Woodward said, disturbing the swelling blackness of his reverie. "I quite despise the secure typist's room, and it wasn't as if anything in the file has actually taken place. I shouldn't have thought a history that never happened could hold any secrets."

He felt himself exhumed from the blackness of his imagination, captivated by a facet of the curious file that he'd not considered previously. "Perhaps Sir Alistair didn't fancy the Soviets getting any grander ideas about their place in history than they presently have. They're a spot of bother most of the time... it wouldn't do for them to have obtained a copy of that file and discovered that they've the potential for being a great deal more."

Alice Woodward appeared to consider this, and she seemed on the point of speaking when a signboard protruding from one of the hedgerows swam uncertainly from the rain before them. She gestured toward it. "Isn't that The Swans?" she asked.

Alec Grey peered uncertainly through the windscreen. The sign depicted two swans, one black and the other white. It resembled the sketch Hugh Somerfield had provided him with, in addition to directions to the inn. He braked suddenly and turned the car into the lane it heralded.

The Swans had no doubt been a small Victorian inn a century earlier, Alec Grey decided, before it had been given siege by a squadron of tradesmen and carpenters. Its heart appeared to be a three-story brick house with a great deal more ornamentation than seemed called for. Its cornices and filigrees had clearly been painted of late — they were now British racing green, and matched the coachwork of the MG. The original structure had grown several appendages that sprawled lazily across a substantial car park and several acres of formal gardens left to grow wild with the cessation of the tourist season. Gravel rattled beneath his tires as he ascended the drive.

The car park was entirely deserted. Alec Grey granted himself a berth nearest the path to the main door and switched off the engine.

"This is quite grand," Alice Woodward breathed, peering up through the windscreen at the building. He imagined that he heard a note of relief in her voice, perhaps at discovering it to be something other than a caravan park in two feet of marsh.

"It's fortunate we've arrived before all the crowds," Alec Grey observed. She smiled and kissed him once again.

He was on the point of winding his window down and reaching outside for the door release when he stopped himself and leant back in his seat.

"There's something I imagine I should ask you," he said uncertainly. "It's my understanding that the tradition of romantic weekends in the country is available in two flavors."

"Oh yes?" she inquired.

"The first involves walking along the seaside and eating a considerable amount of candy-floss." He turned to regard her, peering into her eyes. "The other doesn't call for any walking to speak of... and no reason to leave the hotel. I... I don't believe the tradition really speaks to mentioning any of this until at least tea time, but we probably should decide whether we'll be having two rooms... or just the one."

Her features were touched with amusement for a moment, or perhaps it had been empathy for his disquiet. She smiled and kissed him, her lips lingering on his for some time. "I'd have thought one room," she whispered.

She giggled as she turned from him. "Are we to pretend to be married?" she asked.

"I believe it's part of the tradition as well," he replied.

She removed a ring from her right hand and placed it on the third finger of her left, turning it so its jewel faced her palm. It served as a reasonable impersonation of a wedding band. "I've always fancied doing that," she said.

"I shall be Robert MacDonald," he said. "You can have any Christian name you like."

She appeared to consider this. "Beryl or Gladys?"

"Beryl," he suggested.

He opened the car's door, walked around and opened hers. "Mrs. MacDonald," he said, gesturing for her to get to her feet. She smiled at this, oblivious to the rain. He was another minute defeating the cover of the luggage compartment and retrieving their cases.

The lobby of The Swans seemed in keeping with its grounds. It had no doubt been freshly painted and admirably appointed at the commencement of the season, but a summer of guests and revelers had clearly wrought upon it some measure of distress. Its walls were stained, its furniture emitted motionless fountains of stuffing and its illumination was growing moldy with the passage of several of its lamps. The building smelled faintly of dampness and stale beer.

The woman behind the front desk had given her entire attention over to a particularly substantial book, and she seemed unaware of them until Alec Grey was before her. She glanced up at him with a start, her eyes growing wide and alarmed before she affixed a suitably professional smile to her face and rose to her feet.

"I'm terribly sorry, sir," she said. "I didn't hear you come in."

Alec Grey smiled. "I didn't intend to frighten you," he said. "I'm afraid we haven't rung ahead, but I was hoping my wife and I might have a room for the weekend."

She returned his smile. "Yes, sir. I think we might just fit you in." She paused, her smile growing wry. "In fact, sir, this is our off season and you can have whichever room you wish."

"Do you have one with a view of the seaside?" Alice Woodward inquired.

The woman seemed amused by this. "It's actually a view of the English channel, but we've few oil tankers at this time of year."

Alec Grey signed the register book with his imaginary persona and the woman placed a key on the desk before him. "It's room 23, up the stairs. I'm afraid I've no one to bring your cases up. It's our off season, you see."

"They're very small cases," Alec Grey said.

She recited the inn's meal times for him. He'd forgotten them before she finished speaking.

They reached the top of the stairs before Alice Woodward succumbed to uncontrollable laughter, which he considered an impressive measure of self-control. "That could have been dreadfully embarrassing," she whispered.

"Have you not registered at an hotel before?" he inquired.

"Not under a made-up name," she hissed. "The woman at the desk might have asked to see your driving license."

"I do have one, you know."

"Do you have one that says Robert MacDonald?"

"Yes," he replied.

She paused at the crest of the staircase.

"I had Technical Services do it up for me several months ago, for a spot of theater with the Soviets," he explained. He took her hand and turned to catch her gaze. Her eyes were bottomless pools of green and gray in the hush of the corridor. "We are spies, Miss Woodward," he reminded her. "We're paid handsomely to be deceitful and untrustworthy."

"Are you paid handsomely?" she asked.

"It's more a figure of speech."

Room 23 was dominated by a neatly-made bed, a narrow armchair and a highboy. Its furnishings left scarcely enough of its floor to circumnavigate the bed. It did offer a private bath, which Alec Grey considered must be the height of luxury at a country inn. Its single window would have opened onto the waters of the channel a hundred yards distant had it not been securely painted shut several decades earlier. He pushed the door to behind Alice Woodward and rested their cases on the top of the highboy.

"This is quite cozy," she said uncertainly.

"I was told it would be," Alec Grey assured her.

She walked to the window and gazed out into the freshening storm. "Did you tell Mr. Somerfield who you were bringing out for the weekend?"

He shook his head. "No," he replied. "I'd trust Hugh Somerfield with my life, but not with my pension."

She grinned and directed her attention to the bed. At length she sat on the far side of it, gazing once more at the window. When she again spoke, she was facing away from him.

"I've a confession," she said, her voice little more than a whisper. "I'm afraid I've little experience with romantic weekends."

She turned to regard him. "The truth is, I've not actually been to a place like this before. I... that is, I've only actually been with one other man... and that was quite some while ago..."

He smiled, hoping his expression would appear reassuring. "That's a comfort," he said. "I've never been to a place like this before either, and I've only been with one other woman."

Her eyes narrowed and she seemed to be considering whether he was having her on. "You said you'd been married."

"I did," he agreed, "but we never came away for a weekend."

"Oh," she said.

She got to her feet and shrugged her cardigan from her shoulders. She fixed his gaze with her own as she undressed, releasing her clothes to the threadbare carpet. She smiled at him, clearly pleased with her resolve, as she slid her knickers over her hips and kicked them toward the foot of the bed. Wordlessly she drew back the covers and climbed beneath them.

"I believe the traditional calls for you to put out the light and get into bed with me," she suggested.

26

J ames Joyce was clearly a far greater threat to the safety and well-being of the English people than the Soviet Union could ever aspire to, Hugh Somerfield considered. What the hell was a 'teargarten,' he wondered angrily, or 'nenuphars.' Finnegans Wake required a second volume to translate its English into English.

He twisted his back unthinkingly, seeking about on the unfamiliar bed for a disposition of his spine that didn't entail its encountering any of the larger hillocks in the mattress. His feet hung over the footboard, and he was distantly aware that they'd probably gone to sleep hours earlier. Where might one come upon a 'Finglas mill' — he thought the phrase might well describe his current lodgings, if he had the faintest idea of what it meant.

He'd sent the boss to The Swans in Kent for a dirty weekend, he mused, recalling the distant hotel. The Swans had known how to maintain a bed, and had understood the exact frequency with which to deliver drink to a gentleman's room that his lady be suspended in a state of optimum inebriation. The Swans had also mastered a proper ploughman's lunch.

He wondered absently who Alec Grey had chosen to accompany him to The Swans. The matter had tickled his curiosity. Even after the inevitable departure of his wife, Alec Grey had expressed no overt interest in the women of Leconfield House. The initial bloody skirmishes of its present crisis seemed an odd time for the boss to fancy a bit on the side.

He'd sent the boss to The Swans, and with an uncharacteristic lack of generosity, the boss had entombed him in an upstairs room of The Three Crowns. It was not so much a public house as a public convenience, he considered, glancing about the water-stained paper and rotted woodwork of the room. The Three Crowns possessed the sole virtue of being the nearest accommodation to the Cornwall time stream project. None the less, if he'd appreciated the full magnitude of the odors from its kitchen and the fumes from its plumbing, he'd have cheerfully driven ten miles further and sought for a proper hotel.

In a far corner of the room, a regular cadence of rain drops plummeted through an unpatched opening in the roof and echoed into a bucket. The bucket was growing full, he observed, which suggested that his landlady would be up presently to replace it. His landlady was an emaciated stick insect with a moustache that would have given an officer in the Coldstream Guards pause. She invariably requested that he assist her with the full buckets, and he made a point of refusing.

He returned his attention sourly to his book. Zoe Stockwell had an infectious smile and she was unusually inventive between sheets, but she would receive a substantial ragging-out for this importunity. That she had on occasion suggested he might do well to expose himself to literature beyond that which was suitable for reading on the tube was hardly an excuse for her to leave it lying about his flat, risking his unthinking collection of it on his way out.

She would no doubt observe that the book had had its title printed clearly across its cover, had he troubled himself to consult it. He permitted himself a minute of consideration as to how best he might rebut her argument. She would owe him dinner at the very least for this outrage.

The Three Crowns itself had been able to offer him nothing further to read beyond a four-day-old copy of The Times with half its pages having been purloined, no doubt to wrap chips, and a bible. He'd dispensed with the former some hours earlier, and even staring Joyce in the face, he'd been unable to bring himself to accept the latter.

He reached unthinkingly to the bedside table and sought across its ragged surface for his packet of cigarettes. When at length he came upon it, it deflated beneath his palm, almost exhausted. He would do well to ration his fags, he decided abruptly. The Three Crowns, he'd discovered to his horror, sold only raw Players and tins of tobacco. He accepted the inevitable torment of his lungs by those medieval implements in time, but he vowed to forestall them for as long as his resolve endured.

What could possibly be described as 'cribcracking yeggs?' Might The Three Crowns serve a plate of them for his tea?

He permitted himself to wonder how David Hollings was getting on with his second masterwork of deception. Alec Grey had recounted the scientist's reservations about the undertaking. The boss had expressed a moment of concern that David Hollings might well recant part way through the weekend, and ultimately prove unwilling to be the author of the destruction of the Soviet time stream facility. Hugh Somerfield had thought the subterfuge clever — very much in keeping with the machinations of Alec Grey's mind — but he'd confessed to serious reservations as to how likely Moscow was to swallow it.

He glanced at his wristwatch. It had just gone half one. David Hollings was yet to ring him, sobbing in anguish and inevitable remorse. Perhaps the day was proceeding well.

He'd labored through three additional pages of his book, comprehending none of it, when the contemplative silence of the room was unsettled by a knock upon its door. He recognized the bony knuckles of his landlady. As was her habit, she opened the door a moment later without having been given leave to do so.

"Mrs. Llewellyn," Hugh Somerfield acknowledged.

"I'm sorry to disturb you," the woman said mechanically. It was clear from her tone that her remorse was a professional courtesy at best.

"Not at all," he said. "I'm afraid I'm still unwilling to assist you with emptying the rain bucket."

She shook her head wearily. "You asked to be called if someone rang and inquired after you," she continued, clearly ignoring his attempt at wit.

He felt his heart thunder in his chest for a moment, deciding that his earlier confidence in Alec Grey's tame scientist had been ill-founded, or at best premature. Hugh Somerfield had been granted leave to appear before David Hollings in any guise from father confessor to lord high executioner if it were warranted, as long as he had a packet of documents for Alice Woodward to photograph when she arrived at Leconfield House on Monday morning. He had little stomach for the work.

He closed his book without troubling himself to mark his place, deciding that one page of Joyce was as good as any other. Mrs. Llewellyn preceded him along the narrow corridor and down a flight of creaking wooden steps that sagged menacingly with his passing. She gestured at a Precambrian telephone handset languishing across the polished surface of the bar.

"Somerfield," he said mechanically as he crushed it to his ear.

The connection rasped with a forceful sigh. "Mr.

Somerfield?" The distant voice was unmistakably that of David Hollings.

"Have you completed your work so soon?" Hugh Somerfield inquired hopefully.

"No… no, nothing like that, I'm afraid," David Hollings said anxiously. "Look, I'm sorry to bother you, but we've had a spot of trouble here, and you're the closest chap about. I wanted to see you… before I rang London."

"What sort of trouble?"

David Hollings paused. "I think it would be best if you popped 'round for a chat," he said. "I'll be waiting to clear you at the gate."

Hugh Somerfield was considering whether to inquire further into the unusual summons when the connection went dead.

"I shan't be needing my tea after all, Mrs. Llewellyn," he said, and he strode to the door.

The drive to the time stream facility occupied a quarter of an hour, and he was several minutes more deciding which of the disused laneways he'd come upon constituted the entrance to the project's compound. He was well out of sight of the road when he encountered a high steel fence pierced by an imposing gate. He eased the car to a stop beside a concrete gate house and awaited the pleasure of its occupants. Two uniformed men emerged, one to inquire after his intentions and the other to direct a particularly troubling rifle at him during the conversation.

He extracted an envelope from his coat pocket and removed his pass from it. The pass was a sheet of paper with his photograph affixed to it and a substantial volume of printing. Amongst its spells and incantations, he knew, was the admonition that it would be transmuted into a pumpkin at precisely 9:00am on Monday, 23 October, and anyone presenting it for entrance to the facility thereafter might find himself doing a stretch of porridge at Wormwood Scrubs.

The guard read the pass in detail, returned to his guard house and finally emerged, pass in hand, to gesture him forward. The gates swung open before him.

The outer perimeter of the time stream facility was but the first seal to be transgressed. He drove into a corridor lined with high brick walls. It ran for some distance before he encountered a second gate. Its guard house had been replaced by a steel door in the brick wall to his right which appeared capable of withstanding a sustained assault by heavy artillery. It opened as he pulled abreast of it. Three guards emerged from this one, two of whom took up flanking positions before his car, their rifles adopting an unhealthy interest in his head.

He presented his pass to the third guard, who scrutinized it, compared his face to the one on the pass and then vanished through the door from which he'd appeared. He was almost five minutes returning.

The guard returned the pass to Hugh Somerfield with obvious reluctance. He was clearly having a tedious weekend, and the prospect of watching a Soviet infiltrator die in a hail of gunfire would no doubt have relieved his growing boredom. He gestured at the gate, which began to swing open.

"Drive on, sir, and turn to your left once you've passed the gate. Stop in location seventeen and wait to be received by Doctor Hollings."

Hugh Somerfield accepted his pass wordlessly and put the car in gear. He was in no way surprised to observe one of the armed guards follow him through the gate, his firearm resting upon his shoulder. He parked as he'd been instructed and switched off his engine. The guard stood behind his car, oblivious to the rain, his head shifting mechanically as he surveyed the compound.

The storm had swelled in intensity beneath bruised

clouds. He snatched glimpses of several hulking brick
buildings between the curtains of rain, tentacles of
immense steel pipes issuing from fissures in the tarmac,
oddly-shaped structures of unfathomable purpose. The
director had suggested he would be unwise to attempt to
ascertain the deeper secrets of the facility, lest he attract
the suspicions of those whose task it was to maintain its
security. Alec Grey had suggested he would be unwise to
do so as he was likely to inflict upon himself a substantial
headache.

He glanced through the rear window of the car. The
guard who'd accompanied him to the car park remained
like a colossus, oblivious to the deluge.

A hunched figure took shape in the lee of one of the
buildings and strode uneasily toward him. The sodden features of David Hollings attained substance and dimension,
weary and fearful. Hugh Somerfield stepped from his car,
feeling the rain seek for entrance beneath his coat. He
turned his collar against the onslaught of the storm and
approached David Hollings.

"What the hell's happened?" he shouted above the
clatter of rain across the tarmac.

David Hollings shook his head. He gestured toward
the building from which he'd come and turned to retrace
his steps. Hugh Somerfield felt himself grow still more disquieted and made to follow him.

There was another guard station just inside the door,
and another expressionless soldier with an automatic
weapon directed at him. To his surprise, the guard
demanded not only his pass, but that of David Hollings as
well, who'd clearly left the building a minute earlier. The
door beyond the guard station was somewhat more substantial than a bank vault, and it swung reluctantly open to
the accompaniment of an unseen electric motor.

"You've not been here before, I understand," David
Hollings said as he passed through the immense door.

Hugh Somerfield followed him into a brightly-lit corridor of concrete and gray doors bearing only numbers and gleaming steel locks.

"Considering what it's required to undertake a visit, I doubt I shall wish to return," Hugh Somerfield remarked.

"This is the most heavily guarded facility in Great Britain, Mr. Somerfield," he said, although there was an unmistakable note of unease in his words. "We all accept the understanding that a modest degree of inconvenience must be born as a result of the importance of the project."

Hugh Somerfield smiled wryly at the back of David Hollings head, wondering as he did whether anyone was observing him through an unseen spyhole in the concrete that surrounded them. It had been his conclusion, within the hegemony of Leconfield House, that the security pre-cautions applied to important files were often the banner of their importance. Officers who fancied their obscure fiefs as vital bastions in the defense of the realm periodi-cally assigned their work MOST SECRET clearance to attest to their invaluable contribution to the continuance of the British way of life.

Had he been responsible for disposing of several bil-lions of pounds for a time machine, he mused, he'd have put the thing behind a bank-vault door as well, Russians or not. If one endowed a thing worth billions of pounds as being deserving of the most heavily guarded facility in Great Britain, the billions of pounds must perforce have been well spent.

David Hollings turned into an intersecting corridor and began fishing about in his pocket for a key. They reached a door with the number 27 painted on it in gleam-ing black characters. The scientist unlocked the door and gestured for him to proceed through it. He found himself at the top of a stairwell. David Hollings joined him, locked the door behind them, and began to descend.

The journey through the arteries of the facility occupied at least as much time as Hugh Somerfield had spent
driving from The Three Crowns. Several additional guard
stations emerged from the concrete and strip lighting,
demanding his pass and that of David Hollings. The
guards were unsmiling, wordless, heavily armed. The
doors they guarded seemed as if they'd have been capable
of withstanding the elemental forces of the cosmos. At
length Hugh Somerfield came to appreciate that they
served the dual functions of denying access to any particularly stealthy Soviet agents who succeeded in penetrating
the outer defenses of the complex, and of containing the
enraged godlings that powered the time stream apparatus,
in the event that one of them sundered its chains.

After what seemed like half the afternoon spent
walking, they came at length to a gray steel door which
guarded a room, rather than another passage or stairwell.
David Hollings extracted a suitable key from his pocket
and ushered Hugh Somerfield within it. It, too, was bright
and formed of concrete, but it was a tangle of pipes, con-
duits, bulging steel vessels and gray crypts with scarlet
warnings of extreme voltage. It appeared to stretch into the
far distance, vanishing behind a subterranean horizon.

"Is this where you've been writing your file for the
Russians?" Hugh Somerfield inquired, his voice little more
than a whisper. The chamber appeared to be deserted, but
there were half a hundred places within earshot which
might have concealed a small cadre of Soviet operatives.

David Hollings shook his head. "I've an actual
office," he explained. "Senior research staff are even permitted chairs. We've a more pressing matter, I'm afraid."

"Alec Grey expended some small effort to impress
upon me that nothing could be more pressing than the
delivery of your work on Monday morning if either of us
expects to still be collecting his wages as of Monday
noon."

"I believe... that is, we have evidence to indicate that there's been a break-in," David Hollings said coldly. The statement bore the tone of an actor's dialog, a line that had been rehearsed rather more often than was called for.

"Here?" Hugh Somerfield inquired, glancing once more about the room. "Are we speaking of a human being getting through all the guards and blast doors we've just been through... without a pass?"

"We are."

Hugh Somerfield permitted himself to consider this. "Crafty," he suggested, refusing to discount the possibility that he'd become involved in the sort of humorous activity that only scientists were sufficiently educated to appreciate. "Do we know who's responsible for this break-in?"

"No," David Hollings replied.

"Or how whoever it was achieved it?"

"No."

"Was something taken?"

David Hollings sighed. "Yes, that's rather the point. We've lost a blank of refined Uranium."

Hugh Somerfield fixed his eyes upon those of the scientist. "Are you certain?" he demanded.

David Hollings appeared to gather his thoughts. "We're reasonably certain," he said hesitantly. Hugh Somerfield resisted the temptation to observe that his statement represented something of a contradiction in terms. "Are you familiar with the first theft of a Uranium blank?"

"Yes... the corpse found in Mayrick Road... I've been briefed."

"When I returned from London, I instructed that procedures be put in place immediately to inventory all of our Uranium, derived materials, containment and transportation apparatus... anything that might be involved in another theft. Our Uranium blanks were inventoried yesterday and the lead containers used to store the blanks were inventoried this morning. As counting the latter involves counting the former as well, the Uranium blanks were effectively counted twice."

"I don't believe I understand the problem," Hugh Somerfield interrupted him.

"The two counts didn't match," David Hollings said angrily, clearly of the opinion that his conclusion might well have been obvious.

Hugh Somerfield regarded the scientist uncertainly. "Someone's bollocksed-up the count," he said. "One of them's been kicked under a desk and forgotten."

David Hollings shook his head. "It doesn't quite work that way, Mr. Somerfield," he said with obvious exasperation. "Uranium is grotesquely toxic. It can only be handled by personnel in protective lead suits, using remotely-controlled machines to manipulate it. Simply removing a Uranium blank from its case requires several members of my staff, an hour of preparation and a sub-stantial volume of paperwork. It's impossible to simply misplace one."

"I would have said that a Soviet thief slipping past your guards would have been equally impossible," Hugh Somerfield suggested.

"As would I," David Hollings agreed. He gestured into the tangle of pipes before them. "Permit me to show you what we've found." He strode forward without further explanation.

The Uranium storage facility was, Hugh Somerfield considered, the only room in the time stream facility he'd thus far encountered that bore a name on its door, rather than merely a number. It also bore several draconian warn-ings about the nature of the material behind it and the likely results of entering it without suitable protection. The phrase 'immediate death by lethal radiation poisoning' seemed sufficiently unambiguous as to render the lock on the door superfluous. None the less, it had one.

Upon reflection, Hugh Somerfield decided he was uneasy merely being in proximity of the room.

"This was unlocked when we discovered the theft," David Hollings explained. "Not only is it unthinkable to leave it thus… it's also impossible. The locking mechanism has a clockwork timer built into it. Three minutes after it's operated, it re-locks itself."

"Can you explain how it came to be unlocked?"

"I had Nicholas Harwell down here… he's our chief of security for the facility. He's examined the lock and he came to the conclusion that it's been picked. Whoever picked it has forced the end of a kitchen match into the clockwork mechanism to prevent it from operating."

Hugh Somerfield stared at the lock for a moment longer. There could be little doubt the unaccounted-for Uranium blank had met with foul play. Sir Alistair Fitzhenry would be inquiring about the legality of ritual disembowelment by Monday tea time.

"There's this as well," David Hollings continued, disturbing the blackness of his thoughts. The scientist took several paces from the door and indicated a small metal container partially obscured by a black valve protruding from the floor.

"What would that be?" Hugh Somerfield asked, hearing a note of weariness in his own words.

"The Uranium blanks are stored in lead fixtures, and the fixtures placed in much larger lead boxes to prevent the escape of gamma radiation. We've found it's easier to have the mechanical hands that move the Uranium blanks grip the small fixtures and then remove the Uranium than it is to attempt to manipulate the Uranium directly when it's in one of the lead boxes. It would appear whoever took the blank discarded the fixture it was stored in."

Hugh Somerfield indicated the warnings on the door to the Uranium storage room. "Wouldn't whoever stole it be easy to identify?" he asked. "We'd be looking for a horribly-disfigured dead Soviet agent having a nap against one of these pipes."

"Whoever took the Uranium blank is unquestionably dead, but he might not be aware of it as yet. The level of gamma radiation emitted by the stolen blank wouldn't be immediately fatal."

"How long would he have taken to die?"

"We have no way of knowing... we haven't undertaken any meaningful research into the effects of hard radiation on human subjects. We were a great deal more interested in ensuring that none of it ever got close enough to human subjects to call for that sort of research."

"Could someone have walked out of the facility with it, if they'd had a pass?"

David Hollings shook his head. "We now have Geiger counters at every guard station," he explained. He appeared to appreciate that Hugh Somerfield hadn't understood what he was referring to. "Radiation detectors. A particle of Uranium the size of a grain of sand lodged in the tread of someone's shoe would set them off. An entire Uranium blank would probably have them screaming like cats."

"Then it's still in the facility," Hugh Somerfield said.

"I'm quite certain it's not. We've searched every meter of this room, visually and with Geiger counters. There's a counter at the door we came in through, the only entrance. We've verified that the counter at the door hasn't been tampered with. The door itself is wired to alert three separate guard stations when it opens. The man on duty at each station logs each occasion of the door opening. All three logs agree. Every occasion of the door being opened is accounted for."

"Is the Uranium storage room door wired as well?"

David Hollings glanced at the door. "It's not," he admitted. "The original design of the facility didn't call for it, as the only door to this area is monitored. I instructed that it be monitored as well as part of the increased security precautions... our Technical Services people were to see to it next week."

"Mention to them for me they're a bit late," Hugh Somerfield suggested.

He glanced about the room, trying to imagine a faceless intruder moving between the shapeless metal titans that dwelt within it. There was another exit from the room, he decided, and someone had discovered it.

At length his attention returned to the discarded lead container. He noticed a stain on the gray concrete it rested upon. It seemed noteworthy in that every inch of the facility he'd been permitted to observe appeared to have been scrubbed hourly.

"What do you have down here that's bright green?" he inquired of David Hollings.

The scientist regarded him uncertainly, and Hugh Somerfield gestured at a small crescent of emerald fluid near the container.

"That's high-temperature coolant," he explained. "It's used in the heat transfer system that maintains the temperature of the time stream reactance chamber when the facility is in operation."

"Someone's trodden in it," Hugh Somerfield observed. "That mark was made by a tennis shoe, I believe. Do any of your staff wear tennis shoes to work."

"I... I couldn't say."

"Would there be anywhere down here where someone might have trodden in this coolant?"

David Hollings glanced about the room. "Yes, I suppose there is. The coolant's under considerable pressure, you understand, and we have relief valves in the feed system. They can vent coolant under some circumstances."

"Show me, if you would," Hugh Somerfield instructed him.

David Hollings crossed the chamber to a network of pipes affixed to its far wall. The pipes had each been painted a different color. "The green ones are coolant," he explained. "If we follow them along, we'll come to a relief valve."

They came to five relief valves before they encountered one that was leaking coolant. A small puddle of viscous green fluid had collected on the floor beneath it. The puddle had been disturbed by several clear impressions of a shoe.

"How long could this have been here?" Hugh Somerfield inquired.

"Maintenance is through at twenty-two hundred hours every day... that's ten at night," David Hollings replied. "It would have had to have been after that."

Several faint impressions of a shoe tread were visible across the concrete floor, fading into ghosts as the fluid dissipated. When Hugh Somerfield glanced away from the last of them, he found himself before a large metal cylinder partially submerged in concrete. It had a dome-shaped hatch atop it, and a great many bolts fastening it together.

"What's this?" he asked.

"That's an access door for the heated water return outflow pipe. It's another part of the cooling system. The superheated coolant exchanges its heat with seawater, which is exhausted through a stainless steel pipe under this room."

Hugh Somerfield brushed his thumb across the metal, and finding it to be of room temperature he placed his palm along its edged and put his weight against the hatch. The metal slid reluctantly before him, screeching its displeasure before it surrendered its purchase and clattered to the floor.

David Hollings gaped at the open pipe. "That's impossible," he spat.

Hugh Somerfield glanced into the blackness of the pipe, seeing nothing in its depths and expecting as much. He walked to the far side of the open pipe and knelt beside the hatch cover. "Someone's taken this thing to pieces from the inside," he said.

David Hollings appeared over his shoulder. "That's impossible," he repeated.

"It would appear not. Someone's crawled up your outflow pipe, dismantled the hatch cover and gotten into this room." He rose to his feet once more.

"You don't understand what you're suggesting, Somerfield," David Hollings said urgently. "It can't be done."

Hugh Somerfield regarded him blankly.

"For one thing, there's a bloody great steel grill at the far end of the outflow pipe where it drains into the sea."

"Is it guarded?" Hugh Somerfield asked, deciding as he did that the answer to his question was clearly evident.

"Of course it's not guarded," David Hollings replied. "It's an outflow pipe."

"We'll have one of your security lads climb down and have a proper look at it presently, but I think we might safely assume someone's been at it with a gas axe, and its bloody great steel grill is lying along side it."

"Even if that were the case, the pipe's less than a meter across. A grown man couldn't fit through it."

"An unusually small man might, or a teenaged boy... or a slight woman, perhaps," Hugh Somerfield suggested.

David Hollings waved dismissingly. "Even so, it would be suicide to try. When the outflow pipe's in use, scalding water rushes through it. Anyone crawling through it would be boiled alive in seconds."

"Does this scalding water flow through the pipe continuously?"

"No... the cooling system's only used when the time stream apparatus is in operation."

"Would I be correct in assuming that happens in accordance with a schedule?"

David Hollings nodded. "There's certainly a schedule for the facility. We plan sessions some weeks in advance to allow for the process of deriving the Berkelium required to access the time stream."

"Does it operate on Saturdays?"

Hugh Somerfield stared at him for a moment, his expression suggesting that he'd not previously considered the issue. "Not as such," he replied at length. "There's a staff of five technicians responsible for maintaining calibration and the integrity of the reactance chamber... they perform their work over the weekend."

"Does this involve making the cooling system work?"

"Yes... yes it does, as it happens. The reactance chamber is brought to temperature and then cooled." David Hollings glanced at his wristwatch. "The procedure is due to begin in about an hour and a half... they'll have to be notified to cancel it."

Hugh Somerfield regarded the scientist and then permitted his attention to return to the hatch cover.

"I know what you're thinking, Somerfield," David Hollings said, "but you can't possibly be right. For someone to have known the times when it was safe to crawl through the outflow pipe, to have known where the Uranium blanks are stored, how to get through the lock... it all would have required a great deal of inside knowledge of this facility."

"I'm certain it did," Hugh Somerfield agreed.

David Hollings winced noticeably.

Hugh Somerfield deliberately looked away from the scientist. "Were I to request it, would you be able to draft me a list of those members of your staff with access to the schedule for the time machine, knowledge of the procedures for storing the Uranium blanks, the name of the firm that supplied the hatch cover and the schedule for anyone who'd be down here... including the lads who sweep the floors?"

"I could... it would be a rather short list," David Hollings replied.

"We at MI5 are particularly fond of short lists," Hugh Somerfield said. "Would Arthur Dunross have been on your list?"

David Hollings appeared perplexed by the question. "Well... yes, I imagine he would have been, save that he's dead."

Hugh Somerfield smiled coldly. "Yes he is, Doctor Hollings," he said, as much to himself as to the scientist. "That's rather the point. Dead men are so very difficult to interrogate. One might even suspect that's the reason Mr. Dunross got to be dead in the first place."

27

Sunday, October 22

There were indeed few oil tankers at this time of year, Alec Grey considered, and it required little effort of will to imagine that they'd journeyed to the seaside. The rain and the swelling mists from the channel had rendered the beach a gray mirage, another couple's weekend seen through a poorly-focused camera lens. He could hear nothing beyond her words and the cadence of their feet upon the overgrown wooden path that flanked the water.

He'd made a point of orphaning his wristwatch upon the bedside table in their room at The Swans. He had little sense of the hour. They seemed at times to have been strolling this beach for much of their lives.

Their shared umbrella tottered uncertainly, and he decided that she'd grown tired of supporting it aloft. "Perhaps it should be my turn for a time," he suggested, accepting it from her.

Her arm sought for renewed purchase across his back.

The channel smelled of salt and decay, its wetness almost that of blood. At times it was an all-but-forgotten taste, threatening to displace the taste of her. He resented its intrusion, deciding as he did that the day had disordered his thoughts to a far greater degree than he'd anticipated.

"Is eating candy-floss not on, then?" she inquired.

He pretended to consider this. "The only thing I've noticed that looked the slightest bit like a candy-floss vendor was boarded up and missing part of its roof," he replied. "I believe they've all fled for wherever it is seaside distractions winter."

"It's probably for the best. I always grow tired of candy-floss part way through, and there never seems to be anywhere to leave the rest of it."

"Perhaps we'll return when the candy-floss is in season," he suggested.

She was silent for a time, and when she spoke her voice was barely audible above the reverberant hush of the storm. "Will we?" she asked.

"If you'd like to."

"I've thought... that is, I believe I should like to ask you a hypothetical question."

He felt himself smile, teased by the rasp of her voice. "What sort of... hypothetical question... did you have in mind?"

She paused once more. "I read a great deal... or at least, I did until quite recently. I shouldn't admit it to just anyone, but from time to time I've permitted myself the occasional penny-dreadful romance. I don't imagine you've ever read such books... one of the things that turns up in a great number of them is the woman saying something she shouldn't and the man running off to join the navy or explore the Amazon, and they never see each other again."

"Sir Alistair wouldn't permit it," he assured her.

She smiled uncertainly. "I thought that if I were to ask you a hypothetical question, and it turned out to be something I shouldn't have asked you at all, it wouldn't have been asked sincerely... and you could avoid the Amazon. From what I've read, they've mosquitoes there the size of badgers."

"That's most thoughtful."

They walked in silence for well over a minute. "Hypothetically, then... I wanted to ask you whether you thought we might have another romantic weekend." She paused, staring into the mist before them. "I... I wanted to ask whether you thought we would see each other a few more times and then discover that we had work to complete or friends we'd not spoken to for weeks... or whether we could become a long-term object of office rumors and have each other to buy Christmas gifts for, hypothetically."

"Hypothetically," he agreed. He glanced away from her, smiling despite a moment of unease that seemed to roll across them both, a damp breeze from the unseen channel. He gazed into the mist, puzzled for an instant at the dread in her words. They'd been nattering on for most of the morning.

"Hypothetically, I couldn't say," he replied, "but hypothetically, I should certainly prefer the latter."

She laughed, the sound like the shattering of glass. He wondered fleetingly if he might reassure her that there was nothing she was likely to say to him that would injure their time together, or cause him to give serious consideration to a career in the navy. It seemed beyond him to suggest it.

"My mother warned me off penny-dreadful romances when I was a child," she whispered. She paused in their procession along the seaside, and when he turned to face her she kissed him. It was a kiss reminiscent of the afterglow of their lovemaking, promising to linger well past nightfall.

They walked in silence for some time, exchanging the umbrella on several occasions.

"Do you imagine any of Hugh Somerfield's girl-friends lose their nerve and make a complete pig's breakfast of asking him simple questions, as I've done?" she asked him.

"I've long been of the understanding that Hugh Somerfield selects girlfriends who are unlikely to ask him questions at all," Alec Grey replied. At times he'd caught himself envying Hugh Somerfield the seemingly unending parade of women which legend had sharing his bed, and it amused him now to think that the legend appeared to have permeated the culture of Leconfield House.

She turned to regard him, her features teased by a smile. "Did it trouble you that I was a virgin but for one?"

"I've not heard it expressed quite like that before," he replied, feeling himself infected by her amusement. "I'm certain it reflects my sheltered upbringing... I've been of the understanding that a woman either was or she wasn't."

She shook her head. "There are many degrees of virginity," she assured him.

"Was he your husband," Alec Grey asked, "your 'but for one?'"

She glanced at him uncertainly, and for an instant he feared he'd unearthed a shard of her past she'd imagined inexorably buried. Her expression grew puzzled, and he decided that she found his question unlikely.

Alice Woodward stared into the rain as if she were surveying the invisible channel, awaiting a ship. "His name was Donald Hughes... Donald Hughes the third, in fact. His father and my father were friends from school. His family has a country estate with a manor house and a stable and half a county to ride across. We visited there some summers, and one summer he said he fancied me... and... and I decided that I was twenty-two, and old enough that I should know what it was like for a boy to fancy me." She turned to face him and she smiled uncertainly. "I... I was with him three times. Once in the stable, once in the rear seat of my father's gray Bentley, and one final time on a settee in the groundskeeper's cottage when the groundskeeper was in hospital having his appendix out. Shortly after that, he decided he fancied the daughter of another of his father's friends, and he never spoke to me again."

He peered into her eyes, watching them grow wet with tears before she looked away from him.

"Perhaps I might arrange to have him up on charges of high treason or accidentally shot," he offered.

She laughed and brushed her hand across her eyes. "It was a very long time ago, and it was something foolish I did one summer." She paused, and after a moment she smiled at him. "I saw him last year... he was at Windermere when I'd gone up for the weekend. Donald Hughes the third presently weighs about twenty stone. He has a great deal of hair on the backs of his hands and very little on his head. He has a wife he loathes and he works for his father as a clerk... and I shouldn't wish to see anything about him changed."

Alec Grey permitted himself to be distracted by a leafless branch washed upon the shore by the retreating tide. It comforted him to learn that the poison of vengeance flowed in her veins, if perhaps only in trace quantities. It was swilled by the cupful by so many of the other distorted phantasms of the looking-glass world they'd chosen to dwell in. Perhaps the memory of Donald Hughes would serve to inoculate her against the poisonous vengeance of those around her.

He paused and kissed her, enjoying the opportunity to gaze into her eyes once more. Hers were features that might have been beloved of painters a century earlier, when painters still depicted women with the conventional numbers of eyes and breasts. He imagined gazing into her eyes staring back at him from a canvas, wondering if their green pools would appear as deep.

"What are you thinking of, Alec Grey?" she asked as her lips released his.

"I've considered a hypothetical question of my own," he replied. "I preferred yours, but it's already been asked."

She smiled and nodded her consent.

"Hypothetically, were we to become a long-term object of office rumors," he began, "I've had occasion to wonder whether I'd be expected to accompany you to Windermere one weekend to have sherry with your family... or whatever it is people do at Windermere."

"I should like that," she replied. She seemed to be wrestling with her laughter. "Sorry... I meant I should like that hypothetically."

"I imagine what I've in fact been wondering was whether I should like that. I've visions of your father greeting us at the door of his baronial manor with a loaded shotgun, demanding to know how a mere civil servant dared have the effrontery to debauch his daughter." He paused, darkly amused by the image. "They do have shotguns in Windermere, I imagine."

"Oh yes," she replied. "My father has a matched pair of Holland and Holland guns. He's ever so proud of them. He goes out for birds in the spring. Of course, he can't shoot for toffee... my mother maintains that the safest place to be when one of his guns goes off is directly in front of it, as he never hits what he's aiming at."

"That's a comfort," he said.

She laughed and took his hand. "It's not nearly as perilous as you might think," she assured him. They walked in silence for a time. When at length she spoke, her voice was alight with mirth, a measure of amusement he was uncertain he could share.

"Do you know, I believe my parents' reaction upon meeting you will be one of relief," she said. "It's very likely to overwhelm them to the extent that they won't notice that you've told them you're a spy when they inquire what you do for a living."

"I'm not actually permitted to tell people what I do for a living," he corrected her. He'd long considered this to be a peculiarity of his profession, as the only people who might have a sinister interest in his activities already knew full well that he was employed by MI5, and no doubt maintained substantial files about him. "I'm not certain I understand why they should be relieved."

Her features contorted with uncertainty for an instant. "My father fears he's destined to be the last of his line," she whispered. "As you'll recall from our first conversation in Sir Alistair's office, my brother Charlie... doesn't fancy women. I've an auntie that's the same way, except she does fancy women... there's a name for that, but I can't recall it. I've not brought many boys home for tea, and I've begun to appreciate that my family harbors doubts about me as well. Far from shooting you, my father might see fit to provide you with a bodyguard to be certain nothing happens to you."

He felt her hand tighten in his, wondering what the gesture signified. He imagined fleetingly being welcomed by her father. Perhaps the older man would insist that he borrow a gun and accompany him into the high fields in search of grouse or pheasant or whatever it was that the gentry blasted into clouds of blood and feathers for sport. If he could arrange to have a few of them painted red with a hammer and sickle displayed on their tails, he'd no doubt bag his limit.

"Did your former wife bring you 'round to meet her parents?" Alice Woodward asked softly.

"Yes," he replied, "yes she did. It was the longest two hours and eleven minutes of my life... and the quietest."

She smiled at this. "Did you not get on with them, then?"

"I remain grateful that shotguns aren't fashionable in Knightsbridge," he replied.

"Only, I've come to appreciate that I'm indebted to your wife," she said. He glanced at her to find she was staring across the channel once more. "If she hadn't left you, we'd not be here. I don't imagine you're the sort who'd come away with me if you were still married."

He considered this. "I believe you're disparaging poor Hugh Somerfield again," he teased her.

She smiled, affecting an air of contrition, and said nothing.

The planks of the path that bore them along the waterside had grown worn, the occasional board showing signs of having been replaced. They were returning to the proximity of The Swans, he decided. The tufts of rye grass and distant trees, spectral watchtowers in the rain, were becoming familiar. He'd noticed them hours earlier when they'd begun their journey, cloaked in awkward silence.

In another handful of minutes, another few footfalls, they would return to their airless room with a view of the channel, and the embrace of its bed, and the fragrance of her hair. He smiled to himself, refusing to permit his imagination any further licentious amusement. He was confronted with the very real danger that he might begin reciting poetry.

"Is there anyone I'm indebted to for your being here?" he asked.

"Andrei Bogdanov," she replied. "It's really quite the strangest irony when you consider it."

He allowed that he'd not done so, and the thought touched him with dark amusement.

Her face appeared suddenly to be overwhelmed by laughter. "Do you imagine Princess Margaret gets to have long walks on the beach with her Russian friend?" she inquired.

He paused for a moment, turning to regard her. "In Leningrad? Perhaps in snowshoes on the shores of Vasilievsky Island."

"I know she's something of a traitor, running off with him to the Soviet Union," she said quietly, "but I've always found it rather romantic... that she'd give up her home and her family for love."

He felt himself smile, and at length he turned to resume walking, feeling her hand grow tight in his. "It wasn't as the newspapers told it," he said, and he heard the rasp of conspiracy in his words. "I don't imagine it's the sort of thing Sir Alistair would have asked you to type."

She glanced uncertainly at him.

"Princess Margaret was involved with an air force officer... Group Captain Townsend, if I recall. The palace was not pleased with the thought of the queen's sister marrying a divorcee twice her age, and in time she was made to end the affair. Shortly thereafter, she met Lieutenant-Colonel Yevgeny Ivanov, an assistant naval attaché at the Soviet embassy in London. The next thing anyone knew, she'd popped off behind the curtain and married him."

She nodded. "That's as I recall it as well."

"The part of her romance that's covered by the act is that Yevgeny Ivanov was actually a colonel in the KGB. He agreed to divorce his wife at the time and court the princess in exchange for a car, a particularly desirable apartment and a dacha outside the city. His file at the registry includes a number of Enigma decrypts in which he describes the princess in... less than flattering terms. There are rumors that he's back with his wife, and only appears with the princess for state dinners and formal opportunities to embarrass Whitehall on television."

She put her hand to face for a moment, and he felt a pang of regret at having sundered her illusion. "Does the queen know?"

"She does not," he replied, "and Sir Alistair's been charged with ensuring that she never finds out. In the event that he proves unsuccessful, I'd imagine enough heads will roll to block the Thames and constitute a hazard to maritime navigation."

He listened to the cadence of their footfalls along the

boardwalk, syncopated with the drumming of rain on their umbrella. "It's rather sad," she whispered.

"Spies don't do what they do for love, Miss Woodward," he admonished her.

"Present company excluded, Mr. Grey."

Their morning's conversation seemed to have guttered as the distant spires and cracking bricks of their hotel swirled from the rain and the fog, dancing lewdly upon the gray threshold between substance and his imagination. He felt gravel crushed beneath his shoes as they left the wooden path, listened to the imperceptible timbre of rain upon the slates of the aged building. The cough of the channel grew hushed as they made for the car park. Ken Bryan's MG remained its sole occupant, he observed, smiling to himself.

That they'd come to be the lone guests at The Swans had been a peculiar counterpoint to their weekend. He'd begun to enjoy the echoing silence of its corridors and the fastidious attentions of what few staff as hadn't broken ranks for an off-season in the Canaries. Perhaps Alice Woodward had grown up knowing the smiling countenances of domestics hovering in the shadows. The sensation had been remarkable for him, an after-dinner liqueur from an oddly-colored bottle with a name no one could remember an hour later.

The woman behind the desk in the lobby of The Swans glanced up as they entered, her expression flickering with disappointment when she appreciated that they represented no fresh custom. He furled their umbrella and smiled his acknowledgement.

"Mr. MacDonald?" she inquired uncertainly as they approached the desk for their key.

"Yes," he replied.

"Someone's rung from London for you," she continued. "At least, I believe it was for you. I'm meant to ask you if you might also answer to the name Alec Grey."

He felt his features grow taut, willing himself to smile despite his sudden unease.

"I've been known to," he replied coldly.

"The chap who called, he said I was to give you a message, sir," she said. "It was an odd message. I think he was trying to make believe he was a Yorkshireman."

"What did the caller say?"

"He said 'you's been pinched,'" she answered him. "Just like that... 'you's been pinched.'"

Alec Grey sighed, and in the corner of his eye he watched Alice Woodward's eyes grow dark as she glanced into the shadows at the distant end of the lobby.

"Thank you," he said at length. "I wonder if I might ask you to make up our bill. I'm afraid we won't be staying to supper this evening."

"Yes, sir," the woman said.

He turned and took Alice Woodward's hand, walking slowly toward the stairs. She said nothing until they'd reached the second floor of the hotel, and when at last she spoke her voice was a harsh whisper.

"Was that Mr. Somerfield who telephoned?" she asked.

"I imagine it must have been," Alec Grey agreed. "I didn't tell anyone where we were off to, but as Hugh recommended this place, he would have known."

"I don't understand the message," she said.

He smiled and kissed her, losing himself in her for a time. When he decided that he could no longer forestall replying to her query, he opened his eyes to find himself staring into hers. She appeared to be studying him in the stolen moments of their kiss, seeking for something that had not chosen to reveal itself in his features.

"I don't understand the message," she repeated.

"U's been pinched," he said. "I should say that the Soviets have stolen another blank of Uranium."

28

Monday, October 23

H e'd read a substantial volume of reports from his subordinates that had described meetings with Soviet sources in public toilets and disused buildings. Upon consideration of them now, he allowed that a conversation with Ivan Nikonov amidst the clatter and smoke of this cafe was hardly a matter to be complained over. The coffee was only objectionable if he drank it.

Alec Grey glanced at his wristwatch. The KGB officer was three minutes late. He willed himself to still his unease. Colonel Nikonov would appear, he was certain, if two of MI5's burlier employees had to frog-march him all the way from Abbots Close.

The morning had unnerved him. He'd listened to the description of Alice Woodward servicing her dead drop at the entrance to the Bond Street tube station as normal men with normal livelihoods listened to football matches on the wireless. Edward Blair had been detailed to telephone him when she appeared. The entire breathless conversation had occupied little more than a minute, but he'd experienced a lifetime of dread before its conclusion. She'd not even stumbled on the steps on this occasion, he reminded himself once more.

She'd have returned to her typewriter by now, fortified behind the walls of Leconfield House. He glanced at his watch, willing the door of the cafe to open and Ivan Vasilievich Nikonov to appear, that he might put a whip to the fetlocks of this day and see it to its stable.

The Russian was another seven minutes arriving. Alec Grey was on the point of casting aside his darkest terrors and sampling the coffee before him.

Ivan Nikonov took his place at the table opposite him, his back to the wall and his palms pressed into the scarred plastic surface as he descended to his seat. He appeared to have aged another decade during the course of the previous weekend. His skin was decidedly gray. It resembled the leather seats of a Bentley Continental that had been abandoned in the sun. Alec Grey smiled to himself for an instant, driving the image from his thoughts.

"You are amused, Mr. Grey?" the Russian demanded accusingly. "What in hell were you thinking, having your people bring me here?"

Alec Grey glanced at Ivan Nikonov, permitting his smile to grow thin. "It's a pleasure to see you again as well, Ivan Vasilievich."

The man before him leant forward, the poorly-shaven tundra of his cheeks swelling into harsh relief. "This is fucking dangerous, Mr. Grey," he hissed.

"I don't feel I'm in any danger," Alec Grey said evenly.

"I... I am in danger. Every time I am seen with you, there is the chance I will be observed. The first time, yes, I understand, the need to make contact. This time... what is it you wish to say to me that could not have been left at the dead drop you arranged?"

"I need your help, Colonel," Alec Grey replied. "It's a matter of some urgency, and I was certain you'd wish to understand exactly how best you can assist us."

The Russian's eyes narrowed. "There is nothing more urgent for me than not being seen in the company of MI5."

"You do appreciate that it's within my power to change that, Colonel," Alec Grey suggested. He met the gaze of the face across the table, holding it for a moment before its owner glanced away. His threat had been crude and guttural, but it had been clearly understood.

"What is it you want, Mr. Grey?"

Alec Grey smiled once more. He considered summoning a waitress, to permit Colonel Nikonov a minute longer to smolder. Upon reflection he decided that the temperature of the Russian's blood was probably satisfactory.

"Saturday last, one of your people burgled our facility in Cornwall and made off with a piece of refined Uranium about the size of a dinner plate," Alec Grey said. It was an irony of the sort which apparently amused Alice Woodward that he was prepared to speak of things to the Russian that he would have stopped at nothing short of murder to prevent the Britons surrounding him in the cafe from knowing. "I should like it returned to us."

Ivan Nikonov tumbled back in his chair as if he'd been slapped. "I know nothing of this," he said darkly.

"I'm quite certain you don't," Alec Grey agreed. "None the less, I'm confident in your abilities to find out where the Uranium has been hidden. Having done so, you'll convey the information to me, our people will return Her Majesty's radioactive materials to their rightful home, and all will be right with the world once more."

"This is not something I am able to do," the Russian said. "You must understand, I have access only to that information which my government believes is required for my activities on its behalf. They would not trust me with... what you have described. I have no need to know such things."

"Someone at Kensington Palace Gardens knows where our Uranium is, Ivan Vasilievich," Alec Grey assured him.

The Colonel shook his head wearily. "Why are you doing this, Mr. Grey?" he demanded. "It is a piece of metal. Unlike my country, as you are aware, you have the ability to create more of it."

Alec Grey sighed, feeling himself grow angry despite his preparation for this morning's drama. "I don't imagine your government has briefed you on the nature of the material that was stolen from us, Colonel," he said. His tale would only be plausible if Ivan Nikonov were as ignorant of the matter as he claimed. "I must confess that I'd not troubled myself to learn much about it either, until it was explained to me recently. Uranium is extremely nasty. It kills people just by being close to them. It burns them alive from the inside. If I were certain you'd smuggled it out of the country, we wouldn't be having this conversation. You can burn alive as many Russian scientists as you like. I shouldn't wish to explain to my superiors how it came to be secreted in the wall of a school or hidden in a supermarket or forgotten on the tube. The resulting stack of dead Englishmen would not please the people I answer to."

Colonel Nikonov waved dismissingly. "My government wants this material very badly," he said. "If they stole it, as you have said, it was on its way to Moscow an hour later. You have nothing to worry about. May I leave now?"

"I'm not permitted to discuss the details with you, Colonel, but we're able to know when the Uranium has left the country. It's still here, and you're going to locate it for us."

"I cannot do this."

Alec Grey paused, restoring his smile like damaged greasepaint. "I make it a point to learn a new word in the Russian language each morning, Colonel," he said. "I've quite a mastery of your language. Would you like to know which word I learned this morning?"

The colonel stared blankly at him.

"My word for today is *gulag,*" he continued. He watched the eyes before him grow haunted. "I can see that you know that word as well. I'm not surprised... I'm certain you know a great many more Russian words than I ever will. I was told that *gulag* is actually an acronym... it derives from *Glavnoe Upravlenie Ispravitel'no-trudovykh Lagere,* the Chief Administration of Soviet Work Camps. Did I pronounce that correctly, Colonel?"

The man before him nodded wordlessly.

"My research chaps inform me that *gulags* are Siberian labor camps where your government sends criminals for whom it feels that a nine-millimeter bullet to the base of the skull would be too merciful. The cold and the brutality and the filth and the food... it's a wonder to me how anyone survives in those places."

"No one does, Mr. Grey," the Colonel said through clenched teeth. "That is the point of them."

"Upon the instructions of my superiors, I'm here to offer you a choice. If you choose to assist us in locating the stolen Uranium, you will be given the opportunity to defect to this country. If you decline our generous offer, Ivan Vasilievich, or if the Uranium surfaces behind the curtain, I will personally burn you to Moscow and you will acquire a first-hand understanding of my new Russian word for today."

"I cannot..."

"Yes, Colonel, you can," Alec Grey interrupted him. "You can expend every asset you have, call in all the favors you can think of and you can locate what's been taken from us. However this turns out, you won't be needing them again."

He leant forward until he was a hand's breadth from the Russian. "When I contacted you last week, Colonel, I envisioned having you as a source for a very long time. Not to put it mildly, your only two options for retirement would have been a KGB bullet or heart failure. Upon the instructions of my superiors, I'm about to let you walk free for the price of a few day's work. Generosity on that level goes against everything I believe in. You would do well to take me up on this offer before I convince the men I answer to that they've taken leave of their senses."

In the corner of his eye, the door to the cafe opened for a moment. The figure who passed through it from the gray daylight beyond resolved itself into the form of Julie Gardner, one of the A4 staff who'd been assigned to keep Colonel Nikonov in a box that morning. She'd been instructed to remain in her car half a block beyond the cafe. That she'd appeared mid-way through his conversation with the Russian could not be attributed to her sudden thirst. He turned slightly and she gestured toward the street. A moment later she returned to the sullen rain beyond the cafe.

Ivan Nikonov parted his lips to speak, his expression suggesting he was uncertain what words might emerge from them. Alec Grey rose to his feet, crushing the man before him into silence. "I believe you know how to get in touch with me," he said, and he turned to leave before the Russian could reply.

Julie Gardner had taken shelter in the doorway of a newsagent's shop across from the cafe. She glanced uncertainly at Alec Grey as he approached her.

"I'm really sorry to've interrupted you, boss," she said hurriedly.

"Don't be," he said. "Ivan Vasilievich was an act of pure desperation. He doesn't know anything, and he never will. We'd have better luck finding what we've lost with a pack of dogs. If it had occurred to me, I'd have told someone to pull me out when you did. You came in right after the dreadful ultimatum part, but before he could work up a compelling level of groveling."

She smiled, clearly at a loss for not being called upon to defend her breach of tradecraft.

"I wouldn't have bothered you, except there's been a message over the radio," she continued. "It had your name on it."

She offered him a folded scrap of paper. He accepted it, gazing at it for several seconds before he appreciated what he was looking at. The street address in Adams Row was that of Alice Woodward. The only other word on the paper was 'urgent.'

"What is this?" he demanded.

"I don't know, boss," Julie Gardner replied. "It was coded for watcher radio... they're usually just names and addresses. It gives the Soviet cryptographers less to work with."

"Yes," he agreed, "yes it does." He knew very well that it did, as he'd instituted the procedures for A4's radio communications.

He glanced into the street. "Where's your car?" he demanded suddenly.

"Just there," she replied, gesturing to the street. "The white Volvo."

"I need you to drive me here," he instructed her, returning the scrap of paper. He began walking briskly toward the Volvo.

"I've been detailed to Colonel Nikonov," she protested, falling in beside him. "Andy Dixon's fond of reminding us that the watcher cars..."

"Andy Dixon's fond of reminding you that the watcher cars aren't to be used as taxis," he interrupted. "I'm aware of that. I instructed him to remind you of it. I'll instruct him to overlook your transgression in this instance."

"And Colonel Nikonov?"

"The second car will have little difficulty keeping him in a box," Alec Grey replied. "He'll be off to Kensington

Palace Gardens in a moment."

They came abreast of the Volvo. She inquired whether he preferred to drive. After a moment's consideration he decided that she was likely the more skilled of them, and certainly possessed of calmer nerves at present. She let him into the passenger's door and took her place behind the wheel.

"I should like to be in Adams Row about twenty minutes ago," Alec Grey said as she summoned the car's engine from its slumber and put the machine in gear. "You may violate any traffic laws you see fit. In the event you notice the Queen Mother crossing the street, sound your horn before you run her down."

Julie Gardner clearly possessed driving skills superior to his own, Alec Grey decided as she began to negotiate the clotted streets. She slipped through the sedentary traffic with the fluid grace of a shark. None the less, the journey occupied almost half an hour, and he experienced every moment of it in perfect relief, every passing building and expressionless pedestrian a still life to be studied and remarked over. The Volvo had barely come to rest before Alice Woodward's house before he'd flung its door open and hurled himself from the car.

The front door was unlocked, and he pushed it before him, stepping uncertainly into the hall beyond it. Had one of his people rushed into an unknown situation with so little concern, he thought fleetingly, he would have ragged them out with a sufficient level of wrath to have blistered paint. Someone spoke in the front sitting room.

Alice Woodward sat before him in a huge arm chair, her features bloodless. She stared at him as he stepped into the room, her eyes suddenly huge. She was flanked by several of his staff, their heads turning as one as he entered. A figure in the furthest corner of the room reached into his suit coat, withdrew a pistol in a flicker of blue steel and

then returned it to its confinement. The man smiled apologetically, his shoulders relaxing.

He willed himself to regard the woman in the chair
before him as another of his staff, the unfortunate amateur
she'd been when he'd first encountered her in Sir Alistair's
office. She stared at him for a moment, clearly uncertain
what was expected of her.

"Miss Woodward," he said, hearing his breath rasp
in his throat. "Are you quite all right?"

She nodded. "Yes," she replied. "Yes... Mr. Grey...
yes, I'm fine."

Alec Grey turned toward the nearest of his people.
Oliver Boyle was a short, athletic Irishman with a crumpled nose that had been broken in an adolescent pub brawl
and a brutally receding hairline. He was unquestionably
armed as well, but as the man closest to Alice Woodward,
he'd not drawn his pistol. In the event that Alec Grey had
been an intruder from the Soviet Union, he would not have
wished to draw gunfire to her.

"Boss," he acknowledged as Alec Grey's attention
fell to him. "The house is secure."

Alec Grey resisted the opportunity to observe that
the front door was hardly secure. "What's happened, Mr.
Boyle?" he demanded.

"Hugh Somerfield's waiting for you in the kitchen,"
he replied. There had been a note of urgency in his words,
Alec Grey appreciated. The group of men before him had
separated themselves from whoever was deeper within the
house. He glanced once more at Alice Woodward, smiled
uncertainly, and turned wordlessly to leave.

The kitchen had undergone substantial reorganiza-
tion since he'd last seen it, earlier that morning. The table
where he and Alice Woodward had shared coffee had been
driven into a corner, followed by all but one of its chairs.
A lone chair stood like the subject of an interrogation in the
center of the room. There was a prone figure on the floor

behind it, his wrists and ankles bound with rope and his mouth stopped with a tea towel. He twisted angrily despite his restraints. Alec Grey stared at him for a moment, realizing as he did that he was observing Andrei Mikhailovich Bogdanov.

Hugh Somerfield approached him from the rear of the kitchen. Two other men remained with the Russian.

"What the hell is happening?" Alec Grey demanded.

"Miss Woodward... she had a guest waiting for her," Hugh Somerfield replied. "Not exactly his sort of neighborhood."

Alec Grey wrested his attention from Andrei Bogdanov. "I think you'd best explain," he said coldly.

Hugh Somerfield crossed the expanse of the kitchen and withdrew two chairs from before the table. He took one for himself and offered the other to his superior. It was substantially less comfortable than it had been earlier, Alec Grey decided.

"I collected her after she filled her dead drop," Hugh Somerfield began, his voice little more than a whisper. He clearly did not wish to be overheard by the Russian. Alec Grey suppressed the growing sense that whatever secrets they were about to discuss were beyond blowing to Andrei Bogdanov. "As she was leaving the tube station, a car passed and splashed her. She was properly soaked, and she asked if we might stop here so she could change. I entered the house first, just as we discussed, and imagine who jumped from the sitting room. He'd a knife and a very surprised look on his face."

Hugh Somerfield smiled, clearly amused despite the gravity of his morning. "A struggle ensued, as they say... he turned out to be a great girl's blouse once I had his knife off him. I tied him up, rang for some additional lads, Olli Boyle had A4 send for you... and here we are."

"Was she hurt?" Alec Grey inquired.

His subordinate shook his head. "No one came to

harm, boss," he answered, grinning wryly. "Not even your humble servant... ta for your concern. Miss Woodward had the sense to stay well back during the disagreement."

"Has he said anything?" Alec Grey gestured toward the prone figure of the Russian.

"Nothing I'd care to repeat in polite company."

"Do you have any idea what he's come here for?"

Hugh Somerfield's eyes narrowed as he leaned forward. After several seconds he reached beneath the table and withdrew a battered Gladstone bag. He unfastened its clasp and emptied it across the kitchen table.

"This is an ugly one, boss," he sighed.

Alec Grey stared blankly at the objects that had emerged from the bag.

"We found the kitchen as you see it now," Hugh Somerfield continued. "His bag was on the table." He reached into the clutter of objects. "He brought a lamp flex with the ends of its wires bare, several scalpels, a leather truncheon, a considerable length of rope... some of it's in use at present... and these." He pushed two cellophane squares toward Alec Grey. They resolved themselves into condom packets. "A most thoughtful rapist," Hugh Somerfield remarked.

"I assume he meant to have it off with her, then tie her to that chair in the middle of the floor and torture her. He's clearly had some experience in these matters, judging by the tools he's brought. I imagine he wanted to avoid doing anything to her that would be... outwardly visible... to avoid the possibility that she'd draw attention to herself and compromise her usefulness as a Soviet agent. Having her up the... having her get pregnant wouldn't have done either."

Alec Grey stared at the tangle of rope and wire and steel on the table, unwilling to return his attention to Hugh Somerfield. "Christ, Hugh," he said, hearing rage in his words, "what have we done? What the hell have we gotten her into?"

Hugh Somerfield regarded him uncertainly. "She's unharmed, boss," he insisted.

He wrested his attention from the table, meeting Hugh Somerfield's gaze at length. "Yes... yes, of course she is," he said. "Well done." He struggled to appreciate the proper disposition of this fragment in the immense jigsaw puzzle of the previous few weeks. He imagined Alice Woodward in the front room. He could not bring himself to turn, to view the lone chair, the struggling figure of Andrei Bogdanov.

"I trust A4 had Bogdanov in a box earlier," he said, struggling to subdue his swelling anger.

"Every minute. He looks for her chalk mark each morning just after eight o'clock... A4's got him on a timetable. When he found it this morning, he was off to Bond Street like a hound with a scent. He emptied the dead drop five minutes after she filled it. He sent the film along to another chap in a brush pass a few minutes later. Two watchers followed the package directly to Kensington Palace Gardens. Mr. Bogdanov was rather craftier... he turns out to have been wearing a reversible coat. A fellow who looks a bit like him was wearing the same sort of coat, turned inside out. He ducked into the old Bond Street arcade... the watchers assigned to him are fairly certain that's where he changed places with his double. They followed the double for an hour before they realized they'd had their legs pulled."

"During which time we may surmise he came here," Alec Grey concluded. "I presume you've not found the Minox cassettes on him."

"We searched him," Hugh Somerfield said. "They're definitely at the Soviet embassy."

Alec Grey exhaled. "That's a small comfort at least,"

He glanced at the kitchen door. "Does... Miss Woodward know what you've found... what Bogdanov had in mind?"

Hugh Somerfield shook his head. "The lads've kept her in the sitting room. She's more nerve than she looks... no screaming, no tears, no difficult questions. I thought it'd be best if you explained it to her... whatever you decide she needs to know."

Alec Grey permitted himself a final moment's consideration of the objects on the table before him. No woman could possibly need to know what she'd been spared, he thought angrily. It was beyond him to imagine speaking to her of the events of this morning.

He rose to his feet. They'd moved Soviet operatives in similar situations. The one on the floor of Alice Woodward's kitchen posed no greater problem. He glanced at Andrei Bogdanov for an instant as Hugh Somerfield abandoned his chair.

"There's a chap in Technical Services named Franklin... Terry Franklin," Alec Grey said. "He'd a few years of medical school before he realized he'd no patience for being surrounding by ill people, and he came to work for us. He's sufficiently familiar with a syringe to know where to stick the sharp end. Ring him... have him lay on an ambulance and two other lads with convincing white coats. I want Bogdanov shot full of horse tranquilizer and taken out on a stretcher. Have Olli Boyle ride with him. Send that bloody bag along as well. When he's gone, you and I and the rest of these chaps will set this house to rights. No one will speak a word of this to Miss Woodward." His final instruction had been sufficiently loud for the other men in the kitchen to hear it. Both of them nodded as he turned to face them.

"I'll see to it, boss," Hugh Somerfield said. He looked once more at Andrei Bogdanov. "Where do you want the ambulance to drop him?"

Alec Grey considered this for a moment. "Balmoral Castle," he replied.

In the closing months of the tenure of his predecessor, Technical Services had been instructed to install an interrogation suite with what its designers would later come to describe as 'all modern conveniences.' It had been the observation of Sir Simon Turnbull, the director of MI5 at the time, that questioning defectors in poorly-lit back rooms and subterranean closets reflected unfavorably upon the capabilities of the British intelligence community. None of his subordinates had been greatly concerned about what defectors and Soviet agents thought of the British intelligence community, but Sir Simon had been a force unto himself, oftentimes with an agenda comprehensible by no one else.

The interrogation suite had been an impressive piece of work when Alec Grey had been introduced to it. It was a broad concrete room with one-way glass in all four walls, adjustable lighting, sixteen concealed microphones each with its own pair of tape recorders and four sixteen-millimeter film cameras to visually record important debriefings.

Lawrence Downs, who'd been tasked by Sir Simon with the implementation of the room, had guardedly suggested that he was uncomfortable with the thought of interrogating Soviet agents in surroundings far more luxurious than their apartments in Moscow. Alec Grey had found little difficulty in agreeing with him, and the interrogation suite had fallen into legend as having never witnessed a single interrogation. He was uncertain how it had come to be referred to by the name of the royal family's castle in Scotland, but he allowed now that the sobriquet seemed appropriate.

"Shall I have Lawrence Downs or Nigel Perry attend to have a word with Mr. Bogdanov?" Hugh Somerfield asked.

Alec Grey shook his head. "I'd prefer this one remain in the family for the moment," he said, conscious of a note of conspiracy in his words. "I'll question Andrei Bogdanov myself. I'm certain I lack Mr. Downs' patience and skills of observation, but I can swing an iron pipe about with the best of them."

29

S usan Pascal felt herself start as the interior of her tiny office echoed with the rattle of knuckles upon the glass of her door. She glanced about uneasily, wondering how long it had been since she'd last withdrawn her attention from the scraps of paper strewn across her desk. She was not unfamiliar with doing so to find that night had fallen during her lapse in attention.

She peered at a small brass clock at the periphery of her desk. Its hands were motionless. She'd clearly neglected to wind it. The knock came again.

"Yes," she said loudly in the direction of the door.

The door swung toward her. Dennis Edminster was a tall man with sandy hair and a perennially bemused smile. He regarded the world through enormous spectacles that rendered him somewhat more avuncular than he might have wished. His work, he'd remarked on occasion, was to uncover Soviet agents and bang them up for fifteen or twenty years. It was a serious matter. He'd usually added that it was largely a serious matter for the Soviet agents in question, and that its seriousness was no cause for any of his staff to lose sleep.

She herself had been instrumental in the 'banging up' of Melita Norwood, who'd worked as a secretary at the Non-Ferrous Metals Research Association in Euston, the

original location of the Uranium extraction facility for
whatever it was that no one was permitted to know about
in Cornwall. Melita Norwood had been little more than a
growing hillock of paper scraps and files for several years,
and Susan Pascal had been disturbed to learn that the
Soviet agent had possessed a face and a voice and hollow,
lifeless eyes upon hearing the pronouncement that she
would spend the next quarter of a century in a cell for her
treachery.

Dennis Edminster pushed the door to and pulled a
steel visitor's chair from the corner of her office. He seated
himself beside her desk. "You sent for me, Miss Pascal," he
said.

"Yes, sir," she replied. "I've discovered something."

Dennis Edminster smiled warmly. "I do so enjoy it
when people tell me that," he laughed. "Who have you discovered?"

Susan Pascal suspected that Dennis Edminster
regarded the Codes and Ciphers division as an enormous
crossword puzzle, crafted and recrafted on a weekly basis
for his private entertainment. She was but the clue for
number seventeen down.

She smiled. "STANLEY," she replied.

He seemed still more pleased. "Your secret admirer,"
he mused. The identity of the Soviet agent who used the
code name STANLEY had been her personal quest almost
from her first day at this desk. The problem of refining the
fragmentary references to him extracted from Soviet intercepts was daunting, but it had captivated her attention.
Most of the researchers in Codes and Ciphers had personal
projects. Dennis Edminster encouraged them.

He leant forward into the puddle of light from her
desk lamp. "Have you determined who STANLEY might
be?"

She shook her head. "No sir," she replied. "I'd have
sent for you a great deal sooner if I had. I've discovered

several critical pieces, though. Would you like to hear what I've found?"

"I shouldn't miss it," he replied.

She exhaled and pushed her current carpet of papers to the side of her desk. She opened a ragged green folder and spread its contents before him. "This is STANLEY," she said. "Shall I tell you his entire story?"

He nodded, glancing at the tangle of papers.

"STANLEY is first mentioned in a VENONA decrypt in June of 1946," she began. VENONA was an American codebreaking project that had intercepted and recorded a vast library of encrypted Soviet radio transmissions during the nineteen-thirties and nineteen-forties, and set about attempting to break into them a decade later. The American cryptographers had discovered the Soviets had periodically reused the one-time pads that had encoded their transmissions, raising the theoretical possibility of working out the contents of the pad pages, and hence the messages they'd been used to encipher. The undertaking had been augmented with computers several years earlier, and while only a fraction of the intercepted Soviet messages had been broken to date, western intelligence had been granted a vast insight into the activities of the Soviet Union beyond the iron curtain.

"In the 1946 message, the sender confirms that PETER has received GOBLET from STANLEY. We don't know who PETER is, although it's reasonable to assume he's STANLEY's controller. GOBLET is also a mystery... we'll probably never know what it refers to."

"Perhaps STANLEY will be good enough to tell us one day," Dennis Edminster suggested.

She smiled to herself and returned her attention to her papers. "The first interesting thing I've learned is in a decrypted Enigma message from June of 1946, sent four days before the VENONA message about STANLEY. In this message, SYNOK has contacted PETER to inform him that GOBLET is ready to be collected. Later the same day, there's another Enigma message from PETER informing Moscow Center that SYNOK has become *glukhoy*... deaf."

Dennis Edminster stared expectantly at her, and she was several seconds appreciating that he'd not understood the implication of her discovery. "Whoever STANLEY is, he used to have the code name SYNOK. He changed code names in June of 1946. The word *synok* is Russian for 'sonny.' It suggests that STANLEY had already been working for Moscow Center for some time by June of 1946, and he'd outgrown his code name."

"Oh... I see," Dennis Edminster said suddenly. "That's quite clever. Is there more?"

"Yes, sir," she replied. "We have a lot of VENONA material that references SYNOK. We've hardly bothered with it, as it seemed that SYNOK disappeared in 1946, and was no longer a current Soviet agent after that time. In fact, he just altered his name."

She adjusted the papers in her file. She found herself regarding a harsh black and white photograph of an older man. It was unusual for her research to include photographs. She was comfortable reducing the characters of her sinister narratives to words and code names.

"This is Michael Straight," she said, indicating the photograph. "Are you familiar with him?"

"Should I be?"

"He's an American. He studied at Cambridge during the 1930s. He was a bit of a pratt... he joined the Communist Party, did the usual bolshie things students did then. When he returned to America, he was given a position by President Roosevelt... his family was close to the Roosevelts. He began spying for Moscow. By all accounts, he wasn't terribly good at it, and within a few years he and Moscow had lost interest in each other."

She smiled and turned Michael Straight face down

in her file, deciding that she no longer wished to have him watch her while she recounted his folly.

"Earlier this year, he was appointed to the President's Council for the Arts by President Nixon. The Americans appear to be rather particular about Soviet spies just now, and Mr. Straight learned he was to be the subject of a background check by their FBI. He decided it would be preferable to admit his youthful indiscretions rather than to have them found out. He wouldn't name any other Soviet agents, but he did tell the FBI a great deal about his days at Cambridge. One of the things he mentioned was his membership in a Cambridge secret Marxist society known as the Apostles."

"Ah, now there's a name I do recognize," Dennis Edminster said. "They were a rather unpleasant lot, if I recall. Aside from being red, they were also largely poofs and drunks."

"Yes, sir," Susan Pascal agreed. "Michael Straight used the Soviet code name NIGEL. One of the early Enigma decrypts refers to SYNOK and NIGEL being apostles. At the time the message was decrypted, our people had no knowledge of the Apostles as an organization, and it was believed the reference was another code name."

"So we know that STANLEY studied at Cambridge."

"It's rather better than that," she corrected him. "We know that STANLEY studied at Cambridge prior to 1935, which is when the Apostles ceased to exist. Apparently Moscow Center felt that having all its future spies begin their careers expressing public sympathy for communist institutions mightn't look good on their CVs."

"Nor would having them all getting drunk and buggering each other," he added. He glanced uncertainly at her, his features growing flushed in the harsh light of her lamp. It pleased her none the less that Dennis Edminster did not feel the need to shelter her from the coarser elements of her work.

He considered the file before her. "This is really quite brilliant, Miss Pascal," he breathed.

"I've one more, if you're not in a hurry, sir," she said.

His smile broadened. "I've all morning, if you wish."

"On 12 October, the Enigma chaps upstairs broke the daily rotor settings for the Soviet embassy. It was quite a busy day, and we got a stack of decrypts. One of them referred to STANLEY and a 'photograph of ships.' I've no idea what that means, but I imagine someone at Leconfield House might do."

He appeared momentarily disappointed, and once again she appreciated that he'd not understood her correctly.

"If someone could be found who studied at Cambridge before 1935, and who had access to a classified photograph of ships that would be of interest to Moscow, we might well know at last who STANLEY is. At the very least, we might create a short list of names."

Dennis Edminster stroked his chin, his smile gradually infusing his features once more. "What will you do with your days if we catch him, Miss Pascal?" he inquired. "You shall have to find yourself another Soviet agent."

"There are a great many of them from which to choose," she said.

He rose to his feet and returned her visitor's chair to its corner. "You've done brilliantly," he said. "I'd recommend you for a pay rise if I thought there was the slightest chance you'd receive one. I trust you'll type up a report of your findings."

"Yes, sir," she said. "By day's end."

"Splendid," he turned to leave. "It's not long until luncheon is served. Would you like a hand?"

She scowled at him. "Thank you, sir," she replied. "I can manage."

He glanced once more at her file. "You're more than

we deserve, Miss Pascal," he said, and he slipped into the corridor beyond her office.

Dennis Edminster had expressed his admiration for her work on earlier occasions, as well as his assertion that she was capable of a great deal more than researching archived Soviet decrypts. At another place, in another life, she thought sourly, she might have agreed with him.

She put her palms against the edge of her desk and put her weight against it until her wheelchair began to slide backward. She grasped its wheels without thinking, propelling herself toward the door of her office. It was scarcely wide enough to admit her chair, and its frame bore the scars of innumerable collisions.

She'd been moved on several occasions to remind Dennis Edminster that she'd been assigned to the research division wholly on the grounds that her access to it did not require that she negotiate any stairs.

30

It had required a substantial volume of coffee and a glass of whiskey from a bottle that Hugh Somerfield had sworn he hadn't possessed to reach his current level of resolve. Alec Grey imagined himself having passed through a number of rooms. He had transcended his desire to kill Andrei Bogdanov, to beat him unconscious, to emasculate him, and finally to burn him to Moscow and send him postcards in Siberia. He felt a reverberant calm envelope him and he was touched with a disembodied embarrassment at his earlier plateau of rage.

He'd been unable to arrange to spend a few minutes alone with Alice Woodward as he and his people had been preparing to vacate her home. Two of his men had remained with her, to escort her back to Leconfield House when she'd changed her clothes and composed herself. He'd stared into her eyes across the sitting room, struggling to remind himself of his more pressing responsibilities. In time, he'd succeeded in convincing himself that her continued safety rested in his addressing his attentions to the Russian who'd meant to assault her.

He glanced through the one-way glass of Balmoral Castle at Andrei Mikhailovich Bogdanov and he drew a deep breath. The air still tasted minutely of fresh masonry and newly painted steel. The interrogation suite was a pharaonic tomb carved well in advance of the demise of its intended occupant, waiting these long years for the arrival of the Soviet agent who now occupied the metal chair bolted to its floor.

Andrei Bogdanov resembled a creature from a bad American film. His wrists and ankles were shackled. A length of chain ran between them through a metal eye welded to a metal table fixed to the floor in the middle of the room. The room was equipped with sufficient illumination to make the Russian resemble a plate of chips at a cafe awaiting its diner. He'd been staring into the featureless surface of the table for some time, his posture one of supplication. Alec Grey considered it pointedly unlikely that Andrei Bogdanov's appearance betrayed his true state of mind. The length of his chains largely determined his disposition.

He drew another breath into his lungs and he stepped through the heavy steel door that admitted him to the distant side of the one-way glass. It closed behind him with the finality of a prison cell. Andrei Bogdanov glanced at him, squinting before the glare of the lamps overhead.

The designers of the room had intended that those of its occupants not chained into their seats be permitted the comfort of viewing those who were with the lights behind them.

"Andrei Mikhailovich," Alec Grey said, and he allowed that he was content with the timber of his voice. He'd known moments of concern that he would utter the Russian's name and fly into an uncontrolled rage, beating the helpless prisoner to a bloody pulp before Hugh Somerfield could enter the room and restrain him.

The Russian leant back in his chair to the extent his restraints would permit him. "Who the fuck are you?" he demanded.

"My name is Alec Grey. I'm surprised you don't recognize me."

Andrei Bogdanov peered uncertainly at him. "You are Alec Grey? You do not look much like your photographs."

"You look precisely like yours, Andrei," Alec Grey said. "Every one of them."

The Russian smiled coldly. "Why have I been brought here?"

Alec Grey permitted his expression to grow bemused. "I should have thought that would have been obvious. You attempted to recruit an employee of Her Majesty's government to spy for the Soviet Union, and earlier today you attempted to do her grievous bodily harm. We frown on that sort of thing."

Andrei Bogdanov's eyes narrowed. "You know about this?"

"Yes, Andrei, of course we know about this. Miss Woodward grassed you out as soon as she'd finished her lunch. Every page she photographed and passed along to you was prepared by us. You've been of invaluable service to MI5."

"Bullshit," he spat. "If what you say was true, you would not be telling me now. You would want my people to continue to believe the papers she copied for us are genuine."

"And so they shall," Alec Grey assured him. "Who do you imagine will tell them otherwise?"

"I will tell them."

Alec Grey shook his head. "I shouldn't think so, Andrei. There are two avenues by which you might exit this building, and I'm afraid neither of them includes an audience with anyone from Moscow Center."

The Russian laughed. "Bullshit. This is England, not the Soviet Union. You have laws here. You cannot keep me in this room. I am entitled to demand to see someone from the Soviet consulate. I am entitled to demand to speak to a solicitor. You know this better than I do."

"Your demands are duly noted, and duly refused."

"I know about English laws, Mr. Grey," Andrei Bogdanov continued. The pitch of his voice had risen noticeably. "I know that you cannot keep me here forever. There must be a trial. I must be permitted to speak to…"

"British laws don't apply to you," Alec Grey interrupted him. The man before him fell silent, staring blankly up at him. "You're an illegal agent of a hostile foreign power, Andrei. We have an entirely different set of laws for you."

"What is this bullshit?"

Alec Grey stepped back and leant upon the one-way glass panel facing the Russian. "When Moscow Center sends someone important to spy on us, the spy in question is fitted with diplomatic papers. I've yet to meet a colonel in the KGB with any diplomatic talents to speak of, but none the less, when we catch them out, we're required to escort them to an Aeroflot and send them home. You weren't carrying diplomatic papers, Andrei. I can say with a comfortable degree of certainty that were we to accuse Moscow of sending you to commit acts of espionage upon British soil, your superiors would deny you'd ever been born. They're certainly not about to inquire after your whereabouts if you turn up missing."

Andrei Bogdanov's lips grew taut, and he said nothing.

"British laws apply to British subjects, of which you are clearly not one. International laws apply to diplomats, of which you are also not one. This leaves me free to create whichever laws I feel are appropriate for you, Andrei."

The Russian forced himself to smile once more. "You are trying to frighten me, Mr. Grey. I have lived in your country for a long time. I know that you cannot do what you say. Tell me what you want, maybe we will have a deal, yes?"

Alec Grey experienced a moment of regret that he'd

not given more serious consideration to Hugh Somerfield's suggestion to have Lawrence Downs in attendance. The veteran interrogator would have been impressed that he'd drawn Andrei Bogdanov to the point of compromise with so modest an effort.

He nodded and glanced away from the hunched figure before him. "I wish to know who talent-spotted Alice Woodward for you."

Andrei Bogdanov laughed, the sound like the barking of an aged dog. "Fuck you," he said. "You know I am not going to tell you that."

Alec Grey returned his attention to the Russian. "I think perhaps you will."

"I think maybe I will take my chances with your laws."

Alec Grey paused for a time, considering the chained man. "Do you recall my telling you that there were two exits from this building?"

The Russian nodded uncertainly.

"One of them is a black van. It will take you to a private cell at Wormwood Scrubs prison. You'll spend several years there, until we're certain that nothing you have to tell Moscow will be of use to them. One day, we'll arrange to exchange you for one of our agents that the KGB has captured, and you'll be permitted to return home."

"Your prisons do not frighten me, Mr. Grey."

"The second exit is as a bucket of ashes flushed down a lavatory."

"Bullshit."

"Very possibly. One never knows what will come floating down the Thames."

"If your superiors learned that you had executed me, it would be you going to prison. You would not risk that, I think."

Alec Grey smiled. "I shouldn't imagine that's a concern. There are no tapes rolling, and everyone behind these windows are my people. No one knows you're here, Andrei, so no one will know when you've gone."

The Russian shook his head. "This is not how the game is played, Mr. Grey. We are professional, you and I. We lie to each other, we steal each others' secrets... we do not kill each other."

"We don't set about to rape innocent civilians, either."

Andrei Bogdanov's expression grew confused. "It was not a personal thing. She is *shalava*... she is just someone's secretary. She is... a pawn in the game, yes? I fuck her, I do not fuck her... why should you care?"

Alec Grey had watched as Terry Franklin had injected Andrei Bogdanov with a stimulant to counteract the effects of the drugs the Russian had been given to sedate him. Even as the man had come to his senses and begun to test the integrity of his chains, Alec Grey had appreciated the inexorable course of their conversation. He'd imagined writing it all out in advance of his entering the brightly lit room and sealing it in an envelope, that he might entice Hugh Somerfield into wagering over it.

He'd known the words he would speak at this moment, despite his resolve to remain silent. He crouched before the table until his eyes were at a level with those of the Russian. "She's my girlfriend," he said coldly. "It is about to become very personal indeed."

Andrei Bogdanov stared at him, his features suddenly bloodless. "Fuck you," he spat. "Do you think you can frighten me, Mr. Grey?"

Alec Grey rose and glanced into the electric inferno of the ceiling. "Mr. Poole," he said to the microphones lurking between the lights. "I wonder if you'd come in here, and bring the key to unlock Mr. Bogdanov's restraints."

In the corner of his eye, the Russian smiled, clearly

pleased with himself. The door to the interrogation suite opened a moment later.

Kevin Poole was the most substantial human being Alec Grey had ever encountered. He was well over six feet tall, and his colleagues were amused to suggest that he had muscle in places few of the rest of them had any substantial volume of skin. His existence, as nearly as any of them had been able to ascertain, consisted of arriving at Leconfield House at nine each morning, leaving Leconfield House at five in the afternoon and then lifting weights until the cycle repeated itself the following day. Alec Grey surmised that the weights in question were almost certainly busses.

It served to surprise fresh additions to Alec Grey's staff that Kevin Poole had studied at Oxford, and was a competent officer. He seemed untroubled by a great number of the operations to which he was assigned involving his breaking things or frightening the living daylights out of people.

Andrei Bogdanov appeared to be on the point of gnawing through his own wrists to escape him as he entered the room.

"Andrei Mikhailovich will be shifting himself to new quarters," Alec Grey instructed Kevin Poole. "I'd like you to release him from the table and escort him down the cor-ridor to the final door on the right, just before you reach the stairs. Take him inside and await my arrival. I shall be along presently."

Kevin Poole nodded. "Yes, boss," he said.

"And do be careful with him," Alec Grey added. "Mr. Bogdanov probably appreciates by now he has nothing left to lose if he attempts an escape... even a wholly futile one."

Kevin Poole nodded his understanding. He unlocked the Russian, winched him from the chair by his chains and led him from the room.

Alec Grey watched the two men depart, permitting

himself to sigh. He felt his shoulders sag. He could imagine himself walking backstage and peeling his costume and
wig from his flesh, discarding the role he'd wrought for
himself. He glanced once more about the shadowless
room. It was merely an interval. A much more demanding
second act awaited the tread of his feet upon the boards.

"Mr. Somerfield, please put out the lights now," he
called to the ceiling. He turned to leave the room as the
first bank of lamps was extinguished.

Hugh Somerfield said nothing during their journey
in the wake of Kevin Poole and Andrei Bogdanov, for
which Alec Grey allowed that he was distinctly grateful. By
the time they caught Kevin Poole up, the Russian had overcome some measure of his terror at the sight of his captor.
He'd begun to struggle against his restraints once more,
and spit obscenities at the huge man who guarded him.
Kevin Poole was clearly oblivious to both.

The room to which Andrei Bogdanov had been led
was one of a number of specialized workshops used by
Technical Services. It was a featureless concrete chamber
with a great many instruments arrayed along its far wall, all
of them dark and silent at present. Its most compelling feature, however, was the rather sinister black sphere that
occupied most of its interior. Perhaps six feet in diameter,
it was fitted with a substantial pressure hatch and a
number of brass gauges. Alec Grey observed as he came
abreast of it that it clearly consumed the attention of the
Russian.

"Do you know what it is?" he inquired absently.

Andrei Bogdanov turned to address him, his chains
rattling as he did. Alec Grey imagined him to be a
Dickensian specter from a hastily-produced film of A
Christmas Carol.

"Why the fuck have you brought me here, Mr.
Grey?" he demanded. There seemed to be mere vapors of
his earlier defiance in his words.

Alec Grey ignored his question. "This is a hyperbaric chamber, Andrei," he explained. "Our chaps use it when they design microphones to plant on the floor of the sea, to listen for Soviet submarines. As I understand it, they can lock their creations inside it and increase the pressure until it's similar to what would occur at a depth of several hundred feet of water. It's very much more convenient than having to actually sink the things in the ocean to see if they work."

The Russian stared at him, his eyes growing haunted.

"It's actually possible to fit a man inside it," Alec Grey continued. "A small man... you'll manage."

Andrei Bogdanov shook his head, forcing himself to smile. "Fuck you," he growled. "Do think being locked in a tiny room will make me want to tell you anything?"

Alec Grey regarded him for a moment. "I don't believe you understand, Mr. Bogdanov," he said. "You'll be like one of the microphones our chaps test in there. Once you're inside, the chamber will be pressurized until you're at the equivalent of several hundred feet of water."

He turned to meet the Russian's gaze. "The air you breath includes all manner of things aside from oxygen. The rather troublesome gas for divers is nitrogen. When they breath air under pressure, the nitrogen becomes dissolved in their blood... as it will do in yours when you're inside that thing. After you've had an hour or two for your blood to become saturated with nitrogen, we'll let you out. With no more pressure to keep the nitrogen in suspension, it will boil out of your blood like champagne when the cork pops. Divers refer to the resulting inconvenience as 'the bends.' I'm told that it's the most intensely painful experience a human being can be subjected to. The pain can extend for hours... in extreme cases even days. It can leave one permanently crippled."

He stepped forward until his face was all but pressed

against that of the Russian. "And the most terrible thing about it, Andrei Mikhailovich, is that it's rarely fatal. When you finally finish screaming and thrashing about, you'll be ready to be stuffed back inside to begin it all over again."

"You will not do this, Mr. Grey," the man before him hissed.

Alec Grey smiled. "Andrei Mikhailovich, you've spied on my country and threatened someone I care a great deal about. In the event that you do not choose to assist us, I'll stuff you into that chamber and I believe I shall enjoy doing so. After you emerge the first time, or perhaps the second, you will tell us everything we wish to hear. Unfortunately, by the time you do, most of the blood vessels in your body will have been torn to ribbons. I'm afraid we have no one here qualified to look after a man in the condition you'll be in, and as you'll no doubt appreciate, I wouldn't be in a position to have you taken to hospital. Mr. Poole here will break your neck when you've told us all you can, and your earthly remains will be disposed of in the furnace we maintain for incinerating confidential papers."

Andrei Bogdanov stared at him for a moment longer, his jaw locked, his eyes glowing like liquid steel. "Fuck you," he spat. "Yes, all right, I will tell you. What I know… it is not worth dying for. Fuck you."

Alec Grey stepped away from him, grateful to be removed from the immediate presence of the Russian. "Mr. Poole," he said, speaking toward the distant end of the room. "Please return Mr. Bogdanov to the interrogation suite and restrain him to the table as before."

"Yes, boss," Kevin Poole said, and he led Andrei Bogdanov into the corridor.

Alec Grey turned to watch the door swing closed. He was conscious of Hugh Somerfield leaning against the wall beside it, having observed the previous few minutes without comment. A lack of comment was an oddity for Hugh Somerfield.

"I'd like you to summon Lawrence Downs now," he instructed his subordinate. "We'll draw up an agenda for him to put to Bogdanov. There are actually just a few matters that are pressing, but I believe it would be worth seeing what else he might be disposed to share with us."

"Yes, boss," Hugh Somerfield agreed, sounding very much unlike Kevin Poole when he'd spoken the same words.

"Bloody hell," Alec Grey whispered, imagining his words to be overwhelmed by the hammering of his heart against his chest.

"Yes, boss," Hugh Somerfield repeated. He was silent for a time, and when he next spoke his expression had grown darker. "I'm not sure I should be asking you this... were you serious... what you said to Bogdanov?"

Alec Grey permitted himself a broader smile. He brushed his hand across his face, feeling it grow slick with his perspiration. His had been a masterful performance indeed, he congratulated himself, if he'd succeeded in convincing Hugh Somerfield.

"We're not the KGB, Hugh," he replied, "even if it's in our interest to pretend to the office on occasion." He gestured toward the black sphere. "The air compressor for that thing's been knackered for months. All the underwater microphone chaps have downed tools and shifted along to Portsmouth to finish up. The only way it could have inflicted pain on Andrei Mikhailovich would be if he'd managed to trap his fingers in the door when it closed."

Hugh Somerfield smiled and shook his head. "No, boss," he said. "I was referring to what you said about Miss Woodward... and yourself."

"Ah..." Alec Grey decided that in other circumstances he might well have cursed himself for his lapse in security. His admission to the Russian had been a worthwhile element of his performance, something to convince Andrei Bogdanov that he was sufficiently enraged as to transgress the laws of his government and the unwritten rules of the great game. He might well have convinced Hugh Somerfield of it as well. He decided abruptly that he'd worn the wig and the greasepaint for far too long this day. He nodded wordlessly.

"She's an attractive girl," Hugh Somerfield said, clearly amused by his discovery. "I imagine the two of you will be quite happy wherever it is Sir Alistair Fitzhenry posts you when he finds out."

"I find that to be a thoughtless observation, Mr. Somerfield, coming from someone who's reputed to have been to bed with half the female staff at Leconfield House."

Hugh Somerfield was clearly pleased by his accusa-tion. "I make it a point to leave the ones with titles in their families alone. An outraged investment banker is a fat fellow with a red face. An outraged OBE is quite a different matter."

"I wasn't aware that her father held an OBE," Alec Grey said.

"Her father?" Hugh Somerfield pushed the door open. "No, boss. The Woodwards' gardener has an OBE. I believe her father is a first cousin to God."

31

The director rose from his chair and reached across his desk, his features creased with a broad smile. Sir Alistair Fitzhenry possessed a face that disguised the origins of its expressions. One could rarely be certain whether they were genuine, or merely affected for the sake of protocol or courtesy.

"Mr. Downs," he said warmly. Lawrence Downs shook the hand offered to him and permitted himself to be directed to a chair.

"Sir Alistair."

"We've not had occasion for a chat for some time," the director observed, returning to his own chair. The room was blue with fumes from the man's pipe, which Lawrence Downs decided was an improvement upon the foul-smelling *papirosi* that Mikhail Zakharov insisted on smoking.

"No, sir," Lawrence Downs agreed.

"I understand you've been conscripted by Mr. Grey to question Andrei Bogdanov... the fellow they brought into custody this morning." Sir Alistair's tone suggested that Andrei Bogdanov had been done for shoplifting, and faced nothing more serious than a stern lecture from a magistrate.

"I have," he acknowledged. "While I've not been

briefed as yet, it's my understanding that Alec Grey has done much of the donkey work. Andrei Mikhailovich has agreed to the interview. I'm looking forward to learning how Mr. Grey achieved his cooperation so quickly."

The director sighed. "As long as you don't put it in writing, whatever it turns out to be," he said quietly. His smile had returned, Lawrence Downs observed, although it had grown notably colder.

"Sir?"

"Mr. Bogdanov behaved rather poorly," Sir Alistair explained.

Lawrence Downs nodded. The great game was played by rules which were understood to be incumbent upon all its participants. While few of them had been explicitly presented to him, he appreciated the gravity of those which pertained to his work. He was not empowered to lie egregiously to the men who sat before him, however much they lied to him. He was prohibited from offering them inducements to speak which he was not prepared to provide them with when they'd ultimately fallen silent. He was forbidden any species of physical duress, however richly some of the Soviet agents he was confronted with might have deserved it.

If Andrei Bogdanov had behaved badly — if he'd abrogated the rules by which their peculiar chess match was played — Alec Grey might well have chosen to deny him the benefits of those rules as a consequence. This too was a matter of which little was said.

"I've read the file on Andrei Mikhailovich Bogdanov," Lawrence Downs observed. "It's hardly surprising."

Sir Alistair nodded, and Lawrence Downs decided he would do well to come to the point of this audience with the director. He was not entirely comfortable in this chair, in this office. He rarely came by for a 'chat,' as the director referred to their briefings, with good reason. It was the province of the director to assume responsibility for dark secrets and monstrous acts that would have beset him with an infinity of sleepless nights.

"Sir, I wished to apprise you of another matter," Lawrence Downs began. "This one involves a Soviet defector I was handed some weeks ago. Mikhail Sergeyevich Zakharov is a former colonel in the KGB. He's proven rather more knowledgeable than we'd initially expected, and no less cooperative than most of his colleagues I've had words with. A problem has arisen, however, and I fear it might have... consequences."

The director seemed unsettled by his tone, and he eased himself back into his chair. Sir Alistair's pipe was belching forth clouds of smoke like an unusually authentic toy railroad.

"Consequences?" he inquired.

"Perhaps I should explain further," Lawrence Downs offered. After a moment's consideration the director nodded his assent.

"I trust you're familiar with Anatoli Golitsyn, one of the Soviet defectors the Americans have," he began. "As it happens, James Angleton sat in on a session with Mikhail Zakharov last week... his presence rather served to underscore Mr. Golitsyn's contribution to our labors."

"I'm not certain I understand, Mr. Downs," Sir Alistair said.

"Anatoli Golitsyn appears to have made it his life's work to brand every defector who's come after him as a plant sent by Moscow to deceive us. Mr. Angleton believes him in this regard... I'm of the opinion that Mr. Golitsyn is either playing silly buggers for his own amusement, or he is in fact the plant. It hardly matters... it has become increasingly difficult for us to know which defectors to trust."

The irony of this situation was clearly not lost on the director, who smiled indulgently. "One might almost suspect this was the effect Moscow was hoping to achieve," he suggested.

Lawrence Downs nodded. "In interviewing fresh defectors such as Mikhail Zakharov, I've attempted to ascertain whether the information they've brought us is consistent with what we know from other sources. Inasmuch as agents who've been planted upon us will have been sent to provide us with lies, spotting the lies puts us well along to spotting the plants."

"I'd be surprised if it were as simple as that," Sir Alistair said.

"As would I, sir," he agreed. "Colonel Zakharov is perhaps a perfect example of this. He's brought us a great deal of potentially exciting material, including some tanta- lizing details about the state of the Soviet time stream proj- ect. He's also brought us four demonstrable and unshak- able lies."

"Four lies?"

Lawrence Downs nodded once more. "I shan't get into the details of the information in question unless you wish to hear them... suffice it to say we have four statements by Mikhail Zakharov that contradict intelligence from other sources we know to be accurate. If it were a single item, we would give serious concern to questioning the corroborating material. Four of them rather points to the colonel telling us incontrovertible fibs."

"Have you brought this to the attention of your defector?"

"On numerous occasions," Lawrence Downs replied. "He's resolute in his conviction that he's telling us the truth."

"I appreciate your problem, Mr. Downs," the direc- tor said. "If you choose to believe that this fellow is a plant and discount everything he says on that basis, we risk dis- carding a great deal of potentially valuable intelligence. If we ignore his four obvious fabrications, we risk accepting as fact an unknown volume of Soviet disinformation."

"It's rather more troublesome, sir." Lawrence Downs withdrew a folded sheet of paper from the inside pocket of his suit coat and placed it on the director's desk. Sir Alistair accepted it warily, clearly appreciating that he would not enjoy its contents. "This was one of the items Mikhail Zakharov has provided us with during the course of his interviews to date."

Sir Alistair unfolded the page and scowled at it. At length he read its contents aloud. "I know there to be an active Soviet agent within British intelligence. He fulfills the function of a head of a department at six of MI." He glanced over the sheet of paper, eyeing Lawrence Downs.

"There is a third possibility, sir," Lawrence Downs offered. "It was suggested by Alec Grey, and some of what Mikhail Zakharov has brought us tends to re-enforce it to a degree."

"Go on," the director prompted him.

"We have noted in the debriefings of Soviet personnel on several occasions of late a sense of... malaise about the KGB. Mr. Grey speculated that the level of morale in Moscow has reached something of a low ebb. He further speculated that the senior officers in Moscow could hardly have been unaware of this situation, and that they would have appreciated a number of defections were inevitable. This would certainly account for the Soviet plants we have encountered." He smiled uncertainly. "Assuming, of course, that we've actually encountered any."

"I believe I recognize the workings of Alec Grey's mind in this," Sir Alistair prompted him.

"Mr. Grey suggested that the KGB might have planted intelligence amongst its own people to damage their credibility in the event they defected. If one were to subscribe to his theory, Colonel Zakharov would have been deliberately provided with some obviously inaccurate information, as would all of his colleagues. At such time as one of them defected and provided us with the deliberate lies, they would be discredited, their genuine intelligence ignored and the potential damage they might have caused by defecting minimized."

The director appeared to consider this for a time, and Lawrence Downs appreciated that he might well merely be attempting to follow its convoluted logic. Alec Grey had explained it several times before everyone in the briefing had fully grasped it. He'd prefaced his assertion with the very real possibility that it might be too convoluted even for the KGB to have implemented. Lawrence Downs had found himself largely in support of it, and his more recent experiences with Mikhail Sergeyevich Zakharov had served only to fortify his conviction.

"The flaw, of course," Sir Alistair said, "is that it would be effectively impossible to distinguish a genuine defector who'd been seeded with disinformation to discredit him from a genuine plant who knowingly tells us lies."

"Yes, sir," Lawrence Downs agreed. "Mr. Grey suggested as much."

"Mr. Zakharov might be telling us the truth about there being a mole in MI6, in which case we could act upon his information and catch the fellow. Alternately, he might be telling us a deliberate or unintentional falsehood, in which case we risk tearing MI6 apart with a pointless mole hunt. Finally, we might choose to discredit Mr. Zakharov's revelation, in which case the putative mole in MI6 will remain active and at large."

"That's the essence of it, sir."

"I can't help feeling that this is one of the reasons my predecessor consumed a bottle of whiskey each evening upon visiting his club," Sir Alistair said. He glanced once more at the page in his hands. "Have you briefed Alec Grey about this?"

"Not as yet, sir," Lawrence Downs replied. "If it's true, I felt that you would wish to decide how to proceed with it."

"This will set him off... we'll have a mole hunt with everything short of beagles and beaters."

"Perhaps it would be for the best if we did, sir," he suggested.

The director regarded him darkly. "Only if there's a mole to hunt, Mr. Downs," he said coldly. He folded the page and pushed it back across his desk. "I shall brief Mr. Grey this afternoon. I should appreciate it if you'd refrain from mentioning this to him before day's end. Under no circumstances are you to speak of it to anyone else."

"I understand, sir."

The director leant forward. He seemed to have become aware that his pipe had gone out, and he laid it on its side before his telephone. "In the poem Gerontion, T.S. Elliot describes 'a wilderness of mirrors,'" he said thoughtfully. "When last I was in Washington, I was surprised to hear your new acquaintance James Angleton use the same phrase. 'We have arrived at a wilderness of mirrors,' he said. Apparently it's a phrase he enjoys, and uses frequently, but I was quite taken by the notion none the less. I fear we are in considerable peril of being unable to distinguish the truth from its many and varied reflections."

"Yes, sir. As you suggested, that presumably is Moscow's intent."

Sir Alistair retrieved his pipe and gestured at Lawrence Downs with its stem. "I can't help feeling that we stand a very good chance of being buried alive in a sea of shattered glass."

32

"**S**omeone will come in here and catch us," she whispered as his lips released her. Her eyes were still pressed shut, her expression touched with foreboding.

"I think that unlikely," Alec Grey said. "People rarely deign to visit my office even when they're summoned to it."

She opened her eyes at length and glanced over his shoulder at their surroundings. "It is rather dark and small," she agreed.

"Efficient of light and space," he corrected her.

"The box that covers my typewriter is less efficient of light and space," she observed. "Couldn't you have had a larger office?"

"They're all dark and small, save for the registry," he replied. The registry, the records division of MI5, was housed on the ground floor of Leconfield House. It had no windows, and it enjoyed the atmosphere of a disused tube station. Staff members who complained of their accommodations were traditionally offered the opportunity of taking up residence on the ground floor.

He relaxed his arms about her and glanced into her eyes. "How have you held up... after this morning?" he inquired.

She smiled fleetingly. "Rather better than I might have imagined," she answered him. "I kept thinking... after your lot came... that I should expect to collapse into tears at any moment, or engage in a proper ladylike faint. I've come to appreciate that I probably shan't do."

"I feel bloody awful over your being involved in this."

Her smile returned and she met his gaze. "I'd prefer you didn't," she said. "I agreed to fill the dead drops, and I was aware even that day in Sir Alistair's office that Andrei Bogdanov wasn't the local vicar. You weren't about to watch Mr. Somerfield have his knife off him... I don't imagine I was in any serious danger." She kissed him once more. "Besides, if I'd not become involved in all this espionage, we shouldn't have met and I'd have missed the opportunity to deceive the management of The Swans."

"It will be something with which to regale our friends in later years," he allowed, "if we can persuade them all to sign the Official Secrets Act."

She stepped back a pace, taking his hands in hers. A sudden shift in location was unwise, he thought absently, considering the hazards of his office. She appeared mindful of where she might safely place her feet. "It's done with now," she said. "Mr. Bogdanov is in jail... or wherever it is you lock up Russian spies. I don't imagine I shall require someone with a pistol to see me home this evening."

He shook his head. "I've assigned you two of them."

"Why is that?" she asked.

Alec Grey sighed. "Andrei Bogdanov handed your film off to another Soviet agent before he paid you a visit. We've no idea who the second man was... save that there was a second man, and he's still about. Someone acting on instructions from Moscow put the wind up Andrei Mikhailovich, and we must assume Moscow still wants whatever it wanted this morning."

"Oh," she said.

He put his arms about her once more, feeling her

breath upon his ear. For a time he expected her to finally succumb to her tears, but she remained silent.

His telephone rang, shattering the dark funk of his office. He permitted himself the indulgence of ignoring it.

"Do you think you should speak to whoever that is?" she asked.

"No," he replied. "They'll ring back if it's important."

"Perhaps the Soviet Union has surrendered. You'd be ever so cross if you had to learn of it in the Times."

He felt himself touched by her amusement despite the gloom that had enveloped them. He released her and reached across his desk for the handset.

"Mr. Grey?" a voice inquired before he had the opportunity to speak.

"Yes. May I inquire who's speaking?"

"This is Lieutenant Tony Righton, sir. I'm one of the men assigned to coast watch."

Alec Grey glanced at a list of names on his desk, locating that of his caller. "Yes, Lieutenant," he said.

"I've been posted near Ayr, in Scotland, sir. I believe I've spotted what you're looking for."

"Have you indeed," he said. "What exactly have you seen?"

"I'm ringing from a pub, sir," Tony Righton said uncertainly. "I'm not certain I should say."

"Don't concern yourself, Lieutenant," Alec Grey assured him. "Please continue."

"This morning two men purchased a rowing boat. The chap who sold it to them said they sounded as if they'd come up from London, and they clearly knew nothing about boats. They refused to say what they intended to use the boat for. The boat's been hidden in a patch of grass near the sea, where two men... I imagine it's the two men who bought it... are keeping watch over it. They have a small package wrapped in brown paper. One of them has

a pair of binoculars, which he uses to look out into the
North Channel from time to time. The other fellow
appears to be poorly. He's gone off into the grass and been
sick several times today."

"Very good, Lieutenant," Alec Grey said.

"Shall I have some of my men collect them, sir?"

Alec Grey paused for a moment. "No, Lieutenant,"
he replied at length. "I should like you to observe them for
as long as they're about. Under no circumstances are you
to approach them. Sometime around nightfall I expect
them to row out into the channel. If you have a very keen
eye, you might spot the periscope of a submarine. Let them
get on with their rowing. I would appreciate your ringing
me tomorrow and letting me know at what time the boat
made its way into the channel."

"Yes, sir," Tony Righton said uncertainly.

"One more thing, Lieutenant," Alec Grey added. "In
the event that something goes wrong, please be certain that
no one approaches the brown paper package. Keep yourself, your men and any passers-by well away from it, and
ring me immediately. Do you understand?"

"Yes, sir."

"Thank you for your time, Lieutenant," he said, and
he rang off.

Alice Woodward was regarding him with a puzzled
expression as he turned from his desk. "I heard most of
that," she said. "What have you just done?"

He smiled despite her growing unease. "I've let the
Russians have our Uranium," he replied.

"That's rather what I thought," she whispered. "Is
Sir Alistair not likely to be cross and wish to see you before
a firing squad when he discovers your generosity. He
might well have me there as well, just for allowing you to
get on with it."

"As a rule, Sir Alistair rarely executes his own
people," Alec Grey replied. "It's bad for morale."

"He'll make an exception, Mr. Grey," she insisted. "Why have you let the Uranium get away?"

Alec Grey began to reply and then stopped himself. "You know as much as I do of this," he said. "Would you like to have a stab at what I might tell the director?"

She eyed him curiously. "Shall I presume you won't use insanity as your defense?"

"Perhaps that would be wise."

"Does this have to do with the papers I photographed this morning for Andrei Bogdanov?"

"It does."

"From what I understood of them, the papers described how the time stream apparatus in Cornwall is adjusted and switched on. Is that correct?"

He nodded.

"You didn't have me give the Russians the actual plans for the machine in Cornwall, did you?"

"No, that would have made me a Soviet mole. I frown on Soviet moles for the most part."

She appeared to consider this. "The papers I photographed were made up so the Russians would think they were real," she concluded.

"They were."

"Something very nasty will happen when they switch on their machine, won't it?"

"Yes," he replied. "Yes, it will."

Her eyes narrowed. "And they require the Uranium to power their machine so something nasty will happen to it."

Alec Grey felt his breath grow still in his chest. "If this were a card game, I'd have just pushed all my money, my grandfather's watch, the deed to my family's castle and the ownership of my first-born son into the middle of the table," he said. "As it is, I've none of those things, and I'm wagering someone else's purse. The Americans call this a 'crap shoot.'"

"How American of them," she said, clearly not understanding the expression.

"I believe it refers to a game of dice," he explained. "This is a considerable gamble. Sir Alistair isn't pleased by it, but he's grudgingly provided his blessing. You may be comforted in knowing he'll be the first one in front of the rifles if it all goes pear-shaped."

"Would we not be better off if they simply never managed to switch on their machine in the first place?" she asked. "It's hardly a threat if it's not plugged in."

The director had suggested as much, and had clung to the hope of the Russian time stream project, bereft of the Uranium to power it, ultimately being modified to make a great deal of tea. It had required a substantial effort of argument and reason to dislodge him from it.

"The Soviets will eventually acquire sufficient Uranium to power their time stream apparatus," Alec Grey explained. "They've been working like madmen to steal the refinement technology from us, and we can only assume that the Americans have found themselves the object of their attentions as well. Perhaps they'll even design a refinement facility of their own if all their attempts to pinch one fail."

"But that could be years from now," Alice Woodward said.

"Yes it could, and by that time they'll have had their people studying the papers you left for Andrei Bogdanov this morning for a good long while. David Hollings was justifiably proud of his work on them, but he was of the opinion that they'd probably not withstand prolonged scrutiny. We'd very much like to have the Soviets start their time stream apparatus sooner rather than later."

"Did you arrange for them to steal the Uranium?"

He shook his head. "No, that would not have gotten past the director. However, once they had it, it became an opportunity too tempting to ignore. Had we intercepted the Soviet couriers, Moscow might have begun to suspect more than we were letting on... and further damaged our chances that they'd use your papers."

"It's fortunate you thought to have the coast watched," she observed.

He smiled coldly. "I'm rather pleased with that," he allowed. "This morning... just before Andrei Bogdanov came calling... I'd a chat with another Russian, Colonel Ivan Nikonov. I imagine you'll be asked to type something for his file presently. I suggested that if he assisted us in ascertaining the location of the Uranium, I might be disposed not to inform his government of certain peculiarities of his character. He rang earlier to say that a submarine would be collecting it. The underwater microphone chaps were of no small assistance in reducing the number of places to station watchers."

She put her arms across his shoulders and kissed him, relenting by inches to a grin which appeared to overwhelm her. "You're most frightfully clever, Mr. Grey," she said.

"That remains to be seen. This entire business hinges on the Soviets testing their time stream apparatus before they suspect we've been having them on. If they were to learn of the true origin of your documents... if they were to so much as discover that Andrei Bogdanov is lodging with us... we'll have done nothing more clever than give them a free supply of Uranium."

He glanced at the door of his office. Despite his assertions to the contrary, it seemed inevitable that someone would come seeking his attention given sufficient time. It seemed incumbent upon him either to propel Alice Woodward to her typewriter, or to lock the door.

"Will we be taking Mr. Bryan's car and going away for the weekend again?" she asked him, her breath tickling his ear as she spoke.

"Yes, I think we should," he replied. "I shall have to

administer an oath upon Hugh Somerfield not to ring me unless he has first-hand evidence of Soviet troops deploying in Piccadilly."

"Will we be returning to The Swans, then?"

He considered this for a moment. "It would be awkward," he decided. "They wouldn't trust us under whichever names we signed in with. There'd be a maid up every hour or so to count the towels. Hugh Somerfield appears to know of quite a number of hotels along the coast... I'll have a word with him."

"He'll become curious about who you're sneaking about with," she suggested.

Alec Grey smiled to himself. "I'm afraid he knows who I've been sneaking about with," he said softly.

She relaxed her embrace and met his gaze. "Does he really?" she asked.

He nodded his head. "You've worked here for a sufficient time, Miss Woodward, to appreciate that nothing can be kept secret for long enough to make keeping it worth the effort."

33

Yuri Modin approached the bench uncertainly. The man who occupied it wore a preposterous felt hat and a flowing tweed coat that suggested a horse blanket. He was almost abreast of the bench when the ungainly hat raised itself like the prow of a rotting ship and STANLEY smiled briefly at him from beneath it.

He glanced with a practiced lack of concern at the cattle market of faces flowing past him, sightless, soulless. He eased himself onto the bench and unfurled his newspaper, affecting an interest in its contents.

"You're bloody late," STANLEY said softly. As his part in this senseless music-hall performance, he produced a magazine from beneath his ludicrous coat and opened it before himself.

"I have been here for a quarter of an hour waiting for you to relinquish the bench so the man I came here to meet could occupy it. You might have observed me passing by several times, if you could see beyond that thing on your head."

"D-D-Do you not approve of my wardrobe?" STANLEY inquired archly. "I think I look very much unlike myself... not an entirely undesirable effect under the circumstances."

"You look like *petuh*... what do you say, like an old queen."

This clearly amused STANLEY. "A great many of the friends of our youth are old queens now."

"If you intend to disguise yourself, you should do so in a manner not calculated to draw attention to your disguise," Yuri Modin chided him.

"Look around you," STANLEY said, gesturing at the enormous chamber they'd come to occupy. "I'm hardly alone."

Yuri Modin shook his head angrily.

"While we're on the subject of poor disguises," STANLEY continued, "why did you insist that we meet in Euston railway station? I feel as if I'm an exhibit at a museum, or an insect pinned to a card."

"Look around you," Yuri Modin replied, pleased with his turn of phrase. "It is very much easier to hide in a crowd. Since work began rebuilding this place, the level of confusion has increased considerably. No one will take notice of two men waiting for a train."

STANLEY grunted, a noncommittal rebuke. Yuri Modin glanced at him from behind his newspaper. He was conscious as he did that while the eyes that rattled about him like toy marbles in an immense sack were, to the best of his observation, dull and void of the spark of intellect, there were a great many of them. He and STANLEY might not be the only men hiding in this crowd.

"Would you care to explain why you've summoned me here?" STANLEY inquired. "I do prefer dead drops... one is so much less likely to find one's self surrounded by policemen."

"This was extremely urgent," Yuri Modin explained.

"They're all growing extremely urgent of late. You're getting to be something of an old woman."

Yuri Modin felt his jaw stiffen. He resisted the urge to observe that at least he wasn't dressed like one.

The pleasantries of their conversation had been seen to. STANLEY was correct in his assessment of the vulnerability of his choice for a meeting. He would do well to conclude their business here and fold himself back into the crowd.

"It is time for you to leave," Yuri Modin said coldly. "It is time for you to visit Moscow."

STANLEY was silent for a considerable span of heartbeats, and at length Yuri Modin wondered whether he'd been understood. When STANLEY eventually chose to reply, his tone was wreathed in irony. "Is it indeed? I think not. The weather's perfectly foul there this time of the year."

Yuri Modin suppressed his swelling anger. "You are in immediate danger of discovery."

STANLEY sighed audibly. "I've been in danger of discovery for t-t-twenty-five years. What makes this day any different?"

"We have information..." Yuri Modin began.

"I'm certain you do," STANLEY interrupted him, "but I do not. You'll need to convince me to leave this green and pleasant land, imperialist bastion though it may be. I may not agree with its politics, but you can't fault the food."

Yuri Modin put his hand to his chin, considering the man in the corner of his eye. He had appreciated that STANLEY would be unlikely to blindly follow his instructions. The degree to which he might reveal the origin of his concerns over STANLEY's well-being was what the English liked to refer to as a 'juggling act.' He himself had never learned to juggle.

"We have sources," Yuri Modin said, his words a harsh whisper from behind his magazine. "We have... a source in the MI5 registry. Our source has informed us that there has been an unusual interest over the past several days in you."

"In me?" STANLEY demanded. "I hardly think I'm mentioned in the registry. It's chock full of spies."

"Interest in references to the code name STANLEY, then," Yuri Modin acknowledged.

STANLEY scowled, his expression suggesting a struggle to marshal his thoughts. "Come now," he said at length. "That's hardly grounds to pack up and flee the country."

"There is a great deal more," Yuri Modin assured him.

STANLEY smiled fleetingly. "Go on, then," he prompted Yuri Modin. "Convince me."

"I would rather not explain these matters in detail..." Yuri Modin began uncertainly.

STANLEY nodded. "I see," he whispered. "You'd prefer that I not know of your more v-v-valuable sources within MI5 just in case you're correct, and Alistair Fitzhenry's neatly shaven young men are poised to snatch me from my bed and seat me under the bright lights. Is that it?"

Yuri Modin nodded, momentarily surprised at the depth of his embarrassment over STANLEY's perspicacity. He would have preferred that his agent merely accept his warning.

"I believe you asked me to defect several years ago," STANLEY continued. "As things have turned out, that would've been premature. I dare say you'd have been in a considerable volume of hot water back home if I'd agreed at the time."

Yuri Modin nodded. "Yes, you were correct to refuse me," he agreed. "This time... this time is different. We know you are suspected. We know MI5 is actively seeking your identity. I will be in, as you say, a great deal more hot water if I permit you to be captured."

STANLEY stared blankly at his newspaper, sheltering beneath his enormous hat. "I don't believe I'd enjoy the experience either," he mused.

"I am permitted to tell you that arrangements will be provided for you to leave England. I can have a submarine meet you at an unpopulated location…"

"I have no intention of crawling into a bloody submarine," STANLEY snapped.

"We can make other arrangements if you wish," Yuri Modin offered, sensing STANLEY's acquiescence. "The important issue is that we make them quickly."

"What of Aileen?" STANLEY demanded. "An Englishman may cast off his country in times of imminent threat of arrest, but it's bad form to discard one's wife."

"She is under no suspicion, and your government cannot arrest her for what it suspects you of. You will be free to send for her once you reach Moscow. We will provide for her transportation to the Soviet Union."

STANLEY frowned. "What am I to do when I arrive?" he pondered. "I hardly think I'll be hired on in my present capacity by the KGB."

Yuri Modin smiled. He'd anticipated his agent's concern several hours earlier, and he'd occupied himself at length with a reply that would satisfy him. "You would be better served worrying about when you will find time to sleep, my old friend," he said warmly. "You have no idea how you are revered in my country. You will be a hero of the Soviet Union. You will be much in demand at official functions. You will lecture to the young officers, you will write textbooks about your experiences in British intelligence… you will see your face on a postage stamp."

"I remain uncertain how pleased I'll be at the prospect of someone's grandmother licking the back of my head every time she wishes to post a letter to her brother in Stalingrad," STANLEY observed.

Yuri Modin was some time appreciating that the man beside him had agreed to his request.

"It is vital we act quickly," he said. He turned the page of his newspaper, suddenly conscious that he'd neglected to do so since the beginning of their conversation. "We have no way of knowing how far along the investigation of MI5 has progressed."

STANLEY shook his head, his expression bemused. "MI5's investigation will no doubt progress at the speed of a pet turtle pulling a locomotive up a slight grade," he said. "Were I to write out a detailed confession of my activities on behalf of the Soviet Union and nail it to the door of Alistair Fitzhenry's office, I would still be assured of a f-f-fortnight at the very least in which to effect an escape."

"I would be comforted, my old friend, if you would effect an escape sooner than that," Yuri Modin requested. "Perhaps tomorrow. You could board the channel ferry to Calais. Some of our people could meet you in France, a comfortable journey east by train... I could arrange for a proper welcome for you when you arrive in Moscow."

"I have affairs to wind down, a few friends I'd like a final drink with..." STANLEY protested.

"If they are truly your friends, they will understand your reluctance to spend the rest of your life in a British prison. You could send them all postcards from Russia."

"With my likeness on the stamps, I presume."

"I cannot help but think they would be greatly impressed."

34

"*Ë b tvoju mat,*" Andrei Bogdanov spat at the Englishman across the table. He reached for the man's throat, hearing the familiar rustle of the chains that bound him to the table, feeling the steel manacles shred the flesh at his wrists. The bright metal was darkened with clots of his blood, so frequently had he strained against his imprisonment. The chains arrested him long before he could provide a meaningful threat to his captor.

The Englishman had introduced himself as Lawrence Downs. For a time Andrei Bogdanov had imagined him to be an insult deliberately inflicted upon him by Alec Grey in retaliation for his abortive rape of Alice Woodward. Lawrence Downs regarded him myopically through an old woman's spectacles. He was a withered gnome of a man, losing his hair, perhaps his teeth as well, his face appearing as if it had been assembled from leftover pieces of more robust men for the amusement of children. His voice was that of a bookkeeper.

Lawrence Downs glanced up at him now and smiled. "I think that very unlikely, Andrei Mikhailovich," he said softly. "I cannot imagine any circumstance that would persuade my mother to sleep with the likes of you."

Andrei Bogdanov felt his eyes narrow as he stared at the Englishman.

"Yes, Mr. Bogdanov," Lawrence Downs continued, "I've a fluent command of Russian. However, in consideration of the no doubt underpaid young woman who will be required to transcribe the tape recording of this interview, perhaps you would do me the courtesy of confining your remarks to English."

Andrei Bogdanov rattled his chains. "Fuck you," he growled.

Lawrence Downs smiled indulgently at him. "On second thought, perhaps a young woman would not be the appropriate staff member to transcribe this interview."

"Fuck her as well."

Lawrence Downs scribbled something on a pad of writing paper he'd perched upon the edge of the table. The Englishman returned his attention to Andrei Bogdanov at length.

"We were discussing your visit to the home of Alice Woodward, Andrei Mikhailovich," Lawrence Downs said evenly.

Andrei Bogdanov shook his head and slammed his fist into the surface of the table between them. The table was a substantial steel platform that had been bolted to the floor, and it appeared to ignore his assault. "We were not discussing anything, Mr. Downs," he said. "You were talking about Alice Woodward, and I was telling you to fuck yourself."

"This is unproductive," Lawrence Downs chided him. "Mr. Grey informed me that you had agreed to cooperate with us."

"Mr. Grey threatened to kill me if I did not agree," Andrei Bogdanov said, hearing the whine of a scolded boy in his words. "I would have agreed to cut off my own *khuy*... that does not mean I would have asked for a knife."

"I've no knowledge of what Mr. Grey may or may not have said to you, Andrei Mikhailovich," Lawrence Downs continued, his voice like the operation of a newly-oiled machine. "I have my instructions as to which items you and I must discuss."

"Fuck your instructions."

Lawrence Downs' features grew creased, his expression momentarily pained by consternation. Andrei Bogdanov permitted himself a taste of satisfaction.

The Englishman consulted his writing pad, flipping through its pages for a time. He glanced up at Andrei Bogdanov. "Perhaps we could return to the identity of the agent who instructed you to attempt to recruit Alice Woodward as a Soviet spy."

"Are you deaf, Mr. Downs?" Andrei Bogdanov demanded. "We have talked about that. No one told me to contact that woman. I chose her because she has a fine ass, because I would enjoy having her in bed, yes?"

"That's not what you told me earlier," Lawrence Downs said. "The last time we discussed your attempt to recruit Alice Woodward, you told me that you had been given instructions directing you to her, but you were unaware of the identity of the author of those instructions."

"Fuck you... I did not say that."

"I'll be happy to have the recording of your earlier reply played for you, if it would refresh your memory," Lawrence Downs offered.

Andrei Bogdanov stared into the featureless steel surface of the table. It reminded him of the steel tables he'd seen cadavers laid out on, on those infrequent occasions when the KGB was unaware of the causes of their death. His fragment of memory was unfortunate. It was a brief leap of imagination to picture himself on such a table.

"I demand to be permitted to speak to an official from the consulate of the Soviet Union," Andrei Bogdanov recited. "I will say nothing more until this demand is met."

Lawrence Downs sighed and leant minutely closer to the table. "You know as well as I that you'll not be permitted to speak to anyone. There's little point in repeating your demand on a regular basis."

"I have rights."

The Englishman shook his head. "No, Andrei Mikhailovich, you do not," he said with apparent reluctance. "I genuinely regret that the people I work for have the authority to do with you as they please. It would be in your best interest to appreciate that."

Andrei Bogdanov beat his fist upon the table once more, his eyes boring into the skull of the man before him. He was disappointed to see no flash of alarm in the expression of Lawrence Downs. "If I was not chained up like a bear in the circus, I would tear off your fucking head," he growled.

"I trust that will serve to explain why you remain chained up," Lawrence Downs said quietly, clearly amused by his observation.

Andrei Bogdanov struggled once more against his restraints, ignoring the discomfort they inflicted upon him. He drew a breath into his lungs, hungry for proof that he was still alive. "I want a cigarette," he demanded.

Lawrence Downs shook his head. "The level of cooperation you've exhibited thus far doesn't warrant your receiving a cigarette, Andrei Mikhailovich," he said. "Perhaps if you'd like to discuss your recruitment of Alice Woodward."

"Push your cigarette up your *zopa*," he snarled.

"As it happens, I don't smoke."

Andrei Bogdanov smiled. "So you were lying to me when you offered me a cigarette if I tell you about Alice Woodward."

The Englishman shook his head. "Not at all. In the room beyond the one-way glass behind you there is a selection of packets of cigarettes. I believe it includes several American brands, which I understand are highly prized in the Soviet Union."

"Give me a cigarette and maybe I will tell you about Alice Woodward," Andrei Bogdanov offered.

A flicker of amusement touched the features of Lawrence Downs, vanishing as quickly as it had appeared. "You know I'm not permitted to do that, Andrei Mikhailovich."

"How would I know that?"

"This is the fifth time you've requested a cigarette. I'll be happy to have the earlier recordings played back for you if you wish."

"Go fuck yourself."

"As you wish," Lawrence Downs said. "The cigarettes will be waiting for you at such time as you change your mind."

Andrei Bogdanov growled and glanced uncertainly about the room. The intensity of the light stung his eyes if he was incautious. The lights had been arranged to illuminate him and his surroundings — the bloodless, grinning Englishman languished in a pool of relative shadow. He was beginning to imagine that he'd spent his life in this room, that his memories of a world beyond it were stories he'd been told by someone else — perhaps by Lawrence Downs, hours earlier. There would no doubt be a tape recording of it.

"How many more times will you keep asking me the same questions?" Andrei Bogdanov demanded.

"Which questions are those?"

"The questions you have asked me all day... about Alice Woodward, about my instructions."

He watched the man before him nod his understanding, the gesture mechanical. "It's not for me to say. I've nowhere else to be. The patience of my superiors is not without its limits, however."

"And what should I expect to happen when their

patience is exhausted?" Andrei Bogdanov continued, pleased to have seized the role of inquisitor for himself, however briefly.

Lawrence Downs drew his hand across his face and glanced away from Andrei Bogdanov, regarding the featureless panel of one-way glass behind him. "I genuinely can't say," he replied. He considered his wristwatch. He was silent for a time, and then he rose abruptly from his chair. He strode to the far wall of the room and opened a small panel set into it. After a moment's consideration, he depressed a button behind it and closed it. Andrei Bogdanov's eyes led him back to his chair like a dog's leash.

"What have you done, Mr. Downs?" he inquired uncertainly.

Lawrence Downs leant forward, his arms resting on the table. He pushed his writing pad to one side and met the gaze of his subject.

"I've switched off the tape recorder, Andrei Mikhailovich," he said. His tone was very much less assured, his manner suddenly conspiratorial. Andrei Bogdanov felt himself grow uneasy. "The technician in the next room will have gone for his tea break. I believe you and I should have a few words before he returns and it's switched on again."

"We have had nothing but words, Mr. Downs," Andrei Bogdanov said.

"There are some things I feel you should know," the Englishman continued. "These are not of my doing. My superiors... I can't agree with some of the lengths they're prepared to go to in order to obtain information from prisoners such as yourself."

"Are you trying to frighten me?"

Lawrence Downs appeared to ignore his question. He glanced at his wristwatch a second time. "My superiors have permitted me a limited time to question you, and they anticipate a degree of cooperation on your part. In the event I fail to provide them with some indication of my success..."

"Will they refuse to pay your wages this week?" Andrei Bogdanov interrupted him.

"Mr. Bogdanov, I will return to my wife and my children this evening, and I will collect my wages and my regular pay rises. Your immediate future will not be as comfortable. I believe it would be in your interest to understand that. I disagree entirely with what will be done to you, but it will be done in the defense of the realm, and my disagreement will not affect your treatment whatsoever."

"Maybe you will tell me what will be done to me, yes?"

"Unless I am able to persuade my superiors that you are displaying some degree of cooperation, they will assign me to another subject and proceed to extract information from you by more direct means. I understand that this may include subjecting you to large doses of drugs, such as Sodium Pentothal and Scopolamine, or physical duress."

"I have had worse things done to me," Andrei Bogdanov said.

"I don't believe you understand me," Lawrence Downs continued. "The procedures that will be applied to you to permit my superiors to learn what you know have... side effects. They leave... permanent evidence. Her Majesty's government cannot be seen to be torturing helpless prisoners... even Soviet spies. At the conclusion of your interrogation, you would be killed and your body disposed of to ensure that our treatment of you was never discovered."

Andrei Bogdanov gestured dismissingly, the motion of his hand restricted by his chains. "Mr. Grey told me the same thing. I was a fool to believe him. I will not be a fool twice in the same day."

"I'm not surprised. Mr. Grey is my immediate superior. He's the man responsible for the deaths of... of a number of your people."

Andrei Bogdanov shook his head. "I cannot tell you things I do not know, Mr. Downs."

"I'm not asking you to, Andrei Mikhailovich. Tell me anything. Tell me something about the man who talent-spotted Alice Woodward. Give me something I can take to my superiors, so I'm able to say you're beginning to coop-erate. It needn't be a great deal, so long as it's true, so long as they're able to verify it."

Lawrence Downs glanced at his wristwatch once more. "Damn," he whispered. "The technician will be returning in a moment." He rose to his feet and crossed the room. "I'm switching on the tape recorder again," he announced.

Andrei Bogdanov regarded the Englishman uncer-tainly as he returned to his chair. His nerves were alight with the need for something to smoke, a swallow of vodka, a glass of tea. The chains about his wrists weighed more than he did, pulling him inexorably beneath the surface of an unseen ocean, drowning him in a pool of light. If it had been Lawrence Downs in this chair, and he in the shad-ows, he would have been at liberty to consider the Englishman's words. They swarmed about his ears, dis-tracting him, dislocating his reason.

The man before him retrieved his pad of writing paper and glanced up at him expectantly.

"I do not know the name of the man who instructed me to recruit Alice Woodward," Andrei Bogdanov said cautiously. "I only know the code name he is called by... STANLEY. His code name is STANLEY."

Lawrence Downs wrote something on his pad and nodded. There was no trace of his earlier conspiracy in his words when he spoke. "Thank you, Mr. Bogdanov. That's a fine beginning."

35

S ir Alistair pushed the door to the briefing room, mildly surprised to find that its lights were switched on. A clutter of voices spilled into the corridor and then ceased as one. The hush of the empty building clutched at his heels as he stepped over its threshold, feeling himself clothed by the illumina-tion.

Alec Grey stood like the subject of a Joshua Reynolds portrait suffering his final sitting. He'd clearly risen from his chair at the first rattle of the door's latch. He was flanked by Hugh Somerfield and Alice Woodward. The air was acrid with cigarette smoke. An ashtray towering like a souvenir ziggurat before Hugh Somerfield suggested the source of the fumes.

Alice Woodward smiled her acknowledgement of him and returned her attention to an untidy litter of pages on the table before her.

"I'm glad they caught you up before you left, sir," Alec Grey said as Sir Alistair pushed the door to.

"I'm not certain I am, Mr. Grey," the director said warily. "I was on my way to my club, and I dare say I'd earned my respite. You do know it's gone eight o'clock at night, don't you?"

"Yes, sir," Alec Grey acknowledged, "and I apologize

for interfering with your evening. I believe you'll agree it was justified."

"Will I indeed?"

Alec Grey smiled. The assurance in his expression troubled Sir Alistair. It was fecund, pungent with foreboding of a great many memoranda to a great many departments.

"Could this not have kept until tomorrow morning?" he inquired.

"I don't feel that would have been wise," Alec Grey replied.

"I was certain you wouldn't," the director muttered. He stepped to the near end of the table and took his customary seat. "Perhaps you would explain what you three are doing here at this uncivil hour, Mr. Grey."

"We're hunting moles, Sir Alistair," Alec Grey said, his tone suggesting that it might have been obvious.

The director sighed and glanced along the table, feeling himself touched with anger. "I do hope you're not serious."

"I'm quite serious, sir," Alec Grey assured him. His voice rippled with amusement. Perhaps it was triumph. The director decided abruptly that he cared little for the distinction.

"Mr. Grey, you have been hunting moles since a week after you accepted your current position. I fail to see the urgency in yet another mole hunt." Sir Alistair grasped the arms of his chair, preparing to rise.

"This is a very different sort of mole hunt," Alec Grey said. "In this case, we've actually caught the mole."

Sir Alistair stared at him for a moment, uncertain that he'd wholly understood what he'd been told. "Mr. Grey?"

"Yes, sir."

He sighed once again and relaxed in his chair. "I see," he breathed. He gestured to the other occupants of the briefing room. "And these... these would be your fellow intrepid mole hunters, I trust."

Alec Grey nodded, clearly amused. "We've been several hours completing our research. Mr. Somerfield has been working with me on this operation for some months. I've asked Miss Woodward to join us because she has suitable security clearance. Honesty bids me say that my initial interest in her services was her being the only one of us with readable handwriting, but she's proven herself quite capable. If she were somewhat taller, Mr. Somerfield might be at risk for his job."

Sir Alistair glanced fleetingly at Hugh Somerfield, who appeared unthreatened.

The director leant back in his chair. "Please don't misunderstand me, Mr. Grey... when I leave this room, preferably before daybreak, will I do so with the definitive name of an actual mole operating within British intelligence? My experience with moles thus far has been that they're rather like mirages... often glimpsed on the horizon, but constantly retreating as they're approached.

"You will have the name of the mole," Alec Grey assured him. "I'll be happy to tell it to you now, if you'd like to forgo our explanation of how we came to arrive at it."

Sir Alistair considered the proximity of the roast beef at his club, imagining the taste of port and the liquid smoke of his pipe. He shook his head to dispel the wraiths of his imagination. "I should damned well wish to know how you've come to choose the prey in your mole hunt."

"I was certain you would, sir."

Wordlessly, Alice Woodward gathered several of pages from the table before her and handed them to Alec Grey. He ordered them and then glanced over them at the director. "Do stop me if this becomes dull, sir," he said.

Sir Alistair gestured for him to proceed.

"As you know, several weeks ago we undertook to

reduce the number of possible candidates. Mr. Somerfield generated a list of forty-nine names, men who had access to sufficient information to have blown several of our recent operations to the Soviets. As the numbers seemed convenient, we created seven convincing files of fabricated documents on subjects we felt would be of interest to Moscow and we circulated them to the names on our list, with seven names for each distribution. We then watched to see if any of the files appeared in the Enigma traffic from the Soviet embassy. One file did so, and as such we were able to reduce the list to seven names."

"I believe you explained this to me at the time, Mr. Grey," Sir Alistair said.

"I believe I did," Alec Grey agreed. "Having done so, the remaining problem was to eliminate six of the names from the new list."

"Eliminating all seven would have been preferable," the director observed.

Alec Grey nodded, and he glanced at the first of his pages. "As you're aware, the seven names on the new list are Douglas Harvey, Kenneth Lawson, Kim Philby, David Prentice, Nigel Thurloe, Peter Willes and Jonathan Wooley. They're ordered here by last name, so as not to spoil the surprise."

The director shot him a reproving glance and considered cautioning him that a Soviet agent in the British intelligence organization was to be treated as the most serious of concerns, no matter how much he and his staff enjoyed their work.

"We were able to eliminate Douglas Harvey immediately, as he was ill when the deceptive files were circulated, and he had no access to them. He didn't return to his desk until two days after we'd discovered text from one of the files in Soviet Enigma traffic. This left six remaining names, and we were able to get no further with them."

"I've intended to ask you, Mr. Grey," the director

inquired, "why you didn't simply circulate additional files to the names on your new list, as you did with the original set of seven files."

Alec Grey appeared to consider this. "After some thought, we decided that we'd pressed our luck in that regard as far as we dared. The sudden appearance of the files was somewhat peculiar. To have another set appear, even amongst a very small group, risked someone mentioning them in conversation and possibly alerting our mole that we were onto him. We would have tried additional files one at time in a few months, had all other avenues of investigation proven fruitless."

"Which I trust they have not," Sir Alistair prompted him.

Alec Grey nodded once more. "Mr. Somerfield and a number of others on my staff assembled a great deal of research that appeared to suggest a Soviet mole, but with nothing to connect some of it to our investigation, it remained a stack of papers and complaints from the registry that we'd failed to return their files on time. The break came this afternoon, from Lawrence Downs."

Sir Alistair allowed that he was pleased by this. While he would not have discounted the work of those members of his staff who spent their days locked in damp rooms with Soviet defectors, it was rare indeed for any of them to summon forth concrete intelligence from their labors. He had on several occasions characterized their reports as a single sentence of fact followed by fifty pages of qualifications.

"Shall I inquire what Mr. Downs told you?"

"He provided us with the code name of the mole," Alec Grey replied. "In point of fact, he provided us with the code name of the Soviet agent who talent-spotted Miss Woodward for Andrei Bogdanov. We chose to assume they're one and the same. I believe you'll concur with this assessment presently."

The director glanced at Alice Woodward. He'd not had an opportunity to speak with her since her confrontation with the Russian that morning. Her composure at the mention of her assailant was at the very least commendable.

"The code name of the mole is STANLEY," Alec Grey said.

Sir Alistair regarded him uncertainly. "I have the sense I'm expected to recognize him."

Alec Grey shook his head. "No, sir," he said. "As it happens, none of us did, at least not at first. However, STANLEY has been mentioned in Soviet enciphered radio transmissions and Enigma messages for a number of years, some of which we've been fortunate enough to intercept and break into. We've never known enough about STANLEY to associate the references to him with a specific individual."

"I understand this is usually the case with intercepted messages," the director observed. "The Soviets are clearly as careful as they're able to safeguard the identities of their spies."

Alec Grey chose a new page from his handful of papers. "There's a woman in Codes and Ciphers named Susan Pascal. She's made STANLEY her private project. She's read every intercept and scrap of paper, and she's learned rather more about him than any of the rest of us. It seems that STANLEY has been working for the Soviets since the 1930s."

The director stared blankly at Alec Grey's untidy collection of papers, disquieted by the thought of a Soviet spy in their midst for so many years.

"Susan Pascal discovered that STANLEY studied at Cambridge, and that he belonged to a secret communist student group that disbanded in 1935."

The director put his hand to his chin. Hugh Somerfield had lit a cigarette without his noticing it, and he regretted having left his pipe in his overcoat. "Does this have some bearing on your list, Mr. Grey?"

"It has every bearing on the list. We can eliminate David Prentice and Jonathan Woolly, as they studied at Oxford. The remaining four names on the list are Kenneth Lawson, Kim Philby, Nigel Thurloe and Peter Willes."

Sir Alistair was several seconds appreciating why the remaining list of names seemed unpleasantly familiar. He'd confronted Sir Simon Turnbull with three of them a week earlier. The former director had yet to contact him. The outcome of this evening's unorthodox briefing would almost certainly compel him to initiate proceedings against Sir Simon. The last thing his office needed was one of its antecedents appearing in the press several times per day.

"You promised me a single name, Mr. Grey," the director reminded him.

"Yes, sir. We can reduce the list further still." Alec Grey directed his attention to Alice Woodward, who slid several additional pages along the table to him. "Kenneth Lawson attended Cambridge beginning in 1943 and Nigel Thurloe in 1939. Peter Willes came to Cambridge in 1921, and he'd graduated before the group in question came into existence. That leaves Kim Philby."

"I imagine I may take it as read that Mr. Philby attended Cambridge during the years when this group was active," Sir Alistair said.

"Kim Philby attended Cambridge beginning in 1929, and left in 1933, Sir Alistair." The director was surprised to find that it had been Alice Woodward who'd spoken to him.

He gestured at Alec Grey's ragged brood of papers. "It's an impressive effort of research," he allowed, "but I'm afraid it proves nothing conclusively. You can't imagine that I'd have Mr. Philby brought in for questioning based on your conclusions."

"Not on what I've explained thus far, sir," Alec Grey

agreed. "Having discovered what we believed to be the identity of STANLEY, we were able to narrow our search considerably."

The director nodded, and Alec Grey continued.

"Susan Pascal succeeded in tracing STANLEY through an earlier Soviet code name, and we can match his activities to events alluded to in Soviet message decrypts for almost thirty years. We found references to him until 1949, after which time no further evidence of him appears in Soviet message traffic we've intercepted until 1951, when he again begins to be mentioned."

The director gestured impatiently. "I'm sorry, Mr. Grey, but that's quite meaningless. We're able to break into only a small fraction of the Soviet messages we intercept. The lack of references to STANLEY could well be explained by his appearing in the messages we were unable to read."

"It could, sir, save that beginning in 1949, references to STANLEY can be found in several decrypts of messages intercepted by the Americans from the Soviet embassy in Washington. STANLEY appears until 1951, after which time nothing more is said about him."

"Once again, the Americans have only succeeded in decoding a relatively small number of their Soviet messages."

Alec Grey selected another page. "Kim Philby was posted to Washington in 1949 as the MI6 liaison to the CIA. He was recalled to London in 1951."

Sir Alistair turned slowly to face Alec Grey, appreciating for the first time that this was not to be another abstract discussion. He felt an iron fist claw at his guts.

"Is there anything more, Mr. Grey?" he inquired blackly.

"Quite a lot," Alec Grey replied.

"Perhaps you would select a small number of representative items, and I shall read the file in its entirety first thing in the morning."

"I thought I might do, sir." He considered his papers for several seconds.

Alec Grey spoke for over a quarter of an hour, describing the shadowy parallel lives of STANLEY and Kim Philby. All but the first few minutes of his narration were redundant, the director appreciated sourly. Alec Grey and his staff had constructed a coffin for Philby with crafts-manlike precision, every plank and nail expertly fitted.

Sir Alistair considered the likelihood that it would carry several additional occupants on its journey to the nether realms.

At length Alec Grey returned his papers to the table and he leant back in his chair. "We have two other items of note, sir," he said. "They're hardly conclusive of them-selves, but perhaps you should be aware of them."

"I'm not sure I could be further convinced of Mr. Philby's treachery," the director said, and he gestured at the other occupants of the briefing room. "If you feel they're significant."

"Susan Pascal makes reference in her report about STANLEY to a recent Enigma decrypt in which STANLEY is mentioned in conjunction with a 'photograph of ships,'" Alec Grey began. "The Codes and Ciphers people who ini-tially read this message assumed that the ships in question were ours. Nothing concerning the Royal Navy has been worthy of clandestine photographs of late... we've not launched a new submarine or deployed a destroyer group in the past few months... and after careful consideration, they marked it NO FURTHER ACTION and filed it."

"It's my understanding that a considerable volume of intercepted Soviet message traffic makes little or no sense to Codes and Ciphers," Sir Alistair said. "We rarely have all the messages pertaining to a specific subject."

"Yes, sir, that's correct," Alec Grey agreed. "I thought this one odd, however, and I sent for the original transcription. It's important to keep in mind that the staff who search for meaning in the decrypts aren't the ones who translate them from the original Russian. The researchers read them in English."

The director nodded.

"There was a slight error in translation for the message in question. One of our people appears to have translated the Russian word *fatograf* as 'photograph,' when it should have been 'photographer.' It changes the nature of the message. STANLEY isn't telling the Soviets about a photograph of ships. He's telling them about a photographer of ships, and we know they're not our ships."

"You've lost me, Mr. Grey."

"And myself for a time, sir," Alec Grey allowed. "Several weeks ago... on 10 October, to be precise... you conducted a briefing about the CORONA cameras the Americans had built to photograph the Soviet Union. You handed around several example CORONA photographs, one of which depicted the Nikolaiev shipyard. I remember remarking on that photograph."

"As do I, Mr. Grey," Sir Alistair said impatiently. "Is this the photograph of ships to which you originally believed STANLEY was referring?"

"Yes, sir," Alec Grey replied. "As per your instructions, everyone who wishes to access the CORONA material is required to sign for it, and every minute of every access is accounted for. That particular photograph appears to have embarked on a remarkable journey. It disappeared for several days after your briefing, and finally revealed itself to have been accidentally slipped into a rather innocuous file about a Soviet factory complex in Volgograd. The file's distribution list indicates that it was briefly checked out by Kim Philby on 11 October."

"I believe I understand," the director said. "Mr. Philby slipped the photograph into this file and then waited until he could gain access to the file with a degree of privacy."

"Yes, sir. We might surmise that he photographed the CORONA picture and passed the film along to the Soviets. The KGB resident at Kensington Palace Gardens would have appreciated the urgency of notifying Moscow of the existence of CORONA, and while he couldn't send the actual photograph by radio, he could describe its con-tents and what Philby had told him of CORONA... the pho-tographer of ships. The Soviet Enigma message that referred to the photographer of ships was intercepted on 12 October."

"You mentioned two additional items."

"Yes, sir, I did. The second was in your briefing ear-lier today, when you informed me that Colonel Mikhail Zakharov had claimed there was a Soviet agent working as the head of a department of MI6. Kim Philby is the head of anti-Soviet counterintelligence. No one else on our list ful-fills that qualification."

"I'm not certain I would wish to include that obser-vation with the rest of your research, Mr. Grey," the direc-tor said cautiously. "There remains considerable doubt surrounding the reliability of Mikhail Zakharov. There is every indication that he could be a Soviet plant."

"I agree, but in this case it's immaterial," Alec Grey said. "It hardly matters whether Colonel Zakharov is telling us that Kim Philby is a spy or the KGB is trying to make us believe that he's not."

The director considered Alec Grey for a moment, relenting by inches to a cold smile. "I don't believe I shall ever wish to play cards with you, Mr. Grey," he said.

Sir Alistair rose to his feet. "I should like you to instruct Mr. Somerfield, and as many additional mem-bers of your staff as you think appropriate, to visit Mr. Philby's home first thing tomorrow morning and escort him here for a chat. I intend to devote the remainder of this evening in prayer to a god I've never put much stock in that Kim Philby can provide us with a convincing rebuttal for your accusations. You three may wish to do the same."

"Yes, sir," Alec Grey agreed.

He turned to leave and then paused, catching Alec Grey in his gaze. When he spoke, his voice was brooding. "It's my understanding that you messed Andrei Bogdanov about earlier today. I'm not troubled by whatever you've done to get him talking... after what he's responsible for, I'd have signed off for anything short of hot irons and thumbscrews. Kim Philby was presented with an OBE by King George and he has more influential friends than you've had hot dinners. I suggest you instruct your people to say 'sir' and 'please' a great deal, and have them refrain from any visible bruising."

"I understand, sir."

"It won't be necessary to apply chains to Mr. Philby, but if he proves to be the traitorous little bastard he appears, you and I will toss a coin to see which of us will garrote him with his own school tie."

36

Tuesday, October 24

Alec Grey imagined his coffee to have the consistency of treacle and the potency of battery acid. Such a beverage would serve as the only reasonable explanation of his remaining awake. He and Alice Woodward had returned to her house in Mayfair some hours after midnight, and he'd hardly shut his eyes before the daylight through her curtains had scoured them open once more. If the dimensions of his office had permitted it, he might have done well to erect a camping bed in the corner for situations such as this.

He dared another swallow of coffee, deciding as he did that it might well have been of greater benefit to his state of consciousness had it been applying itself more fully to its task. Desperate times called for desperate drinks.

The gallery of files and photographs that languished untidily across his desk smirked and teased at him. They were all middle-aged men who appeared as if they'd deliberately pickled themselves in inexpensive scotch rather than pay full price for their later embalming. Each of the pictures had been captured with a very long lens — the subjects were clutched in sharp focus, with everything around them blurred and watery.

They were all aging nonces and pornographers, he decided angrily, resisting the urge to sweep the lot of them to the floor. He glanced at the list Edwina Pearson had provided Hugh Somerfield with, curious to discover that none of the faces seemed in keeping with the innocuous names they corresponded to. One of them almost certainly knew why Arthur Dunross had been discovered in a Docklands hotel with a bullet through him.

He was still seeking absently for a flicker of guilt in one of the motionless expressions before him when his divinations were unsettled by a knock at his door. The handle turned without his leave and Hugh Somerfield entered. His hair was ragged and he seemed on the point of breathlessness, a condition Alec Grey could not recall noticing previously.

"I don't believe MI5 permits running in the corridors, Mr. Somerfield," he said, affecting the air of a long-forgotten headmaster.

"Philby," Hugh Somerfield gasped.

Alec Grey directed him to his visitor's chair. Unaccountably, he considered, it was not waist-deep in purloined files and fistfuls of paper.

"Philby," Hugh Somerfield repeated as he eased himself into the chair. "He's done a runner."

Alec Grey felt his own breath grow still.

"We arrived at his house this morning... his wife said we'd missed him by twenty minutes. He'd packed a case and left for the train... he'd said he was taking the ferry to France."

"Bloody hell," Alec Grey spat.

Hugh Somerfield shook his head apologetically. "No, boss," he said. "I telephoned the local nick at Dover. They met Philby as he was leaving the platform. Olli Boyle and Trevor Graves drove like madmen for the coast. They have him and they're on their way back."

Alec Grey stared at Hugh Somerfield for a moment longer, deciding as he did that he'd forgotten to breathe. "You're certain?"

"Yes, boss," Hugh Somerfield assured him.

He leant back in his chair, considering the infinite detail in the decay of his ceiling. "Bloody hell."

"The director should be pleased."

"I wonder," Alec Grey mused. "Someone will have tipped Kim Philby that we were onto him. I feel the cold death-grip of a new list of names."

"I don't think so," Hugh Somerfield said. Alec Grey returned his attention to his subordinate. "I'd a long chat with Aileen Philby. She told me he'd returned home mid-afternoon yesterday with several tickets and he set about packing his case. He told her he'd be away for a week… he wouldn't say where he was going. It wasn't uncommon for him to vanish from time to time. The thing of it is, as nearly as I can tell, he arrived home at least half an hour before Andrei Bogdanov told Lawrence Downs about Philby's code name. At the time he made his plans to do a flit, not a single one of us had any reason to suspect him of anything. I can't help feeling he just realized he'd run his string out about as far as he dared, and that it was time for him to vanish for good."

Alec Grey considered this for a time, and at length he permitted it to comfort him. The prospect of a mole hunt involving Lawrence Downs, Alice Woodward, Hugh Somerfield and Sir Alistair Fitzhenry as prospective Soviet agents was beyond him to entertain. He was beginning to lose his reason, he reflected. He recalled yarning on to Alice Woodward about his people observing imaginary Russians in the shadows — he feared he was at the point of doing so himself.

Hugh Somerfield appeared to have regained his composure sufficiently to have found his cigarettes. Alec Grey decided that he was sufficiently relieved as to permit one of them to be ignited within the domain of his office.

"Who are this lot?" Hugh Somerfield inquired, gesturing at the files scrawled across Alec Grey's desk.

"They arrived this morning. These are the photographs I asked to have taken of the naughty bookshop owners."

Hugh Somerfield craned his neck for a better view of the men. "Oh yes," he said absently. "I'd forgotten about them with all the recent excitement. Are they still worth bothering over? It seems as if we have all the spies locked up... or at the mortuary."

Alec Grey nodded. "I believe so," he replied. "One of these chaps most likely had something to do with Arthur Dunross being shot. If he did, he's involved with Moscow in some capacity. I'd like a word with him, if only to be certain that we actually do have all the spies locked up or at the mortuary."

Thereafter, he thought sourly, I'd enjoy the opportunity to visit him on occasion at Wormwood Scrubs for twenty years to life.

"You can't tell much of anything from a photograph," Hugh Somerfield observed. "There was a picture of Kim Philby in a frame at his house. He was smiling... he resembled someone's uncle. I looked for a brass plaque under it that read 'devoted father and secret Soviet agent,' but I couldn't find it. Do you think Aileen Philby knows what he's been up to?"

Alec Grey considered this. "I can't imagine she does," he replied. "She was one of the ladies of Codes and Ciphers when they met, if I recall. She'll be shattered when she learns her husband won't be home for a while."

He returned his attention to the photographs before him, pleased to have something to distract himself from his consideration of Kim Philby as more than a code name and an agent to be questioned. "You can't tell much of anything from a photograph," he agreed.

"Can you tell anything more from their files?" Hugh Somerfield inquired.

"They don't have files... at least, not in the proper

sense. That's rather the problem with innocent people who've never done anything more treasonous than reusing a postage stamp. They've nothing to put in a file. In that respect, they're effectively indistinguishable from genuine spies who've not been found out as yet."

Hugh Somerfield leant back in his chair and applied his attention to his cigarette for a time. He'd smoked it to its end, disposed of it in Alec Grey's lone pot plant, dead for longer than either of them could recall, and set fire to a second one when the damp silence of the room was invaded by another knock at its door. Alec Grey shouted his acquiescence that it be opened, and was unnerved to discover Sir Alistair Fitzhenry at the far side of it. He rose uncertainly to his feet.

"I'm sorry, sir," he began with little enthusiasm. "I wasn't aware it was you."

The director smiled. "Good door, Mr. Grey," he observed. "Entirely opaque."

"Yes, sir."

"I've someone here I'd like to introduce," Sir Alistair continued. He gestured into the corridor and a second figure entered the office. He was disturbingly cadaverous, and he glanced around the stygian gloom through large black-rimmed spectacles. Despite his lack of volume, Alec Grey observed, he appeared acutely aware that the room had not been intended to accommodate four grown men unless they all undertook to inhale sharply.

He'd had occasion to meet few Americans, and it still amused him to observe that they all wore neckties like school children. Hugh Somerfield, upon returning from his lone assignment to Washington the previous year, had remarked upon the outdated fashion. Britons hadn't done so for decades, and the tie at the throat of his visitor could not have identified his origins more clearly if it had been cut from white stars and red stripes.

"This is James Angleton of the CIA," Sir Alistair said.

"I understand you two haven't actually met."

Alec Grey reached across his desk, accepting James Angleton's hand. The American seemed for a time intent on crushing the bones in his. He smiled amiably.

"I've heard a lot about you," he said. "It's good to put a face to all the files."

Alec Grey returned his smile. "And you, sir," he said. He'd heard a great deal about the head of counterintelligence for the CIA as well, not all of it wholly believable.

"Mr. Angleton is returning from a week in Germany, and he's paid us a second visit," the director continued. "We're doing a tour of Leconfield House."

"Mr. Angleton is probably one of about three people on earth with sufficient clearance to take such a tour," Hugh Somerfield observed from his chair. Sir Alistair seemed to notice his presence for the first time, and introduced him to James Angleton as 'one of Mr. Grey's employees.' James Angleton ignored him entirely.

"I'm headed over to MI6 when I'm done here," the American said to Alec Grey. "I have an old friend over there... we like to sample the local whiskey when I get to this side of the ocean. You're welcome to join us."

Alec Grey regarded him for a moment. Behind James Angleton, Sir Alistair's features grew bloodless and he shook his head determinedly. Alec Grey forced himself to suppress his amusement as he appreciated the font from which sprang the director's sudden concern.

"I'm afraid I'd have to decline your invitation," he replied. "I've a number of files here I've to clear up."

James Angleton nodded, and after a moment's consideration he glanced at the photographs spread across Alec Grey's desk. He walked around the end of the desk to afford himself a better viewing of them.

"Who are these guys?" he asked.

"Bookshop owners," Alec Grey replied. "We believe one of them might have some affiliation with Moscow."

"One of them sure does," James Angleton agreed, "but I don't think you have to worry about him." He stabbed at one of the photographs with a skeletal index finger. "This one's dead."

"I think you're mistaken, sir," Alec Grey said.

James Angleton shook his head. "This is Morris Cohen... I'd recognize the little bastard anywhere. He was involved in the spy ring that tried to send documents about the early research for our time stream facility to the Soviets. He disappeared along with his wife Lona a few years ago. We have reason to believe the Soviets executed them both to make sure they couldn't be arrested and get offered a deal."

Alec Grey took the photograph from his desk and read the notation on its back. "This is Peter Kroger. He runs a bookshop at 190 The Strand. He has a wife named Helen and he lives in Ruislip. He's originally from Canada. This photograph was taken Friday last."

"He's originally from New York City," James Angleton insisted. "If he isn't dead, he's well worth watch-ing."

Alec Grey smiled. "Is he indeed?"

James Angleton shook his hand a second time. "Good to meet you," he said, and he permitted himself to be ushered from the office by Sir Alistair.

Hugh Somerfield watched the two men leave. When Sir Alistair had pulled the door to behind them, he returned his attention to Alec Grey. "Well bugger me," he said with affected enthusiasm. "The next chap who com-plains that all the Americans ever send us is syphilis and undrinkable beer is going to have a few words with me."

Alec Grey ignored his observation. "You might have stood up, Hugh," he said.

Hugh Somerfield shook his head. "No fear. I wasn't going to risk striking the director of counterintelligence for the CIA with my elbow and cracking half his ribs. You'd think someone at Langley would've been assigned to feed the poor blighter more than once a month."

Alec Grey smiled. "I'm told he gets by with a liquid diet."

"And that's another thing," Hugh Somerfield continued, gesturing with his cigarette. "What came over Sir Alistair when Angleton offered to buy you a drink? I thought the old man would be turning green next."

"I don't believe Sir Alistair has informed Mr. Angleton as yet about the current disposition of his old friend at MI6."

Hugh Somerfield gazed at him uncertainly. "Boss?"

Alec Grey reached across his desk and retrieved one of the files he'd consulted the previous night. He opened it, and after some consideration he withdrew a large black and white photograph. He slid it across his desk to Hugh Somerfield.

The photograph was almost ten years old. It had a typed caption affixed to it with sticky tape that identified it as having been taken at a restaurant in Washington D.C. named the Occidental Grill. It depicted a somewhat younger James Angleton sitting at a table, raising a glass to the camera and smiling broadly. His drinking companion seemed equally cheerful. Despite the intervening decade, Hugh Somerfield would have had little difficulty identifying the other occupant of James Angleton's table as Kim Philby.

37

The day promised to become ugly. Peter Kroger sat behind his till, staring blankly at the pedestrians oozing past the windows of his shop. He'd seen no trade since he'd opened up. His only distraction had been an aging fellow who'd looked as if he'd warranted a clerical collar. The man had strode into the shop, realized what in fact it sold and slunk away with his coat drawn up around his ears and his eyes staring at his feet, clearly hoping that no one he knew might observe him leaving so deplorable an establishment.

Peter Kroger had chuckled to himself, savoring the moment's amusement like a glass of gin with only a few sips left, tumbling around its bottom.

He considered the possibility of venturing amongst his shelves and locating something deplorable for himself. He decided at length that he lacked sufficient enthusiasm to get to his feet.

He'd wholly lost himself in the gray parade beyond his window when the shop door opened once more. He turned his attention from the street to find a woman entering his premises. Women with a taste for what he purveyed were sufficiently unusual as to warrant his consideration. This one seemed decidedly out of place. She was well along into her fifties, and she had the air of someone with a family name, but the lack of a husband to support it.

She couldn't have been more out of place if she'd come in wearing a bright red wig and clown's nose, and he grew certain that she would prove far more outraged and embarrassed than the old gentleman who'd preceded her. He felt himself touched with disappointment when she ignored his shelves of books entirely and made directly for the till.

"Mr. Goldman?" she inquired. Her accent aligned itself with her appearance, Peter Kroger decided abruptly, cloying with the scent of the middle class. "Mr. Abraham Goldman?"

Why were all the imaginary personae he created for himself named Abraham, he wondered fleetingly. He nodded, smiling as pleasantly as he knew how. "Yes, madam," he said with affected warmth. No one should be addressing him by that name, and certainly not an aging matron from Ealing.

"I was told to come," she said uneasily. "Mr. Lonsdale told me to come here and ask for you… if it were urgent."

"Mr. Lonsdale," Peter Kroger said, in a tone which might or might not have been questioning. He felt his heart against his ribs, suggesting a trapped animal struggling to escape its cage.

"I'm to tell you my name is TINA," she continued.

"I see," Peter Kroger said. He glanced into the street, thinking as he did that it was a senseless gesture. If the woman had come as the vanguard for the police or MI5, there was hardly likely to be a black van parked outside his door.

"I find it odd that Mr. Lonsdale would have sent you here in person," he said at length. "Mr. Lonsdale prefers sending letters."

She nodded. "Oh, I know," she agreed, her voice

dropping in volume to a harsh whisper. "I would have used the dead drop. I normally use the dead drop. I've been using it for ages."

Peter Kroger studied the uncomfortable woman. If she was the source who used the code name TINA, she was a clerk of some kind working for MI5. He'd been servicing her dead drop for over two years. He'd not met her in that time, and he'd never intended to. It seemed portentous and more than a little suspicious that he might be doing so now.

"Letters are so much more convenient," he continued.

She nodded once more. "Mr. Lonsdale... he said that if something urgent happened... something that was too important to wait for the dead drop... I should come here and tell you directly. I hope you don't mind."

Peter Kroger re-inflated his smile. He would have preferred to tell the stupid woman that he minded very much, that her presence in his shop imperiled them both. It was not his place to instruct Moscow's assets on the nuances of tradecraft, he reminded himself. "What's so urgent, madam?" he inquired.

The woman produced a scrap of paper from the pocket of her coat and glanced at it. Peter Kroger resisted the impulse to curse her aloud, or to snatch the paper from her hand and swallow it. "A file came down this morning," she said quickly, and then she seemed to stop herself. "I don't know... I'm not sure what the proper code name is for the man it was about."

"Don't worry about that," Peter Kroger prompted her.

"His name is Andrei Bogdanov." She had some difficulty pronouncing the unfamiliar name. "I believe he's been arrested, or captured... they have him in custody, after he was found in the home of a woman named... Alice Woodward. He's believed to be a Soviet agent. I couldn't read the entire file, of course, but I feel certain he's a very important agent."

"I see," Peter Kroger said.

"I hope you'll inform Mr. Lonsdale that I've been of help to the cause."

"Yes, madam," he agreed.

"Good morning... comrade," she said, smiling uneasily. She turned and left the shop.

Peter Kroger permitted his eyes to pursue her through the front door, hearing it close behind her with a sense of relief. She could be nothing other than genuine, he decided. British intelligence could not have successfully recruited so scatterbrained a woman to use as a plant if it had canvassed every tea shop and sanitarium in the country. Clearly her access to sensitive files granted her value — the contents of her skull most assuredly would not have done so.

It was unusual for one of his sources to confide the name of a Soviet agent to him, rather than merely a code name. Andrei Bogdanov. He spoke it aloud several times, that he might better remember it. Unlike his recent visitor, he was sufficiently astute not to commit it to paper.

He glanced about the hushed interior of his shop, tasting the dust and silence of the place as if it were a particularly old wine. It was coming to taste disturbingly like a vintage one of his father's friends had made in his basement when he'd been a child, and inflicted on the rest of his family.

The arrest of Andrei Bogdanov, whoever he was, seemed sufficient grounds to close up the shop and return home. Helen would be pleased by his unexpected appearance in the middle of the day. Moscow would not be at all pleased by his news, but they would afford him their grudging thanks for his hasty dispatch of it.

A devoted servant of the cause could aspire to no more.

38

Alec Grey waited as one of the soldiers unlocked the door they were guarding. Wordlessly, the man withdrew his pistol and handed it to his colleague. He then opened the door and verified that the man it had been locked to imprison was where he'd been for much of the morning, seated at the table that constituted the room's only significant element of furniture. He gestured for Alec Grey to enter.

Kim Philby sat in a chair behind the table, which permitted him to view the door. He was crouched over the table, resting upon his elbows. His suit coat had been discarded in the corner of the room, his shirt stained with sweat. He glanced up as Alec Grey entered, his eyes sunken and etched in blackness.

Alec Grey pulled the unused chair toward himself and descended into it, to gaze into Kim Philby's eyes. They were disturbingly bloodshot. They regarded him with a smoldering venom of outrage and fear. The man's breath was sour with the revenants of drink.

Hugh Somerfield had wanted Kim Philby to perspire and squint under the lights of Balmoral Castle, but Alec Grey had thought otherwise. The man before him was not a Soviet defector, and not an imported Russian agent. Philby knew the drill. Philby would have seen the hand behind the lights and the tape recorders and the bolted-down chairs. He'd no doubt shaken it in friendship often enough.

This room lacked one-way glass and a microphone hidden in its ceiling. Perhaps it was not what Kim Philby had expected to be confined to, Alec Grey pondered as he watched the features before him harden and grow cold. Perhaps he'd simply floated unnoticed below the surface for so many years that he'd long since discounted the likelihood he'd ever be exposed and locked up at all.

Alec Grey withdrew a brown paper sack from beneath his arm and extracted a bottle of Glenfiddich single malt from it. He placed the bottle at the distant end of the table, observing with a moment of satisfaction how Kim Philby's eyes followed it to its destination.

"Have you come along t-t-to explain what I'm doing here?" the man before him inquired calmly. He smiled almost as an afterthought. Sir Alistair had been of the opinion that Philby's stammer was a useful barometer to gauge the state of his nerves. The director had also allowed that long before it indicated Kim Philby was reaching the limit of his own nerves, it would have frayed those of whoever was interviewing him.

"It's over, Mr. Philby," Alec Grey said evenly.

"Is it? What exactly is over?"

Alec Grey gazed at the lined, stiff features across the table. "We know you've been spying for the Soviets all these years. We know about PETER. We know about STANLEY."

A spark of ill-concealed surprise flashed in Kim Philby's eyes for an instant. His smile flickered and was re-ignited. He affected an expression of confusion, but it was badly performed, singularly unsatisfactory.

Alec Grey permitted himself a moment of self-congratulation. The code name PETER had been something of a gamble, a fragment of a deciphered Soviet message.

Philby had just verified it with more certainty than an entire month's worth of Enigma rotor settings.

"I haven't the f-f-faintest idea w-w-what you're talking about," Kim Philby said.

Alec Grey sighed. "Mr. Philby, we should understand one another. You'll have observed that this is not an interview suite. It has no microphones. No one is listening to us speak, and nothing we say will be recorded. This may very well be the last time anyone is able to offer you such an assurance."

"I have n-n-nothing to say that I wouldn't wish to have recorded."

Kim Philby glanced fleetingly at the bottle of whiskey, and Alec Grey smiled. "I don't think you're being entirely truthful, Mr. Philby," he said. The phrase and its tone were the property of Lawrence Downs, who could deliver it with the precision of Olivier and the menace of an automatic rifle with its safety switched off. Kim Philby's eyes narrowed.

"You can't seriously sit there and suggest that I've b-b-been a b-b-bloody spy. I've worked in British intelligence since before you were b-b-born."

"Then you'll know it has an unblinking memory."

"What are you on about?"

"Every spy makes mistakes... little mistakes, most of them. The information you've passed to Moscow was read, filed, forgotten. Your mistakes were recorded, accumulated and poured over. It's taken a very long time, but STANLEY's file has grown taller than you. You should have done a runner when you had the chance."

"You're mad," Philby said, gesturing dismissively.

Alec Grey shook his head. "Not mad, just angry. You've done a substantial degree of damage over the years. I dread to think the number of people you've betrayed."

"You must b-b-be thinking of someone else."

He leant back in his chair. "I don't imagine I need

explain to you how an interrogation is conducted," he began. "I appreciate that in all likelihood I'll leave you in a short while, and someone with more skill in these matters than myself will take my place. I'm certain you know Lawrence Downs... he does a fair number of these things. Mr. Downs or someone like him will be by to put all the evidence before you, ask you about the details, fill in the gaps."

"I don't think I shall have anything t-t-to say to Mr. Downs," Philby said smugly.

"There are those who choose not to speak to the interrogators," Alec Grey agreed. "In your case, it will be inconvenient, but immaterial. At such time as Lawrence Downs informs me that he can proceed no further with you, you'll go to trial."

Kim Philby smiled coldly, fixing Alec Grey in his gaze. "Pull the other one, Mr. Grey," he hissed. "It has bells on."

"Mr. Philby?"

"If I were a Soviet agent, you wouldn't bring me to trial... you wouldn't want the p-p-public to know what bloody fools you've been."

"I don't recall saying anything about a public trial. There'd be far too much classified information involved to allow that. We're permitted to conduct proceedings such as yours in camera." Alec Grey leant forward. "I believe we both know that a substantial amount of the classified infor- mation in question would be used to bury you up to your neck."

"I know nothing of the s-s-sort."

Lawrence Downs had spent a quarter of an hour predicting Kim Philby's behavior and recommending Alec Grey's responses to it. Thus far, his guesses had been suf- ficiently accurate as to have engendered accusations of collusion in any other circumstance. Lawrence Downs had observed that a man in a locked room finding himself accused of high treason had a severely restricted palette of responses with which to paint himself an exit. The object of Alec Grey's visit, he'd insisted, was not to back Kim Philby into a corner, but to entice him to the door.

Alec Grey gestured toward the ceiling. "There are no microphones in here," he reminded Kim Philby. "I invite you to climb onto the table and examine the wiring if you wish. Nothing we discuss in here will appear at your trial."

The man before him glanced away. His smile became that of the many photographs of Philby that Alec Grey had considered the previous evening. It was disarming, unaffected. It was said to have charmed its owner out of innumerable tight scrapes and sticky situations. Alec Grey considered observing aloud that it was not operating as promised on this occasion.

"If you're as clever as your file suggests, Mr. Philby, you'll ask yourself what I've come here for."

Kim Philby returned his attention to Alec Grey. "I believe you have some p-p-preposterous n-n-notion that I'm going to confess to being a spy, and you'll enjoy a substantial pay rise."

"Lawrence Downs deals with confessions."

He watched Kim Philby's expression grow minutely less resolute. "Perhaps you've come to gloat, Mr. Grey," he suggested.

"Not on company time."

"Very w-w-well, then... what is it that you w-w-want?"

"I want to read your tea leaves, Mr. Philby," Alec Grey replied. The expression seemed decidedly theatrical, but Lawrence Downs had insisted it was appropriate. "I want to tell you your future."

"You want to provide Alistair Fitzhenry with a bloody scapegoat," Kim Philby barked. "You want to blame someone for MI5's b-b-blown operations and missed opportunities. You need there to be a Soviet mole, because the alternative would be admitting that no one at Leconfield House can find the Soviet Union on a map without instructions."

Alec Grey smiled. "What do you think of my choice of drink, Mr. Philby?"

Kim Philby paused and stared at him. At length he directed his attention to the bottle. "I'm very much in favor of single malts," he replied uncertainly. He appeared to be on the point of requesting that Alec Grey pour him a glass when he observed that no glasses were present. By all accounts, he would have cheerfully swallowed it directly from the bottle.

"I'd like to tell you your future," Alec Grey repeated. "In fact, I'd like to tell you of two possible futures." He leant across the table and grasped the bottle. "This only appears in one of them."

"Do I d-d-detect a threat, Mr. Grey?"

Alec Grey nodded. "Yes, you do. It's one I suggest you take seriously."

Kim Philby's expression sagged. "Go on, then," he said reluctantly. "Tell me my future."

The bottle of whiskey appeared to have become the property of Lawrence Downs, Alec Grey reflected, who'd had the better of their wager. Kim Philby had all but admitted to the charges of espionage. Alec Grey had been adamant that Philby wouldn't have owned to his treason with a pistol in each ear. He was a moment remembering what Lawrence Downs had suggested he do next, having thought the prospect of persuading Philby to entertain the notion of confession singularly unlikely.

"You are unquestionably the most damaging Soviet agent to ever have operated within British intelligence," Alec Grey began, conscious that his words had adopted the manner of a recitation. Kim Philby smiled despite himself. "At least, we may hope you are. You represent the most profound possible risk to the security of the nation. The magistrate at your trial will believe this unquestioningly when he's completed a review of the evidence against you."

Kim Philby's smile evaporated, and Alec Grey continued. "We will request that you be confined to a secure cell at Wormwood Scrubs. I'm not certain you'll have seen one of them — it's a room six feet by nine feet, with a solid steel door, no window, a bed bolted to the wall and a lavatory. You'll be provided with enough food to keep you alive, nothing to read, nothing to do and out of concern for the defense of the realm, you'll be permitted to speak to no one. That bottle of whiskey will be the last one you'll ever set eyes on."

He leant forward slightly. "Sir Alistair maintains that you'll be provided with expert medical attention to ensure that you spend as many years in there as is humanly possible. I'm certain I need not mention that no possibility would exist of your being involved in an agent exchange in the future."

"You've s-s-succeeded in describing the prospect in sufficiently unappealing detail, Mr. Grey," Kim Philby interrupted him. "I've begun to appreciate that you mean to offer me an alternative."

"That's extremely perceptive," Alec Grey said coldly. "Under the correct circumstances, I might be prepared to leave the door to this room unlocked and send the guards off to have their tea."

Kim Philby's expression grew perplexed. "I think that unlikely," he said. "Alistair Fitzhenry apparently wishes to have my head to mount on his office wall."

"Sir Alistair can be persuaded to decorate his office with a painting from the National Portrait Gallery."

The man before him sighed, corrupting the air between them with alcohol fumes. "Shall I ask what you imagine I would be p-p-prepared to give you in exchange for my freedom?"

"The lot," Alec Grey replied.

Kim Philby glanced at him and cupped his hand to the side of his head. "Once more, old son, for those of us who've left their ear trumpets in their desks."

Alec Grey felt himself touched with amusement despite his contempt for the aging spy. "You'd agree to an extensive debriefing with Lawrence Downs and several of his colleagues. You'd review every second of your life, beginning in the womb. You'd provide us with every secret you've betrayed to the Soviets. You'd burn every Soviet agent in the west you know of. At such time as I'm convinced you've been pumped dry, you'd be put on a train and sent east."

Kim Philby's eyes grew wide. "That's not much to ask," he said acridly. "Do you actually imagine I'd agree to all t-t-that if I were a lifelong spy for Moscow?"

"It would depend upon how much more life you imagine yourself to have," Alec Grey replied.

He rose from his chair and collected his bottle of whiskey. It was Lawrence Downs' bottle of whiskey, he reminded himself, and Lawrence Downs richly deserved it. "I think I shall leave you to consider your future, Mr. Philby. I'll return in an hour or two and see how you're getting on."

Kim Philby glared up at him. "I don't imagine you'd like to leave that behind," he said, indicating the bottle.

Alec Grey shook his head. "If you'll be spending the next thirty years as a teetotal, you'd as well begin as you mean to carry on." He turned and shouted through the door to the guard to be released.

39

The bruised skies above Ruislip poured their venom upon the head of Hugh Somerfield as if they'd divined his purpose in striding beneath them. The rain was colder here, he mused as he walked, and it had infiltrated his collar and run down his back. It was the Soviet agent of rain, insidious and not to be trusted.

There was a green Ford Anglia half a block from him. He made for it with renewed haste, imagining himself being dissolved by the effluent of the suburban skies and flushed into the drains beneath him. Colorless houses wreathed in beds of flowers left to die in the first frigid breaths of winter loomed beside him, each sufficiently like the other as to be distinguishable only by its street number.

The Anglia sheltered two occupants. One of them had shifted to its rear seat. He opened the passenger-side door and propelled himself within.

"Mrs. Gardner," he said, smiling through a curtain of rain flowing from the rat's nest of his hair.

"Mr. Somerfield," Julie Gardner acknowledged. "I see you've had my message." She hadn't turned to consider him — her attention remained captivated by a particularly unattractive bungalow across the street.

"Is that it, then?" Hugh Somerfield inquired.

"45 Cranley Drive," she said. "The one with the make-believe Tudor windows and the brick arch over the front door."

He ran his fingers through his hair. "I'm not certain I understand what your interest is in it. I assume you're not intending to come out here and hold backyard parties with the neighborhood dentists."

"That's where Peter Kroger lives," she explained. "I was assigned by Alec Grey to keep an eye on him this morning."

Hugh Somerfield nodded, conscious as he did that she would be unable to see him. "Yes, the naughty book salesman," he said. "I believe the boss had you in The Strand, watching his shop full of naughty books."

She turned to regard him for a moment, and then she resumed her consideration of the house. "The books weren't going anywhere," she said. "The same couldn't be said for my subject."

"Peter Kroger left the shop, then?"

"It was all rather odd," she said. "It's a grotty little shop, and almost no one visits it. Shortly before noon, a woman appeared and walked in. Perhaps ten minutes later, Mr. Kroger shut up the shop and left. He hailed a taxi, rode in it for about fifteen minutes, got out, hailed another and so on, until he arrived here."

Hugh Somerfield discovered that he'd extracted his packet of cigarettes from his coat without thinking. He considered them for a moment and then returned them to his pocket. "It's not unheard-of for men to return home in the middle of the day," he said. "The taxis are a bit odd."

"What's odd is the woman who visited his shop," Julie Gardner said. "It took a while, but I remembered where I'd seen her. I kept thinking it was in one of the photograph books at A4, but it wasn't. It was in the registry at Leconfield House."

"Do you mean she was on file?"

"No, I mean she was bloody well working there. She's a clerk."

He glanced around the interior of the car. The woman in the rear seat smiled uncertainly, her face a mask of confusion. Julie Gardner would have been assigned one of A4's new staff members, he decided. Whoever she was, she couldn't be making a great deal of sense of what was transpiring. He was uncertain he was either.

"I don't imagine you've thought of a plausible explanation for all this being a strange coincidence," Hugh Somerfield asked.

"Not unless I were to believe in flying saucers and people from Mars as well," Julie Gardner replied. "Mr. Grey told me that Peter Kroger definitely is a Soviet agent, not that he's suspected of possibly being one. He also provided me with a file to read... said what his little shop was about, amongst other things. I've a difficult time imagining that woman, whoever she was, taking time off work and journeying all the way from Leconfield House to buy a naughty book. Besides, from what I could see through his window, she didn't even look at the books... she just spoke with Peter Kroger."

"I'd have to agree," Hugh Somerfield said. "Has anything happened since he returned home?"

She shook her head. "A woman appeared at the door about a quarter of an hour ago... Mrs. Peter Kroger, perhaps. She looked along the street and returned inside."

"The curious thing about the Russians is that they never work alone," Hugh Somerfield mused. "Peter Kroger will have a Soviet controller... perhaps he is a Soviet controller. Alec Grey had rather hoped to watch him until all players of this little company had appeared on stage, and we could roll up the lot."

"That's what I was instructed," Julie Gardner agreed. "There's something odd about this one, though... the Soviets are usually slow and careful. They don't change their behavior as Mr. Kroger did unless they have something important on their minds."

Hugh Somerfield stared through the rain-streaked windscreen at 45 Cranley Drive, struggling to imagine what could be transpiring behind its walls. Had they enjoyed the luxury of time, he appreciated, someone from Leconfield House could have arrived to mend the Krogers' telephone or inspect their gas main and undertaken a quick look 'round. He glanced uncertainly about the interior of the car. To a man in Peter Kroger's line of work, none of its occupants could have looked more like employees of MI5 if they'd been wearing name badges.

"Would you like to stay and watch the house for a few hours, Mr. Somerfield?" Julie Gardner inquired.

He shook his head. "There's a matter which you're not cleared to know of," he replied. "Suffice it to say we don't have a few hours."

"Are you considering rolling up the Krogers now?"

His gaze bored into the walls of 45 Cranley Drive. "It's something of a conundrum, Mrs. Gardner," he said. "If we do nothing, a rather important bit of information may well reach Moscow, which we'd very much like to see avoided. If we stamp in there with a brace of policemen, Mr. Kroger's comrades in arms will most probably leg it."

Julie Gardner turned to face him, her features twisted with a wicked smile. "It's dreadfully lonely at the top, Mr. Somerfield," she said with affected sympathy. "This is why you're paid so much better than I."

Hugh Somerfield glanced at his wrist watch, appreciating as he did that time was hardly the issue. If Peter Kroger had been informed that Andrei Bogdanov was a guest of Her Majesty, the problem of preventing him from sharing his newly-found insights would remain an hour hence. Alec Grey's delicate gamble to set back the Soviet time stream project dangled upon the frayed thread of secrecy. It would require no more than the mere breath of suspicion to sunder it, and persuade the Soviets to re-examine Alice Woodward's papers.

Rolling up a few additional Russians would be a poor consolation at best if Peter Kroger's purpose was as it appeared.

Alec Grey was sequestered with Kim Philby. The boss would not be available to consult on this matter. It hardly mattered. It would have required longer to locate a telephone box and explain the nuances of his morning's travels to Alec Grey than Peter Kroger had granted him.

He would permit himself a minute to re-examine the problem, he decided, gazing at the orbit of the second hand beneath the crystal of his watch. He felt Julie Gardner's eyes upon him, listened to the brittle clatter of rain against the steel above him. Such minutes fled past him like racehorses, terminated by the bloody necessity of his determining the fate of the nation.

Hugh Somerfield smiled to himself. He wasn't being paid nearly enough.

40

The director stared across his desk through eyes like gun barrels, his features blurred by the smoke of his pipe. "I believe you've lost your bloody mind, Mr. Grey," he snapped.

It was unusual to experience Sir Alistair raising his voice, Alec Grey reflected, and despite his having anticipated the director's reaction to this audience, he found himself unsettled by his display of pique.

"Sir?" He appreciated that it would be most efficient of the time and tempers of both combatants to permit Sir Alistair to fully vent his rage before their conversation resumed.

"I don't give a damn what Kim Philby is prepared to tell us. That traitorous little bastard is going to spend the rest of his days in a cage."

"Yes, sir," Alec Grey agreed. "That would unquestionably be one possibility."

"I am unwilling to entertain any others." Sir Alistair clamped his pipe between his teeth, the gesture final and intractable.

Alec Grey regarded the director for a time. Regrettably, this was an interview for which Lawrence Downs had been unable to offer him guidance on the tactics and strategies he might employ to prevail against his subject. Moments after the door to the director's office had closed behind him, he'd come to appreciate that this was to be a battle. As with all his jousts against the steel and tobacco of Sir Alistair Fitzhenry, he'd entered into it in the best traditions of single combat, unsupported and largely unarmed.

The director was to be a more stalwart adversary today than most, he appreciated. He was clearly sufficiently incensed by the discovery of Kim Philby's treachery as to have submerged his reason in a lake of vitriol — he was enjoying its gasps and pleas as it drowned.

"To know what Philby knows, sir," he said reflectively. "To have insight into what he's betrayed to Moscow..."

"You're forgetting who he's betrayed to Moscow," Sir Alistair interrupted him. "I've been reviewing files of defectors and agents who've disappeared after their existence became known to Philby. There are dozens of men and women who went to their deaths at the hands of the KGB thanks to Philby... slow, painful deaths, Mr. Grey. Kim Philby should count himself damned lucky that we don't deal with spies as do the Russians."

"Yes, sir," Alec Grey agreed. "I'd bring them all back from their graves if it were within my power to do so, and treat each of them to five minutes alone with Philby. As it is, I'm forced to content myself with furthering what they died for."

Sir Alistair shook his head angrily. "I don't believe we can trust Kim Philby's account of the information he's betrayed to the Russians. Even if we could, it's behind the curtain. There's no calling it back."

Alec Grey nodded. "I'm not concerned that Philby would try to mess us about, sir. He's lived inside British intelligence for long enough to appreciate that we'll be able to verify some of what he tells us, and he has no way of knowing which of his facts will be checked. He'd be more

of a fool than he appears to risk telling us any fibs, or omit-
ting anything that might return to haunt him." He paused
and considered the grim visage of the director. "We might
yet recover our secrets from Moscow."

Sir Alistair's eyes narrowed and he laid his pipe on
his desk. "I hardly think that's likely, Mr. Grey."

Alec Grey nodded once more. "Perhaps we can't
recover them," he acknowledged, "but we might discredit
them."

The director appeared as if he were on the point of
speaking when he stopped himself. He gazed at Alec Grey
for a time. "How's that?" he inquired at length.

Alec Grey leant back in his chair. "Are you familiar
with the aircraft carrier Hermes?" he inquired.

Sir Alistair retrieved his pipe and gazed over it at
Alec Grey. "I believe so," he replied, clearly at a loss to
understand the sudden shift in their discussion. "I'm not
certain I see what bearing it has upon the matter of Kim
Philby."

"She's one of several Royal Navy ships upon which
GCHQ maintains a presence," Alec Grey continued.
"When she sails on maneuvers, GCHQ technicians sail
with her to monitor Soviet signals intelligence... radio
transmissions and such. She's to some extent our equivalent of those preposterous Russian fishing trawlers
with more aerials than nets. The Soviets know as
much about what the Hermes is up to as we do about
their trawlers... I've never quite understood her usefulness."

"I don't think I do at this moment either, Mr. Grey,"
Sir Alistair growled.

"One of the wireless operators aboard the Hermes is
a young fellow named Kevin McLough. He's quite capable
with radio equipment... he's also spying for Moscow."

The director's features grew darker.

"It's not something to be greatly concerned over,"

Alec Grey assured him. "We've been aware of Mr. McLough's activities almost from the start, and we're entirely grateful for his presence. The captain of the Hermes knows what he's up to as well. We make sure nothing of any importance is sent by wireless when Mr. McLough is on duty. In the event something urgent turns up, we can send the Hermes an agreed-upon innocuous message that will instruct her captain to relieve Mr. McLough."

"Would it not be preferable to arrest this chap and lock him up?" Sir Alistair asked impatiently.

"No, sir, it would not. Kevin McLough allows us to feed disinformation to Moscow through a source the Soviets are very proud of. Intercepted Enigma messages indicate that everything he sends them is swallowed whole."

"You may have strayed from your original purpose, Mr. Grey," the director said. "We were discussing your rather unpalatable suggestion that Kim Philby be permitted to trade for his freedom."

"Yes, sir," Alec Grey acknowledged. "I was thinking that we might grant Philby the promise of his freedom, but not permit him to enjoy it."

"Are you suggesting that we enter into an agreement with him and then renege on it?" Alec Grey studied Sir Alistair's expression as he spoke. The director seemed untroubled by the thought.

"No, sir. While I can't help thinking that Philby deserves no better, it wouldn't serve us were it to become known we can't be trusted."

He leant forward, suppressing a cough as a tendril of smoke from the director's pipe clutched at his face. "I'm suggesting that we let Philby defect to Moscow. In six or eight months, we'd transmit some intelligence to the GCHQ people on the Hermes that would cause Moscow to believe Philby has been working for us, rather than for

them, and that he's sent them thirty years worth of western disinformation. We'd be certain to do so during Kevin
McLough's watch. Moscow would have no choice but to
question everything Philby's sent them, and having a
degree of suspicion just this side of madness, they'd almost
certainly discredit the lot."

"And Philby…"

"And Philby might talk his way into a Siberian labor
camp if he's as clever as his reputation suggests, but I'd
put a week's wages on his getting a bullet to the back of his
skull."

Sir Alistair put his hand to his chin, his expression
softening. "It sounds somewhat dodgy, Mr. Grey," he said
at length, his pipe still clamped between his teeth. His tone
suggested that he wasn't quite as adamant about Philby's
fate as he'd expressed himself five minutes earlier.

Alec Grey returned to the embrace of his chair. He
carried a final sword to thrust into the bloody heart of Sir
Alistair's reluctance, and while he would feel like a cad for
unsheathing it, he appreciated that the director's guard
would never be let down further than it was at this
moment.

"There's something to be said for our not having
Kim Philby about, sir," he said quietly.

Sir Alistair withdrew his attention from his pipe.
"And why is that, Mr. Grey?"

"There's an expression I've heard about our relationship with the Americans… the only time we come first in
the UKUSA intelligence sharing agreement is in its name. If
Philby's in Wormwood Scrubs when the people at Langley
learn of his activities, they'll demand to have a word with
him. They'll claim, perhaps rightly so, that we sent them a
Soviet spy for the three years Philby served in Washington,
and that based on our assurances, they gave our spy unfet-
tered access to a great deal of very sensitive material. Men
like J. Edgar Hoover and James Angleton will shout loudly

enough to be heard in London without bothering with a telephone… and it will be a very long time indeed before we see any further cooperation from across the sea."

Sir Alistair exhaled a distended cloud of smoke. The director detested his oftentimes servile relationship with Washington. The American intelligence agencies had superior resources, more staff and legal authority to ensnare the Soviets in a way his own people could never hope to. The CIA periodically made overtures to Leconfield House and praised the state of its contribution to the great game, but no doubt was permitted to exist as to who had contributed the majority of its stakes, or who held most of its cards.

Alec Grey watched the director pivot upon the spearpoint of his indecision. "Clever as they are, the Americans would have a much more difficult time interviewing Kim Philby if he were lying in a grave in the woods outside Moscow."

Slowly, as if he were a mechanical toy for which the winding key had been misplaced, the director nodded. "I wish you to appreciate, Mr. Grey, that if this matter were to go pear-shaped, the mandarins of Whitehall would unquestionably become involved. You and I would have to answer for what's been said here today. In my case, I would enjoy the company of my wife full time, which I dare say she would favor. You, on the other hand, would find yourself so deep in the fires of hell as to require an asbestos hat. I trust you fully understand the risk we're both taking."

"Yes, sir," Alec Grey said coldly. "Lions to the left, tigers to the right. I'm not greatly concerned."

"I fail to see how you could be otherwise."

Alec Grey smiled. "Our letting the Russians get away with our Uranium promises to go pear-shaped long before we turn Kim Philby loose. One can only be sentenced to hell once."

Sir Alistair scowled. "You clearly don't fully appreciate the resourcefulness of Whitehall when it's seeking
revenge," he muttered.

Alec Grey rose to leave, and he was surprised to see
Sir Alistair gesture him back to his chair. "There's another
matter I wish to bring to your attention, Mr. Grey," he
said. "It's hardly comparable with your intent to assist in
the defection of the empire's most treacherous Soviet spy,
I'm certain, but you will wish to know of it."

"Yes, sir," Alec Grey agreed.

"This concerns your recent recruitment of Miss
Woodward to deceive Moscow," the director continued.
"Alice Woodward has been on my staff for several years,
and during that time she's been quite exemplary. She's
also been extremely quiet. She arrives at work, bangs away
at her typewriter and returns home each evening."

Sir Alistair sighed and gazed uncertainly at the wall
beyond Alec Grey, gesturing with the stem of his pipe.
"Over the past week or so, Miss Woodward's demeanor
has changed. She's very much more... cheerful than I've
seen her in the past. Office rumor and gossip has it that
she's finally found herself a fellow to go out with. God
knows I'm pleased for her, but she couldn't have chosen a
worse time. Whoever he is, he's bound to be a security
risk. You'll want your people to have a word with her, find
out what they can about this chap... and see to it that he
doesn't blow everything she's accomplished to the
Soviets."

Alec Grey listened to his heart thundering in his
chest. He wondered fleetingly if Sir Alistair could be aware
of his relationship with Alice Woodward, and had chosen
this moment to speak of it as a token of retribution over his
handling of Kim Philby. In reflection, it seemed unlikely.
The director wasn't sufficiently devious. It probably constituted a character flaw, considering his position.

The similarity of his current situation and that of a

schoolboy being called before his headmaster for inappropriate language was disturbing. At the very least, it was
amusing. Alice Woodward would unquestionably be
amused this evening when he recounted this fragment of
his conversation with the director for her.

"No, sir," he began. "He's not a risk to our security."
He leant back in his chair, recalling his prediction that Sir
Alistair's head was very likely about to explode.

41

H ugh Somerfield held the handset of Peter Kroger's telephone to his ear, thinking as he did that he might wish to cover it with a hand-kerchief. Could a tendency toward spying for Moscow be in some way contagious, he wondered absently. Peter Kroger hadn't been entirely gracious in the hour following his capture. He could see the man and his wife through the corner of his eye in their sitting room, scowling at their handcuffs beneath the brooding gaze of several policemen.

Alec Grey answered his telephone with a single word, his surname. Even that sounded weary. Hugh Somerfield imagined him having concluded a titanic struggle with Kim Philby. He'd not known his superior to lose his rag, but a traitor of the stature of Philby might well have sundered his resolve at last.

"Somerfield, boss," he said. "Have you a moment?"

He heard Alec Grey sigh, chiding himself. He was wont to ask such a question when he wished to convey troubling news.

"What's happened, Hugh?"

"I'm ringing you from 45 Cranley Drive," he said. "We've had a spot of bother with the Soviets."

"I recall assigning Julie Gardner to watch Peter

Kroger, Hugh," Alec Grey said. "I don't believe I told her anything about burgling his home."

"It's rather worse than that. Mr. Kroger and his missus are in the next room, as are a substantial number of coppers." He paused, and when Alec Grey said nothing, he recounted Julie Gardner's surveillance of Peter Kroger's book shop.

"I see," Alec Grey said at length. He fell silent for a moment, and Hugh Somerfield struggled to imagine him crouched in his matchbox of an office, gazing at its ceiling. "I can't say I'd have proceeded any differently, Mr. Somerfield," he said at length. "I've decided not to assign you to search for explosives in Belfast."

"That's extremely good of you, boss," he said.

"Have you found anything in the Krogers' home?" Alec Grey inquired.

Hugh Somerfield felt himself smile despite his disquiet at the morning's developments. "Yes, I believe we've found the lot."

"I think you'd best explain that."

"Several lads from Technical Services are on their way to tear up the floors and knock holes in the plaster, but even left to our own devices, Mrs. Gardner and I have cracked on quite successfully. Mr. Kroger owns several copies of The Reluctant Maiden, for one thing."

"Is one of them missing a corner of page 217?"

"I've not had a chance to look," Hugh Somerfield replied. "I thought it best not to ask one of the ladies to open them, under the circumstances."

"Please be certain you see to it when there's a moment. I imagine we should send someone along to his shop as well. Is there anything more?"

"There is. Mrs. Gardner's suspicions appear to have been correct. Mr. Kroger was keying Morse code into a tape recorder when we arrived at his house, and we found a burst transmitter."

He heard Alec Grey exhale. "That should please Sir Alistair," he said.

Burst transmitters were what Hugh Somerfield considered to be a typical Soviet innovation. When the first one had been discovered over a decade earlier, its simplicity had confused the MI5 boffins assigned to dissect it for almost a week. Moscow had clearly appreciated that having its agents send short wave radio messages was potentially hazardous, even if the messages were enciphered. Radio signals could be triangulated, and the location of a transmitter revealed if it operated for a sufficient time. The KGB had sought for a system that would reduce the time its spies had to spend on the air.

A burst transmitter consisted of a tape recorder connected to a wireless. The tape recorder had two speeds — normal and inaudibly fast. Messages were keyed in Morse code, recorded on tape and played back at extremely high speeds for transmission. Ten minutes of Morse could be sent in as many seconds. A single burst transmission was typically over with before anyone else knew it had begun.

It was assumed that when it was received by Moscow, a burst transmission was slowed down on a second tape recorder and transcribed.

"Do you know what Mr. Kroger was about to tell Moscow?" Alec Grey inquired.

"Yes, boss," Hugh Somerfield answered. "We have his original text, the one-time pad he used to encipher it and his tape." He unfolded a page of ruled paper and considered it. "He makes reference to an agent by the name of TINA, who we shall assume is the woman from Registry Julie Gardner observed this morning. He says that Andrei Bogdanov has been apprehended by MI5, and must be assumed to have been compromised. There's some additional stuff about his being in need of funds."

"Is there any indication he managed to get his message off to Moscow?"

"I'm quite certain he didn't have the chance. I don't believe he'd finished recording it. His transmitter uses valves, and they were all stone cold. As burst transmitters pretty well require that whoever's intended to receive them be listening at an agreed-upon time, and as short wave reception improves after the sun's gone down, I should say Mr. Kroger was waiting for nightfall before he sent his message."

"I'm pleased to hear he kept to his schedule," Alec Grey said, with considerable relief in his voice.

"As am I."

"Mention to Mrs. Gardner that she's single-handedly saved civilization, if you would, and have her come by for a visit this afternoon. I'd like her to take a stroll through the registry and see if she spots anyone she recognizes."

"Yes, boss."

"Thank you, Hugh," Alec Grey said quietly. "This was very nicely done indeed."

"Thank you," he said. "Can I ask what..."

Something rattled at the other end of the connection, interrupting his question.

"If it's not urgent, I should probably ring off," Alec Grey said. "Oliver Boyle's just come in flapping his arms about and rather red in the face. I should probably see what he wants before he does himself an injury."

Hugh Somerfield grinned at the image. "Yes, boss," he said. "As soon as the Technical Services people have arrived and there's a van to deliver the Krogers, I'll start back to Leconfield House."

Alec Grey rang off and Hugh Somerfield returned his attention to the interior of 45 Cranley Drive. MI5's people would no doubt be spending several weeks between its walls. Its current occupants wouldn't be returning home for at least thirty years.

42

Alec Grey replaced the handset of his telephone and smiled uncertainly to himself. His nascent week was hanging together by threads and tatters, he mused, but it was thus far hanging together. Oliver Boyle was clearly out of breath, and his face was a luminous mask of perspiration. He gestured for the man to have a seat, but he remained standing.

Oliver Boyle was clearly not smiling, and presently neither was Alec Grey.

"Andrei... Andrei Bogdanov," the man gasped.

"I think you should calm yourself, Olli," Alec Grey cautioned him. "If you don't live long enough to collect your pension, it will go to some cabinet minister, and none of us wishes to see that happen. What of Andrei Bogdanov?"

"He's done a bunk," Oliver Boyle said. "He's escaped."

Alec Grey shook his head uncertainly. "That's not possible," he said flatly.

"He's gone."

"Andrei Bogdanov was in a prison cell this morning, then he was in a van, then he was to be locked in a concrete room with doors thicker than this bloody office. He had chains on his wrists and ankles the entire time."

Oliver Boyle inhaled deeply. "I've not been told the details, boss," he said. "He was locked in the transport van this morning to carry him to Balmoral Castle. There was a chap from F Branch in with him, Victor Speaks. Not exactly his line of work, but he was handy. As far as I know, Bogdanov had Speaks' pistol off him... he shot Speaks, and the chain on his ankles, and then the lock out the back of the van."

Alec Grey stared at Oliver Boyle. "You can't be bloody serious," he barked. "No one's permitted to carry a pistol in proximity to a prisoner."

"Yes, sir," Oliver Boyle agreed. "Victor Speaks... perhaps he forgot."

"Is Mr. Speaks still alive?"

Oliver Boyle nodded. "He's in hospital. The doctors say he'll live."

"He'll wish it were otherwise by day's end," Alec Grey muttered. He glanced about his office for a moment. "I need you to get some things in hand, Mr. Boyle. Have you caught your breath?"

"I have, boss."

"I want all the telephones running into the Soviet embassy in Kensington Palace Gardens faulted. I want it done twenty minutes ago, and if the post office gives you any grief over it, you have my permission to ask Sir Alistair to speak with them personally. Fault the telephones at Colonel Nikonov's private brothel as well, and any other residences we know to be occupied by Soviet personnel. I want the embassy surrounded by our people... and any policemen you need. I don't want a bloody mouse getting in there unless it's signed the act. If Andrei Bogdanov appears without a prominent white flag and his arms outstretched in abject surrender, he's to be shot dead."

Oliver Boyle's eyes had grown wide. Alec Grey fixed them in his gaze. "I believe you understand the urgency of ensuring that Andrei Bogdanov not be permitted to communicate with Moscow, or anyone likely to do so on his behalf."

"Yes, boss."

Alec Grey considered the matter for a moment longer. "I've forgotten how many lads are assigned to Alice Woodward, but I want them doubled. If she goes anywhere near an outside door, I wish to have armed men around her, and I wish to be notified."

Oliver Boyle nodded. "Only, I don't think she's about," he said.

Alec Grey caught his eye once more. Oliver Boyle appeared to compose himself. "The rain let up half an hour ago, and she usually walks out to have her lunch. I've been assigned to her several times, and that's what she does." He glanced at his wristwatch. "She'd have left a quarter of an hour ago."

"Bloody hell," he said, hearing a note of panic ripple in his words. He gestured to Oliver Boyle. "Get on with it, man."

Oliver Boyle fled his office almost as desperately as he'd entered it. Alec Grey located a pistol in the upper drawer of his desk and followed him a moment later.

The scrap of grass that Alice Woodward favored with her lunch hours was five minutes along Curzon Street. Alec Grey could see the clutter of policemen and curious pedestrians who currently occupied it from two blocks distant. He began to run, distantly conscious that he was waving his revolver about as he did. He was almost as breathless as Oliver Boyle had been when he reached it.

He recognized one of the constables, and was comforted that the fellow didn't seem greatly troubled by his pistol. He pushed through the milling faces, briefcases, raincoats, hearing the rasp of his chest. The policemen had arranged themselves in a phalanx around the still form of a man in a dark gray suit lying face-down in the muddy grass. His right hand was stretched before him, clutching a pistol identical to the one Alec Grey held.

A crumpled flower of waxed paper lay discarded on the nearest of several ragged wooden benches, partially concealing two sandwiches he'd watched Alice Woodward assemble that morning.

The constable glanced at the body between them and shook his head slowly.

He struggled for an instant to view the essence of the departed Russian agent. He'd stepped from behind a tree, surprised Alice Woodward's protection, shot the man with Victor Speaks' pistol and then put it to Alice Woodward's head. Perhaps he'd stolen a car to carry her off in.

London stretched away from him in all directions, a carpet of streets and buildings that seemed to meet itself on the far side of the earth. His rage and desperation howled in his ears, deafening him.

The Russian hadn't made for his embassy, Alec Grey considered. He forced himself to repeat the thought several times more. Andrei Bogdanov had squandered his pearl of freedom on abducting Alice Woodward. He grasped the image of the coarse, unshaven man, the chained figure before him in the interview suite. Andrei Bogdanov had no use for the girl, but he certainly had use for almost everyone surrounding her.

The Russian hadn't made for his embassy because he was astute enough to appreciate that he'd never reach it. Andrei Bogdanov required assistance, and he had no illusions about it being provided by Moscow.

Alec Grey pushed through the crowd once more. He stepped into Curzon Street and began walking until he encountered a taxi. He flung himself through its rear doors and shouted an address in Adams Row to the driver. As the car began to move he pressed himself into its seat, conscious of the pistol still in his hand, struggling to prevent it from trembling.

The door of Alice Woodward's house was ajar. He pushed it before himself, hearing it crack against the wall behind it. He stepped into the gloom of the front hall. He'd left a raincoat hanging on a peg beside the light switch the night before. With an effort of imagination, he might have smelled the fragrance of the coffee they'd shared that morning. He took a pace forward, the pistol raised, his anger steadying his arms.

Andrei Bogdanov was poised upon the edge of the settee in the front sitting room. Alice Woodward had been discarded against one of its arms, her arms and legs bound with strips of cloth, her lips forced apart by a white hand-kerchief. Her eyes were huge and wet with terror as he entered the room. Victor Speaks' pistol was two inches from her ear.

"Mr. Grey," Andrei Bogdanov said woodenly. "I did not expect you here for hours."

Andrei Bogdanov was dressed in prison overalls. The manacles that had been intended to prevent his escape still clutched at his wrists and ankles — he'd clearly shot through his leg chains, but he'd been unable to defeat the locks that secured them. Alec Grey noticed a number of screwdrivers and kitchen knives on the coffee table between them, suggesting that he'd tried his hand at pick-ing them.

His posture was distorted, almost comical, as he directed the pistol at Alice Woodward with both hands. A length of chain dangled pendulously between them, rat-tling, swaying uneasily.

The Soviet agent's features were dark, ragged with at least a day's beard and no doubt a paucity of sleep. He smiled, the expression an effort of will.

"Do you always arrive home with a gun in your hand, Mr. Grey?" he asked. "Drop your gun, or I will shoot her now."

Alec Grey placed his pistol on the seat of a nearby

chair. Andrei Bogdanov scowled at it. He'd clearly wished it further removed from its owner.

"Why have you come home so early, Mr. Grey?" he inquired. He relaxed his arms, withdrawing his pistol from Alice Woodward and directing it at Alec Grey. After several seconds he permitted it to fall to his lap, clearly grateful at not being compelled to keep it aloft.

When Alec Grey failed to reply to his question, the Russian continued. "You are more clever than you look, yes? You found the *govniuk* who was intended to be guarding your woman while she ate her lunch and you knew to come here. I am impressed. I thought we would have to wait until it was the end of the day."

Alec Grey willed himself to be calm, to regard the sitting room and its occupants with what little of his reason as hadn't deserted him. Andrei Bogdanov gestured with his gun, indicating that he was to distance himself from the chair where his pistol lay. He moved several paces to his right.

The Russian smiled once more, his eyes alight. He returned the pistol to his lap, his chains rattling softly.

Andrei Bogdanov's arms were still chained. Alec Grey commanded his attention to the flicker of steel in the gloom of midday. The Russian had shot through his leg chains, but he'd left the chain that confined his arms. It couldn't have been easy driving in such a posture while keeping his pistol directed at his captive. One bullet would have severed them.

He suppressed a smile as he contemplated Andrei Bogdanov. Victor Speaks' revolver had presumably held six bullets when Andrei Bogdanov had overpowered him. He'd put one bullet through Victor Speaks, one through his leg chain, two or perhaps three through the van lock and one through Alice Woodward's minder in the park. There was every possibility that his pistol was empty. At worst, a single round remained in it. The Russian had not shot through the chain that bound his wrists either because he could not, or because he was loath to expend his final shell.

"I knew you would arrive," Andrei Bogdanov said. "Shall I tell you how I knew? When I was here yesterday, I walked around all the rooms of this fine house. I saw that Miss Woodward does not sleep alone. I saw her man's clothes, a razor beside the sink. When you told me about your... feelings for her, I knew whose clothes and razor they must be. I knew you would come. I am clever as well, yes?"

Alec Grey directed his attention at the Russian, ignoring the motionless figure of Alice Woodward. Andrei Bogdanov had behaved cleverly, he conceded. He'd used his almost indefensible situation to direct the attention of his opponent to his captive, rather than to his almost complete lack of weapons. The man before him was waiting, he appreciated, waiting for him to speak, to express his concern for the girl, to shout his rage and desperation across the sitting room.

"What is it you want, Andrei Mikhailovich?" Alec Grey inquired patiently. The Russian's smile flickered and evaporated at the familiar use of his name. He'd been addressed thus throughout his interrogation. Lawrence Downs had wished the inappropriate familiarity to remind him that his captors were at liberty to define the posture of their relationship.

"What I want is to have these fucking irons off my hands," Andrei Bogdanov howled. "What I want is to be out of your fucking country." He paused and appeared to compose himself. "What I want is to say thank you for your hospitality, Mr. Grey."

He gestured at Alice Woodward with his pistol. "I think all of us will go to the bedroom now, yes? I will take off Miss Woodward's clothes, and I will hold her over the bed, and you will watch while I fuck her. I know she will

scream and say rude things about me at first, but I think
maybe she will enjoy it. I think maybe she will make noises
for me that she has not made for you. When I am finished
with her, I will give her back to you... if you still want to
have her. Maybe she will not want to have you after she has
had a Russian *khuy* inside her."

Alec Grey caught Andrei Bogdanov's gaze, watching
the Soviet agent's smile. There was a faint twitching of the
muscle below his left eye. His jaw was taut, his arms like
longbows as they bore his pistol.

"When I have finished fucking your woman, Mr.
Grey, you will arrange for me to leave England, yes? I will
return to Moscow, I will inform my superiors of your
invented documents, I will be awarded the Order of Lenin
and I will be given my own apartment."

Alec Grey scowled and shook his head. "Are you certain that's what you want, Mr. Bogdanov?" he inquired.

The Russian's smile collapsed once more. "What are
you asking me?"

"Haven't you read the documents Miss Woodward
left at your dead drop?"

Andrei Bogdanov rattled his chain, moving his pistol
uncertainly. "I do not read the films, Mr. Grey. I pass the
films along, someone else reads them."

Alec Grey smiled and exhaled, the gesture seeming
embarrassingly overacted. "That might not have been
entirely in your interest, Andrei Mikhailovich," he said.

The Russian glared at him, his confusion crawling,
insect-like, across his features. "What are you saying, Mr.
Grey?"

"I'm saying that I don't think you'll be welcomed as
a hero in Moscow," he replied. "You provided the KGB
with instructions for the final configuration of your time
stream facility, so they could make it active."

"If you say so," Andrei Bogdanov agreed uncertainly.

"In fact, you provided the KGB with instructions we created to blow it to hell. An hour ago, they did just that," he lied. "I'm told that the resulting explosion was detected by seismographs as far away as California." He smiled, peering into the Russian's eyes. "You have personally orchestrated the most devastating catastrophe your country has suffered since the Russo-Japanese war in 1905. If I were to arrange to send you back to Moscow, I believe your government would award me the Order of Lenin."

Andrei Bogdanov rose from the settee. "You are inventing all this, Mr. Grey," he said, a pleading whine having infected his words.

"That's the lamentable aspect of our business, Andrei Mikhailovich," Alec Grey said, sensing the stellar dust of his fabrication coalescing around them. "Trust is such a rare commodity. Well you might ask yourself why I permitted Miss Woodward to take her lunch outside with only a single minder. I'm afraid I leapt to the conclusion that the whole sordid affair was done with, that your people would have far more pressing issues to concern themselves over than her." He shook his head in what he hoped the Russian would perceive as a gesture of regret. "I admit I'd not included your escape in my considerations."

Andrei Bogdanov took a pace toward him, stepping around the end of the coffee table. It was a pace further removed from Alice Woodward, Alec Grey considered, measuring the footfalls between them. The Soviet agent's eyes were crucibles of molten iron, wet with rage or desperation.

"You are lying to me, Mr. Grey," he snarled.

"No, Andrei Mikhailovich," Alec Grey said calmly. "I'm offering to protect your life in a room with very thick walls and very strong doors. Prison is far less objectionable when you consider what the KGB will do to you when they catch you up."

Andrei Bogdanov screamed, the sound of his terror a

sudden detonation within the walls of Alice Woodward's sitting room. He raised Victor Speaks' pistol to the level of Alec Grey's eyes and clutched at its trigger. Its hammer snapped upon a spent shell. He cursed unintelligibly in Russian and cast the empty revolver across the room. His chains rattled like enraged serpents as he flung himself toward his tormenter.

The Russian drove his head into Alec Grey's chest, hurling them both into the far corner of the sitting room. The walls danced maniacally about them. Alec Grey tasted blood washing over his tongue and the stale funk of panic on Andrei Bogdanov's breath. Something crashed in the periphery of his attention, a vase or a pot plant. Andrei Bogdanov's contorted features resolved themselves before him, clouded with his shock and his sudden inability to catch his breath.

He freed one arm and levered the Russian from his chest. Andrei Bogdanov swung at him, his fist arrested by the chain that still bound it. Alec Grey struck his jaw, driving him back. The room echoed darkly with guttural obscenities.

He'd almost risen to his feet when Andrei Bogdanov launched himself from the floor. He felt the Russian's chain tighten around his throat, heard the man curse in his ear. He clawed at the steel, succeeding only in entrapping his fingers beneath it as it grew tighter. He felt himself begin to choke.

Andrei Bogdanov was twenty pounds heavier than he, Alec Grey realized desperately, and the KGB had no doubt instructed him at length for situations such as this one. Tentacles of scarlet and black began to invade his perception. The face howling before him became indistinct. He coughed, feeling his lungs ignite. His free hand thrashed in the periphery of his attention, snatching fistfuls of air.

The Russian twisted him, altering the geometry of

the room. In the extreme distance, the minute figure of Alice Woodward writhed upon the settee, desperate, drowning in her hopelessness. Andrei Bogdanov smiled and turned once more, clearly pleased that Alec Grey had appreciated his intentions.

Alec Grey drove the ball of his fist into Andrei Bogdanov's ear and his knee into the Russian's belly. The effort required his last wisps of breath, and for a moment he was certain he would lose consciousness as a result of it. He heard the Russian curse once more. The chain at his throat grew slack and he clawed at it, seized by disorientation and the betrayal of his muscles. In a moment he would very likely have a superb view of the floor, he thought fleetingly, and he struggled to locate Andrei Bogdanov in the dark tunnel of his vision before it rose to embrace him.

The Russian was on his knees, his arms clasped awkwardly to his stomach. He was clearly devoting his entire being to regaining his feet. Alec Grey felt himself awash in panic, his veins flowing with acid. He wrestled with the flickering shards of detail to which the sitting room had been reduced. He was several seconds appreciating that the chair upon which he'd deposited his pistol was immediately to his left.

Andrei Bogdanov hurled himself forward once more. Alec Grey clutched at his revolver. There would not be an opportunity to aim it. He stumbled back and brought its butt down upon the Russian's skull. The man tumbled forward, senseless, descending upon Alice Woodward's coffee table. The protest of shattering wood sounded like rifle fire.

Alec Grey almost succeeded in dropping his pistol as he sought to orient it in his numbed fingers. He directed it at the Russian for a time, but it became clear that Andrei Bogdanov intended to recline upon his bed of splinters for the present. He willed his legs forward, to cross the room, to free Alice Woodward, to find a telephone and awaken from this treacherous nightmare.

He was an eternity untying her, his hands defying him.

"Are you all right?" he asked, his voice rasping in his throat. "Did he... did he hurt you?"

Alice Woodward shook her head. "I'm fine," she breathed.

He got to his feet and put his arms around her.

"Are you... I believe you're bleeding, Mr. Grey," she whispered.

"I'd not be at all surprised, Miss Woodward," he said, smiling to himself.

He felt her arms tighten across his back. "I thought he'd kill you," she said.

"I believe that was what he had in mind."

He lost himself in her for a time, convincing himself by inches that she was still breathing, that he could hear her heartbeat above his own. She clung to him, trembling. He felt the blood return to his flesh. The house grew still, a neglected garden overgrown by the distant muttering of a clock and the footfalls of traffic through the open front door.

He all but ignored the first rattle of wood. Belatedly he appreciated that he'd been standing with his back to the motionless form of Andrei Bogdanov, having assumed him to be unconscious. Alice Woodward twisted in his arms and he released her. He pushed her to one side and snatched his pistol from the settee.

Andrei Bogdanov struggled to his knees as Alec Grey aligned the barrel of his revolver with the Russian's forehead. The man before him paused, considering the weapon as he might have done an unidentifiable curiosity at the back of a junk shop. He smiled, the expression ugly and contemptuous. He braced his hand upon one knee and put his weight against it.

Alec Grey squeezed the trigger of his revolver, feeling it kick at his palm. The sitting room thundered with its report. He tasted the burnt flint of cordite. Alice Woodward screamed. A perfect ruby disk appeared between Andrei Bogdanov's eyes. The Russian stared lifelessly past him for an instant before his hands slipped from beneath him, his form dismantling itself as it lapsed back upon the shattered wood from which it had ascended. The obverse of his head was largely missing, the back of his overalls a tangle of blood and brains.

The aftershocks of his body striking the floor seemed to reverberate in the sitting room for the remainder of the afternoon.

Alec Grey replaced his pistol on the settee. Alice Woodward returned to his arms for a time. It seemed beyond him to speak.

"Shall I ring 999?" she inquired softly, relinquishing her embrace.

"I think he's past medical attention," he replied. "Perhaps it would be better if our lot saw to this."

"I was rather thinking of you, Mr. Grey," she said. She smiled, clearly amused that they'd continued the affectation of formality.

"I believe I shall survive," he offered. He glanced at the body of Andrei Bogdanov. "I don't imagine the same can be said for your furniture."

"I've never liked it. No one in my family has."

Sir Alistair would in all likelihood not even request his explanation of the death of Andrei Mikhailovich Bogdanov, Alec Grey considered. The director would ascribe it to his defense of Alice Woodward and himself... or perhaps the defense of the realm, the defense against which no appeal could be sought. Lawrence Downs would unquestionably lament the passing of his most promising subject in recent memory. A great deal of intelligence might have been extracted from the mind of Andrei

Bogdanov, had Alec Grey not deposited it in bloody clumps across Alice Woodward's oriental carpet.

He permitted himself a glance at her. She knew differently, he appreciated, and one afternoon as they walked the deserted beaches of Kent in the off-season or stole away in Kenneth Bryan's MG or tested the patience of the Official Secrets Act over her father's expensive wine ten years hence, she would unquestionably ask him why he'd put a bullet through Andrei Bogdanov, rather than merely clubbing him back to insensibility and returning him for additional debriefing. She would be beyond deceiving.

In the official report of his soul, he allowed, he would be compelled to write that he'd killed the Russian for the certainty that he would not step from behind a tree once more and take her away at gunpoint. He found it darkly troubling that he could summon no measure of hatred for the creature on the floor before him, and no satisfaction at his death. Andrei Bogdanov was an unshaven, bloody chess piece, now toppled in defeat beyond the edge of the board.

The Russians were inordinately fond of chess.

43

The director had retired to his club for the evening, Alec Grey considered, which was unquestionably for the best. The corner of the Technical Services workshop that had been conscripted as a reliquary for the secret possessions of Peter and Helen Kroger would not have impressed Sir Alistair as being secure. A long steel table that appeared to have formerly seen service as a marksmanship target had been installed to display the artifacts of 45 Cranley Drive. Several of his staff had been installed to discourage the curiosity of the hulking, misshapen gnomes of this stygian realm, at least until the intelligence had been culled from the machinery.

Even at this late hour, an occasional figure in a soiled white coat could be observed peering intently over a rack of gauges and oscilloscopes, soldering iron in hand like a dagger, curious at the wonders he was being denied.

Hugh Somerfield periodically entertained himself by taking the mickey out of Technical Services. Doing so was hardly sporting, Alec Grey chided himself, and he vowed to refrain from his further ill-use of the men who labored here.

He returned his attention to the table and its odd bits of treachery. Each of them had been placed upon a sheet of paper describing its original location in the Krogers' home and in some cases its presumed purpose in being there. Some of the pages bordered upon the preposterous.

One of the men he'd stationed at the periphery of the table rose from his chair at length, which he'd come to appreciate typically heralded the approach of one of the Technical Services staff hoping to snatch a glimpse of this rampart of secrecy before he was instructed to leave. He glanced at the source of the intrusion to discover that it was attired inappropriately for the workshop. Hugh Somerfield slipped between two racks of unidentifiable devices.

"Good evening, boss," he said, clearly pleased with himself.

"And to you, Hugh," Alec Grey replied.

Hugh Somerfield glanced at an unoccupied chair against one wall. "I understood Miss Woodward was down here with you. Has she left for home?"

"Miss Woodward has gone off to make tea," he replied. "Miss Woodward has speculated upon the possibility of never again leaving Leconfield House without an armed escort... several of them, at last reckoning." He permitted himself to be amused by this, by the dark irony of Alice Woodward's expression as she'd suggested it.

Hugh Somerfield's expression grew troubled. "I've heard what happened... with Bogdanov," he said quietly. "How's she managing?"

Alec Grey smiled, hoping to dispel his subordinate's concern. "Remarkably well... probably better than I."

He watched a flicker of apprehension leap upon Hugh Somerfield's features, hanging there by claws in his flesh for a moment before it scuttled away into the dark corners of the workshop. He'd watched a similar transformation of character in everyone he'd encountered this afternoon.

"Before you inquire, Mr. Somerfield, I'm quite unin-jured, save for a few scrapes and bruises. I hasten to remind you that I shot Mr. Bogdanov, rather than the other way 'round."

"It can't have been pleasant."

"It's nothing that a large whiskey and a substantial volume of coffee wasn't capable of addressing. Lawrence Downs poured me a glass from the bottle I lost in a wager with him earlier... I find there to be a pleasing symmetry in that."

Hugh Somerfield appeared to relent to his character-istic amusement. He turned his attention to the table between them.

Alec Grey followed his eyes. "This is quite the Aladdin's cave of Soviet equipment," he mused.

"There'll almost certainly be more of it," Hugh Somerfield assured him. "They were still tearing up the floors when I left. I understand they've discovered a hidden cellar under the kitchen."

Alec Grey reached across the table and picked up a tin of Yardley's shaving talc. "I've been wondering about this one since I arrived," he said. "Have the Yardley people been spying on us as well, or did Technical Services just bag the lot and intend to sort it all out later."

Hugh Somerfield smiled. "I'm quite taken by that one." Curious, Alec Grey handed him the tin. He extracted a penny from his trouser pocket and used it to pry the bottom from the tin. "It has a secret chamber," he explained. "They've hidden microfilm inside it. It's proba-bly radio schedules... a very large lens is no doubt called for."

"Shall I ask how you decided it was something other than a tin of shaving talc?"

"It's like a number of things we found at the Krogers'," Hugh Somerfield observed. "It's almost full of powder, but the tin itself is scratched and banged up as if it'd been used for months. It's what you'd expect... having gone to the trouble of altering the tin, they wouldn't chuck it away when whatever's in it was used up. They'd buy a new tin, refill the old one and chuck the new one away."

"I assume our lads will be examining every tin of soup and packet of biscuits."

Hugh Somerfield nodded. "And no doubt writing enough reports to fell half the trees in England." He permitted his attention to wander across the table for a time. At length he returned the tin of shaving talc to its page and picked up a small glass vial of black powder.

"This one's bloody clever," Hugh Somerfield said.

"Is it indeed?" Alec Grey inquired. He glanced at the page it had rested on, but it offered him nothing more than a description of a secret hollow carved into a table leg.

"We found some of this on a tape recorder attached to a wireless in the Krogers' kitchen. It turns out to be very fine magnetic iron powder. When Peter Kroger recorded a transmission from Moscow, rather than listening to the Morse, he could dust this stuff on the tape. It sticks to the bits with sound, and he could read the Morse directly. Considering the transmissions would have been nothing but digit groups, it no doubt went a long way toward reducing the number of garbled messages."

Alec Grey nodded, unable to share Hugh Somerfield's admiration for the KGB's resourcefulness.

He turned and walked to the distant end of the table. He paused before a metal tin that had been discovered in the Krogers' cellar.

"Was there photographic equipment at 45 Cranley Drive?" he asked Hugh Somerfield.

"Bags of it. We found a complete darkroom in the cellar... several of those odd spiral tanks for processing Minox films. There's also what appears to be a camera for producing microdots. It's bloody huge... when I left, they were still trying to work out how to get it up through the trap door into the kitchen without taking it to pieces. If Peter Kroger ever turns talkative, I wouldn't mind inquiring how he got it down there."

"I'll see to it someone asks him," Alec Grey said wryly, feeling himself infected by Hugh Somerfield's enthusiasm. He opened the metal tin and removed one of the strips of negatives it contained. "I believe these are Minox films," he said.

Hugh Somerfield drew closer and considered the diminutive sequence of negatives. "Yes, boss," he agreed.

"I borrowed a microscope from one of the boffins here," Alec Grey continued. "You wouldn't want to try to read a great deal of text through one, but it was suitable to glance at the titles. These are photographs of a report David Hollings wrote about enhancements to the gaseous diffusion Uranium refinement process they've got going in Cornwall."

He watched Hugh Somerfield's amusement over his hoard of captured Soviet espionage equipment vanish. "Bloody hell," he whispered.

"Yes," Alec Grey agreed. He gestured at the tin of negatives. "Most of this stuff is about Uranium refinement, as nearly as I've been able to tell. It's all been nicked within the past few months."

"That would be down to Mr. Philby, I imagine," High Somerfield suggested.

Alec Grey shook his head. "That's the disturbing part of this. I'll wager another bottle of whiskey that Kim Philby wasn't on the distribution lists for any of this stuff. There's no reason for him to have been... it's technical as hell, and it has no bearing on anti-Soviet counterintelligence."

Hugh Somerfield regarded the tin of negatives for a time. "If you're suggesting we've banged up the wrong man, boss, you should know that Philby was in with Lawrence Downs all afternoon. He's cracked like an egg.

Mr. Downs' staff can't write the stuff up fast enough." He took a step closer to Alec Grey, and his voice dropped to a harsh whisper. "He's named Sir Anthony Blunt as another Soviet agent."

Alec Grey glanced at his subordinate. "Anthony Blunt is the Surveyor of the Queen's Pictures, and a personal friend of the royal family."

"Yes he is... but fifteen years ago, he was with MI5."

Alec Grey forced himself to abandon his consideration of the repercussions of Kim Philby's revelation. He had a sense that more of them were to follow. He shook his head, willing himself to resume his earlier conversation.

"I've no doubt we've banged up the right man, Hugh," he said, dangling one of the negative strips between his thumb and forefinger. "Unfortunately, we don't appear to have banged up enough of them."

"Boss?"

"There would seem to be at least one more mole," Alec Grey explained. "I find myself unwilling to imagine who it might be just at the moment, considering the distribution lists of these papers."

Hugh Somerfield seemed to require a moment to appreciate what had been said to him. "Oh... I see," he said at length. "Another mole hunt."

"With an exceedingly large gun."

The director would not be pleased, Alec Grey considered, and he resolved to give the matter his full attention the following day.

Alice Woodward returned to the workshop at length, bearing two cardboard cups of tea. She greeted Hugh Somerfield and offered to fetch one for him. He smiled and declined, and after she'd tasted hers she announced herself in agreement with his reluctance to accept one of his own. She appeared able to manifest little interest in the Krogers' possessions. She returned to her chair by the far wall of the workshop and extracted a book from her handbag — a penny-dreadful romance, Alec Grey decided, based on the lurid illustration on its cover.

"Will we have to share this lot with the Americans?" Hugh Somerfield inquired without extracting his attention from the table between them. "It was Angleton who put you onto Peter Kroger, after all."

Alec Grey nodded. "It would seem appropriate." He felt himself touched with amusement. "I dare say President Nixon would be disposed to pinning medals on yourself and Mrs. Gardner for your handling of the Krogers."

Hugh Somerfield seemed uncertain whether he was intended to take the suggestion seriously. "Clever chap for an American president," he mused. "The only member of his cabinet he appears to trust is that objectionable dog he keeps having himself photographed with. One can't help thinking we'd all have been a lot worse off if the other fellow'd won their election." He paused for a moment in concentration. "Connolly?"

"Kennedy."

Hugh Somerfield nodded. "The one who screwed himself out of the White House," he said, his voice clearly having dropped such that it not be audible to Alice Woodward.

Alec Grey permitted himself to smile at this. Sir Alistair had expressed a considerable degree of concern in the months preceding the previous American election at the prospect of Washington finding itself in the hands of what the Americans euphemistically referred to as a 'democrat.' He'd been visibly relieved when a newspaper photograph of John Kennedy and one of his female campaign staff staring from their bed in a Chicago hotel room had effectively decided the matter. The candidate had agreed to an interview, but one of his assistants had invited the reporter in question to John Kennedy's rooms an hour earlier than John Kennedy had been expecting him.

Alec Grey and Hugh Somerfield hovered about the

battered steel table, examining each of its contents. Alec Grey felt his interest in the exercise dissolve. He began to consider who to assign to make enlargements of the Minox negatives, who was to be entrusted with taking the Krogers' machines to pieces.

He didn't notice one of his staff rise from his chair. A white coat approached the table, to be intercepted by a dark gray suit. The man seemed undeterred by the obstruction.

"Is one of you gents Alec Grey?" the technician inquired.

"This is Mr. Grey," Hugh Somerfield replied. "You know you're not permitted in this area."

"Right, guv," he said, clearly oblivious to the restriction. "Only, they sent me down with a message for Alec Grey."

Alec Grey stepped around Hugh Somerfield. "Go on," he instructed the technician.

The man scratched at his thinning hair with considerably more enthusiasm than seemed appropriate for a mere itch. He withdrew a slip of paper from a pocket of his coat and consulted it. "There's been an explosion inside the Soviet Union," he began. "It occurred at 1932 hours. Initial triangulation places it roughly at sixty-five degrees north by thirty-two degrees east, below Murmansk, near Finland. At almost exactly the same time, a monitoring station in Finland that had been tracking a radio signal at 1420 megacycles reports the signal abruptly ceased." The technician glanced up from his page. "Does any of that lot mean something?"

Alec Grey smiled to himself. Hugh Somerfield confiscated the technician's slip of paper and instructed him to leave.

"Christ," he said. "Was that the Soviet time stream installation blowing itself to bits?"

Alec Grey felt himself overwhelmed, uncertain what

he was experiencing. "It does rather sound like it," he replied. He was teased by the urge to have someone call California and determine whether seismographs there had registered the explosion.

44

Wednesday, October 25
Russo-Finnish Border

Despite cold-weather gear that he'd imagined capable of keeping him comfortable during a protracted trek across the Antarctic, the interior of the helicopter was numbingly cold. He flexed his fingers periodically, certain that if not for the deafening noise of the machine, he'd have heard the cracking of his knuckles. Five minutes into the flight he'd renounced all hope of conversation with his fellow passengers and contented himself with a detailed surveillance of his feet.

Alec Grey imagined himself having spent most of his life in unheated aircraft. The central heating, objectionable coffee and cloying cigarette smoke of Leconfield House seemed a half-remembered luxury of another age, or perhaps an ancestral legend whispered to him in his sleep.

He glanced around the cabin. Hugh Somerfield was entertaining himself by leaning toward the pilot and peering through the windscreen. David Hollings had been ill into a paper sack shortly after they'd lurched drunkenly into the air, and he seemed decidedly green now.

Alec Grey was growing increasingly suspicious of the balance of his own mind. Sir Alistair had questioned his reason at the prospect of giving the Soviets a supply of Uranium. It hardly compared, however, to clandestinely flying into their country to investigate what had become of it.

The director was sitting vigil beside a wireless at the moment, he imagined, as was Alice Woodward. He felt his eyes grow wet, thinking that they were at considerable risk of freezing. His breath grew still in his chest. He'd not seen her cry since they'd first met in the director's office. Her abduction by Andrei Bogdanov had not been sufficient to bring her to tears, but she'd sobbed into his shoulder when he'd explained his destination. They'd stolen a quarter of an hour alone in the director's briefing room — he to assure her of his certain return, she to plead with him to direct someone else to steal into hell in his stead.

He could no longer recall when he'd come to curse himself for the paras and the helicopters and the charts and the Geiger counters. The realm had no bloody right to imagine him willing to perish in its defense.

The realm had no bloody right to leave Alice in tears, he mused, warmed minutely by his preposterous assertion. The realm believed differently.

It would be an effort of will to recall now the precise moment when he'd appreciated the opportunity afforded him by a confluence of stealth and meteorology. He and Alice Woodward had stepped outside Leconfield House to escape the thickening haze of Hugh Somerfield's cigarettes. The weather had become unseasonably cold over the previous few hours, and there had been gray veins of snow tracing the margins of Curzon Street. He'd watched her breath become anthracite clouds between them, her features cast into cubist shadows by a street lamp.

It had been midnight before the director had arrived, his displeasure at having been roused from his bed almost tangible as he'd accepted his chair at the end of the briefing room's table. He'd regarded the map of north-western Russia sprawling before him as he might have done the death warrant of a close friend awaiting his signature.

The remote location of the Soviet time stream project, Alec Grey had explained, had become the point of convergence of two weather systems. The Murmansk peninsula had accumulated almost as much snow in the previous twenty-four hours as it had during the entire winter of 1960. A second storm front, swelling north from Moscow, was assailing the area with high winds and a shroud of ice. What few roads as existed in that barren corner of the Soviet Union were impassable.

It would be another day, perhaps two, before the two storm fronts collided almost atop what he presumed were the remains of the time stream facility. Until they did, the only avenue by which to approach the installation was from the west — from Finland.

The fragments of signals intelligence which had escaped the storm had confirmed that the Red Army had been immobilized. There was no sign of activity within a radius of two hundred miles of the time stream facility. He'd risen to his feet and leant over the map, his fist a giant oak rooted in the tundra of Murmansk. It was a bizarre jest of God, he'd observed, that the Soviets could not have sent so much as a radio message to the facility, while Finnish aircraft could reach it easily in under an hour.

The director had not appreciated the joke, he thought absently, recalling Sir Alistair glaring at him through eyes still not wholly bereft of sleep.

With the benefit of time and forethought, he'd continued, the opportunity to inspect the remains of the Soviet facility would have been the province of MI6, or perhaps better still, the Americans, who appeared to enjoy being shot at. There had been the opportunity to arrange neither. In a day the storms would shift, the Soviets would dig out and the patch of calm that lead like a well-marked ambush from the border of Finland to the time stream facility would be closed forever.

He'd nominated himself, Hugh Somerfield and David Hollings as the only personnel quickly to hand with the security clearance and sufficient knowledge of the time stream research to make the operation worth undertaking. Sir Alistair had appeared ready to rise up from his chair and drive them from the briefing room with it.

He'd hardly slept since the briefing for the director. David Hollings had been en route from Cornwall by the time Sir Alistair had arrived, and he'd tentatively arranged for transport from High Wycombe to Finland. The director had not been pleased by his temerity, and he'd been ill-disposed to consider his assertion that the operation was unavoidable.

In the coming week, he imagined, Sir Alistair would attribute his eventual agreement to his being deprived of sleep. Alec Grey wondered absently who the director had telephoned to arrange for the helicopters and the squad of British paras awaiting them at Rovaniemi. He'd been informed as they'd stumbled onto the tarmac that the Finnish air transport that would take them within sight of the Soviet border would be landing at a location they were not permitted to know the name of.

Sir Alistair's final wish for his safety had been his assurance that in the event of his capture by Soviet forces, MI5 would have Kim Philby to offer up as a bargaining chip. The prospect had not served to reassure him.

The howling of the rotors changed its pitch minutely. Alec Grey glanced around the cabin, aware as he did that its other occupants had simultaneously done so as well. Hugh Somerfield had returned to his seat, and he gestured to the invisible ground below them. David Hollings seemed to be casting about for another paper sack.

The helicopter landed in what appeared to be a vortex of snow. Alec Grey gazed through its windscreen, certain for a time that his understanding of the local weather had gone dreadfully wrong. The storm abated as the rotors wound to a halt. One of the paras unlatched the door beside him and assisted him to his feet.

The day was eerily still. He struggled to work his legs, listening to the whispering silence of the bleak land-scape. There were few trees, and much of what might have once been alive was entombed in drifts and peaks of snow. The air was almost painfully cold. He gasped, feeling his heart slow.

He ducked his head instinctively as he stepped to the far side of the helicopter. The machine had been conceal-ing the object of his being here. The desolation that greeted him was beyond anything a Russian winter might have wrought.

The explosion of the time stream apparatus had been more savage than even David Hollings had predicted. The facility appeared to have consisted of several single-story brick buildings surrounded by a twelve-foot high steel fence, topped with razor wire. All but one of the structures were heaps of gravel, and much of the fence hung in tat-ters. There were several dark forms in the snow which he took to be the partially-buried corpses of people who'd been slain by the blast.

One of the paras approached him. The man was an ambulatory munitions store, every pocket and pouch of his coat thick with hardware. Alec Grey recognized him as the commander of the unit. The man had not offered his name, and he'd been sufficiently astute not to inquire after it.

"We're here, sir," he said.

"Thank you... I'd noticed."

"You understand, sir, my orders are that you and your people have precisely thirty minutes on the ground from right now. In thirty minutes plus one second, anyone who isn't back in the helicopters will be dragged there by his nose." The man smiled briefly beneath his snow hood, but it was clear that his threat was anything but idle.

"I understand," Alec Grey said.

"I've detailed four men to accompany you. Our information is that there isn't a living Soviet soldier within a hundred miles of this location. In the event that our information is incorrect, you're to return to the helicopters at the first sign of trouble."

Alec Grey nodded.

"I've been ordered to see yourself, Mr. Somerfield and Mr. Hollings alive and back to Finland, even if no one else gets out, sir," the commander added gravely.

"Let's see if we can't keep it from coming to that," Alec Grey offered.

"I'd appreciate that, sir."

The commander turned and walked into the snow. He had other matters to concern himself with in the coming half hour. Those of his men who weren't assigned to guard Her Majesty's spies would be arranging packages of plastic explosives and detonators. By the time the helicopters re-crossed the Finnish border, what remained of the Soviets' attempt to access the time stream would be ashes.

Alec Grey stepped forward into the snow, locating Hugh Somerfield and David Hollings in the lee of the next helicopter. Hugh Somerfield appeared to be attempting to light a cigarette, contrary to the wishes of the winter that had enveloped him. David Hollings was operating what he took to be a Geiger counter, apparently unconcerned by what it revealed. The scientist had predicted as much. Berkelium decayed to half its initial level of radioactivity within four and a half hours of its creation, and half of that in another four and a half hours. He'd predicted radiation no more worrisome than that of a dentist's X-ray machine. Alec Grey had previously been comfortable in his ignorance that dentists' X-ray machines involved any radiation at all.

Alec Grey gestured toward the nearest gap in the

fence surrounding the ruined time stream facility and began to make for it. The snow clutched at his uncomfortable boots, and he felt himself begin to struggle for breath before he'd reached it. Four ghostly figures in white coats and carrying rifles converged on him as he walked.

The lone intact building had hardly escaped the wrath of the forces unleashed by the time stream facility. Its windows were tangles of shattered glass. Its door hung by a single hinge, and was swinging erratically in the breeze. A man in a white shirt, his face a mask of blisters and welts, lay motionless just beyond the entrance, staring lifelessly at the ceiling. Alec Grey stepped over him uncertainly, imagining him returning to life and calling out in alarm.

David Hollings followed him into the hush of the building. The darkness was pierced by the needle of a torch, and then another. He located his own in one of the pockets of his coat and sought for its switch through his glove. At length he dared remove the glove.

"Bloody hell," Hugh Somerfield said from the darkness behind him.

Alec Grey felt his words claw at his throat. He pushed the sleeve of his coat along his arm and he glanced at his wristwatch. Nine minutes had expired.

There were more bodies. Some of the Russians had clearly died instantly, crouched over their desks and equipment consoles like the discarded toys of a petulant child. The ones who'd been at the center of the building appeared to have survived the explosion for a time.

He listened to the hush that surrounded him. At length he noticed the faint crackle of David Hollings' Geiger counter, and he made for the sound. He located David Hollings and Hugh Somerfield at the distant end of the building, in an office that had escaped the worst of the cataclysm. Its former occupant was mercifully absent.

The room was not a great deal larger than his own office. It contained a desk, a file cabinet, a long table, a pot plant that had clearly succumbed to inattention far more rapidly than his own. There was a framed photograph of Nikkita Khrushchev looking uncomfortably dyspeptic clinging to the far wall at an impossible angle.

David Hollings turned as he entered the room, momentarily blinding him with the beam from his torch. "I believe this is what you were after," he said.

"What have you found?" Alec Grey inquired.

"This appears to have been the office of whoever oversaw this place... my counterpart, I imagine. I've found photographs of pages from a number of reports I've written, drawings of various components of the Cornwall apparatus." He paused and glanced uncertainly around the room. "I've found the final set of papers you had me prepare as well."

Alec Grey detected a note of accusation in David Hollings' words, struggling as he did to ignore it.

"The odd thing is," David Hollings continued, "all this stuff's in English."

"It's not that odd," Alec Grey explained. "Moscow likely didn't trust its translators with its time stream intelligence. It made sure this place was staffed with people who could read English... probably not an uncommon ability amongst scientists."

Hugh Somerfield gestured to him from a corner of the office. "I think you need to see this, boss," he said. Alec Grey pushed past David Hollings.

He followed the beam of Hugh Somerfield's torch to where it intersected with his hand. It glared from a glass vial that appeared to be empty. Hugh Somerfield shook it and it emitted an all but inaudible rattle.

"What've you found, Hugh?" he inquired.

"Ricin pellets," Hugh Somerfield replied. "They're identical to the one that came out of Konstanin Bolshakov.

I've found a microscope as well, if you'd like to have a proper look at them."

"I'll take your word for it," Alec Grey allowed. "It seems like a peculiar thing to have about in this place. I can't help feeling the umbrella that's supposed to have delivered them would have seemed out of place up here."

David Hollings summoned him once more, and he turned from Hugh Somerfield.

The scientist was clearly disturbed by what he'd discovered. He was seated before the office table. A substantial stack of pages rested before him. They were like most of the other documents in the facility, photographs printed on thin paper. "This shouldn't be here," David Hollings said tonelessly.

Alec Grey peered over his shoulder. He was several seconds appreciating why the document appeared familiar. When last he'd seen it, it had been typed on blue stationary. He'd undertaken to read it largely to please Alice Woodward, having initially been convinced that it would bore him to distraction.

"It's the manuscript you recovered from the time stream," he breathed.

"How in hell did they steal this?" David Hollings demanded. He began to flip through the stiff pages as Alec Grey permitted himself glimpses of their text. He'd turned several dozen of them before Alec Grey noticed a tangle of handwriting on the back of one of the pages. He snatched it from David Hollings. The notes were in Cyrillic, and he was a minute understanding them.

He returned the page to its place on the table and stepped back into the center of the office. David Hollings rose from his chair and turned to face him.

"What's wrong," he asked. "What've you found?"

"I know what they were doing here," Alec Grey replied, unable to compel his eyes to focus on the figure of the scientist.

"I should think we all do," David Hollings said.

"No... no, we don't. We could never have imagined it."

"I'm afraid you've lost me."

He stepped across the room and returned with the vial of Ricin pellets. David Hollings wouldn't appreciate what they were intended for, but it was suddenly beyond him to care. "They were attempting to access the time stream... to project these back in time," he continued. "A substantial distance back in time, as you'd say."

David Hollings shook his head. "I still don't understand."

"They were attempting to assassinate the ancestors of Ira Rosen."

http://www.stevenwilliamrimmer.com

Afterword

While this novel is a work of fiction, a number of its characters are based on real individuals. The lives of these men and women were somewhat different from what has been described herein. I am indebted to *The Encyclopedia of Espionage* by Norman Polmar and Thomas B. Allen for assistance in verifying many of the following details. Any errors which have crept in are, of course, mine.

Kim Philby (STANLEY) was perhaps the most damaging Soviet agent in British intelligence during the cold war. He was one of the Cambridge spy ring. He was offered a post in Section V of the Secret Intelligence Service, MI6, in 1941. After World War II, he served as the MI6 liaison in Washington. Suspicion about Philby's communist sympathies while at Cambridge, his association with Guy Burgess and Donald Maclean – who defected to Moscow in May 1951 – and a growing body of evidence from decoded Soviet radio messages prompted MI6 to recall Philby to London and conduct a secret hearing in which he was charged with espionage. The charges were not substantiated, but Philby was dismissed from MI6 in July 1951. He became a foreign correspondent for The Observer in the middle east, and moved to Beirut. In 1961, Anatoly Golitsyn, an officer with the KGB, defected to the United States, bringing with him fresh evidence that Kim Philby was a Soviet agent. Philby was summoned to London. He vanished from Beirut and appeared in Moscow in July 1963. He remained there for the rest of his life, dying in 1988. His likeness appeared on a 5 kopek postage stamp issued by the Soviet Union in 1990, shortly before it collapsed.

Peter Kroger was born Morris Cohen in New York City. He and his wife Lona were ardent communists and active Soviet agents. On July 17, 1950 – the day that Julius and Ethel Rosenberg were arrested for espionage – Morris and Lona Cohen left the United States. They traveled for several years, eventually reaching New Zealand, where they adopted the identities of Peter and Helen Kroger, a Canadian couple who had recently died. They arrived in England in 1954 with their new identities. Peter Kroger opened an antiquarian bookshop at 190 The Strand in London, where he specialized in somewhat extreme works of pornography. The Krogers lived at 45 Cranley Drive in the suburb of Ruislip until January 1961, when they were arrested by MI5 and subsequently convicted of espionage. On October 24, 1969, they were released to the

Soviet Union in an agent exchange. Lona Cohen died in Moscow in 1992, and Morris Cohen in 1995.

Yuri Modin (PETER) was a handler for the members of the Cambridge spy ring, including Kim Philby. He was an officer in the NKVD, one of the predecessors of the KGB. In June 1947, he and his family were assigned to London as the NKVD resident. He assumed the cover of a Soviet press officer. He was instrumental in the escape of Guy Burgess and Donald Maclean in 1951. He left Britain himself in 1958. Anthony Blunt eventually identified him as a KGB officer, making his further presence impossible. He was reunited with Kim Philby, Guy Burgess and Donald Maclean in Moscow, where he assisted Philby with his autobiography, *My Silent War,* published in 1968. He wrote his own memoirs, *My 5 Cambridge Friends,* which was published after the collapse of the Soviet Union, in 1995.

Guy Burgess (HICKS) was a member of the Cambridge spy ring, which included Kim Philby and Donald Maclean. He appears only in passing in this book. After graduating from Cambridge, he became a journalist for the BBC, and did occasional work for MI6. He was hired by MI6 full-time in 1939. He was an active double agent, providing information both to his Soviet controllers and to British intelligence. In 1944, he was hired by the British Foreign Office. Burgess was a flamboyant homosexual and often appeared in public extremely drunk. In 1950, he was posted to the British embassy in Washington, where he lived with Kim Philby and his family. A year later, Philby learned that Donald Maclean was about to be exposed as a Soviet mole. He convinced Burgess to behave disgracefully enough to be immediately recalled to London, where he could warn Maclean. Guy Burgess and Donald Maclean fled England on May 25, 1951, defecting to the Soviet Union. Burgess died in 1963.

Donald Maclean was a member of the Cambridge spy ring, which included Kim Philby and Guy Burgess. He too appears only in passing in this book. His career and his espionage are similar in many respects to those of his friend Guy Burgess, but Maclean was a serious diplomat and an equally commit-ted spy. He served as the first secretary at the British embassy in Washington. He had access to secrets of the British atomic weapons program after World War II. However, he was also the subject of FBI surveillance as a result of his increasingly public drinking and alleged homosexual activities. He returned to London in 1948, and was posted briefly to Cairo. He was recalled in 1950. The stress of his double life had made him increasingly erratic and he periodically drank him-self into unconsciousness. In 1951, he and Guy Burgess defected to the Soviet Union. Donald Maclean became fluent in Russian, and worked in Moscow until his death in 1983.

Anthony Blunt (JOHNSON) was a member of the Cambridge spy ring, which included Kim Philby and Donald Maclean and Guy Burgess. He worked for MI5 during the second world war, during which time he betrayed the identities of every active MI5 officer to the Soviet Union. He later became famous as an art historian. He was a personal friend of Queen Elizabeth, and was named the Surveyor of the Queen's Pictures. He taught art history at Oxford, Cambridge and London University. Unlike the other Cambridge spies, Blunt chose not to defect to the Soviet Union. He was revealed as a Soviet agent by Michael Straight in 1963, and he confessed to charges of espionage in 1964. His activities were not officially revealed by the British gov-ernment until 1979. He died in 1983.

James Jesus Angleton was the head of counterintelligence for the CIA for two decades. He became convinced that west-ern intelligence had been compromised by a number of secret Soviet agents – moles – working within it. His mounting paranoia was fueled by a series of Soviet defectors, each of whom claimed that the others were intentional plants sent by Moscow to deceive the west. He was forced to resign in 1974. A year later he was awarded the Distinguished Intelligence Medal, the CIA's highest decoration. He died in 1987. He was a long-time friend of Kim Philby, prior to Philby's defection.

Boris Hagelin is often erroneously credited with the invention of the Enigma code machine, much beloved of the producers of World War II espionage films of late. In reality, the machine was invented by Arvid Damm. Hagelin acquired the company that owned the design of the machine and began marketing it under the name 'Glow Lamp Ciphering and Deciphering Machine Enigma' in 1923. The machine was intended for use by banks and international businesses that wished to be able to communicate securely with their foreign offices. It was adopted by the German military during World War II. Hagelin also developed cryptographic machines for the United States military during the war. The company he created, Crypto AG, remains one of the world's most successful cryptographic technology firms. Its head office is located in Zug, Switzerland. Boris Hagelin died in 1983.

Anatoli Golitsyn was a KGB officer who defected to the CIA in December 1961. He convinced James Angleton, the head of counterintelligence for the CIA, of the existence of a number of Soviet moles in his organization. While he could not name the individuals in question – he provided only vague descriptions of their functions – his allegations were extremely corrosive to morale and effectiveness among the western intelligence agencies. Angleton instigated a series of mole hunts based largely on his information, and began to suspect other Soviet sources. In 1989, Golitsyn wrote a book entitled *New Lies for Old,* his observations on the cold war.

Gordon Lonsdale was the cover for Conon Molody, a Soviet agent. In 1955, having assumed the identity of a Canadian businessman, he moved to London and set up a spy ring that included Peter and Helen Kroger. He was arrested in 1961 and returned to the Soviet Union in 1964 in an agent exchange. He died in Moscow in 1970.

Sir Percy Sillitoe was the head of MI5 from 1946 through 1953. A former policeman from South Africa, he is remembered largely for his directorship of MI5 being a 'golden age' for secret Soviet agents. He returned to South Africa after leaving MI5, where he was hired by De Beers to investigate diamond smuggling. He died in 1962.

Melita Norwood was a Soviet agent spying on British atomic weapons research. She was never caught. Her existence became known in 1999. When she was revealed as a former Soviet agent, she was a great-grandmother living in Bexleyheath, a suburb of London. She died in 2005.

Michael Straight (NIGEL) was an American studying at Cambridge in 1934 when he was recruited as a Soviet agent by Anthony Blunt. He later returned to the United States, where he worked at the State Department. In 1963, as part of his appointment to a high-level political post, he was subject to a background check by the FBI. Fearful that his earlier communist affiliations would be revealed, he confessed his activities. Among his revelations was the identity of the "fourth man" in the Cambridge spy ring, Anthony Blunt.

C. H. Page was a vice-consul at the British embassy in Istanbul. In August 1945, he was contacted by Konstantin Volkov, an NKVD intelligence officer who wished to defect. He offered information about a mole within British counterintelligence. Page forwarded the information provided by Volkov to MI6 in London, where it was received by Kim Philby – the mole Volkov had been referring to. Philby notified Moscow of Volkov's attempt to defect. Konstantin Volkov and his wife were abducted by agents of the NKVD, returned to Moscow and presumably executed.

Sir Francis Walsingham was the head of the intelligence service for Queen Elizebeth I, and her secretary of state.

Yevgeny Ivanov was a lieutenant-colonel in the GRU, Soviet military intelligence. He was assigned to the Soviet embassy in London in 1960 as an assistant naval attaché. He shared his mistress, Christine Keeler, with John Profumo, then the British Secretary for War. The ensuing scandal toppled the government of Harold Macmillan. He returned to Russia in 1963. His autobiography, *The Naked Spy,* was published in 1992, shortly before his death.